Praise for the work of
USA TODAY and NEW YORK TIMES
bestselling author
CYNTHIA EDEN

"A fast-paced, sexy thrill ride
you won't want to miss."
Christine Feehan on *Eternal Hunter*

"Cynthia Eden's on my must-buy list."
Angie Fox, *New York Times* bestselling author

"Eden's unsurpassed creativity shines!"
Larissa Ione, *New York Times* bestselling author

"Fast-paced, smart, sexy and emotionally wrenching—
everything I love about a Cynthia Eden book!"
HelenKay Dimon on *Broken*

By Cynthia Eden

BROKEN

Forthcoming

TWISTED

CYNTHIA EDEN

BROKEN

AVONBOOKS

An Imprint of HarperCollinsPublishers

AVON BOOKS
An Imprint of HarperCollins*Publishers*
195 Broadway
New York, New York 10007

First Avon Books mass market printing: April 2015

Avon Trademark Reg. U.S. Pat. Off. and in Other Countries, Marca Registrada, Hecho en U.S.A.

HarperCollins® is a registered trademark of HarperCollins Publishers.

Printed in the U.S.A.

10 9 8 7 6 5 4 3 2 1

I want to dedicate this book to all of the fantastic romantic suspense fans out there. Thank you so much for all of the support that you have given to me!

And for my husband . . . Nick,
you truly are my best friend. Thanks, bestie!

ACKNOWLEDGMENTS

I'D LIKE TO THANK THE WONDERFUL STAFF AT AVON for all of their incredible support! In particular, Lucia and Nicole—you ladies rock!

I was thrilled to have the opportunity to write this story. *Broken* is set in Dauphin Island, Alabama, a place that is very near and dear to my heart. No, there are no serial killers on the island, and bodies haven't been discovered there in the aftermath of any hurricane (the story is fictional, after all!), but Dauphin Island is an amazing place, full of mystery. Each time I visit this beautiful island, I return home feeling recharged and happy.

I've got so many terrific friends on Dauphin Island. People who work there and folks who are lucky enough to call the island home. So to Joan, Mendel, Greg, and Carrie—thanks for sharing your paradise with me.

Happy reading, everyone!

BROKEN

PROLOGUE

SHE COULD SMELL THE OCEAN AND HEAR THE pounding of the surf. She could see the sky above her, so very blue and clear, but she couldn't move at all.

Her body had gone numb hours ago. At first the numbness had been a blessing. She'd just wanted the pain to stop, and it had. She didn't even scream any longer. What would be the point? There was no one around to hear her. No one was coming to help her.

Seagulls cried out, circling above her. She didn't want them to fly down. What if they started to peck at her? *Please, leave me alone.*

Her mouth was dry, filled with bits of sand. Tears had dried on her cheeks.

"Why are you still alive?" The curious voice came from beside her because he was there, watching, as he'd watched for hours. "Why don't you give in? You know you want to just close your eyes and let go."

She did. She wanted to close her eyes and pretend that she was just having a bad dream. A nightmare. When her eyes opened again, she'd be someplace different. Someplace without monsters.

He came closer to her, and she felt something sharp

slide into the sand with her. A knife. He liked to use his knife. It pricked her skin, but then he lifted the knife and pressed the blade against her throat.

"I can end this for you. Do it now. Just tell me . . ." His words were dark. Tempting. "Tell me that you want to die."

The surf was so close. She'd always loved the ocean. But she'd never expected to die like this. She didn't *want* to die like this. She realized the tears weren't dry on her face.

She was still crying. Her cheeks were wet with tears and blood.

"Tell me," he demanded. *"Tell me that you want to die."*

She shook her head. Because death wasn't what she wanted. Even after all he'd done, she didn't want to stop living.

She didn't want to give up.

The knife sliced against her neck. A hoarse moan came from her lips. Her voice had broken when she screamed and screamed. She should have known better than to scream.

That was what he'd told her. *You should know better, sweetheart. It's just you and me. Until your last breath.*

Her blood mixed with the sand. He was angry again. Or . . . no, he'd always been angry. She just hadn't seen the rage, not until it was too late. Now she couldn't look at him at all. No matter what he did to her, she *wouldn't* look at him.

She didn't want to remember him this way. Actually, she didn't want to remember him at all.

Her gaze lifted to the blue sky. To those circling seagulls.

I want to fly, Daddy. She'd been six the first time

she'd come to the island and seen the gulls. *I want to fly like them.*

Her father had laughed and told her that it looked like she'd lost her wings.

She'd lost more than that.

"I want to fly," she whispered.

"Too bad, because you're not flying anywhere. You're going to die here."

But there was no death for her yet, and she wasn't begging.

The gulls were blurry now, because of her tears.

He'd buried her in the sand, covering her wounds and packing the sand in tightly around her. Only her head and some of her neck remained uncovered. Her hands were bound, or so he thought.

But she'd been working beneath the sand. Working even as the moments ticked so slowly past, and he kept taunting her.

He had taken his time with this little game. Tried to break her in those endless hours.

She wouldn't be broken.

Her hands were free. If he'd just move that knife away from her neck . . .

He lifted the knife and stabbed it into the sand—into the sand right over her left shoulder. She choked out a cry as the sharp pain pierced her precious numbness.

"You'll beg soon," he told her. Then he was on his feet. Stalking away from her. "They all do."

He'd left the knife in her shoulder and made the mistake of turning his back on her.

She'd lived this long . . . if she was going out, she'd fight until her last breath.

Her fingers were free. She just had to escape the sand.

The heavy sand that he'd packed and packed around her.

Burying me.

She could feel the faint cracks start to slip across the sand as she shifted. Her strength was almost gone, but she could do this. She *had* to do it. If she didn't, she was dead.

He was turning back toward her.

Move! The scream was in her head, and she managed to lunge up. Her right hand grabbed the hilt of the knife. She jerked the blade out of her shoulder and surged to her feet even as the sand rained down her body.

He was yelling, screaming at her. She didn't care. She charged forward and slammed the knife into his chest. Their eyes met. It was the only time she'd looked into his gaze since the torture had begun.

She saw herself reflected in his stare.

He fell, slumping back. She didn't stop to see if he was still alive. She didn't care. She raced for the edge of the beach, for the little boat that was anchored just off-shore. Then she was stumbling into the surf. The water was icy against her skin, and she knew her blood was turning the water red.

She wasn't afraid of sharks. Men were the killers. Men just like—

"Don't leave me!" His bellow.

He was still alive. He was coming after her.

She fell into the boat. Fumbled. She'd been around boats her whole life. She could start the motor, even with hands that wouldn't stop trembling. She could start—

The motor growled. She shoved the throttle forward. The boat surged away from that little beach, jumping, bouncing over the waves.

He was still shouting. She was laughing. Crying. Not looking back.

She would never look back. Never. He hadn't broken her. Hadn't killed her.

She gazed up at the gulls. *I want to fly.*

Then the boat hit the rocks. Heavy rocks that she'd known were out there, but she'd tried to maneuver around them too late. The boat twisted and shot into the air.

And, in the next instant, she really was flying. Flying and then slamming face first into the water. The water was so red.

Her blood.

She tried to kick back to the surface. She wouldn't give up.

But her body was so tired. The numbness . . . it had vanished. Pain was back. A deep agony that cut into every muscle.

The surface was farther away. She could just see the outline of the gulls above her.

I want to fly.

She tried to swim. Tried to reach the surface. She didn't want to die.

But she didn't have the strength to fight anymore. The waves rolled around her, and the seagulls vanished.

CHAPTER ONE

HER STOMACH TWISTED AS EVE GRAY GAZED UP at the imposing building centered on the busy Atlanta street. Heat rose from the pavement, seeming to surround her. Someone bumped her from behind, and she took a quick step forward.

Just one step, then she caught herself.

Her heart was racing so fast, too fast, and her palms were sweating. She brushed her palms over her narrow skirt, and then Eve took just a moment to smooth down her hair.

This was it. The moment she'd been waiting for. The people inside would either help her or—

No, there is no option. They have to help me.

She straightened her shoulders and headed through the big swinging doors. She kept her gaze focused straight in front of her as she marched toward the elevator. She needed to go up to the fourth floor. Suite 409.

The elevator doors opened silently. Men and women in expensive business clothes climbed on and off the elevator. Eve kept her chin up. Her clothes were older, faded, too casual for this office building, but it wasn't like she had a lot of choice.

There were *no* choices for her.

The elevator dinged, and she hurried out onto the fourth floor. The lush carpet swallowed her footsteps. Then, a few desperate moments later, she was standing in front of a heavy, wooden door. Across the door, golden letters spelled: LOST.

Her lips curved in a smile that just felt sad. *Lost.* Yes, that was exactly what she was. And she desperately needed the people inside that office to help her.

Eve turned the doorknob with trembling fingers and crept inside. A perky receptionist glanced up at her, showing a smile that flashed huge dimples. "Welcome to Lost, how may I help you?"

Eve had to swallow twice in order to ease the dryness of her throat. "I need to speak with Gabe Spencer." He was the man she'd read about in the paper. The tough ex-SEAL who'd made it his new mission to create LOST.

LOST . . . the Last Option Search Team. This office and all of the personnel in it had one function, just one—to find missing people. To search for those that the authorities had already given up on.

The receptionist, a pretty girl with sun-streaked blond hair, gave a small shake of her head. "I'm sorry but do you have an appointment, ma'am?"

"No." And Eve knew that the perky lady was about to tell her to hit the road. So Eve shoved her hands into her oversize bag—the only bag that she had—and yanked out a carefully folded newspaper. She smoothed out the folds and offered the paper to the receptionist. "I need to talk with Mr. Spencer about this." *This* being the series of murders that had been highlighted in the *Atlanta News* three weeks ago. Seven women had been abducted. Tortured. Killed.

Their murderer hadn't been caught.

"We don't . . . um . . . we don't really hunt serial killers here at LOST," the receptionist said with wide eyes. "I'm not sure what you think Mr. Spencer can do for you—"

The office door opened behind the receptionist. At the soft sound, Eve glanced up automatically and saw a man—tall, handsome, powerful—filling that doorway. His hair was jet-black, thick, and still military short, even though she knew the guy wasn't active with the SEALs any longer.

Gabe Spencer.

She'd done research on him at the local library. Found his picture. Read his bio, again and again. Thirty-four. Single. Master's degree in criminal justice. He'd been a decorated SEAL, but he'd left the Navy after his sister had been abducted a few years ago. Gabe had made it his sole mission to find Amy and bring her home.

He had brought her home, just not alive.

His gaze was a bright, intense blue, and that gaze focused sharply on Eve. She shifted beneath his stare as uncertainty twisted within her.

He was handsome. No, almost *too* perfect. But his features had looked softer in the pictures she'd seen online. In person, his jaw was sharp and square, his cheeks high, his nose a strong blade . . . and his lips were sensual. The man had a deep, powerful appeal that seemed to fill the air and—

And she was just staring at him. Heat stained her cheeks. *What is wrong with me?*

"I don't think we can help you," the receptionist told Eve, giving a sad shake of her head.

But Eve wasn't really paying attention to the blonde any longer. She was too aware of Gabe.

Gabe was still staring straight at her, too. His gaze

dipped from her face down to her toes—the toes that peeked out from her high heels—then it slowly rose to study her face once more. His voice was a deep rumble as he asked, "Have we met, Ms. . . . ?"

She almost laughed at his question. "I'm afraid that I don't know if we have."

One dark brow lifted as confusion flashed in his blue gaze.

"I'm here to meet with you, Mr. Spencer." The words came out in a rush, but this was her chance. She had to take it. Eve grabbed her newspaper back from the receptionist. "Please, can you spare a few minutes to talk with me?"

That bright stare seemed to weigh her. Eve tensed. She was used to people assessing her. It was all they seemed to do lately. Assess. Judge. Find her lacking.

"She doesn't have an appointment," the not-so-perky-now blonde said. "I was just telling her—"

"Melody, I think I can spare a few minutes," he said, and stepped back. Gabe gave a little wave of his hand, indicating the open door. "If you'd like to come inside, we can talk privately."

Eve's knees were trembling as she hurried forward. At least she didn't trip or do anything to embarrass herself. *Yet.* This meeting was important. No, this meeting was *everything.* She had to get Gabe Spencer to help her. If he didn't help her, she had no idea what she'd do next.

The office smelled of leather. A bright expanse of windows looked over downtown Atlanta. Gabe's desk was huge, taking up a third of the room. She sat across from that big desk, sinking into one of the leather chairs. She expected him to assume a position behind his desk. Instead, he strode toward the left side of the desk, the side close to her, and he paused. His arms crossed over his chest as his gaze raked her once more.

"Is someone missing?" His question was low, sympathetic.

Eve gave a small nod, then offered him her newspaper.

Frowning, he read the headline. "The Lady Killer?" Gabe shook his head. "I know they recovered some bodies after the last hurricane swept through that area, but I don't see—"

"They haven't recovered all of the bodies. S-Some are still missing." Her fingers twisted in her lap. According to the newspaper, there were seven suspected abductions and murders. But only four bodies had been found so far.

Three women were still missing.

His gaze scanned over the article. Then, after a few moments, he glanced back up at her. "You want me to find one of the missing women?"

He wasn't getting it. "O-Open the paper."

Frowning, he opened it. Pictures of the missing women were inside. Grainy pictures. Black and whites but . . .

"I don't need you to find a missing woman."

"That's what we do." His gaze was on the photos, not her. There was a slight southern drawl beneath his words, just a little growl of sound, barely noticeable. "We search for the missing. We—" He broke off and she saw his gaze widen. Slowly, very, very slowly, that bright blue stare came back to her face. This time she felt his stare like a physical touch on her.

Eve licked her lips and said, "I don't need you to find a missing woman . . . because I'm pretty sure . . . I think—I think I *am* one of the missing. I'm one of the Lady Killer's victims, only I'm not dead like they say in the paper."

Gabe Spencer wasn't talking. So Eve let her words tumble out. She didn't want him to think she was crazy. She needed his help too much. "I'm not dead. I just . . . I don't remember anything. I can't remember anything that happened to me before June third of this year."

"And what happened on June third?" he asked, voice lacking all emotion.

"That was the day I woke up in St. Helen's Hospital." She'd woken to a room of white. To the sterile scent of cleaners and disinfectants. To the steady drone of machines.

And it had felt . . . *wrong.*

I should have heard the waves. Should have smelled the ocean. Those had been her first thoughts, but after them, she'd remembered nothing of her life. No names. No faces. No memories at all.

He just stared at her.

Her heartbeat thudded in her ears. "I'm not lying." Desperation cracked beneath the words. "You can check at the hospital, and they'll verify everything that I've told you."

Dissociative amnesia. That was what one of the doctors had told her she had. She'd sustained a strong blow to her head. Some memory loss was common after an injury like that.

But she wasn't just talking about *some* memory loss. She'd lost everything.

"I need your help," Eve told him, and she knew it sounded like she was begging—she was. "Because what's missing . . . my life is missing. *I'm* missing." She stood on trembling legs and went to his desk. She looked down at the paper that had fallen to his desktop. Her fingers touched the picture of the beautiful smiling woman. A woman that *could* be her. "If that's me, then

I want to know what happened." She glanced over at him. "I want my life back, Mr. Spencer."

"Call me Gabe."

A hard order as his gaze traveled carefully over her every feature. She couldn't read the expression in his eyes. She wanted to, so badly.

"Have you gone to the police with your story?" he asked.

Her lips tightened. "The abductions and murders happened along the southern Gulf Coast. Not here in Atlanta. They don't see the connection." And she believed the detective that she'd spoken with had just thought she was crazy. Since one of her endless doctors had been giving her a psych evaluation at the time, the cop had probably felt pretty justified in that opinion.

A faint line appeared between Gabe's brows. "No one has escaped from the Lady Killer."

"No one that you know about." Her fingers were shaking when she lifted them up to her neck. She pulled her hair back and pointed to the raised flesh, the long, white scar that slid around the left side of her throat. Usually, her hair covered that scar. She didn't want people staring at it and asking questions she couldn't answer. But this time . . . the scar could actually help her. Maybe. "I think that I got away from him."

In the next instant, Gabe was in front of her. To be such a big guy, he sure could move quickly. When his warm, strong hands touched her skin, Eve flinched, totally unprepared for the hot surge of awareness that shot through her. For months her body had been poked and prodded by dozens of specialists. She'd felt nothing. Been too numb. But one touch from Gabe . . .

Her gaze darted to his face. There was no sexual awareness in his gaze. No, his eyes were narrowed and intent on the scar that slid around the left side of her neck. "I—I have more scars," she whispered. She'd been ashamed of them at first, so many injuries, but if they were proof, if they could help her . . . "Someone used a knife on me." Long, deep slices. Two on her stomach. One on her thigh. One on her back. One on her left shoulder.

His fingers were caressing her neck, lightly stroking her skin.

He was tall, had to be about six-foot-three or six-foot-four, so she had to tilt her head back to fully meet his gaze. "Help me? Please?"

Their faces were so close. If someone came inside that office, they'd probably think they were embracing. *Lovers.* And, for just the briefest of moments, she did see a burning flash of awareness in Gabe's eyes. A surge of heat. Desire.

Her body tensed.

That flash vanished from his gaze. "Let me learn more," he said, voice guarded, "then I'll see about taking the case."

She nodded, refusing to let her hope slip away. But there was just one more thing. Unfortunately. She kept her chin up as she confessed, "I don't have any money. I can't pay you. I mean, if you take—" Her cheeks burned as she tried to press on. "I can work for you. I can help at LOST, I can do anything, just—"

Help me stop being no one.

Gabe seemed to shrug that concern away. "We'll work out payment later. *If* I take your case."

He stepped away from her. She immediately missed the warmth of his body. What was wrong with her? She didn't react this way to men. She didn't react this way to anyone.

"I'll need to see your medical reports. Need to know

where you were found before you were brought to the hospital. *Who* brought you in. I'll want to talk to all of your doctors."

Eve nodded quickly. "Right, of course."

A muscle flexed along his hard jaw. "If you're lying to me, you'll come to regret it very quickly."

The words held a silken menace.

"Why would I lie?" Eve whispered. Who would want this life? No, not a life. *Nothing*.

"Because the woman that you claim to be, the woman in that picture . . . Jessica Montgomery . . . her family is very, very wealthy."

It wasn't about the money. It was about being *someone*.

"I look just like her." Her words were hoarse. There was no way she and that woman could share the same face. That wasn't a coincidence.

"All of the Lady Killer's victims are similar in appearance. Blond hair, green eyes, mid-twenties." A pause. "Beautiful."

She shifted uncomfortably before him. "If I'm not her, then I'm still someone. My life is missing. Just . . . I want it back. I want to know what happened to me."

After a long, tense moment, he nodded, but said, "Sometimes, you should be careful what you want in this world. If you are one of the Lady Killer's victims, what do you think will happen next?"

Goose bumps rose onto her arms.

"From all accounts, he stalked these women. Chose them specifically. They are his targets. His prey. Wonder how he'll react when he realizes that one of his victims got away?"

She could feel all of the blood draining from her head. For just an instant she could smell the scent of the ocean. Could hear the cry of a seagull.

No, that wasn't a seagull. It was a scream. *My scream?*

Her mouth had gone dust dry with fear, but she still managed to say, "I—I want my life back."

"Then let's get started." His head inclined toward her, and Eve wondered if she'd just passed some kind of test. And if he had been deliberately pushing her, she couldn't help but wonder . . . what would have happened if she'd failed his test?

THE GORGEOUS BLONDE with the bedroom eyes and the never-ending legs lived in a homeless shelter.

Gabe watched her from his position across the street. She didn't realize that he'd followed her from LOST. The woman who'd called herself Eve Gray—but who claimed to be someone else entirely, perhaps Jessica Montgomery—had seemed oblivious to everyone and everything as she made her way back through the busy Atlanta streets.

She hadn't taken a taxi. Hadn't jumped into a waiting car.

She'd cut through the streets. Carefully counted out change for a bus.

And hadn't even noticed him slide onto the same bus with her.

Her head stayed down for most of the trip and she didn't talk to anyone. There were plenty of men who stopped to give her admiring glances. When you looked like her, it would be hard not to attract attention.

Oval face. High cheekbones. Small button of a nose. Lips red and plump. And those eyes . . . one look, and he'd found himself edging closer to her. Wanting to touch. *Needing* to touch.

That sure as hell wasn't the way he normally acted. His iron-tight control was legendary. He didn't look into a pair of big green eyes and think . . .

Want.

Not usually. But today he had.

He'd wanted. So he'd brought her into his office, even though he had three other appointments waiting. He'd brought her inside so he could get closer to her. Gabe had inhaled the light, sexy scent of her. Watched as her long legs moved a bit nervously beneath her skirt.

Then he'd heard her story.

He had been enraged when he'd seen the scar on her neck. The rush of rage hadn't been expected. He'd heard some brutal stories during his time at LOST, but his elemental fury at just seeing her scar . . . *What the hell had been up with that?*

She could be bullshitting him. It wouldn't be the first time someone had come in LOST with a bogus story. There were plenty of people out there willing to lie, steal, or even kill in order to get what they wanted.

And what they wanted? It was usually money.

The kind of money that Jessica Montgomery's family had in freaking spades.

A homeless shelter.

Gabe recognized the building on Lortimer Lane for exactly what it was. He just hadn't expected Eve to stop there, but she was rushing inside as if this were a normal routine for her. As if she belonged there.

Her medical files were on their way to his office. He'd be going to see her doctors soon. But right then . . .

Gabe found himself walking across the street and following her into the shelter.

He'd just stepped inside the doorway when a big, hulking, giant of a guy shoved one hand against his chest. "Where you think you're goin', buddy?" the man demanded, his voice a rumble that sounded like thunder.

Gabe raised his brows. "I need to talk with Eve." He

threw her name out, waiting for a response. If Eve was a regular there, then—

The man's hand slammed harder into his chest. Gabe didn't so much as move as the guy barked, "You stay away from Eve!"

Ah, this hadn't been part of the plan. The man's face was flushed a deep red, his bald head glinting, and it looked for all the world like he was about to start swinging punches.

Gabe figured he could take the guy, but fighting his way inside the shelter hadn't been on the day's agenda.

Guess the agenda just changed.

"Pauley, stop!" Eve's voice. High. Scared. Then she was there, running back toward them with a clatter of her high heels.

That was when he noticed that her heels were old, scuffed. The top and skirt that molded to her body so well—showing off her high, round breasts, and slim hips—the outfit hugged her so tightly because it was the wrong size.

Not her clothes.

Eve put a hand on Pauley's hunched shoulders. "He's a friend, Pauley."

Pauley's gaze darted to her. He shook his head and didn't move his hand from Gabe's chest. "No one . . . no one's supposed to follow you . . . Guarding door. I always guard."

"Yes, you do." Now her voice was soothing. She smiled at the man. Pauley looked like he was in his early forties. Tattoos slid down his arms. Dozens of them. Faces. Symbols. "And you guard us all very well. But it's okay for Gabe to be here. He won't hurt me."

The guy hesitated a minute longer, then slowly dropped his hold.

Gabe caught the fast exhalation of breath from Eve. "Thank you, Pauley," she whispered. "I'm so glad you're here to keep us safe."

Pauley shuffled back and resumed what Gabe now realized was his guard position at the door.

Eve bit her lip. She probably didn't mean to look sexy. He shouldn't have found her sexy. But there was something about her . . .

I followed her. Tracked her down. Not for the case. Because I couldn't let her leave. He'd passed off his appointments to his right-hand man, Wade Monroe, just so he could be free to track Eve.

"We need to talk," Gabe heard himself say.

"I'm assuming so." She offered a faint smile. "Since you followed me." Her cheeks held a pink tint, as if she were embarrassed. "Maybe we could talk outside?"

"Where's your room?" Gabe asked instead, just to see her response.

The pink deepened. "We don't . . . we don't have rooms here. Just beds." Then her chin lifted. Determined pride was there, in her eyes, in her posture.

Pauley had taken up his position a few feet away. Since the guy was so close, they didn't have much privacy, and Gabe definitely wanted privacy with her. Actually, he wanted her completely alone. "You're staying here?" Just so he was clear.

Eve nodded. "Ever since I got out of the hospital." She eased back and stepped into a small corridor. He followed her. "It's not exactly easy to get work when you don't have a real name, much less a social security number. And no work means . . ."

No money.

She cleared her throat. "I'm sure you understand."

Yeah, he did. Gabe looked around the old building.

In the next room, he could see a row of cots. Not beds. Cots. "You shouldn't be here." For some reason, the fact that she was there . . . it pissed him off. She didn't belong there.

Where does she belong?

"It's better than being on the street." Her chin was still up. "And you're going to help me now, right? You're going to help me get my life back? Once I know who I am, then I can get out of here. I can get my name. Get a job. Get a home."

Not a shelter.

His gaze locked with hers. He wanted her out of that place right then.

"You're helping me?" Eve pressed.

Dammit. He hadn't even started the research on her. The woman could be playing him. If she was, she'd regret it. He'd make sure of it. But for that moment . . . with Pauley muttering behind them . . . with a social worker frowning and heading toward them . . . all Gabe could say was, "Yes, I'm helping you." He'd find out all of her secrets. Good, bad, and everything in between. Maybe she'd regret it. Maybe he would. But from this moment on he and Eve would be tied together.

Until the case was closed.

GABE RETURNED TO LOST, adrenaline pumping through him. He spared a glance for the receptionist, Melody Gaines. "Call the team into my office."

Eyes wide, she nodded and reached for her phone.

He hurried inside his office, the memory of Eve's intense gaze following him. The memory of *her* following him.

When she didn't have any memories of her own.

He dropped into his chair. Rubbed a hard hand over

his face. He'd never taken a case like this before. Normally, his team *found* the missing. They started with a case, found the person . . . or sadly and far more often, they found the person's body. The remains.

This time, they were starting *with* the body. A very live one.

A faint knock sounded at his door, then the heavy wood opened and Victoria Palmer poked her head inside. A small pair of glasses perched on her nose, and she had her long dark hair pulled back at the nape of her neck. "We've got a new case?" Excitement hummed in her voice.

He nodded.

She rushed inside. "Do I have to wait on the others, or can you spill now?" Nervous energy seemed to bubble just beneath her surface. That was the way she always appeared. Tense, moving, on the verge of . . . something.

"You don't have to wait long," a low voice drawled from the doorway. "We're here." And Wade Monroe strode inside. Not an excess of energy from him. Slow, deliberate steps.

Dean Bannon followed right on his heels. Dean's assessing gaze landed on Gabe. "I'm guessing this has to do with the pretty blonde?"

"What blond?" Victoria demanded. "I didn't see—"

"Sarah's out on another case today," Gabe said, referring to the psychiatrist he kept on staff at LOST. "So go ahead and shut the door. I'll brief her later."

Dean shut the door. Gabe's team—his *top* team—because there were dozens of other support personnel who worked for LOST, closed in. They took the chairs around his desk and waited for their intel.

Gabe's gaze swept over them. Each team member

had been chosen because of the specific skills he or she possessed. When Gabe had started LOST, he'd wanted the best personnel working for him. He knew that his team was truly the last chance for many families. Those families *deserved* the best.

So he'd stolen Dr. Victoria Palmer away from Stanford. The forensic anthropologist was using her talents in the field now, and not just in the lecture hall. As for Wade Monroe, the decorated ex-Atlanta detective could dig to the truth faster than anyone Gabe had ever seen. Wade didn't mind getting his hands dirty. In fact, the guy seemed to relish that part of the business. Wade wasn't afraid of danger. He thrived on it. And his personal loss had made him a prime candidate for a position at LOST.

"You're keeping us in suspense," Dean murmured, his voice calm and flat. Totally without emotion or accent.

Dean had been working with the FBI when Gabe approached him. An agent in the Violent Crimes Division, Dean had known all about the real monsters who hunted in the world. And he knew how to *hunt* those monsters. With LOST, Dean had the chance to do plenty of hunting, without so much red tape holding him back.

As for the missing team member . . . Sarah Jacobs . . . Sarah was just as vital to the LOST unit. She had a fistful of degrees, but it was her experience as a psychiatrist and a profiler that mattered most to Gabe. When they tracked the missing, Sarah created victim profiles and profiles for their abductors. Their killers. Dean hunted the monsters, but it was Sarah who got into their minds. She went into the terrible, dark places that most people feared.

And as for Gabe . . . his job was to work in the field.

To take the knowledge that the team gave him. To find the missing. To work with his team and local law enforcement to close the cases.

And, of course, his job was also to finance the whole business.

Gabe gave a slow nod. "We've got a new case."

"Who does the blonde want us to find?" Wade pressed. "Hope it's not her husband." He gave a low whistle, one that had Gabe's eyes narrowing. "Because that woman was—"

"Off-limits," Gabe growled.

Wade's brows shot up.

"That woman," Gabe gritted out, "*is* the case." Then he pushed Eve's newspaper toward them. "She says her name is Eve Gray—no, actually," he corrected, "she doesn't *know* her real name. Eve is just the name she's using now." A name they'd given her in the hospital? He'd have to check on that.

"You're losing me, boss," Victoria said, even as she peered at the paper. "What does this 'maybe' Eve want us to do?"

"That story's about the Lady Killer case." Dean had stiffened. "The FBI's been tracking him for months. Ever since those bodies washed up after Hurricane Albert."

Hurricane Albert had been a vicious storm that struck early in the season, blasting across the southern Gulf Coast.

"We're going to find one of his victims? One that's still missing?" Victoria asked, then gave a low whistle. "Talk about high profile."

"We may have already found a victim." Gabe pointed to the black and white picture in the newspaper.

The room got very, very quiet.

"Eve doesn't remember anything before the third of

June. According to her, she woke up in a hospital, with no memories whatsoever."

"Sarah needs to be here," Wade said, sitting a little straighter. "She could tell if the woman was faking or—"

"Eve Gray wants us to find out who she really is."

Frowning, Victoria glanced up at him. "What does your mystery blonde have to do with the Lady Killer?"

"One of the Lady Killer's suspected victims is Jessica Montgomery." Twenty-six. Blond. Green eyes. Five-foot-six. Last seen down on the Alabama Gulf Coast—on Dauphin Island. "And Jessica Montgomery happens to look *exactly* like Eve Gray."

"Define 'exactly,'" Dean said as he began to lean forward.

"A dead-on match." Gabe met Dean's eyes. He knew the ex-FBI agent would understand the importance of this case more than the others. Dean had worked plenty of serial cases during his time at the Bureau. He knew how hard it could be to stop a serial. How unlikely it was that a victim could survive an attack, but if a victim did survive . . .

"If that's her," Dean's voice was tight with tension, "then she could lead us to the Lady Killer. We could find him."

"And to the other missing victims," Victoria added, her fingers tapping on her chin. "She would have been at his kill scenes. She would have seen everything."

Seen everything and then blocked it all from her mind?

"*If* she's telling the truth," Wade threw out. Because Wade would be the suspicious one. Pretty face or not, Eve wouldn't just automatically be accepted by him. "You want me to start the check on her?"

Gabe nodded. "Tear into every detail of her time at St. Helen's Hospital. Rip into her life."

The new life that she had. The life that had begun just months ago.

The order was cruel, but it had to be done. Before they could start connecting any dots that might exist between Eve Gray and Jessica Montgomery, they had to find out as much information as they could about Eve's "recovery" at St. Helen's.

Gabe had seen enough families with broken hearts. He wasn't just going to call up the Montgomerys and tell them that their missing daughter had been found.

His team would investigate Eve. Tear into her life. Learn her every secret. If she checked out, *then* they'd move forward.

And for Eve, that would be the time when the real danger began.

I hope you're ready for what's coming. Because if she truly had escaped a killer once, she might not be willing to put herself in the target zone again.

But if she turned out to be Jessica Montgomery, there wouldn't be much of a choice for her. The media would find out about her survival. The FBI would rush in.

And the Lady Killer would know that she was still alive.

EVE WOKE, HER heart racing in her chest and sweat covering her body. She grabbed the thin blanket and clutched it tightly in her hand. On the cots beside her, the other women kept sleeping. Soft snores filled the air. Faint mutters as Sue Smith talked in her sleep. Sue always talked, asleep or awake. Those mutters should have reassured Eve. *I'm not alone, others are here.*

Eve's gaze searched the darkness. She couldn't remember her dream, never could. But that was just normal . . . since she couldn't remember anything.

She rose from the cot, moving quickly. She always slept in her clothes. Sweatpants and a loose top. The men were down the hall, housed separately, but . . .

But they made her nervous. Most of them did, anyway. Just not Pauley.

She went to Pauley, because she knew that he'd be up, too. He never could sleep at night. He said the darkness reminded him too much of his time in battle.

She wasn't sure where or when Pauley had battled or even if he'd actually been in a war, but Eve never questioned him. He didn't question her story about having no past, so why should she question him?

Eve found him by the front door, in his usual guard position. He looked like a big dangerous shadow, but she knew he wouldn't hurt her. Pauley was gentle on the inside, good, but . . . damaged. She knew that, too.

He spoke slowly. Moved slowly.

It didn't matter. He was her friend.

"Someone's watching, Ms. Eve."

Pauley's quiet voice had her smiling at first, but then, as his words registered, her smile froze. "Wh-What do you mean?"

"I can feel the eyes. Just like I felt 'em in battle. The enemy's out there. He's watching."

She looked out of the window. Saw only streetlights. Darkness. "The doors are locked, right?" And they did have a security guard at the shelter. Except James spent most of his time sleeping. Pauley was a much better guard.

"Locked. Checked 'em all." Pauley rocked forward onto the balls of his feet. "Four times."

Her smile spread again. "Then I'm sure we're safe. Especially with you on duty." She said the words easily, but a chill still seemed to be icing her skin.

"Not safe. *Watching.*" He put his hands against the door and leaned forward. "I should go patrol."

He was going to open the door. Go outside. "No!" The sharp order broke from her, and Eve wasn't sure why. She grabbed Pauley's big hand in hers and held tight. "Stand guard in here, with me."

He gave a hard shake of his bald head. "Need to patrol. *Patrol.*"

But the darkness was scaring her. *Watching.* What if Pauley had seen someone out there?

Her left hand rose to her throat. Brushed lightly over the raised scar. A scream echoed in her mind. "Stay in here with me," Eve whispered.

Pauley glanced down at her, frowning.

She could confess to him, as she couldn't to anyone else. "I'm scared, Pauley," she said. Scared because she'd just taken a very dangerous step with her life. Eve Gray had no past. So she had no enemies. Nothing to fear.

But Jessica Montgomery? That woman had been a victim. She'd been hurt. Attacked. Left for dead?

The authorities were sure that Jessica Montgomery had been abducted by the Lady Killer, a sadistic serial killer who was still on the loose. Still hunting.

Still looking for Jessica?

She knew her hand held too tightly to Pauley's arm. "Stay inside," she said again. It was too dark outside. And, like a child, she was very much afraid that . . .

Monsters waited in the dark.

CHAPTER TWO

W HEN EVE WAS BROUGHT INTO THE HOSPITAL, she had lacerations on her stomach, her upper thigh, her back, and her shoulder." Dr. Ben Tyler leaned forward as he glanced first at Eve, then back toward Gabe, who didn't like the way the doctor's gaze seemed to linger a bit too long on Eve. Or the way it warmed every time it touched her. "She had suffered a concussion, and she was unconscious for almost three days before she opened her eyes."

Eve's body was tense. The doctor had agreed to talk with Gabe, but only if Eve stayed in the room.

"And who brought her in?" Gabe asked.

The doctor's face tensed. "She was found at a rest stop, just outside of Atlanta. A mother and her young daughter discovered Eve. She was . . . sprawled on the floor of the bathroom."

Eve flinched. Gabe almost reached for her hand. Almost.

Instead, the doctor stood, walked around his desk and put a comforting hand on her shoulder. The doctor was about Gabe's age, mid-thirties, with blond hair and dark eyes. Those eyes were lingering on Eve again.

Watch the bedside manner, Doc.

Gabe cleared his throat, okay he gave a rough growl, and the doc's gaze jerked back to him. Gabe asked, "So no one knew how Eve wound up at that rest stop?"

"I think the police talked with the security guards there. Interviewed some truckers, but . . ." The doc's hand tightened on her shoulder. "No one was able to discover anything for certain. Eve was found around four A.M. The place was pretty much deserted then."

So she'd just fallen out of the sky and wound up at a rest stop? Hell, no, there had to be more to that story. Maybe Wade would be able to find out exactly how she'd gotten there. The guy was already talking with his contacts at the Atlanta PD. Soon, he and Gabe would know everything about Eve's "discovery" at that rest stop.

"I don't remember anything about that place," Eve said. "I wish I—" She stopped and shook her head. There were shadows under her eyes. Shadows that hadn't been there yesterday. Had nightmares kept her up? Something else?

"You operated on Eve when she was brought in," Gabe said slowly, watching for a reaction on the doctor's face.

Dr. Tyler nodded. "I'm just glad I was here to help her."

Gabe would be glad when the guy got his hands *off* Eve. The guy's bedside manner was far too cozy. Intimate.

"Did she say anything in the O.R.?" Gabe pressed. "I know some patients can talk when the drugs hit them—" He broke off when he saw the brief flicker of the doctor's eyes. *She had spoken.* "What did she say?" Gabe pushed.

Dr. Tyler glanced back down at Eve. "Uh . . . it's probably nothing . . . it seemed so odd . . . just gibberish . . ."

Eve tilted back her head and stared up at him. "What did I say?"

He swallowed. "You said . . . 'I won. Tell the bastard . . . I won.'"

Wasn't that interesting? "Anything else, Doctor?"

Dr. Tyler dropped his hand from Eve—*fucking finally*—and moved back a few steps. "Everything else is in my report. The location of the wounds. The number of stitches. The—"

"Amnesia?" Gabe inserted smoothly. "Because that's the main issue, right? The fact that Eve can't remember a single thing about her life."

This time the dress that she wore was a little too loose, but the dark green just made her eyes seem to sparkle even more. Her shoes were the same. Black heels. Slightly scuffed. Clinging tightly to her arched feet.

"The term is 'dissociative amnesia.'" Hell. Now the guy was sounding pompous. Just the kind of shit attitude that Gabe wasn't in the mood to deal with right then. "It's common after an injury to the brain—"

He'd already done some research on amnesia that morning, and he'd spoken with Sarah—the lady knew all about the brain's mysteries. "It's not common to lose a whole life."

The doctor frowned. "Ah, no, it isn't." He wasn't sounding quite so pompous then.

"Was her injury that severe?" Gabe had to ask the question. The woman had no money. Nothing that she could claim.

So why not try to be someone else? Maybe Eve was running from something or someone, and by faking memory loss, she thought that she could escape from her past.

He wouldn't trust her. As a rule, he only trusted his LOST team members. Everyone else . . . well, he knew to be cautious.

He'd been burned before. Both during his time as a civilian and when he'd been a SEAL. Sometimes, pretty faces were the best at hiding lies.

And sending innocents to their deaths.

"Ah . . . brain injuries can be tricky to—"

Gabe raised a hand. "She had a concussion. It's in your big stack of files. You did MRIs, CT scans . . . all the works. So just tell me, did the injury cause her amnesia?"

Dr. Tyler's gaze hardened as a tight anger seemed to boil beneath his carefully controlled surface. "I can't make that diagnosis with absolute certainty. Not with the severity of her case and her . . . other injuries. It's quite possible that a . . ." Now his gaze slid to Eve once more, and the anger bled away. "It's possible that an . . . intense experience may have triggered Eve's amnesia."

Intense experience? Like say . . . an attack by a serial killer?

"Eve was attacked," the guy said flatly. "Someone spent a great deal of time hurting her. Her body was covered in bruises. Three fingers on her right hand were broken."

From the corner of his eye Gabe saw Eve flex her right hand.

"There is no doubt in my mind that she suffered a traumatic event, and, though I'm no psychiatrist—"

Good thing he had one on his team.

"—it could be possible that Eve's amnesia is a defense mechanism. Maybe she just doesn't want to remember what happened to her."

Eve surged to her feet. "You're wrong, Ben."

Ben? Not Dr. Tyler? *Too cozy.* And oddly damn annoying.

"I want to remember what happened to me. I want to remember it more than anything else." She exhaled on a hard breath and her shoulders trembled. "But I can't." Then she turned and marched from the room.

Gabe didn't follow her. Not at first. There were other questions that he still needed to ask the good doctor. "No one ever appeared to claim her?"

The other man's focus was on the door. *Still staring after Eve.* A muscle flexed in the doc's jaw. "No."

"Her picture was released to the paper." His research had already turned up that story. "You're telling me that not one single person came forward then?"

"Not one single person," Ben said, voice flat. He started to head for the door.

Gabe moved into his path. "Are there other injuries I need to know about?"

"Read the files. I—"

"You seem awfully . . . involved in Eve's case." And he could understand the temptation. A woman like Eve. Sexy. Vulnerable.

The doc had fallen under her spell.

I won't fall.

"I don't like your implication," Ben snapped immediately as his cheeks reddened. "She's my patient. *My* responsibility."

"Not anymore she's not." The words were blunt. "From now on she's mine."

Ben's gaze burned into his own. "Now who sounds involved?"

Gabe shrugged. "Eve's hired me to help her. That's what I'm going to do."

The doctor crossed his arms over his chest. "Eve has no money. How could she hire you to do anything?"

"Don't you worry about our payment plan," Gabe murmured. The doc might be a problem. There was no ring on the guy's finger, and the man had been spending a whole lot of time with Eve. Getting a little too close with the patient? "Now tell me," Gabe said, getting back to the part that mattered, "are there other injuries?"

Understanding dawned on the doc's face. "You want to know if she was . . . sexually assaulted."

Gabe just waited.

"Not that we could determine."

His breath eased out.

"We had police here with us when she was brought in, but there was *no* evidence left behind to link with her attacker. Even her open wounds looked as if they'd been washed." The doc's lips tightened, then he added, "Actually, she . . . she smelled like saltwater when she came in. If I didn't know better, I would have thought she'd just been pulled out of the ocean. Her hair was even still wet."

Gabe absorbed this information, then gave a slow nod. "Thank you, Dr. Tyler. My team will be in touch." He turned away and reached for the door.

"Eve's been released from my care." The words were low. "Technically, she's not my patient anymore. Anything between us . . . there's nothing wrong with a relationship."

Gabe knew his shoulders had tensed. The doc shouldn't have pushed right then. Glancing back, Gabe leveled a hard stare at the guy. "She's not your patient. She's *my* client." *And you need to stay the fuck away from her.*

But the doc wasn't backing down. The fellow took a step toward him. "If Eve wants me, if she needs a—a friend, I'll be there for her."

"You don't want a friend," Gabe fired, annoyed. "You're looking for a bedmate. Keep looking," he advised. "This woman . . . she's not for you."

He grabbed for the doorknob.

"Is she for you?"

The doc really wanted an ass-kicking. Pity he was supposed to be above that now. Having a corporate image could be such a pain in the ass some days. Gritting his teeth, Gabe managed to say, "Thanks for the help, Doc. Now stay the hell out of my way."

Before he gave into the urge to say or do anything else, Gabe opened the door and stalked outside. Eve turned toward him, her face pale, her blond hair sliding over her shoulders.

She glanced at him, then over Gabe's shoulder. The doc hadn't followed him out. Good.

Gabe took Eve's hand. "Let's go."

Her heels clicked on the floor. "I hate the smell of this place," she whispered.

Yeah, he'd spent more than enough time recovering in the VA hospital after his last mission with the SEALs. He could understand. To him, hospitals smelled like death and weakness.

Her gaze met his. "Did that . . . help you?"

Yes. But instead of replying, he said, "There's someone that I want you to talk with." Eve seemed to be double-timing it in order to keep up with his steps, so he slowed down.

"Who?" she asked, as her fingers curled around his hand.

He glanced down at her hand. Small, so delicate next to his much bigger, darker fingers. "Someone who will be able to tell me if you're lying."

"You . . . you think I'm playing you?" She didn't sound hurt, though, just curious.

Gabe shrugged.

"If you think that, why are you here with me?" She stopped suddenly in the middle of the hallway. Two orderlies had to swerve around them.

He faced her. "I'm here because I don't know what the truth is." His lips lifted in what he knew would be a mocking smile. "It's a quirk of mine. When I see a puzzle, I have to solve it."

"Is that what I am to you?" A faint furrow appeared between her brows. "Some kind of puzzle that you want to figure out?"

He didn't know what she was, yet. He only knew that he was drawn to her. That he wanted to help her. If her story turned out to be true . . .

"You're my client," Gabe said, the words soft as he leaned in toward her. From the corner of his eye he'd noticed that Dr. Tyler had just stepped out of his office. The guy was watching them. Gabe put his hand on her shoulder. "For now, that's the only thing that either of us needs to focus on."

For now . . . but later, later the game could change.

He led her down the hallway and out of the hospital. Away from the scent of death. A scent that stirred no memories for her, but reminded him too painfully of all that he'd lost.

ANOTHER DOCTOR. SURE, the lady in front of her—the woman with the wide, dark chocolate eyes and light gold skin—wasn't wearing a white lab coat, but Eve still recognized her for what she was. After spending so much time in a hospital, it had become too easy for her to weed out the doctors.

"Eve, I'd like for you to meet Sarah Jacobs," Gabe said, waving toward the other woman. Sarah stood, offering her hand. The lady was about Eve's height, but with short black hair.

Sarah's gaze was assessing as it slid over her features. "Nice to meet you, Eve," she murmured. Her palm was cool, soft.

Eve forced herself to smile in return. They were back at LOST, in Gabe's office, and Eve knew an interrogation was about to begin. "I've done this before," she said, feeling like she had to warn the other woman.

Sarah's brows rose. "Excuse me?"

"You're a—a shrink, right?"

Sarah gave a little nod.

Eve's gaze slid to Gabe. He was watching her so intently. Poor guy. He was about to be disappointed. "I've talked with three shrinks already. You're just going to tell me that I'm blocking some traumatic event." Her hand lifted and her fingers smoothed over the scar on her neck. That move was becoming a habit for her. "But I didn't need to be told that bit, I figured out the traumatic event part just fine on my own." When you woke up to find yourself covered in stitches, concussed, and with a broken hand, figuring out that you'd been *traumatized* was fairly easy.

Sarah's lips curled in what Eve knew was probably supposed to be a reassuring smile. It didn't reassure Eve. "I'm not here to diagnose you," Sarah said softly. "I'm just here to talk."

Lie. But Eve would play the game. Gabe thought that she was pretending. Well, she'd show him just how wrong he was. She glanced around the room. Saw the two chairs that had been moved to the side. She headed for the nearest one and sat down quickly. "Is he . . . is he going to watch?"

Silence.

Eve raised her eyes to meet Gabe's once more.

"Do you have a problem with me being in here?" he asked. His voice was such a low hard rumble. Every time she heard him speak, part of her tensed. Not because of fear but because of something else . . . something she didn't want to think about too much, not then. Not yet.

But Sarah carefully cleared her throat and said, "She may be able to speak more freely if—"

"I want you here." Eve cut across Sarah's words. "I don't have anything to hide from you." She tried to calm her racing heartbeat with a few slow breaths. "I want you to help me, not to constantly be thinking that I'm lying to you."

He inclined his head. "Then I guess that's settled."

Sarah sighed. "Guess so." Then she was coming across the room and taking the chair next to Eve. Her stare swept over Eve's features. "You should know that I spent the morning reading all of the medical reports on you. And I'm very sorry for all that you've suffered."

Sarah seemed like a nice woman, but there were shadows in her eyes. A lingering darkness that put Eve on alert.

"Don't worry," Sarah said, and Eve knew the woman's sharp stare had caught the tightening of her muscles, "I really just want to talk."

For now.

"If we're just talking . . ." Her voice sounded a little too high, so Eve took another deep, slow breath and grabbed onto her control with both fists. " . . . then tell me . . . what is it that you do here at LOST?"

Gabe took a seat behind his desk. His leather chair creaked. "Sarah is the one who helps us to understand the criminals who abduct and kill . . ."

I can smell the ocean.

"And I also help figure out why those perpetrators selected their victims." Sarah's voice was mild, a soft contrast to Gabe's harsh words.

Eve focused on her, trying to block Gabe, but he seemed to be dominating the room. Pulling her attention to him. "You think I'm one of the Lady Killer's victims?"

"That's what *you* think, isn't it?" Sarah asked.

And Eve knew the shrink session had begun. Because every time she met with a psychiatrist, the shrinks didn't answer her questions. They just turned the questions right back around on her. Pushed to learn all of her secrets. Pity she didn't have any secrets to give them. If only.

"What do you want to know?" She was ready to cut through the bull. If Gabe wanted this interview to make sure that she was legit, fine. She'd do it. But she didn't want to waste any more time. *Let's do this.*

"We're going to start simply," Sarah said. "Tell me, do you know who the president of the United States is?"

Like the others hadn't asked her that. "Since I saw him on the news last night, yes, I have a pretty good idea about the president's identity." Now, did she vote for him? *No clue.*

Sarah's expression didn't alter. "Why are you using the name Eve Gray?"

"Because I didn't want to be Jane Doe?" The response sounded flippant to her own ears.

Sarah just stared back at her.

Do better. This lady is sharp. Eve cleared her throat

and said, "Eve was the first woman, right? A blank slate? I picked her name because I was blank, too."

"Blank . . . but you still know about the story of Eve."

"Just like I still know that the sky is blue, the way I still know the pledge of allegiance, the way I can remember to count in French." She shrugged. "The facts are there, spinning in my head, but I don't have any personal memories."

Sarah had a notepad in her lap. When had she grabbed that? And the woman was scribbling now. Eve straightened her shoulders as she tried to see into that notebook. She even craned her neck a bit, but . . . *no dice*.

"I'm going to say a few words . . . with each word, tell me the emotion that you immediately feel."

Uh, sure.

"Home."

Eve waited for an emotion. Nothing came.

Sarah lifted a brow.

"I don't feel anything," Eve whispered. Was she messing up?

"If you don't feel an emotion, then does any association come to mind? If it does, just say it."

Eve felt like she was failing a test. She bit her lower lip.

"Let's try another one," Sarah said. "Hospital."

An emotion hit Eve this time. "Anger."

Sarah's pen scribbled quickly. "Knife."

"F-Fear. Eve hated the stutter that slipped from her.

"Ocean."

A scream built in her throat. "Death."

Her eyes darted around the room, and Eve saw that Gabe was still watching her. His eyes were so bright and blue.

Her breaths were ragged. Why? *Just a little word association game.* This should have been a piece of cake.

Give the responses that were expected, then move on to the next part of the interview.

"You're going great, Eve," Sarah murmured, "and I have a few more questions for you now."

Wonderful. Not.

"How did you celebrate your sixteenth birthday?"

"I don't remember."

"How old were you the first time you kissed a boy?"

I haven't kissed anyone. I don't know what it's like to feel lips pressed against my own. Her gaze was on Gabe, and her eyes dropped to his mouth. "I don't know." Her words were husky.

"How did the fingers on your right hand get broken?"

She flexed those fingers, still feeling the slight tightness there. "I don't know. I guess—I guess whoever stabbed me broke them." That made sense, right?

Sarah was still scribbling. Gabe was watching her like she was under some kind of microscope—*I am*—and she was starting to sweat.

"What's your favorite piece of Impressionist art?"

"Monet's *A Corner of the Apartment*," Eve replied immediately. In her mind, she could suddenly see that art. So beautiful. A crystal clear image.

"What was the subject of that piece?"

"Monet's son Jean," Eve said at once. Her eyes narrowed as she considered the image in her mind. "I always thought he looked a little lost in that big room. His mother sits behind him, but it's Jean that's the focus of the painting. The colors Monet used push for a tranquil feel." Her lips twisted. "It's a look into Monet's life."

Sarah wasn't scribbling now. She was gazing straight at Eve. "That's some . . . rather specific knowledge that you possess."

Now Eve was the one to frown. "I . . . didn't . . ." How *had* she known all of that? And the image that had been in her mind . . . it hadn't been a picture from the pages of a book. It had been the *real* art. As if she'd seen it somewhere before. A museum?

"It seems you know a bit about art," Sarah added.

Yes, she did. Her heart was suddenly beating faster. None of the other shrinks had asked anything about art. "How did you know to ask me that?"

Sarah cleared her throat. "I have a few more questions . . ."

Eve leaned forward and caught Sarah's hand, stopping the pen before it could scribble across the page. "I think . . . I think Gabe should leave now." Because this wasn't like the other interviews. Not anymore. She felt vulnerable, exposed, and having that intent gaze of his on her every second . . .

Too much.

She couldn't maintain her control with him focusing on her like that. His stare was like a touch that she could feel against her skin.

"Why do you want him to leave now?" Sarah asked.

Of course, another question.

"Because he's making me nervous." The truth. "I thought it would be fine if he stayed in here with us, but I'm too . . . aware of him." She could *feel* him. His eyes on her.

Gabe rose to his feet. His head inclined toward her, then he stalked for the door. "I'll wait outside until you're done, Sarah."

Eve watched him leave, and when the door shut behind him, she finally eased out a low breath. Her hands flattened on her thighs.

"You're very . . . attuned to him," Sarah observed.

Eve wasn't sure that attuned was the right word.

"Is that the way you are with all men?"

Eve flinched. Talk about a probing question. "No." She met Sarah's stare. "I actually . . . don't like being too close to most men." The men who stared at her with lust in their eyes. The men who had gazes that tracked over her body as if they were imagining her naked.

"Why not?"

"They want what I can't give." The awareness was instinctive to her.

"Sex?"

Eve swallowed. "That's personal, I—"

"Believe me, things will get a lot more personal if you stay with the LOST team. You aren't allowed to have secrets with us." The words were a warning.

"I don't have secrets," Eve denied. How could she have secrets when she didn't remember her life?

"Everyone has them."

She certainly believed that Sarah did. She could see those secrets in Sarah's eyes. "You're good at your job, aren't you?"

"Yes."

An actual answer. Eve hadn't expected that. Surprise rippled through her.

"I'm good at understanding killers," Sarah continued as she tilted her head to study Eve. "Maybe too good."

Goose bumps rose on Eve's arms. "How do you know the killers so well?"

What could have been pain flashed in Sarah's eyes. "I guess you could say it's in my blood."

Eve had no idea what that was supposed to mean.

"Are you afraid of Gabe?" Sarah asked as her pen poised over that notepad.

And back to the questions. *Sarah's* questions. "No."

Lie. Her lips pressed together for a moment, then she admitted, "Yes."

"Why?"

"Because he makes me feel . . ." Eve wasn't sure how to explain this. Not sure what to say, but . . . "He makes me feel like I want more."

No, not more. *Him.* He stirred an awareness within her that she wasn't sure she should be feeling. Need, lust . . . in the void of her life, did she even have room for those?

"And Gabe doesn't remind you of anyone?"

Her breath came a little faster. "No."

"When he touches you—"

"Gabe hasn't—"

Sarah held up her hand. "I just mean casually. When his hand brushes against you or if he takes your arm, how does that make you feel?"

Alive.

"Eve?"

"I'm probably supposed to say it makes me feel safe, right?" That was what the LOST team was about. They were the good guys. Good guys equaled safety.

Sarah's eyes held hers.

"I don't feel safe when he touches me. I don't ever feel safe." Fear was the only companion she knew. "But when I'm near Gabe, I also don't feel dead."

Sarah put down her pen. "And do you feel . . . dead . . . a lot of the time?"

"I feel like I've drowned." *Soft.* "I feel like I walk through life like a ghost."

"Until Gabe touches you . . ."

She fisted her hands in her lap. "I don't want to be dead." Her heartbeat was too fast. The drumming sounded too loud as it echoed in her ears. "Can you help me? Can you *please* give my life back to me?"

GABE POUNCED THE minute Sarah slipped from his office. "Well?"

Sarah glanced back over her shoulder. She'd pulled the office door shut, and Eve was sealed inside. "Let's take a little walk."

Gabe turned. Saw Wade heading toward them. Gabe motioned toward the door. "Make sure she doesn't leave."

"The blonde's in there?" Wade saluted. "Don't worry, I'll keep her busy."

Gabe grunted and followed Sarah back to her office. He'd thought Eve might be more relaxed if she talked with Sarah in a place she'd been before, but . . . hell, Eve had appeared so brittle during the interview that it looked as if she'd break apart any moment.

So much for helping her to relax.

Sarah pushed open her office door. "I have to do more research on her. This was just a preliminary session."

He held up his hand. "Save me the spiel, Sarah. I know how the deal works. I'm not looking for a full profile on the woman right now. I just want to know . . . do you think the amnesia is real?"

"Based on the medical reports, the conversations I had with the other psychiatrists—"

She was about to drive him crazy. *"Sarah."*

"I think it could be real."

Could be?

"But some of her affect . . . it's off."

Now that revelation had his muscles locking.

"I felt like she was telling me what she *thought* she

should be saying. Almost like she was following some kind of script." Sarah shook her head, then rubbed the back of her neck. "The only time I felt like I was seeing the real woman was when she talked about you."

They'd talked about him? Gabe wasn't sure what to make of that revelation. Just how had he worked his way into the conversation?

"I think you may be a trigger for her."

She sure seemed to trigger some primal responses in him.

"And you're attracted to her, aren't you?" Sarah pressed.

"Sarah, the woman is gorgeous." Understatement. With those legs and curves, she was more like a walking wet dream. "I'm betting most men are attracted to her." The doc at St. Helen's sure had been. Jerkoff.

"But she's not attracted to most men. She's attracted to *you*."

Now that news was interesting and arousing. But Gabe made himself say, "I don't have sex with clients. The woman is—"

"Unusual. Not our typical case at all."

Sarah sounded confused. Definitely *not* a typical situation for her.

Gabe crossed his arms and waited.

"By all accounts, Jessica Montgomery was a gifted artist."

So the conversation had just taken a one eighty. He figured Sarah would bring things back around, eventually. She usually did. He just had to wait for her to connect her dots.

Sarah put her notepad on her desk. "Your Eve has a strong grasp of art history. I asked her a series of questions at various points during the interview—all related to art facts that I had to research before the session with her—and she easily answered them all."

Interesting. He'd done his own research. "Jessica Montgomery received her master's degree in art history from the University of Alabama," he said. So if Eve actually was Jessica, that art knowledge would make sense.

"And Jessica Montgomery was right-handed," Sarah said. "If you want to hurt an artist, well, I think breaking the hand she uses to paint would be a perfect way to start your torture."

Gabe kept his expression blank. "The other four bodies that were recovered showed no signs of broken bones."

"No, they didn't." Her voice held that faint, distracted air that she got when she was trying to slide into a killer's mind.

"So why would Eve be different? If she were a victim of the Lady Killer—"

"The Lady Killer's signature is torture. Control. His M.O. is that he stabs his victims, but the crime isn't about the stabbing. It's about hurting his victims. Establishing his control and dominance." She rubbed her arms, as if fighting off a chill. "If Eve is one of his victims, then he went a step further with her. He let his attack get very personal."

Gabe wasn't liking this news. Not at all.

"The personal nature of that attack would suggest that she isn't some random victim to him. She matters. He'll view her differently, especially once he learns that she survived his attack."

He wanted the simple truth. "Is she for real? Is her story—"

Sarah gave a slow nod. "I think it's time we contact

the Montgomery family. We can get their DNA and find out if Eve is their daughter or if she's someone who is very, very good at lying."

Good enough to fool even Sarah?

Because no one had ever fooled Sarah before. Not witnesses and not even cold-blooded serial killers. She got into all of their minds, and she didn't stop until she'd learned every secret that they possessed.

CHAPTER THREE

NIGHT HAD FALLEN OVER THE CITY ONCE MORE. Gabe eased his car to a stop near the shelter, his fingers tightening around the wheel. He didn't want to leave Eve alone in that place.

He let his attack get very personal with her.

The Lady Killer was still out there. Eve's picture had circulated in the newspapers a while back. What if the killer already knew that she was still alive? What if he was hunting her even now?

Gabe had recently learned a great deal about the so-called Lady Killer. Thanks to Dean, he had gotten access to the FBI's files on the serial. The Lady Killer stalked his victims—wealthy socialites—for weeks as he played with them. He broke into their homes. Took small possessions.

Then he took their lives.

Plenty of people had access to the shelter. It would be so easy for a stranger to walk inside and get to Eve. *So easy.*

"Did I pass your tests?" Eve asked him, her voice guarded.

Gabe glanced over at her. A faint glow from the streetlight spilled into the Jag, illuminating her face.

"Do you think I'm a con artist or a victim?"

"I think you're a woman who has been hurt." No denying that. "One of my team members, Wade Monroe, is contacting the Montgomery family. We'll get DNA from them and find out—"

"If I'm Jessica." There was hope in the words. Enough hope to break his heart.

Gabe nodded.

"When will we know?"

It would take a few days, even with the strings that he could pull. "As soon as possible," he said, not wanting to give her a specific timetable.

"Thank you." Then, just like that, she was across the car, giving him a tight hug. "Thank you."

His arms wrapped around her, an instinctive response. She smelled faintly of flowers, a sweet scent that teased his nose, and her body was soft against his.

She tried to pull away, as if realizing what she'd just done.

For an instant he was tempted to hold her, to keep her close.

She's a client. Focus.

He let her go, but his body ached.

"I . . . um . . . I should get inside."

Yes, she should. While he was still clutching tight to his control. The control that said he shouldn't push her. Shouldn't want her so much. Not when she'd already been hurt so badly.

Her fingers reached for the door.

"Let me," he said, voice rumbling, and Gabe climbed from the Jag. In seconds he was on the passenger side, opening her door for her. She rose, and her body brushed against his.

He stepped back. *Distance.* He seriously needed to put some distance between them. But even with some fast steps back, he could still smell that light and sexy scent that clung to her body. And he still wanted her.

"Your shrink asked me a lot of questions about you," Eve told him as she stood temptingly close.

Gabe inclined his head. "I'm sure—"

"I think she wanted to know why I respond so much to you."

Oh, hell, she'd just said . . . He cleared his throat even as part of his body surged in quick response to *her*. "It's a tense situation, you're—"

"You don't look at me as if I'm a victim."

He stopped talking.

"I mean, you know what I am, but you still look at me and seem to just see me . . . as a woman."

"Others see you the same way." Doc Tyler sure did. Bastard.

"It's different with you," she murmured as she stepped even closer to him. Her head had tilted back so she could look into his eyes. "I don't know what I've felt for other men before."

Why did the idea of others have his body knotting with tension?

"But I know that when I see you, I want." A hushed confession. "I just . . . I needed to tell you that."

And he needed to make his self-control a hell of a lot stronger. Her lips were just inches from his, and he wanted her mouth beneath his. Wanted her lips open. Needed to taste her.

"You're the first man I've wanted since I opened my eyes in that hospital."

He could actually feel his control splintering. *Client. Cli*—

"You probably don't want me. I—I might not be your type."

Now her gaze had fallen, as if in embarrassment. Had she really just asked if she was his type? She was probably every damn man's type.

"But you make me feel normal again, so I had to tell you—"

His fingers curved under her chin. "Eve . . ."

Her smile was a little too big. Too bright. "I don't think I can handle anything else right now, I'm . . ." She pulled away. Stumbled onto the sidewalk. "I just wanted to tell you how I felt," she told him again.

Then she walked into the shelter, her steps hurried. As if she were running.

From him.

He stared after her. She wanted him.

And she was so fucking beyond his reach.

"EVE."

She frowned at the voice. A hard, dark voice that was familiar to her.

"Eve, wake up."

Hands were on her, shaking her lightly.

Not a dream.

Her eyes flew open and she rose with a scream on her lips.

But a hand was there, choking back the scream. She punched out, fighting, kicking.

"Eve, shh . . . I'm trying not to wake everyone in the place."

That voice . . . it was Gabe's voice. She stopped fighting. Blinking, she let her eyes adjust to the darkness. Gabe was on the edge of her cot, leaning over her.

Snores and faint, sleepy mutters came from the others in the room. He'd slipped inside but hadn't woken anyone.

The thought chilled her. She'd thought that she was safe there. Because she wasn't alone. *Safe.*

Only he'd gotten right to her. Put his hands on her. Been close enough to kill.

If Gabe had been the killing kind.

Her heartbeat thundered in her chest.

But he wasn't a killer. He was a protector. She could trust him.

"Don't be afraid."

Too late. "Why are you here?" Her voice was a rasp. She needed her heartbeat to slow down. The frantic beat actually hurt her chest.

"Because I want you to come with me." He glanced around at the others in the room. "I don't . . . this place isn't secure enough, Eve. If the Lady Killer's out there and we start stirring up your past . . ."

He could come for me.

That thought didn't have her heartbeat slowing down any.

"Get your things," Gabe ordered, his voice low. "And let's get out of here."

He didn't understand, and it was humiliating to admit, but, "I don't have any other place else to go." She did odd jobs for the shelter's manager. The lady paid her under the table. It was the only way that she could get any cash.

"You're coming with me."

Eve scrambled back on the cot as she tried to put some space between them. His words were mere whispers, but they screamed in her mind. Was this about what she'd said earlier? She shouldn't have told him that she wanted him. Now he thought that she wanted sex.

I do.

But, not—

Gabe swore. "Stop it. Whatever is going through your head, just stop." His fingers curled around her wrist. "I've got a spare bedroom at my place. Until this situation is sorted out, I want you close. I want to make sure you're safe."

She was a situation, huh? That was better than being a problem case. The nurses at the hospital had called her that when they thought she couldn't hear them.

Only she had always heard them.

"I'm not leaving here without you," Gabe growled. "So either I'm about to bunk down here on the floor—I don't think your roommates are going to like that too much—or you're going to get your things and come with me."

She pushed back the covers. He frowned, and she knew he'd seen the clothes she wore. So she liked to be prepared. She didn't want to be caught off-guard.

He won't see my body. I'll have on clothes and he won't see.

She stilled as the thought pushed through her mind. Where the hell had that just come from?

"Eve?"

"I'll come with you." Because she trusted him. He was the good guy, just as she'd thought during her interview with Sarah. Good guys didn't hurt anyone. Good guys saved the day. Everyone knew that. She slipped from the bed, then bent near the floor to grab her bag. "I'm ready."

He took the bag from her. "This is it?"

"Yes." Two dresses. A shirt and a skirt. A pair of jeans. Underwear. One pair of high heels. She grabbed her tennis shoes from their position at the foot of her bed. *This is everything I own.*

In the shadows, it looked as if his face tightened, but

he didn't say anything else. Just reached for her elbow. Gabe held tight to her as they made their way, not to the front of the shelter where she knew that Pauley would be standing guard, but toward the back of the building.

"I—I'll need to tell the manager." She didn't want Georgia to think that she'd vanished. Though plenty of others had wandered from the shelter in the weeks she'd been there.

"I'll take care of notifying her tomorrow."

And tomorrow, she'd come back to see Pauley. She'd tell her friend good-bye.

Then Gabe was pushing open the back door. She frowned. "Wasn't the door locked?"

"I took care of the lock."

He seemed to be fairly skilled at taking care of things. But were good guys supposed to pick locks?

The Jag waited in the darkness. She stilled and found that she couldn't move forward.

I shouldn't leave with him.

"Do you trust me, Eve?" His voice was low, right near her ear. She could feel his breath lightly blowing across her skin.

She wanted to nod and say that she trusted him, but . . . she wasn't sure. To just walk out into the night with him—that thought terrified her.

"I just want to keep you safe."

Her head turned as she looked back at the shelter. "I didn't feel safe there." She could whisper this confession now. "I felt like someone was watching me."

His fingers tightened around her elbow. "Get in the car, Eve." Not so gentle and soft anymore.

She moved woodenly and climbed into the car. Her body sank into the soft leather seat. Gabe shut the door behind her, and then they were heading down the alley.

Only Gabe hadn't turned on his headlights. They were easing away silently in the dark.

Unease tightened her stomach. Why did they need to sneak away? "Gabe?"

"Better safe than sorry," he muttered, and the Jag slipped from the alley.

She glanced behind them. Saw only darkness. A shiver slid over her. She'd just left the only place that she'd known as a home.

"Trust me," Gabe urged her. "I'll keep you safe."

She wanted to believe him. Wanted that so badly, but deep inside, a small voice whispered . . .

You've heard that promise before from a man, and it was a lie.

PAULEY ROCKED BACK and forth on his feet. The night was quiet, so quiet.

He liked the quiet.

Ms. Georgia had told him that he should sleep when it was dark and quiet, but he didn't like to sleep. When he slept, he had bad dreams.

Dreams of guns and screams. Of deserts and men dying.

He rocked faster. His fingers drummed against his thigh. Drummed fast like the shots from a gun.

But he didn't hear any shots.

It was quiet.

He liked the quiet.

His gaze swept from the left to the right. He'd told Ms. Georgia that he'd stand guard tonight. He watched the street. Made sure no one came too close to the shelter.

Made sure no one got in.

There was a creak of sound behind him, and he turned, expecting to see Ms. Eve. But she wasn't there.

Ms. Eve didn't like the quiet either. He knew . . . when she'd first come to the shelter, she'd woken, screaming in the night. It had taken four days for her screaming to stop.

Now, Ms. Eve didn't always sleep at night. Sometimes she liked to come up to the front with him. Liked to stand guard with him.

The faintest rustle reached his ears. A sound that didn't come from behind him. But . . . outside. On the street.

It could have been nothing.

Have to guard. Have to protect.

His job was to watch the shelter. Ms. Georgia said it was an important job.

His hand rose to the locked door. He'd heard a rustle like that last night, but Ms. Eve hadn't let him go outside then.

He glanced over his shoulder once more. Ms. Eve was sleeping. Everyone was sleeping in the quiet. Everyone but him.

Have to guard.

He opened the door. Headed outside. His gaze swept to the left. To the right. There were thick shadows near the side of the building. Shadows that were moving.

Pauley tensed because that shadow—it was a man.

"I need to get inside," the man said as he crept closer.

Pauley put his body in front of the door. "I don't know you." He didn't. Pauley knew everyone who came to the shelter. Ms. Georgia introduced him to everyone.

"I need to see the woman."

There were a lot of women in the shelter. "I don't know you," Pauley said again. The man hadn't stopped walking. Pauley shoved his hand against the man's chest and stopped him.

"She's blond, early twenties . . ."

Pauley frowned. Only one blond woman in the shelter. "Ms. Eve's sleeping."

"Is she . . . ?"

Pauley shook his head. "I don't know you." Ms. Eve's friends shouldn't be coming there at night. He pushed hard against the man's chest, sending him stumbling back. "Leave."

The man hunched his shoulders. "I need to see Eve."

Pauley fisted his hands. Ms. Georgia said he wasn't supposed to fight anyone, that he'd get in trouble for fighting, but no one was getting inside his home. He was the guard. "Go away."

The man stared up at him. The man had angry eyes. Pauley didn't like his eyes. He liked Ms. Eve's eyes. They were kind.

"You shouldn't get in my way," the man said.

Pauley wasn't moving. "Shouldn't . . . come to my house." Because it was his house. His family. He protected them.

The man charged at him. Pauley lifted his fist, ready to fight no matter what he'd promised Ms. Georgia but . . .

Something hard and sharp slid into his chest. Pauley gasped, the pain familiar. Reminding him of another time, another place.

The gunfire had been so loud. He hadn't seen anyone come close, but the enemy had snuck up on him even as the gunfire blasted. Had sliced with a long blade.

A blade like this one.

Guard.

Protect.

Another stab in his chest. Pauley's legs were sliding down. He hit the pavement. He felt cold. He should ask

Ms. Georgia for a blanket. Maybe Ms. Eve would give him one, she'd given him hers to use before.

He opened his mouth to call out for her, but he found that he couldn't speak.

So quiet . . .

His breath rustled out.

I like the quiet.

HE SLIPPED THROUGH the dark hallways of the shelter. Eased past the sleeping men and women. He knew who he wanted. Knew he had to see her with his own eyes once more.

A turn, then a few more steps . . .

The knife was in his back pocket, still stained with the fool's blood. He hadn't wanted to attack him, but the man had messed up everything.

He'd had to get inside the shelter. Had to find her.

He turned, and the last room was before him. He'd searched everywhere else. Seen no sign of the blond woman.

There were four beds in this area. Women slept in three of them. The fourth bed . . .

Empty.

Rage began to churn within him. The bed shouldn't have been empty. She should have been there, waiting for him.

One of the old women started talking in her sleep. He backed up quickly and darted into the shadows.

No Eve. She wasn't there. *She. Wasn't. There.*

His teeth snapped together. He didn't run back for the entrance. He didn't want to see the man's body again.

A mistake.

There had to be another way out. He fumbled with the doors. Hurried.

Where was she?

He'd caught sight of her before. Knew that she'd been staying at the shelter. But she'd left, just as he came for her.

Eve.

He tasted the name. He rather liked that name.

He'd find her again. She wouldn't get away.

No one ever got away.

The knife in his pocket was a familiar weight. *I'll find you, Eve.* His promise.

She could run, but she wouldn't escape. There was no escape. Only death. When he found her, he'd make her beg for death. She'd cry and she'd plead and she'd offer him *everything.*

And then, after he'd enjoyed the sound of her cries, she'd die for him.

CHAPTER FOUR

Eve couldn't make herself move out of the doorway. "This is . . . really nice." Her voice sounded lost, almost scared, so she cleared her throat. And her words were rather lame because *nice* was a serious understatement. When Gabe had said that he was taking her to his place, she'd expected an apartment. Maybe a little house. Her expectations had been *way* off.

Gabe lived in a penthouse. One that gave him a huge, 180-degree view of the Atlanta skyline. She could see all of the glittering Atlanta lights from her perch right there—mostly because he had giant floor-to-ceiling windows that seemed to stretch around the entire place.

His hand pressed lightly into her lower back. "I've got a top-of-the-line security system installed here. You'll be safe."

Eve made herself step forward. Her knees felt a bit shaky. *I don't belong here.* "Let me guess . . ." she murmured. "You installed the system?"

He laughed a bit as he shut the door behind them. His laugh was like his voice. Deep, rumbling, sexy. "Guilty." He reset the security system, then he just . . . stared at her.

She should say something. Do something. But her hands were twisting in front of her and her mouth had gone dry.

I'm alone with him. And, as he closed in on her, Eve realized that she'd never been more aware of him. He was tall, so tall, and his muscles stretched the T-shirt he wore. This guy was powerful and strong, and she wished that she knew more about him.

Why did I leave with him? She should have stayed at the shelter.

"It's all right," Gabe told her softly. Could he see the fear on her face? "You're safe with me."

She didn't feel safe right then. "Maybe I should go back to the shelter." She felt so out of place in that penthouse. *Too rich. Too . . . everything.*

"I circled back to that place three times before I came in and got you." His jaw hardened. "And it was so easy to get inside. Too easy. If you are Jessica Montgomery, a target is going to be on you. The Lady Killer *will* come after you."

Those words were not what she wanted to hear.

"I'll keep my hands off you." His hands were off her. He wasn't touching her at all. Just standing about a foot away. "You don't have to worry about that."

Eve shook her head. "I wasn't worried." And she hadn't been. Not even a little bit.

The lights were on in his penthouse, and his blue eyes seemed to blaze even brighter at her words.

"I, um, I should have said thank you." Now her cheeks heated. "You're really going above and beyond for me. Especially considering that I haven't paid you anything." Shame burned through her. "Maybe I can start doing some paperwork or filing at LOST for you. I could—"

"Eve."

She liked the way he said her name. Liked the roughness of his voice.

"Wait until we figure out what the hell is going on. Then we'll talk about payment."

But she didn't like being so indebted to him. To anyone. "I didn't expect this." Her hands rose helplessly to indicate their surroundings.

His face seemed to soften. "It's just a home, Eve."

No, it wasn't. Her home had been a shelter. This place was something entirely different. A whole other world.

"I did some government contracting over the years that turned out to be quite . . . lucrative."

She thought that might be a serious understatement.

"But LOST is what matters most to me."

Her gaze held his. There was a sincerity in his voice that couldn't be doubted.

"And, Eve, I *will* help you." Those words sounded like a vow, and the tension between them just increased. But then he pointed to the hallway on the right. "The guest room is that way." Then his hand moved to the left. "And my room—if you should need me—is over there."

I do need you. She'd bared her soul to him earlier. Told him how she felt. He'd stared at her with a clenched jaw and glittering eyes. Did he want her? She didn't know. The man was so hard to read.

But . . . he tempted her.

I'll keep my hands off you.

That had been his promise. Not hers. So Eve put her hand on his chest. It was rock-hard. Seriously—*hard.* She leaned onto her toes and pressed a quick kiss to his cheek. "Thank you."

He was as still as a statue before her.

Embarrassed now, Eve started to pull back.

In a flash, his hand flew up and his fingers locked around her wrist. As she stared into his gaze, Eve stopped breathing.

He wants me.

She could see his desire. Right there. In his eyes. In the hard lines of his face.

"You can only push so much," he warned.

She wanted to push him more.

But Gabe shook his head and stepped back. His hand freed hers. "You're a client." It sounded as if he were trying to remind himself of that fact. He turned away from her. Ran a hand through his hair. "Get some rest. Tomorrow is going to be a long day. One of my LOST agents, Wade Monroe, he's already made contact with Pierce Montgomery."

She didn't say anything. She'd met Wade. After her interview with Sarah, Wade had come into the office and, well, she was pretty sure that he'd been there just to keep an eye on her. He hadn't said much, just watched her. Unnerved her with his golden eyes.

She knew Wade, but Pierce Montgomery? He was—

Gabe looked over his shoulder. "Jessica's brother."

Eve swallowed.

"The guy lives in Birmingham, so it won't take him long to travel here. After Wade talked to him, Pierce insisted on coming to town. He wants to meet you."

Jessica's brother.

"DNA will prove if you're Jessica. And a brother— he'd know his own sister."

Her fingers were trembling.

"So get some sleep," he advised again, his voice even deeper. "And maybe tomorrow you'll even get your life back."

Maybe she would.

And that thought terrified her.

Eve turned away and hurried toward the guest room.

"Eve?"

She stopped.

"If you need me, I'm here."

He didn't mean the words to be a sensual promise. She was sure he didn't, but . . . *I want him.*

She went into the guest room. Closed the door and slumped against the wood. *What is happening to me?*

Ben had been in her life for weeks, and the doctor had made his interest obvious. He was handsome, charming, and he made her feel *nothing.*

But Gabe . . . Gabe touched her and . . . she melted.

Her breasts were tight, aching, and a hot, sensual yearning had filled her sex.

All from his touch.

What is wrong with me?

She had to get herself back under control, right away. Too much was happening. Too much was at stake. Pierce Montgomery was coming to town. He could tell her if she really was Jessica or if she was just a stranger to him.

Desire, need . . . that could wait.

It can wait.

She hurried toward the bed. Climbed up on a mattress that was as soft as a cloud. She kicked away her shoes but didn't undress. She never did, not when she slept. She hadn't bothered to turn on the light—in that room with its big windows, there was no need for extra light.

She lay in that bed, too aware of the silence. There were no other people near her. No snores. No Sue talking in her sleep. There was only silence. Unnerving, total silence.

Gabe is close by. So close.

She stared up at the ceiling. *I'm safe here.*

Her breaths came, a little too fast and ragged.

Tomorrow, I might get my life back. Tomorrow . . .

She just had to get through the night first.

HER SCREAM TORE through the night. High, terrified, and abruptly cut off.

Gabe leapt from his bed and ran to her. His bare feet flew over the hardwood floor of his penthouse and he shoved open her door. *"Eve!"*

She was sitting straight up in bed, still wearing her T-shirt and jogging pants. Her hair streamed over her shoulders and her body shuddered. "I'm sorry! I—I haven't done that in weeks." Eve jumped from the bed. "I'm sorry." She backed away from him, edging toward the wall.

Gabe's fist slammed into the light switch and illumination flooded that room. Eve's eyes were wide, stark, the green terrified and—and her cheeks were wet with tears.

As he stared at her, her hands lifted and she quickly swiped away the tears. "I didn't mean to wake you." Her back hit the wall. "I'm so sorry."

He advanced toward her.

Eve tensed.

"It's okay," Gabe told her, lifting his own hands in what he hoped was a reassuring manner. "You were probably just having a nightmare. That happens." It happened to him plenty.

He could almost feel her terror filling the room.

"I'm sorry I woke you," she said again. Her face was far too pale. "I—I used to wake the others in the shelter. If I hadn't stopped . . . stopped screaming, they were going to make me leave. Ms. Georgia said there wasn't a choice and I—"

She broke off.

He was right in front of her. He wanted to pull her into his arms and hold her. Her scream had sent adrenaline and a killing fury surging through him. When he'd heard her cry, he'd been afraid that the killer had found Eve. That she was in danger, hurt, and he hadn't been able to get to her fast enough.

"You scream a lot?" he asked her carefully.

"Sometimes," was her hushed confession, "when I sleep."

"How did you stop screaming at the shelter?"

Her gaze lowered. "I just . . . I didn't sleep much. Didn't sleep too deeply. Pauley . . . he likes to keep guard out front. I spent some nights out there with him."

No wonder she'd seemed so on edge when she first walked into his office. The woman had been living in terror for weeks. "You felt safe here," he realized, "and you let yourself sleep." A deep sleep that had let her nightmares slip in.

"I'm sorry—"

He touched her. Wrapped his arms around her shoulders. *So much for keeping my hands off her.* "Don't apologize again."

Her lashes lifted as she met his stare.

"Don't," he told her. *Her eyes are fucking gorgeous.* "Not to me, do you understand? You have nothing to apologize for. Everyone has nightmares." He could feel the heat of her skin through that thin T-shirt.

"You don't." She gave a laugh that seemed to be part laugh, part sob. "I bet you don't fear anything or anyone."

"That bet's wrong." And his left hand slid down her

arm. Gabe caught her fingers. Lifted them to his chest. He'd run right from bed, and he only wore a pair of black boxer shorts. He put her hand on his bare chest, so close to his heart. Over the thick scars that would always mark him. "We all have nightmares."

Her breath caught. Her gaze lowered to his chest, and he saw her eyes widen.

"There's a reason I'm not a SEAL anymore. The last mission almost took my life." He'd been trapped in that hospital bed for weeks. He turned carefully, giving her his back. Her fingers trailed over his skin. "He shot me in the back first. When I fell, he kicked me, rolled me over, because he wanted to see my face." Gabe turned back toward her. "He smiled and he aimed his weapon at my heart."

Her hand lifted again, and her fingers pressed to his wound. The scar that reminded him to be careful who he trusted.

Enemies were everywhere. Far too often, they hid in plain sight.

"He thought I couldn't fight back. He was wrong. Even as he fired, I shot my weapon, and we were both soon on that ground, bleeding out."

Her fingers seemed to scorch him.

"Medics got to us. At first they thought I'd be paralyzed. That first bullet had come so close to my spine . . ." *He'd wanted to paralyze me. To make me weak. Easy prey.* "But in a war zone, you don't always get a perfect shot. He missed my spine and he missed my heart." *I was always a better shot than you.* "I didn't."

Eve didn't remember the life that gave her nightmares. Gabe could never forget his past. Only in his nightmares the bullet hadn't missed his heart.

And his teammate had been laughing when he shot him.

"Nightmares can't hurt you."

She still had her hand on his chest. Her touch made him too aware, it— *Bullshit*. Hell, she just made him aware. His boxers were stretched to capacity right then even though he was talking about the second worst night of his life.

The *worst* night? That had been when he found his sister's body.

And that night caused other nightmares. Nightmares that he'd never escape.

"Scream if you want," he told her, rolling back his shoulders but not stepping away from her. He liked her touch too much. "I don't mind."

Her lips trembled. He wanted those lips. Wanted her mouth beneath his. Wanted to know how she'd taste. Would she be as sweet as she smelled? Would her lips part beneath his? Would she lick him, arch toward him?

She needs comfort now. Back the fuck off.

He sucked in a deep breath. "I should go now." He should. Damn well should.

But Eve had just bent forward. Her lips pressed to his scar. Gabe's whole body locked down. Her lips feathered over him.

And desire erupted. *Fuck me—*

Eve pulled back, flushed. "I—I'm sorry. I don't know what I was thinking! I shouldn't—"

"Told you," Gabe managed to rasp out. "You don't apologize to me. But I'll sure as hell need to apologize to you . . ."

"To me? Why—"

"For this." And his control was gone. She'd pressed her lips to him, and there was no holding back. He had to taste her. His head lowered toward Eve's and his mouth took hers. Her lips parted, just as he'd wanted them to do. Soft, silken lips, and his tongue swept into her mouth. He should have made the kiss gentle. He *knew* that he should have been more careful—

Her tongue licked against his.

Screw careful. He pushed her back against that wall. Caged her there, and just feasted on her. Her taste wasn't sweet—it was rich and sensual. Like the chocolate he'd always snuck as a kid. And he wanted more. So much more.

His body pressed to hers. He could feel the tips of her breasts—her tight nipples—thrusting against his bare chest. She had to feel the thick erection pushing against her. He wanted *in* her.

He caught her hands. Lifted them and pushed them back against the wall. He drove his tongue past her lips again, and when she moaned he greedily drank up that sensual sound.

Get her naked. Get her in the bed. Take and—

Gabe jerked back. His breath heaved out, and his cock seriously protested his move.

"Told you . . . sorry . . ." The guttural words were all he could manage. Shit, he should have known it would be like that. He touched her, he tasted, and he went nova.

He retreated, one fast step back.

She was standing there, her hands still up against the wall, looking like the sexiest woman he'd ever seen.

Gabe took another step back. "It won't happen . . . again." He wished his voice didn't sound like a growl, but he was too far gone for much else.

Her right hand slowly moved. Her fingers pressed to her lips.

She needed to say something.

"You're a client . . ." Now he was rambling. And still wanting *in* her. "I don't have sex with clients."

Her hand fell.

"I don't—"

"I can still taste you," she said.

Shit. His cock was so hard he ached—for her.

"You're the first man to kiss me."

Okay, she was about to break him. If he didn't get out of that room in the next five seconds, he wouldn't be leaving.

And I like being her first.

A primitive surge of possessiveness had risen within him. He was in serious trouble because he sure wanted to show her all kinds of firsts.

Get. Out. Of. The. Room.

Because he knew Eve could have another lover out there. A boyfriend. God fucking forbid, a husband.

If she isn't Jessica Montgomery, then she's someone else. Someone who may have a family waiting.

Desire and anger churned within him.

I don't want another man to be waiting on her.

He was almost to the door.

"I didn't realize . . . what I was missing."

His eyes squeezed shut. He needed to keep walking instead of freezing and picturing her naked. Seeing her beneath him in that bed.

"Is desire always that powerful?"

His hands gripped the door frame. Hell, at least she wasn't terrified any longer. "No." His reaction to her had gone far beyond the norm. He didn't usually touch a woman and go from zero to sixty in two seconds flat. He'd have to be careful around her. So very careful. She tempted him too much.

"Then why is it like that between us?"

Hell if he knew. But keeping his hands off Eve was going to be even harder now that he'd had a taste of her.

He stepped out of the room. Started to pull the door shut.

"You don't have to apologize to me, either."

She'd crossed the room on soundless steps. He looked up and got caught in her gaze. A gaze that could probably make a man beg.

"I'm glad you kissed me. I wanted you to do it."

If he didn't get out of there, she would be beneath him in that bed.

She smiled then, and her face lit up. "Thank you for teaching me about desire. I was so scared, then you came in . . ."

He cleared his throat. "You don't have to be afraid."

"Not when you're close."

He hesitated. Maybe she should be afraid of him. If she knew half of the things he wanted to do with her. *To* her . . .

Client!

"Good night, Eve."

"Good night, Gabe."

He closed her door. Didn't move. He could hear her, moving around in that bedroom. *I can taste you.*

He could still taste her, too.

He needed a fucking cold shower.

"TAKE A BREATH."

She glanced up at Gabe's low voice. They were back at LOST, specifically in *his* office, and Eve was so nervous that she worried she might actually pass out. She'd thought about sitting down in that lush chair of his and putting her head between her knees. Seriously, she was getting that desperate. Maybe she could find a paper bag to breathe into.

Gabe shook his head. "You're not breathing."

Her breath rushed out.

"He's on the elevator. He'll be here in a few minutes."

He . . . Pierce Montgomery. The man who might be her brother. Gabe's associate, Wade Monroe, was escorting him up to meet them. She'd been calm, mostly calm, anyway, until about five minutes ago.

Then the nervous panic had set in.

He could be my brother.

"Stay beside me," Gabe told her, voice quiet. "The whole time. If the guy looks familiar to you, if you have any flashes of him . . ." His fingers caught hers. " . . . then squeeze my hand."

She was going to hold tightly to that hand, like it was a lifeline. *It was.*

"It will just be me, you, Montgomery, and Wade. We'll be the only ones in here for this meeting."

Eve knew he thought his words would make her feel better. She actually didn't care if a hundred people were in there. She was sure her knees would still be shaking no matter what.

"Wade's an ex-Atlanta police detective," Gabe continued softly. She wondered if he was just talking in an attempt to distract her from her fear. If so . . . *keep talking.* Maybe that strategy would work. "He and I are also old friends. When I opened LOST, I knew I had to bring him on board."

"Old friends?" Now he had made her curious. She wanted to know as much as she could about Gabe.

He nodded. "We met in the third grade. He, hell, once upon a time, the guy had a serious crush on my little sister."

There was a quick knock at the door.

"You ready for this?" Gabe asked her.

No. Not even a little bit, but Eve nodded.

"Come in," Gabe called.

The door opened. She expected it would be Pierce Montgomery. Instead, Wade Monroe stood on the threshold. He was tall, broad-shouldered, with golden eyes—deep, sharp eyes that reminded her of a jungle cat. His hair was dark and a little long, and his face looked as if it had been carved from stone. Seeing him just made Eve tense even more.

"Gabe." Wade inclined his head, then advanced. When he entered the room, she saw the man who'd been waiting behind him.

Not as tall as Wade or Gabe, the man in the doorway had a golden, sun-kissed tan. He was fit, but with more of a casual strength than with Gabe's steely muscles. His hair was blond and cut to fall perfectly around his face. And his face was classically perfect. High cheekbones. Square jaw. Green eyes.

Eyes that were on her.

And as he stared at her, some of that golden glow seemed to leave his skin.

The man took one tentative step toward her. "Jessica?"

She wanted to squeeze Gabe's hand, but not because she recognized the blond male before her. Just because she was terrified.

The guy advanced toward her with slow, halting steps. Eve straightened her shoulders and tried to look less terrified than she felt. The man wore a suit that fit his body, as if it had been cut just for him. *It probably was.*

She was wearing her worn high heels and the best clothes that she owned—the same clothes she'd worn when she first met Gabe.

"Pierce Montgomery?" Gabe said, his voice making her jump, then slid partially in front of her. "I'm Gabe Spencer. Thank you for coming in to see me today."

Pierce was craning his neck so he could still stare at Eve, but he quickly shook Gabe's hand. "After the call I received from your man there . . ." He nodded his head toward the ever watchful Wade. ". . . how could I stay away?"

Eve kept staring at him, searching for some familiar sign, but she saw nothing. Their hair was the same shade of blond. But their eyes were two different greens. Her gaze was a deep, dark green. And his was light, almost a blue-green.

Gabe turned to glance back at her. There was worry in his stare. She notched up her chin. *I'm okay.*

His fingers squeezed hers.

She didn't squeeze back.

Slowly, his left hand slid away from hers.

"This is the lady Wade told you about . . ." And he stepped to the side so Pierce Montgomery would be able to see her fully.

Pierce sucked in a quick breath. "The resemblance is . . . remarkable." He stared at her as if she were some bug under a microscope. His gaze slid over her, inch by slow inch. From the top of her hair . . .

"Her hair is a bit longer than Jessica's . . . Jessica always liked to keep hers right at her shoulders . . . and the shade is a bit darker . . ."

. . . to her face.

"The eyes . . . they look like Jessica's . . ." Pain roughened his voice then. He cleared his throat. Lifted his hand as if he'd touch her, but then his fingers fisted.

"Th-The height is right, but she's . . . thinner than Jessica. Jessica never liked model chic." His lips lifted then and his green eyes warmed a bit. "She said she'd rather have her burgers and her curves, and men who liked stick figures could kiss her ass."

Eve swallowed. *Am I her?*

His smile faded. "Jessica?" He leaned toward her.

Eve found herself leaning back, away from him.

"Do you . . . do you remember me?" Pierce asked softly as his gaze searched hers.

Sadly, she shook her head. "I—I don't."

He stiffened. "Say something else."

"I don't remember you. I don't remember anything about my life before I woke up in that hospital."

He stepped back, a quick, fast move. "Her voice is wrong. Everything else . . . it *could* be her, but the voice is wrong. Too husky. Jessica didn't sound like that." He gave a hard, jerking shake of his head. *"Jessica didn't sound like that."*

Wade moved from his position near the door, a small ripple of his shoulders that drew her gaze because she was frantic to look away from Pierce. *He's saying that I'm not his sister.*

"In Eve's medical file," Gabe said softly, "the doctor noted that she'd suffered bruising and a deep laceration on her neck."

Her hand rose. Traced the scar. Pierce's eyes followed that movement. Sympathy flashed on his face.

"There were also . . . nodules discovered on her vocal cords. The doctors said she'd endured some damage to her vocal cords. Damage that could come," Gabe's own voice lowered, "from excessive screaming."

Eve flinched, but she'd heard those words before. When she first woke in the hospital, she'd barely been able to speak at all. Her voice had improved, and she'd thought it was perfect again.

It's not perfect to him. Because it wasn't *her* voice. Jessica's.

"A DNA test can settle this," Wade announced as he marched toward Gabe's desk.

"I told you . . ." Pierce's gaze was still on her face. "I don't have any of my sister's belongings. Keeping them was too painful. I don't have any of her DNA that you can use for a match."

"We have you, Ace," Wade said, and slapped Pierce on the shoulder. "We can compare you and Eve to see—"

"Jessica Montgomery was not my biological sister."

Eve shook her head. *What?*

"She was adopted." His lips tightened. "I was four when my parents brought her home. A perfect, blond-haired, green-eyed girl, as if they'd ordered her off a menu." Anger hummed in those words. "Another accessory for them . . ."

Adopted.

"My parents died ten years ago. Their boat sank on a trip to the Keys. It's just been me and Jessica since then." He retreated a bit more. Shook his head. "Though it was really just the two of us all our lives, anyway. Me and Jess. Us against the world." There was so much grief in his voice that she ached for him.

But she didn't *know* him. Didn't recognize anything at all about him.

"I wanted to walk in and call you a fraud." His words were stark and his gaze seemed tortured. "And I wanted to walk in and call you . . . *my sister.*" He yanked a hand over his face. "But I don't know. I. Don't. *Know.*"

Eve didn't speak. What did she have to say? *Welcome to my world. I wake up every day not knowing.*

"Her birth mother," Wade said suddenly. "If you

have her adoption records, we can find her. We can get DNA to—"

"I have no records for my sister's adoption." Pierce's shoulders slumped. "I have nothing at all of her anymore. It was all too painful. Looking at it all just reminded me of what I'd lost. What that bastard out there *took*."

Her heart was racing in her chest. Her palms were sweating, and her breath came far too quickly.

"May I . . . may I touch you?" Pierce asked her.

Gabe stiffened. "Look, I don't think—"

"Yes," Eve said. Because maybe she'd feel *something*. Maybe his touch would make her remember. Spark an image. Create a connection.

His hands were shaking a bit when he touched her cheek. His touch was cool. Light.

And she felt *nothing*.

"You could be her," he whispered, the words ragged. "And I should know, shouldn't I? I should know my sister." He swallowed, and the faint click was almost painful to hear. "But I don't."

The office door flew open behind him.

Gabe surged forward. "This is a private meeting—"

"Sorry, Gabe." It was Sarah, her cheeks flushed and her voice sounding too high. "But there's a news story that just came on the air. I thought you needed to hear about it."

"We're in a meeting, Sarah. I'll be right out—"

"It's about her shelter."

She saw Gabe's shoulders stiffen. "What about it?"

Sarah's stare edged toward Eve. "A man was killed there last night. An ex–army officer named Pauley McIntyre—"

"Pauley?" Eve broke away from Pierce and all but ran to Sarah. She grabbed onto the other woman's arms. "Someone hurt Pauley?"

Eve realized that Sarah was watching her too carefully. Almost assessing her. *Isn't that what she always does?*

She shook the woman. *"Pauley!"* her voice snapped out. The woman could assess her later.

Sarah blinked. "He was stabbed last night. The police think it was a robbery gone wrong."

No. That made no sense. "Pauley didn't have anything a robber would take." She yanked her hands away from Sarah, too aware of a sharp, blinding pain in her chest. In her heart. "Pauley . . . Pauley guarded the shelter."

He was always on guard.

Always.

She'd passed so many nights in the front of that shelter with him. Neither of them had cared much for sleep. Or the dreams that haunted them.

"A . . . shelter?" Pierce's voice had risen. "You were in a shelter?"

She didn't look back at him. "He's not dead." Her words were a plea to Sarah. "He's not." *Tell me he's not. Tell me this is a mistake. Not Pauley. Pauley is sweet and good and he keeps me safe. He—*

"I'm sorry," Sarah said, and there was a kind of desperate horror in her gaze. "I didn't realize you were close with him." A bit awkwardly, she tried to pat Eve's shoulder. "I thought Gabe needed to know because he'd wanted a watch put on the shelter. I didn't mean to just—"

Eve pushed past her and ran out of the room. Gabe was calling her name but she didn't look back. She was going to lose it. Going to break down and cry, and she couldn't cry in front of them. Not in front of Sarah. Not in front of Pierce Montgomery. Or Wade or—

She ran into the bathroom, grabbed the edge of the sink, and the tears erupted.

Pauley.

GABE WAS RUNNING after Eve. He—

A hard hand grabbed him. He spun around and saw Pierce Montgomery frowning at him. "I don't understand . . . are you saying that woman has been living in a shelter?"

He needed to get to Eve. Gabe gave a grim nod.

"I—I . . . *what am I supposed to do?*" Pierce asked, his face tense. "I don't know if she's Jessica. I don't know—"

Gabe yanked away from him. "Wade, keep Pierce company." Wade would understand that order actually meant: *Don't let the guy leave. Not until I get back.*

Then he was out of the office. Sarah was at his side, hurrying to keep up with him. "I'm so sorry! I didn't realize that was her friend. I just . . ." Her breath huffed out. "It was too much of a coincidence. A murder at *her* shelter right after you'd ordered surveillance there. I had to tell you. I thought you needed to know!"

He didn't see Eve. She wasn't in the lobby. Wasn't in the break room. "You did the right thing." *Where are you, Eve?* He turned to the left. Saw the sign for the ladies' restroom.

"Uh, Gabe—" Sarah began. "That is the *ladies'* room."

He ignored her. He shoved open the bathroom door and rushed inside. "Eve?"

She spun at his approach.

Tears were on her cheeks again. He *hated* to see tears on her cheeks.

"Eve . . ." He stood there, just inside the women's restroom, and felt so lost and helpless and couldn't stand that she was hurting.

He despised feeling helpless. When he felt that way, he wanted to fucking destroy someone.

Or something.

"I—I need a minute, okay? Just give me a minute." She was swiping at her cheeks. Trying to hide her tears.

"Don't hide anything from me." Gabe took her into his arms. Pulled her against his chest. Held her tight. "Don't ever hide from me."

She cried then, in his arms, and he knew that he was in trouble. Because she was under his skin. Cutting right through his careful guard. *Getting to him.*

As she cried, his thoughts twisted.

I'll break anyone who hurts her. Make them beg. Make them bleed.

He'd always known he walked a dangerous edge. That edge had made him a good SEAL. It made him a deadly adversary.

It made him too lethal.

"He was my only friend," she confessed.

He held her even tighter.

"He had no money." Her words were so low that he had to strain in order to hear them. "He lived in a shelter. Why rob someone in a shelter?"

You didn't rob in a damn shelter. You didn't rob the homeless . . . But a killing . . . in Gabe's experience, there was always a reason for that.

"I'll find out what happened," he promised, and pressed a kiss to her brow.

"Gabe." She whispered his name. "What if it's because of me?"

All of his instincts were already screaming that same thing at him, and Eve had obviously connected the dots.

She pulled back. Stared up at him with gleaming eyes. "You took me from the shelter because you thought I might be in danger. I felt like someone was watching me there." Her gaze searched his. "Pauley always guarded the entrance . . . *what if someone killed him because that person was looking for me? What if it's my fault?*"

"I'll find out," he said again. Wade had connections that they could use at the PD. If it were a real robbery gone wrong, they'd know. And if Pauley's death turned out to be something more, then Gabe wouldn't stop until he brought down the killer.

Because he was quickly realizing that, for Eve, he would do just about any damn thing.

CHAPTER FIVE

WADE MONROE PACED IN FRONT OF THE morgue. He'd always hated that place, but back in his homicide days, he'd sure spent plenty of hours down there.

He'd done his best to give justice to the dead. Some days, he'd succeeded in that job. Other days, he hadn't.

The morgue's door swung open, and Dr. Gus Bane stood in the doorway. Gus's skin was a light coffee, and the gray grizzle of stubble lined his jaw. He frowned at Wade. "You're not supposed to be darkening my door these days."

Wade shrugged. "And you're supposed to be retired and living down in Florida." A grim smile curved his lips. "So I guess neither of us wound up where we were *supposed* to be."

Gus grunted. "Wife left me. Gotta pay alimony now."

"She found out about the mistress, huh?"

Gus glared.

"Easy. I brought a peace offering." Wade lifted his bag. "Still got that sweet tooth?"

Gus snatched the doughnuts. "They better have chocolate on them."

"Always." Wade followed the guy into the morgue. The place was icy, and the smell—it always made him feel a little sick to his stomach.

Gus carefully put his bag down on his overflowing desk. "What do you want, Monroe?"

"A homeless man was brought in this morning. Stab victim. He was—"

"Pauley McIntyre." Gus's brows lowered. "Ms. Georgia was in here earlier. She identified him for us."

There was some familiarity in the coroner's voice. "Uh, Ms. Georgia?" Wade pushed.

"She runs the shelter on Lortimer."

"And you know her because . . . ?" He waited for Gus to answer.

Gus just stared back at him. Right. The guy didn't spend all his time with the stiffs in the morgue. If the rumors were true, Gus was supposed to be one serious ladies' man.

Hence the divorce. And the alimony payments.

When the silence stretched a beat too long, Wade said, "I need to know about his case."

"Not much to know." Gus headed into the back, where the bodies were kept. Wade locked his shoulders and followed him. "Two stab wounds. One to the heart. One to the gut."

"He went fast?"

"Fast enough. The man sure didn't suffer long."

They were in front of the freezer—well, that's how Wade had always thought of the place. A series of big, heavy lockers lined the right wall. Bodies were in those lockers. As Wade watched, Gus bent and pulled one of them open. More cold air slipped out, and so did a body that had been bagged and tagged.

"I heard it was a robbery," Wade murmured.

"That's what the detectives upstairs are saying." Gus's voice held no inflection. "But seeing as how he was wearing boots with holes in them and threadbare clothes, I'm not so sure that theory works."

Wade held his stare.

"But I just determine COD," Gus told him. Cause of death. "The cops run the investigation."

Wade understood exactly what Gus was saying and what he wasn't. "He's a homeless man—"

"And not the rich businessman who was killed in that hit and run last week. Guess who's going to get front page coverage for a while, and who'll get sent straight on to the cemetery."

Right, Wade thought. That was another reason why he had left the PD. "It wasn't a robbery."

Gus shook his head. "This guy who did it knew what he was doing. There were no hesitation wounds, and Pauley—he didn't even have time to fight back."

Hell. "He was ex-military—"

"And I would say he was taken down in less than a minute. No one even reported hearing him scream."

Wade looked down at that zipped body bag.

"And the wound to the gut," Gus's voice roughened, "the killer twisted the knife."

Shit. "Maximum pain." Even if the guy did go quickly, he hadn't gone easily.

"Cases like this don't keep public attention long. On the news one day, gone the next." Gus sighed. When Wade looked at him, he realized Gus's gaze had turned distant. "I've seen so many dead cross my table. I've wondered about the lives they had before the end. Wondered if they were happy. Wondered if they fought to live a bit longer." He shook his head. "This man didn't have the chance to fight."

Every detail he learned about Pauley McIntyre's murder had Wade feeling more and more uneasy. If a guy didn't have anything to take, why rob him? And the kill—so professional . . .

At the same shelter where Gabe's girl was staying.

Yeah, this shit didn't feel right, and Wade knew better than to ignore his instincts.

"Thanks, Gus." He turned away.

"I can unzip the body, if you want to see him."

Hell, no, he didn't want that. Wade had always hated the bodies. He headed for the door. "Enjoy the doughnuts."

"I will." A pause that stretched until Wade was almost out of that too cold place. "And . . . Wade?"

He glanced back.

Gus's face was somber. "Find his killer. Everyone deserves justice."

Damn straight they did.

He hurried into the hallway, pulled out his phone and had Gabe on the line in less than thirty seconds. "I think we have a problem . . ." he began.

A big one.

"I WANT TO go with you." Eve glared at Gabe as he grabbed his keys and headed for the penthouse door. He'd taken her back to the penthouse, and she'd managed to pull herself together, and now that she was back in fighting form, well, fighting was exactly what she wanted to do. "If you're going to the shelter, take me with you."

At the door of the penthouse, he turned toward her. "You really want to go out there and see the spot your friend died? See his blood still staining the ground?"

Eve flinched but said, "I want to help. Pauley deserves my help." She hurried toward him.

His hands closed around her shoulders. "It might not be safe, okay? Shit, I need to find out what's happening. It's too big a coincidence that a guy at your shelter was killed—killed by someone who is too well acquainted with using a knife."

The scar on her neck seemed to burn.

"You're safe here. I want you to stay *here*. Wade and I are going to canvas the area around the shelter and see if we can find anyone who might have seen something last night."

"Didn't the police already check—"

"We're going to check again." His voice was grim and his gaze was steady. "And I want you to stay here."

It was because she'd broken down and started crying at LOST. Now he thought she was weak. "I'm not," she muttered.

His brows rose.

"I'm not weak."

"Uh, I don't remember saying you were." His left hand lifted. Curled around her chin. "In fact, weak is the last word that comes to mind when I think of you."

His words surprised her, and, damn him, he used that surprise to his advantage as he quickly stepped back. "Stay inside, and I'll be back soon."

"Gabe—"

But he was already gone.

HE WATCHED GABE Spencer leave, driving his Jag far too fast. The man should be more careful. Fast drivers often had deadly accidents.

He stared up at Gabe's building. He already knew the

man had a penthouse at the very top of that place. The guy liked to look down at the city. It was a pity he didn't seem to realize that dark parts of the city could look back up at him.

When Gabe had left, Eve hadn't been with him.

Are you up there, Eve? Are you waiting for me?

He needed to eliminate the threat she posed. He'd already messed up by taking out that homeless bastard. That kill hadn't been planned, and the aftermath of that death had left him feeling raw, unsettled.

I need to kill her.

Everything was falling apart around him. Chaos. He couldn't have chaos. He needed his order. Order would only be restored when she was dead.

He'd known about her for months, ever since he'd seen that first image in the paper. But Eve hadn't known about him. He felt safe, and it had been amusing to realize that she was out there, a total blank slate. There'd been no rush to eliminate Eve. Not when she had no fucking clue who he was.

And to see the mighty fall, as she had . . . fall to live on the very streets. It had seemed fitting. Death would have been too fast then, and he'd felt she should live a bit longer, in her pathetic, confused misery.

Then he learned about her visit to LOST.

You can't stir up the past, Eve. Your past is dead and buried. Soon, you will be, too.

He whistled as he headed across the street. The doorman at the building had just slipped away. Perfect, perfect timing.

Now . . . to just get to Eve . . .

EVE PACED. AND she paced some more. Gabe had given her a phone, one that was placed on the table just a few feet from her. She'd protested when he gave it to her. *Something else I need to pay him back for!* But he'd insisted she needed to always have a phone close to her, for safety.

She should have felt safe right then. Up high above the city, in Gabe's penthouse . . . "Fortress," she muttered. But she didn't feel safe. She just kept thinking about Pauley, over and over again. And—

The doorknob rattled.

Eve stopped her pacing. She glanced toward the door. That sound had been so faint. Maybe she'd imagined it.

She crept toward it.

And as she stared at the doorknob, she saw it turn.

No, impossible.

It was turning.

"Gabe?" She called out his name instinctively even as she grabbed for the phone on the table. Her fingers locked tightly around it.

There was another lock on the door. Higher, thicker. And . . .

It was turning, too.

She ran to the door. Put her eye to the peephole. *It's just Gabe. It's just Gabe. He forgot something. It's just—*

She saw a man wearing a black ski mask in the hallway. She screamed, and the fingers of her left hand flew out and she flipped the lock back in place. The top lock. The bottom lock.

For an instant there was stillness and silence as her scream died away. And then the locks started to turn again.

GABE'S PHONE RANG just as he reached the shelter. He glanced down at the screen, frowning when he saw

Eve's name flash across it. He swiped his index finger over the phone. "Eve, I'll be back in—"

"Someone's trying to get inside!" Her voice was loud, frantic.

"What?"

"A—A man in a ski mask. He's at the door."

Fuck, fuck, *fuck*. He ran back to his car. Gunned the engine and shot out of there. The call fed through his Bluetooth system, and the too loud and desperate sound of her breathing filled the Jag. "Hit the button for the alarm, Eve. Hit the panic button, *now*."

"I did! Nothing's happening!"

Had the bastard somehow disabled his alarm?

"Gabe, I'm scared, I—"

Then he heard the crash. And Eve's scream.

EVE HAD HAULED a chair in front of the door and shoved it under the doorknob, but the chair hadn't done any good. The guy had just kicked in the door and sent the chair flying across the room.

He stood there, appearing to fill the doorway. He was in black from his head to his boots, and as she stared at him, her scream still seeming to echo around her, he pulled out a knife from a sheath at his side.

"No," Eve whispered.

"*Yes . . .*" His hiss of sound.

She knew Gabe's penthouse was the only one on that top floor, so there wasn't anyone to hear her screams. There wasn't anyone there to help her.

I was supposed to be safe here.

He was stalking toward her, and she was just standing there.

The hell I am.

Eve snapped out of her stupor and grabbed for the

nearest lamp. She hurled it at him then. It hit him in the chest, but he didn't stop advancing.

She jumped over the couch. Grabbed another lamp and threw it. Her arm was surprisingly good, and the lamp pummeled into him.

He'd followed her movements, just as she'd hoped. And now that he wasn't blocking the door . . .

Eve ran for it. He snarled and reached out for her, his fingers tangling in her hair. She screamed again as she kicked back at him, slamming hard with her foot.

Pauley taught me that move, you bastard! On one of their long nights, when neither had been able to sleep.

The attacker's hold loosened and he swore.

She grabbed the chair he'd sent flying when he burst into the penthouse, lifted it up and whirled back toward him. As hard as she could, Eve shoved that chair at him. The chair legs hit him in the chest and he grunted.

"Stay away from me!" Eve yelled. She could see his eyes. They were dark, muddy, furious.

"*Never . . .*" That same low rasp that sent chills racing over her. An unnatural rasp.

He knocked the chair out of his way and swiped out with the knife. The blade missed her arm by an inch as it sank into the door frame. Eve stumbled back and ran into the hallway.

The elevator was at the end of that hall. If she could get to it, she'd be safe. Ten feet away. That was all. It looked as if it were just ten feet away.

He tackled her.

They hit the floor together. He was behind her and she was scrambling on her stomach, trying to get away from him.

But he wasn't letting her go.

"Beg . . ." he whispered.

Beg to die. Beg to . . .

"No!" Eve yelled, and twisted beneath him. She tried to claw for his eyes because those were all she could see. Those dark, dark eyes.

Those eyes are wrong.

"Beg . . ."

"WAYNE, GET UP to my penthouse *now*," Gabe snarled to the doorman as he drove hell fast. "My . . . guest is being attacked. Get up there!"

"Sir? D-Do I need to call the police?"

"I'm calling them. You get to her. Get to her!"

Wayne slammed down the phone. As soon as the line was clear, Gabe gave instructions for his phone system to call 911. He needed Wayne to get upstairs to Eve. Because by the time the cops got there, it could be too late.

It *can't* be too late.

"Nine-one-one, what is the nature of your emergency?"

He stomped down on the gas pedal and shot through a yellow light. "A woman is being attacked! She needs help, *now*."

SHE SHOVED HER nails toward his eyes. Her fingers slipped through those eye holes on his mask as she attacked.

But he reared away from her, and he drove his fist into her side.

Eve cried out but she also managed to get her knee up. She drove it into his groin as hard as she could.

"Bitch!"

"Bastard!" she shouted back, and then punched him. Punched him so hard that her whole hand hurt. He'd fallen back, holding his groin, and she used that instant to dive for the knife he'd dropped.

They both leapt to their feet at the same time, only she was the one holding the knife.

Her breath heaved out as they faced off.

Then he laughed. The sound was low, insidious. Familiar?

Terror seemed to choke her in that instant because the walls of that hallway vanished. The gleaming marble floor disappeared.

She could have sworn that her feet were sinking into sand, and she thought she heard the rush of waves against a shore.

"Stay away from me," Eve whispered as she backed up a step.

"Never."

Something dinged behind her, and Eve jerked. She looked back over her shoulder. *The elevator!* The doors were sliding open.

She turned and ran for that elevator, ran as fast as she could toward the man she saw standing there, with bright red hair and scared eyes, wearing the same blue uniform she'd seen another doorman wearing earlier.

She slammed into him and they both stumbled back. He tried to steady her so they wouldn't both fall, and then the doorman looked over her shoulder. He screamed.

Eve whirled around, the knife still in her right hand. With her left, she frantically pushed the button to close the elevator doors.

The man in the ski mask was walking toward her. Not running. Just . . . walking. Like one of those crazy guys from some sort of slasher flick.

When did I even see one of those? That ridiculous, random thought blasted through her head just as—

Just as he whispered, "I'll see you again, Jessica . . ."

Then the elevator doors closed.

GABE BROUGHT HIS Jag to a screeching stop. He jumped from the vehicle and ran toward his building. Several police cruisers were already there, their bright lights illuminating the scene in a swirl of blue. Some people from his building were outside, clustered together in groups, talking softly.

He didn't give a damn about those people.

Where was— "Eve!"

He ran for the main door, but a uniformed cop jumped in his path.

"Sir," the cop began, "you need to—"

"Gabe?"

Eve's voice. Eve's fucking perfect, beautiful voice. He whirled to the right and saw her and Wayne, the doorman, standing next to one of the police cruisers. Gabe rushed to her side and then yanked her into his arms. He held her tight, probably crushing her in his too hard grip, but he couldn't ease his hold.

I was afraid I wouldn't get to her in time. Not just afraid, fucking terrified.

"It was him," Eve said, voice breaking. "It had to be him . . . the Lady Killer. He found me." She was shaking in his arms. He wanted to pick her up, to take her back to his car and just get her the hell away from that place. Take her away from anyone and anything that threatened her.

Footsteps pounded behind him.

"Dammit, man," Wade snapped. "Do you know how hard it is to keep up with your fast ass?"

He knew that Wade had followed him back from the shelter.

"Talk to the cops," Gabe said without letting go of Eve. "Find out what they know." Because Wade always had an in with the Atlanta PD.

"Will do," Wade said, his voice softer now. "Is she all right?"

"Yes." Eve pushed against Gabe's chest. When she looked up at Gabe, there were no tears in her eyes and her expression was stark, determined. "She's all right."

Damn straight.

He wanted to kiss her right then.

"I'm not all right," Wayne muttered, sounding seriously aggrieved. "There was a man in a ski mask up there! I thought we were going to die! But she had the knife . . ."

A knife?

"He got away," Wayne exhaled heavily. "That crazy freak got away. The cops can't find him, and I was on duty, so this is gonna be on me, and I—I need a damn drink." Then Wayne headed off, apparently in search of that drink, only the cops caught him before he could and started questioning him.

"Uh, a knife?" Wade lingered next to Gabe's side.

Eve gave a slow nod. "It was his. The man in the mask. When we were fighting, I—I managed to take it from him. The cops have it."

And she'd thought she was weak? Hell, no. From the very first, he'd known she was a fighter.

If she'd escaped from the Lady Killer, she had to be a fighter.

"He called me Jessica."

Gabe thought his heart stopped for a moment, then it was racing in a frantic, double-time rhythm. "You're sure?"

She nodded. "Ask Wayne. He heard it, too. The man in the mask called me Jessica."

Dammit.

"I told you, he was the Lady Killer." Her head tilted

back as she stared up at him. "He knows I survived, and he's come back to kill me."

"That *won't* happen," Gabe swore.

But her mouth curled in the saddest smile he'd ever seen. One that made his heart ache. "He said he'd see me again. He's going to keep coming. He's going to kill me."

"No, he's not."

Her expression didn't change.

There was so much fear in her eyes. He hated that fear.

"We're going to stop him," Gabe told her, needing her to believe him, wanting to make that fear vanish. "We're going to hunt him down. He won't hurt you or anyone else ever again."

Her fear didn't lessen, and Gabe knew that Eve didn't believe him.

He'd prove the truth to her. He wasn't going to just sit back and let the asshole out there control them. He was a hunter by nature, with deadly skills that had been fine-tuned courtesy of Uncle Sam.

If the Lady Killer really was the one after Eve, then he would stop him. He would stop *anyone* who ever tried to hurt her.

Gabe pulled her against his chest once more and held her.

SHE WAS STILL a fighter.

He watched from the shadows as the police questioned the building's tenants. The doorman. Eve.

Only Eve isn't your real name, is it?

Gabe Spencer was there, touching her too much. Standing too close. He knew the man was screwing her. Why else would she have been in his penthouse?

Gabe kept his body close to Eve's at every moment. Possessive bastard. Eve didn't belong to him.

She belongs to me.

Just as all of the others had been his. His to torture. His to treasure.

He'd barely gotten out of that building before the cops arrived. Eve's flight down the elevator had given him just enough time to vanish. Good thing he'd disabled the cameras in the building when he'd taken the liberty of disabling Gabe Spencer's entire security system.

He knew better than to make mistakes. Mistakes were sloppy.

He planned his attacks. Planned every detail.

So he just had to make a new plan for Eve. But . . .

But it wasn't going to be fast.

He'd thought, at first, to just kill her. Yet as soon as she screamed for him, the past had surged back. Her scream was so hauntingly familiar.

My Jessica . . . still alive.

He didn't believe in miracles. Didn't believe in heaven or hell. Just believed in the power he possessed.

But something had brought Jessica back to him.

And a quick kill wasn't in the cards for her. *That* was why he'd let her escape. He could have killed her, and Gabe would have returned to her broken body.

That's not the way for her.

He'd lost Jessica once, he wouldn't lose her again.

CHAPTER SIX

YOU DIDN'T HAVE TO GET ME A HOTEL ROOM FOR the night," Eve murmured. She was so tired that she worried she'd collapse, but sleep was the last thing she wanted to do right then. *If I close my eyes, I know I'll just see him.* "Especially a room like this."

Talk about swank. The place was huge, and it just . . . smelled expensive. Everything gleamed there, and she was afraid to touch anything.

"I chose this room because it's the safest one. It has a private elevator, accessed by key card. I've got a guard downstairs. *No one* will be getting up here tonight."

Because he was in full-on protective mode. She had realized that fast after they left his building.

"Wade will find out what happened to the security at my place. The guy we're after took it off-line, but he would have left some sort of trail behind." Gabe nodded. "We'll find that trail."

Maybe. *Will that happen before he finds me again?* Eve shook her head. "I can't just wait for him to come after me. I need to do something."

Gabe stood just a few feet away from her. They'd talked with the cops for hours, waited while the PD conducted their investigation, but there had been no sign of her attacker. He'd just vanished.

"If he's really the Lady Killer—" Gabe began.

"He is!" She was dead certain. "I told you, he called me 'Jessica.'" There was finally someone out there who knew her—and that man wanted her dead. Figured.

"And did you remember anything when you saw him?" Gabe seemed to be choosing his words very carefully. "Did anything come back to you? Any flashes? Any memories?"

Her eyelids flickered. "Yes."

Surprise flashed on his face and he took a step toward her. "What?"

"His voice . . . what he said, it was familiar." Terror rose, but she shoved it back, hanging tightly to her control. *I'm safe. I'm with Gabe.* "He wanted me . . . to beg. When he said that . . . I—I could have sworn I'd heard those exact words before. 'Beg me, beg me,'" she whispered.

A muscle jerked in Gabe's jaw. "What else?"

"For an instant it seemed as if my feet were in the sand, and I—I thought I heard the ocean." Okay, now that sounded absolutely insane. She realized that. No wonder shrinks were being shoved her way every time she turned around. She'd been in a penthouse, for goodness' sake, not on a beach.

"Dauphin Island," Gabe said with a nod.

Goose bumps rose on her arms. She remembered that place from the newspaper stories she'd read. Four of the Lady Killer's victims had been found on Dauphin Island, after a hurricane rolled through and uncovered the bodies—or what had been left of them—from beneath the sand.

"You think I was there."

"Jessica Montgomery was. She had a home on the island."

Jessica . . .

"I want to go there." Eve stepped forward. Grabbed his shirt. She probably grabbed it a bit too hard. "I need to go there."

His gaze searched hers. "From what Sarah was able to determine, that island is the killer's hunting grounds. He feels most powerful there. He may—"

"Attack again?" Her voice held a brittle edge. "Like he's not doing that here." Her hands had fisted around the material of his shirt. She had realized that with the killer out there, she had no safe place. So whether she was in Atlanta or down at Dauphin Island, she'd be vulnerable. *He can get to me.* "I want to go down there. I want to see her home."

If he wouldn't take her, then she would go on her own. She'd hitchhike, walk, crawl if she had to do it, but she wasn't just going to keep on in this terrible void of *nothing* while that psycho hunted her.

Gabe studied her, then said, "I'll put in a call to Pierce Montgomery. We'll need his okay to get you in her place."

Pierce. Her breath came faster. She'd run out on him earlier and hadn't looked back. Mostly because there had been pain in his eyes, so much pain as he stared at her.

And when she'd found out about Pauley, the pain had overwhelmed her.

After her attack, there could be no more pretending. No more calling it a coincidence. Pauley was murdered by a mysterious attacker with a knife, then that masked man had come after her.

His death is on me.

"He died because of me," Eve said.

Gabe frowned at her.

"Pauley. That bastard—he was hunting me at the shelter. He *found* me, and Pauley got in his way. His death is on me!" Her voice was rising. She shook her head and tried to grab her control back even as she forced herself to let go of her clawlike grip on Gabe.

"His death isn't on you. His death is on the man who stabbed him."

I had the knife in my hand.

Gabe seemed to read her thoughts. "The police are going to check that weapon. If they find Pauley's blood on it, if they find any evidence we can use, you can bet that Wade will be calling us first thing."

She made herself nod. "Pauley—" Eve broke off because saying his name hurt. "He mentioned a sister once to me."

"Gina."

Surprise pushed through her. "Yes."

"I've already contacted Gina, and I've made arrangements for Pauley's body to be sent back home to her."

"How did you find her?"

He laughed then, the sound low, sexy. "Baby, finding people is my business. Gina wasn't trying to hide from anyone, so tracking her down took me all of thirty minutes." His laughter faded. "And I knew you'd want him to go home."

She did. She wanted him to have peace. "Thank you." It seemed like she was always saying that to this man.

"Don't thank me," he said, the words curt. "Dammit, I'm the one who put you at risk." And he was the one curling his fingers around her shoulders. "You wanted to go with me, but I left you at that penthouse. *I left you.* If he'd killed you, what the fuck would I have done?"

She couldn't read the emotion glittering in his bright blue eyes, and a new, desperate tension seemed to fill the air around them. "Gabe?"

"I won't leave you again. Wherever we go, we'll go together."

Eve's breath left her in a quick rush. "Dauphin Island." That was where she wanted so desperately to go. If Jessica's life had been on that island, then she had to see the place.

But Gabe hesitated. "If it's really the Lady Killer, if he's the one after you, then he'll follow you there."

She already knew that.

"If he follows," Gabe continued, "then he'll find me at your side." A grim promise.

She'd been on her own for so long. Scared and constantly trying to hide the fear that seemed to eat at her day and night. "Why are you doing this?"

His jaw hardened even more. "It's what I do."

"But I can't even pay you." Her laugh was bitter. "I have nothing. Pierce Montgomery—if he is my brother—he didn't even recognize me. So there's no money coming in from that end." She licked her lips and said once more, "I have nothing."

"You have one hell of a lot more than you think."

He was so close to her. The heat of his body was warming her and chasing away the cold that had wanted to consume her.

"And as for Pierce Montgomery . . . maybe there's a reason why the guy didn't choose to recognize you."

Choose?

"A lot of money is at stake in the Montgomery family. With Jessica dead, all of that money is his, but if his sister suddenly comes back from the grave . . ."

He'd have to split the fortune. But she shook her head.

"There was real emotion in his voice when he talked about Jess—Jessica." There had been so much pain there. The man had seemed to long for his sister. *Us against the world.* Wouldn't that bond matter more than money?

"You should get some sleep." A new note had entered his voice. Gruff. Guarded. "You take the bed and I'll take the couch."

She didn't want to sleep. If she slept, more nightmares would just come to torment her. Images that didn't make sense to her but still left her terrified.

He turned his back on her and paced toward the window. "Go. If we're going to Dauphin Island, then we should leave tomorrow. I don't want to stick around the city while someone is hunting you."

She glanced toward the bedroom.

Then back at him.

When she took a step, Eve wasn't heading for the bedroom. She was heading for Gabe. The thick carpet swallowed her footsteps, but as she drew closer to him, she saw her reflection in the window's glass. He had to see it, too, and the stiffening of his shoulders told her that he knew she was coming in close.

"Eve . . ." His voice definitely held a warning edge. "Go to the bedroom."

"I don't want to sleep."

His hands lifted. Pressed to the glass. "And you don't want to be around me much longer right now. My . . . control . . . isn't what it should be."

"You always seem to have perfect control." Did she resent that? Eve knew she had no right to resent anything when he was helping her so much, but she did. Her control was barely holding on, while he always was—

"I keep thinking about what could have happened to you. On *my* watch. I think about him hurting you." His hands fisted over the glass. "And it makes me want to destroy him."

Her hand lifted and she touched his shoulder. He was so tense beneath her touch, his muscles locked and hard as stone.

"And I just keep thinking about you." His voice was deeper, rougher. "About how much I want you and how I need to keep my hands *off* you."

"Because I'm a client?"

"Because there could be someone out there with a claim on you. A lover. A husband."

She stared at her hand on his shoulder. Her left hand. Her ring finger was bare, and there was no sign of a tan line to indicate that she'd once worn a ring. "I don't think there's a husband."

But a lover? If there had been a lover, wouldn't he have come looking for her?

"Any lover . . ." Gabe said, the words close to a snarl, "who didn't move heaven and earth to get you back in his bed would be damn insane."

Her breath caught.

"I'm trying to keep my hands off you . . ." His head turned and he looked over his shoulder. At her hand. "But then you touch me, and all my plans shoot to hell."

She couldn't move.

"Eve." He shook his head. "You need to stop touching me. You need to walk away in the next five seconds because that's about as long as I'll be able to stop myself."

She could barely draw in a breath. Eve was still scared, but it was a different kind of fear now. Not terror because of that bastard out there. But a wild, rushing fear because she didn't know what would happen next with Gabe. "St-Stop yourself from what?"

He turned toward her. Caught her hand in a steely grip. "From taking what I want."

Eve stared into his eyes, and mentally, she counted . . .

Five.

Four.

Three.

Two.

One.

"Eve . . ."

"Time's up," Eve told him, then she leaned forward, making sure that her breasts brushed against his chest because she definitely wanted to touch him, and her lips pressed to his.

It was the adrenaline driving her. Adrenaline and desire. She hadn't desired a man since she'd woken in that hospital—not until she met Gabe. She'd looked into his eyes, gotten caught in his gaze, and *wanted.*

She wanted him right then. Naked. *In* her. Wanted him to lift her up against that window's glass and plunge into her.

Because then she wouldn't be a victim. She'd be a woman taking her pleasure. A woman with her lover. A woman just like any other.

His hands closed around her waist and he pulled her against him. There was no missing his arousal, and for a moment a darker fear surged through her.

No, no, I won't let this be taken from me!

She parted her lips. Her tongue slid over the crease of his mouth. She licked lightly and then—

He growled low in his throat. It was such a sexy, animalistic sound. His tongue slid against hers and the kiss became wilder, hotter. She didn't know what her other lovers had been like, but Gabe Spencer sure knew how to kiss. Just his touch was setting her on fire.

She wanted his clothes gone. Wanted hers out of the way. Passion, lust, was burning so brightly within her, and she was afraid the feelings would vanish and she'd be cold again.

But Gabe was lifting her into his arms. Carrying her. His strength had her gasping into his mouth because he held her so easily, and he just kept kissing her. Tongue. Lips. He was perfect. She could feel heat pooling between her legs.

I'm getting wet for him.

And he was definitely aroused for her.

He shifted her body, and in the next moment Eve felt the soft dip of a mattress beneath her. He pulled back and stared down at her with eyes that glittered.

She kicked off her shoes. Her legs were bare, and the dress she wore clung so tightly to her. She wanted that dress gone. Quickly, she sat up and twisted, trying to find the zipper.

"Let me." His words were a sensual growl as his big hands slid behind her and he eased the zipper down. His fingers—the tips slightly callused—followed the trail of the zipper down her spine, and she shivered at the delicious feel of his hands on her.

Then the dress was gone. He'd pulled it off her and tossed it to the floor. For a moment Eve was self-conscious. Her body wasn't perfect. Not with those still pink scars on her shoulder, her stomach, and her thigh. She'd *never* be perfect.

"You are so fucking beautiful."

He made her feel that way.

Eve slid back down on the bed, stretching out before him. She still wore her black bra and panties, and Gabe was just . . . watching her. Staring at her with a blue gaze so intense and hungry.

His hand lifted. His fingers traced along the edge of her bra strap, down, down to the lacy cups that held her breasts. She'd been so proud to find that bra in the thrift shop. Something nice. Something feminine.

But she'd never imagined a man like Gabe would see her wearing only that underwear set.

Her nipples were tight aching peaks. She wanted him to kiss them. "Gabe . . ."

His eyes were on his hands. The hands touching her with such careful restraint.

He still has his control.

"Take off my bra, Gabe," she heard herself say. "I want your hands on me."

The black of his pupils expanded, swallowing that bright blue. And then he was pushing the bra aside, expertly unhooking it as she arched toward him and—

His mouth closed around one nipple.

Her breath hissed out, and her panties—they definitely got wetter. And while his mouth was on that breast, his other hand slid to the other aching peak. He strummed her nipple, a rough caress of his fingers, and she nearly bolted right off the bed.

Pleasure. Need.

"Gabe!"

He licked his way to her other breast. Sucked the nipple. Had her gasping and trying to hold back a moan.

"So responsive . . ." His dark voice made her shiver. "So . . . delicious . . ."

Then he was kissing his way down her stomach.

Some distant part of her couldn't believe this was happening. She'd only known Gabe for a few days. She shouldn't be doing this.

Sex was too intimate, she shouldn't be with a stranger. Yet . . . he was the only one she wanted.

I don't care if I've known him for a few days or forever. I want him.

He parted her legs. Slid between her splayed thighs. His hot breath blew against the crotch of her panties.

"G-Gabe?"

He kissed her through the panties.

Her hips jerked.

Instantly, his hands were on her hips, holding her down, keeping her just where he wanted her.

"I told you . . . delicious . . ." And he kissed her through the panties.

Eve's eyes squeezed shut as her body shuddered. It was too much. Oh, damn it was—*not enough*. And he wasn't done. One hand stayed locked on her hips, and the other hand shoved her panties to the side. When he jerked the crotch of the panties, the back of his fingers slid over her clit. His touch had her whole body tensing because she knew her release was close.

She couldn't remember what a climax felt like, but she was sure that she'd be finding out very soon.

He put his mouth on her. Eve's head tipped back as she gasped out his name. He was licking her, kissing her sex, stroking the most intimate part of her body, and it was *incredible*.

No, there was no room for fear or embarrassment. There was only room for pleasure.

And when his thumb pressed to her clit just as he licked her once more, her climax hit. It wasn't some gentle bubble of release. It was a full-on avalanche of pleasure, enough to wreck her, enough to make her moan and shake and shudder and wonder why the hell she hadn't been having sex sooner.

Because the others weren't him. I need Gabe.

"Look at me." His demanding voice had her eyes flying open. She hadn't even been aware that she'd closed them.

Gabe had risen above her and now stared down, his face etched into tight lines of lust.

As she stared at him, his hand lowered to the snap of his jeans. He yanked them open—

His phone rang.

No. *No. Absolutely not!* She shook her head. That had *not* just happened. She locked her legs around his hips and pushed toward him. She wanted Gabe inside of her, right then. Right there. To hell with anything else. This was too good.

The phone rang again. Louder. Longer and—

Someone was pounding at the door. Not the bedroom door, but the main door that led to their room. Only no one should have been given access to that room. They were supposed to be safe there. Gabe had said a person would need an access card just to get on the elevator that reached their floor.

What was happening?

His eyes glittered down at her. She could easily read the frustrated desire on his face.

And he pulled away. He jumped from the bed and stalked toward that pounding.

Eve rose from the bed, too, only she was moving far more slowly than he was. She ran a shaking hand through her hair and looked around the room. Her clothes. She'd need her clothes. She'd need—

"Wade, what the hell are you doing here?" Gabe snarled.

She yanked on her dress. Didn't bother with a bra but she tried to fix her panties.

"Sorry, Gabe." She could hear Wade's voice clearly. "He insisted."

"Because I had to see her!"

She froze because that *wasn't* Wade's voice. It was the voice of the man she'd met earlier, at LOST. The man who *could* be her brother.

Pierce Montgomery.

Eve found herself hurrying toward the bedroom door.

"I heard about what happened," Pierce continued, voice cracking a bit. "Eve was attacked. Nearly killed."

She pulled open the bedroom door. The squeak of its hinges seemed incredibly loud to her as she peeked out.

That squeak must have been loud to the men, too, because their heads turned at the sound. Gabe. Wade. Pierce. They were all staring at the darkened bedroom. Swallowing, Eve opened that door wider. She was decent, but she knew her hair was tousled, her cheeks were no doubt flushed, and her dress wasn't exactly pristine anymore. Not that it ever had been.

The others will know what we were doing.

Gabe took a quick step, placing himself in front of Pierce. "She's been through hell tonight. She was resting, and Eve needs to go back to sleep—"

"Jessica?" Pierce's voice sounded so hesitant then. Weak. Scared.

He eased around Gabe and stared at her. She was in the bedroom doorway, nervously shifting from one foot to the other.

The first time she'd seen Pierce in LOST, she thought he seemed perfect. Hair exactly in place. Suit pressed.

Everything about him had screamed poise and confidence.

This time he was different. His hair looked as if he'd yanked his hands through it a dozen different times. His shirt was haphazardly buttoned—two buttons were in the wrong holes, and as he hurried toward her, there was no missing the fear on his face.

He pulled her into his arms. "I could have lost you again."

The words were whispered into her ears.

Eve shook her head. "You said . . . you don't even know I'm Jessica." She should feel something for him. A connection. If she'd known this man her whole life, he should make her feel safe. Or happy. Or loved. Something.

But she didn't feel anything when he held her.

She looked over his shoulder and saw Gabe staring at them with narrowed eyes.

We were making love. Gabe made me feel . . . he makes me feel everything.

"I'm afraid for you to be her." Pierce pulled back. Stared down at her with a green gaze gone stark with emotion. "And I'm afraid for you not to be her." His breath heaved out. "I *mourned* her. When Jessica vanished, I—I knew something terrible had happened, right from the start. We always talk. I know every secret she has. She knows mine. No one has ever been closer to me." His arms were so tight around her that they almost bruised her. "And it never hurt more to know that I'd lost her." His jaw locked. "It felt like that bastard who took her had cut out my own heart."

And, finally, *finally,* she did feel something for him. Pity. "I'm sorry," Eve whispered. The last thing she wanted to do was hurt this man in front of her. She didn't want to hurt anyone. All she wanted was to learn the secrets of her past.

But what if my past winds up hurting too many people?

Gabe edged closer to them.

Wade stood a few feet away, his gaze not missing a thing, but the ex-detective wasn't saying a word.

"Wade told me about the attack on you, and I had to see for myself that you were all right." Pierce swallowed quickly. Then he seemed to grow even more uncertain as he stared at her. "The hair is a little darker, just a shade or so . . . but Jessica always stayed in the sun so much, it made her hair appear even blonder."

She'd barely spent any time outside. She'd worked her jobs at the shelter, gone to all of her doctor visits—

"The voice . . . it's huskier. Not hers."

Gabe rolled his shoulders. "I already told you—" he began.

"But your eyes . . . your eyes are *hers*." Then Pierce jerked away from her. He ran a hand through his already tousled hair. "I just . . . I don't want to lose Jessica again. I'm not sure I could survive that." His hand fell to his side. Fisted. "I want my sister back."

Her lips pressed together because she didn't know what to say to him. *I want my life back.*

Pierce turned to face Gabe. "What can I do? Every resource I have . . . I'll put it at your disposal. I want the truth. I need it." His hand was still fisted. "And that twisted freak who did this? The Lady Killer? *I want him dead.*"

Now Wade did advance, stepping away from the wall with a quick shake of his head. "Murder isn't the answer, Montgomery." His gaze cut quickly to Gabe.

"No matter what you might think." Then his stare returned to Pierce.

Pierce's laugh held no humor, only bitter pain. "Tell that to the other families. You think they don't feel the exact same way I do? The FBI told us that the Lady Killer tortures his victims. For days."

Eve's breath came harder. Faster.

The scent of the ocean stung her nose. An ocean that wasn't there.

"He gets off on their pain," Pierce said, the words sharp with anger. "And he's not going to stop. Some fancy-ass FBI profiler told me it was doubtful that the guy *could* ever stop. Some compulsion bullshit." His southern accent was growing more pronounced with each word. "So what do you think should really happen to him? Life in a cage? Or a swift trip to hell?"

"It's not your call to make," Wade gritted out.

"Isn't it?"

Her palms were sweating. The pleasure she'd had with Gabe had vanished, and cold fear had come back to take its place.

"We want justice," Gabe said. There was no emotion in his voice—so at odds with the furious rage barely contained in Pierce's voice. "And we know that's what you want, too."

Pierce grunted. "What I want is not to have dreams about my sister—dreams of her screaming and dying every night."

Eve's body trembled.

Gabe crossed to Eve's side. His shoulder brushed against hers. "We're going to Dauphin Island."

Pierce's eyes seemed to double in size. "Are you kidding me? That's where he got her! That's where—"

"I was just attacked right here in Atlanta," Eve said quietly, amazed that her voice came out so level. "Here or there, if it's the Lady Killer after me, he's going to keep hunting."

From the corner of her eye she saw Gabe tense.

"Being in a familiar place . . ." Gabe's voice had a distinct edge now. "Our psychiatrist said that could spur her memory."

Pierce frowned at that.

Eve had been told the same thing by other shrinks, so she wasn't surprised to hear that Sarah had given him advice to visit a familiar place. *Only back then, I hadn't known which places might have actually been familiar to me.* Then, the whole world had seemed foreign to her.

It still did.

Gabe kept his focus on Pierce. "By going down there, my team and I will have the chance to conduct our own investigation."

A muscle jerked in Pierce's jaw. "So you think you're going to find the killer, and what—use her as bait?"

"Hell, no," Gabe denied instantly. "Our number one priority is her safety. But we also find the lost, and there are still victims down there who are missing. We *can* find them. We can find that killer, and, yeah, we can put him in a cage so that he won't hurt anyone else again."

Pierce's gaze slid between her and Gabe. There was suspicion in his stare. "You sure have developed what seems like a very personal interest in this case." His chin jutted up. "I've done my research on your group. You're not exactly cheap, so how—"

"My interest in this case isn't your concern. Neither is my fee. That's already been paid."

The suspicion just deepened in Pierce's gaze.

"We want access to Jessica's home on the island," Gabe said.

Pierce blinked, seemingly caught off-guard. "But . . . but her home is for sale." He looked down at his hands, still clenched into fists. "I packed everything up. Packed up Jessica's life . . ."

"But her home isn't *sold* yet, right? The condo is on the market, but no one has made an offer yet."

Pierce looked back at Eve. "It just . . . hurt. Going in there. Seeing you—*her*—everywhere. The paints. The brushes." His eyes closed. "I could even smell Jessica inside. Lilacs. She always smelled like lilacs." His voice trailed away.

Silence.

Eve remembered going to the drugstore with the first bit of cash she'd earned. And buying lilac body lotion.

Pierce sucked in a deep breath and then straightened his hunched shoulders. His gaze was like a touch as it slid over her face. "Jessica?" There was a question in that name. An almost desperate hope.

She just stared at him.

His lips pressed together and he gave a grim nod. "You can stay at the condo. There's furniture in it—not Jessica's, but furniture that the real estate agent put in for staging. Stay there. Do whatever you . . . need to do."

"Thank you," Gabe said. "We appreciate your cooperation."

"Cooperation? Screw that. Guilt is eating me alive." Pierce's gaze dropped to his hands again. "I felt like it was my fault. Jessica was my sister. I was her big brother. I was supposed to protect her. *I* was supposed to keep her safe. I didn't."

Eve stepped toward him because his pain was almost

palpable. She reached out and tentatively touched his shoulder.

He froze. "I want you to be her. I . . . miss her." So much pain was there. Pierce exhaled slowly and his gaze lifted. "Anything you need, anything I can do . . . I'll give you full access."

"Thank you," Eve whispered. She didn't want to hurt this man before her. She wanted to help him because it was obvious to her that he'd been through hell.

"I haven't gone down there, not since I put the condo unit up for sale. Jessica always loved that island. I see her *everywhere* there. A ghost." His head tilted. "But you're not a ghost, are you?"

Eve didn't know what she was.

Pierce cleared his throat. "I, um, I have to go to New York . . . stupid damn merger that's been in the works. But I'll fly back and meet you all down there. I'll be there as soon as I can be."

"That's not necessary," Gabe told him. "We don't need you for our investigation on the island."

"But I need to be there." The faint lines near Pierce's eyes deepened. *"I owe it to Jessica."* His hand lifted. Curled around hers. "I'm so glad you're all right," he whispered. "I didn't . . . I didn't want to go through all of that again."

Wade cleared his throat. "Okay, man, you saw her. You talked to her—that was the deal. Now it's time to get the hell out of here." He came forward and put his hand on Pierce's shoulder. "Let's go." Wade glanced over at Gabe. "He was at LOST, waiting outside. The guy was desperate."

"I can *hear* you," Pierce muttered. "But, yes, I am a desperate man. You would be, too, if you'd lost your sister."

Gabe stiffened.

"I tried calling, but I couldn't get you," Wade said quietly to Gabe, but Eve caught his words.

She too heard the phone ring, but she'd been . . . distracted at the time. She could feel her cheeks sting.

Gabe followed Wade and Pierce to the door.

But before leaving, Pierce glanced back at her. "There's . . . something else." His gaze shifted to Gabe. "Something *you* need to know."

Gabe waited. No change of expression crossed his face.

"My sister's lover is down on that island."

Eve felt her heart stop.

"So if you're looking for familiar surroundings to jump-start her memory, that place—and Trey Wallace—hell, that should do it."

Trey Wallace. The name meant nothing to her.

Gabe's fingers curled around the edge of the door. "Her lover?" His voice was as cold as ice.

"That cop is the only guy she kept around long. She'd date other men but always go back to him in the end. She loved him. She told me that." His head turned and he stared at Eve. "Maybe I couldn't make you remember anything, but Trey could be a different story. You're never supposed to forget your first love, right?"

She had forgotten. Everything and everyone.

Pierce cleared his throat. "Fair warning, Gabe, you won't be able to step foot on that island without him coming for her."

A shiver slid down her spine.

"Thought you should know that," Pierce said, voice low, hard. "Because of that *personal* interest you have in the case."

And then he was gone. After one last, long look at

Eve, he'd hurried into the hallway. Wade was right on his heels.

Eve found that she was frozen to the spot, mostly because she was too aware of the dangerous tension that seemed to now cling to Gabe.

Slowly, carefully, he shut the door. Locked it. Reset the alarm. His hands flattened against the wooden door. "You should go to bed. You need your rest."

He didn't even look at her as he said those words.

Her hands twisted together in front of her. "I thought we were going to be together."

His shoulders stiffened. "You could already have a lover out there."

"I don't know him." Trey Wallace was a man without a face to her.

"I had my team do a background search on Jessica. They didn't find any current relationships for her. They told me that she'd broken up with a lover a few weeks before her disappearance." He sucked in a deep breath. "They didn't know you were in love with anyone."

He's my lover . . . only if I am Jessica. "I don't know him," Eve said again, and made herself step forward. One foot. Then the other.

But before she'd reached him, Gabe drove his fist into the door.

Her breath caught and she froze.

"Go back into the bedroom. Shut the door. And count yourself lucky we were interrupted."

She shook her head, but he still wasn't looking at her, so he didn't see the protest.

"Because if I'd taken you, it wouldn't have mattered to me who you loved, you'd be mine." His laugh was harsh. "What the hell does that say about me?"

"Gabe—"

"You make me feel things I shouldn't. My reaction to you isn't normal. It's not safe." He pushed away from the door. Stalked toward the window overlooking the city. *Still* didn't look at her. She needed to see his eyes, but he wasn't giving her that glimpse into his emotions. "You're a client, and I almost fucked you."

Were his words supposed to hurt her? Because they did. "I wanted you," she said. *I still want you.* "And I don't know why you're acting so surprised that I might have been with a lover before." Now she was the one marching toward him. There wasn't anything frozen about her then. She was filled with a fierce fury. She grabbed his arm, spun him around, and *made* Gabe look at her.

Desire and guilt. That's what she saw in his eyes.

"I don't care who you were with before me," she told him flatly. "You had lovers. I had lovers. And you know what? Maybe we were *in* love with them. That doesn't make it worse—it makes it better. It makes it better to know that we can both care about other people." Her breath heaved out as her heart raced like a galloping horse in her chest. "But that's the past. You actually remember your past—bonus for you—but I don't. The fact that I can't remember doesn't change what's happening right this moment. I am here now, with you. I want you. Not some guy named Trey. *You.*"

He moved to touch her. His hands lifted, but then he dropped his arms. "You might change your mind when you remember him."

Is that what he was afraid of? "And maybe I won't."

His jaw was locked tight. "I'm a possessive bastard," he told her.

What?

"I want you so much that I'm fucking about to explode right now."

That was good.

"But I can't have a taste and walk away." He gave a hard shake of his head. "That's not who I am."

She didn't even know who *she* was.

"If I take you, there's no going back. I won't be able to go back."

He was warning her again. Maybe she should be afraid. She wasn't. "And when I take you," Eve told him as she tilted her head to stare deeply into his eyes. *So bright.* "There will be no going back."

His face hardened even more as he stared down at her. "I can still fucking taste you."

Oh . . . wow.

"It doesn't seem like it, but I am honestly trying to be a damn gentleman for you right now."

He was?

"If I were in love with you . . . and you slept with another man, I think I might just go insane."

She licked her lips.

His gaze fell to her mouth. "Fucking. Insane."

"I don't know Trey—"

"Tomorrow, you will. Tomorrow, *everything* will change."

She wrapped her arms around her stomach, suddenly feeling cold.

"I should have kept my hands off you."

Eve turned away from him. Headed toward the bedroom. "I wanted them on me." She'd wanted more than that. She'd wanted him *in* her. She still did. Would she still want him tomorrow? Not if he kept acting like a *dick*.

"Eve."

This time she was the one who didn't look back at him.

"I want you more than I've ever wanted any woman."

Good to know. She'd hate to see how he acted if he didn't want her.

"I won't turn away again. I *can't*. If I get you under me in bed. If I get you over me—if I get you any damn way, you're mine."

Eve stopped at the bedroom's threshold. She already knew she wouldn't be getting any sleep that night. If she closed her eyes, nightmares would just chase her.

"You need to be able to choose . . . you need to know what you might be giving up for me."

She stared into the darkness of that bedroom. "And what would you give up for me?"

Silence. But that was an answer, wasn't it?

She headed into the bedroom. Shut the door.

Then thought she heard the soft growl of one word.

"Everything."

CHAPTER SEVEN

THE WATER STRETCHED BEFORE HER, GLINTING with the afternoon sunlight. Eve found herself leaning forward toward the dashboard, struggling to get a desperate glimpse of the island up ahead.

They'd flown to the Mobile, Alabama, airport. Gabe had been her silent companion during that too-short flight. They'd barely seemed to get up in the air before they were heading right back down. Mobile had been a blur of traffic as they headed down Airport Boulevard, then to the interstate. But, all too soon, they'd left the bustle of the city behind them. Now, all she could see was water—and one seriously large bridge looming dead ahead.

"It used to be called Massacre Island," Gabe said, his voice low and quiet and his eyes on the bridge. A tall beast of a bridge. A metal sign to the right indicated they were heading over the Intercoastal Waterway. "Seems way back when, French explorers came upon the island and found what looked like a large pile of bones. They thought they were looking at the mass grave of about fifty people."

Their rented SUV started climbing over the bridge. Seagulls flew next to them, seeming to race their vehicle.

They slowly reached the high crest of that bridge, and Eve's breath stilled. "It doesn't look like hell." Not some terrible massacre site.

She saw white beaches. Beautiful white, gleaming beaches that stretched and looped. She saw heavy marshes. Sail boats, their white sails a bright contrast to the dark water.

"The Massacre Island name didn't exactly stick," Gabe said as they descended on the other side of the bridge. "The French started calling the place 'Isle Dauphine,' and, over time, the name became Dauphin Island."

She couldn't tear her gaze off that island.

Home.

The one word whispered through her mind.

"The place has seen a lot of tragedy. That oil spill a few years ago hit the people here real hard, and hell, that recent hurricane sure didn't do any good for them."

"And finding out that a serial killer had been hunting here? Like that was good news?" The sharp edge of her own voice surprised her.

As they headed off the bridge, they passed a police cruiser parked near a big wooden sign that proclaimed: WELCOME TO HISTORIC DAUPHIN ISLAND.

Ice seemed to cover her cheeks, then fast, hot pricks of heat ignited across her skin, melting the ice away.

Gabe slowed the SUV. "Are you okay?"

Her hands had flattened on the dashboard.

To the right, she could see a heavy fishing boat returning to the island. Long nets hung near the deck of that boat.

Another marina waited to the right. So many ships— some polished and sleek, some old and showing the ravages of time.

"I—I need to get out." She couldn't breathe in that SUV.

"It's all right." He was trying to soothe her. She didn't want to be soothed.

A scream was building in her throat, and Eve was afraid it would break free at any moment. And if she started screaming—

Will I ever stop?

"The condo is less than five minutes from here at a tower called Dauphin View. Hell, the whole island is only fourteen miles long. We can—"

"Stop the car."

He yanked the wheel to the right, taking them into the parking lot of a gas station, and he hit the brakes, bringing them to a jarring halt.

At once, Eve jumped out of the SUV. The scent of the ocean hit her. That salty air surrounded her, and the cries of seagulls filled her ears.

Those cries sounded like screams. Her screams.

"No," she whispered, shaking her head and shuddering. Some teenagers were walking out of the gas station. They frowned at her.

"Lady, are you okay?" one called out.

Before she could answer, Gabe was there. He caught her hands in his and swore. "You're ice cold."

No, she wasn't. She was burning up. Burning from the inside. "B-Bakery . . ."

"What?"

Her heart hurt because it was beating so fast and hard. She tried to pull away from him, but he held her in an unbreakable grip, so Eve tilted her head to the left. "There's a bakery there."

He glanced to the left. "I don't see one."

"Down the street. About twenty feet. There's a bakery there." She knew it with absolute certainty.

His hold loosened on her, and Eve broke away. She tore from his arms and ran across the street. A car honked and brakes squealed.

"Eve!" Gabe roared her name.

Only that's not me . . .

She rushed past a church, past a row of houses, and then she saw the bakery. The scent of fresh cinnamon rolls teased her nose, and she hurried up the porch steps. The bakery was a converted house, with an overflowing parking lot as folks rushed after the sweet scent that hung and tempted in the air.

Eve shoved open the door. A bell jingled lightly over her head, and for an instant, she almost lost her balance as the world seemed to go off-center around her. There was a long, snaking line of people leading up to the bakery counter. The hum of voices filled the air.

I know this place.

The bell jingled again. "Jessica!" Her name was louder, far more demanding.

She felt a hand on her shoulder as he whirled her around to face him.

It isn't Gabe.

And it slowly dawned on her that the name the man had just called hadn't been Eve.

Jessica.

She was staring up into a pair of warm brown eyes. The man's handsome face had been kissed by the sun, and his brown hair held streaks of blond, no doubt also from the sun. He smiled at her as she stared up at him, and slashes—not dimples, but slashes—flashed in his cheeks. "I'll be damned . . . *it's you!*"

The bakery had gone dead silent around them.

Eve shook her head.

The bell jingled again. Over the man's shoulder she saw Gabe's tense face. Worried, his blue eyes locked on her.

But then the man who'd called her Jessica, who wore a policeman's uniform, leaned forward and kissed her.

His mouth touched hers with familiarity, with skill, but—*it felt wrong.* She struggled against him, pushing frantically with her hands and twisting her head away.

"Jessica?"

"Get those fucking hands off her, *now!*" Gabe's voice. And he wasn't waiting for the brown-eyed man in the cop uniform to comply. He grabbed the guy and shoved him back.

Eve's hand slapped against the nearby wall as she drew in deep, shaky breaths of air.

"Buddy, you don't want to assault the chief of police," the man snarled.

Gabe took up a stance right in front of her. "And when a woman shoves you away, you damn well need to learn how to back off!"

Everyone was staring at them. Eve's frantic gaze flew around the bakery. The two little old ladies behind the counter had frozen, their mouths wide-open.

"We're causing a scene," Gabe said flatly. "Let's take this outside."

Before, Eve had been so desperate to get *inside* the bakery. Now she was stumbling as she pushed her way out. The sunlight seemed even brighter, even hotter when she stepped onto the porch.

"Jess, I thought you were dead!" The cop was following on her heels. "Everyone did. Hell, I've got FBI agents who've been breathing down my neck for months. Ever since you vanished after the party at the marina . . ."

"You're Trey Wallace." Gabe was right beside Eve. They'd now moved a few feet away from the bakery's sprawling porch and were in the shadows of a massive oak tree. A light breeze blew over Eve's face, but that breeze didn't cool her down.

"Yeah, I am, and who the hell are you?" Trey demanded.

Gabe reached into his back pocket and pulled out his ID. "My name's Gabe Spencer, and I own an organization called LOST."

"LOST," Trey repeated softly. A hint of a southern accent rolled faintly through his words. Not a thick twang, a rough growl. Deep and dark. "I've heard of that group. You—you find the missing. You found my friend Kenneth Longtree's daughter when she went missing during a spring-break trip to Mexico."

Gabe nodded. "I remember her."

Trey's gaze shot to Eve. "Did he find you, Jessica? Is that what happened? He found you and brought you back to me!" He took a step toward her, his arms outstretched.

Gabe stepped into his path and shoved a hand against the guy's chest, his fingers barely missing the badge clipped there. "Easy there, slick. In case you didn't get that message before, the lady doesn't want you touching her."

A furrow appeared between Trey's brows. "Why aren't you saying anything, Jessica?"

"I—" She cleared her throat and tried again. "I don't know what to say."

Those brown eyes narrowed. "Your voice is different." Now he looked suspicious. His gaze raked her. "Your hair's different. The color's too dark. And you . . . you're too thin."

Maybe he was about to say that he'd mistaken her. That she wasn't Jessica.

Gabe's fingers tangled with hers. Trey's gaze dipped, noting that movement. "She doesn't remember her past," Gabe explained. "She walked into my office in Atlanta a few days ago. She wanted my help to find out just who the hell she really is."

Trey's gaze was on their fingers.

"Because, maybe," Gabe continued quietly, "she *is* Jessica Montgomery. The woman the FBI thinks fell prey to the Lady Killer." He paused a beat. "Or maybe she isn't. But we're down here because we thought the people who knew Jessica the best—the people here where she lived—would be able to tell us the truth."

Trey's stare finally lifted from their locked hands. His eyes met hers. "We need to take this back to my office. Gossip on this island runs like wildfire." He motioned back toward the bakery. "And we've already given them enough of a show for the day."

His police cruiser was parked a few feet away, its door hanging open.

"I saw you run across the street," he murmured to Eve. "At first I thought you were a ghost. You've sure as hell haunted me enough days and nights."

She swallowed.

"Jessica—"

"Eve," she blurted. "Please . . . just Eve." Because she didn't feel right answering to another woman's name. She'd talked with the nurses at the hospital, and they'd come up with that name together. Sure, it might just be random, but it was hers. *Eve because I was a blank slate, and Gray . . . because the skies had been so gray and stormy after I woke in that hospital.*

But Trey shook his head. "I know you. You think I'd

forget the only woman I've ever loved? It's you. *It's you.*"

Her frantic heartbeat filled her ears because he was staring at her with absolute recognition on his face.

SHE WAS BACK.

She could have stayed away. Could have run, but she'd come home.

To me.

Jessica knew exactly what she was doing, and he could hardly wait for the true fun to begin. She'd changed in the last few months. Those months that she'd spent away from him. There was more of a fight to her now, oh, he knew that. He had the bruises to prove it.

He'd turned her into a fighter. He'd taught her to dole out pain. To hurt others.

He'd always wondered if, deep inside, she might be more like he was. Now, he knew the truth.

You are perfect.

No fear. No shrinking violet. Even with her mind twisted, she was fighting her way back to him.

She should be given a reward for that. Some help, so that she realized she was truly on the right path.

A path that led to him.

And he knew just how to show her the way. A demonstration would be necessary, but where . . . *where* could he find the right tool to help his Jessica? Especially on such short notice.

I like to hunt longer, to build up the anticipation.

But for Jessica, he'd make an exception.

"THE FBI TOOK over a huge chunk of my precinct and the town hall." Trey sat perched on the edge of his desk. Gabe noted that the man's eyes kept drifting to Eve. Lingering on her far too much.

Eyes up, buddy.

"When those bodies were found on the old golf course, hell, it sure stirred things up down here." Trey exhaled. "It's supposed to be paradise, you know? That's how we bill it to the tourists. Come get away in paradise. We don't tell them to escape to hell."

Yeah, he could see where that wouldn't fly with the tourism industry. "How many FBI agents are still here?" Gabe asked. He'd have to make contact with them ASAP.

"Two. And they have a team of techs digging up that old golf course, looking for more bodies." His hand curved around the edge of his desk. "The golf course used to be part of the old country club here on the island. It shut down years ago, but the owners didn't want to see some high-rise take its place, so they just kept the property empty. The course backs right up to the beach. The view there is killer."

It had been.

As if realizing what he'd just said, Trey coughed a bit. "We, uh, left the area alone, thinking it was safe. My unit is small and we just patrolled there occasionally. We had no idea that some twisted jerk was dumping bodies out there."

"Especially since he was hiding them so well," Gabe noted.

Trey nodded. "When Hurricane Albert hit early in the season, the storm took away nearly eight feet of that beach near the golf course, and during the clean-up, we found—"

"Bodies," Eve finished softly.

Gabe thought she looked too pale, but she was definitely holding it together. Not surprising. He already knew how strong she was.

"What was left of them, anyway," Trey muttered. "But the FBI folks told me that sand slowed down the decomposition rates so they were able to make fast IDs on the remains and to figure out just what the freak out there had done to them."

Gabe saw Eve flexing the fingers of her right hand. The fingers that had been broken. Then she lifted her hand, and the tips of her fingers skimmed along her neck.

Along her scar?

"My team is coming down to the island," Gabe said, aware that his voice came out too rough. "I'd appreciate your cooperation as we investigate."

Trey's brows climbed. "You think you'll be able to find out more than the FBI?"

Yes, he did. "I have a former FBI agent working for me. Dean Bannon will be here tomorrow—and my forensic anthropologist, Victoria Palmer, will be with him." He rolled back his shoulders. "Victoria is the best in the business. If she can get access to the remains—"

"They're not here any longer." Trey's lips thinned. "But she can see all the reports I have. And . . . and the FBI is still searching in the sand. Trying to see if there are any . . . more bodies." He'd hesitated there at the end.

Eve stiffened. "You mean they are trying to find Jessica Montgomery's body, right?"

"You—she—fit the killer's profile." Trey's voice was quiet, and his gaze was still far too watchful as he focused on Eve. "With more women still unaccounted for, they have to search. They can't give up." A pause. "*I* can't give up." His gaze slid back to Gabe. "So, yes, you'll be getting your cooperation from me. I want to do everything in my power to stop this bastard. No one kills on my island. *No one.*"

Gabe nodded. If the police chief hadn't agreed to help him, he would have found a way to go around the guy. Dean already had an in with the FBI team working the case. But it was good to know they'd be getting cooperation.

"We'll be staying at the Montgomery condo," Gabe said as he rose and reached for Eve's arm. "Pierce Montgomery knows that we're trying to uncover her past and stop the killer, and he—"

"He doesn't want you to be Jessica."

The cop's words stopped Gabe. He glanced back at him. *He's watching her again.*

"I saw him, after you vanished," Trey explained. "After we all started putting the pieces of the puzzle together and we realized what had happened . . ." He straightened. Walked toward her with a slow stride, almost as if he were afraid he'd frighten her if he moved too fast.

If you go in for another kiss, man, you're done.

"Pierce was torn up. The guy was shattering right before my eyes. Hell, you were all he ever had. Sometimes, you told me that scared you. Because you were afraid of what would happen to him without you."

You.

Eve shook her head. "You can't know that I'm her. Pierce—he wasn't sure. Like you said, my voice is wrong, my—"

Trey reached out and brushed back her hair.

Gabe was the one to stiffen now.

But Trey was just staring at the scar on her neck. "He slit your throat. Just like he did to the others."

She pulled her hair back to cover the scar.

"Pierce is afraid. He knows it's you, though, or he

never would have given you access to the condo. Jessica's home."

"Do you have any of Jessica Montgomery's possessions?" Gabe asked, making sure to keep any emotion out of his voice. The cop had enough emotion for them all. "We need a DNA sample for comparison—"

"And since you were adopted," Trey murmured, "you can't just be compared with Pierce."

Surprise flashed over Eve's face. "You . . . you knew?"

"We didn't have secrets."

Jealousy ate at Gabe. This was what he'd feared. That there was someone else out there, someone waiting for Eve. Someone that she loved.

He'd wanted her so much the night before. So much that need and lust had clawed right through his control. If Wade and Pierce hadn't interrupted, there would have been no going back.

Part of him wondered if it was already too late.

I don't want to give her up.

"I don't have DNA samples," Trey said. "No possessions. But I can prove in five seconds if you're Jessica Montgomery."

Gabe knew he wasn't going to like where this was going.

"How?" Eve asked.

Trey smiled at her. "Easy, sweetheart. All you have to do is strip."

Gabe lunged for him.

"Hold up!" Trey's hip rammed into the desk as he backed away from Gabe. "Jesus, man, calm down! I didn't say she had to strip *for* me!" He motioned toward the door on his right. "There's a bathroom in there! She can change and use the mirror to check herself."

But Eve shook her head. "Check myself? Look, I don't have any tattoos. My scars are all . . . fresh. The doctor said—"

"No, shit, of course, you don't have tattoos. You went to get one on your eighteenth birthday and you passed out when you saw me get mine." He jerked up the sleeve of his shirt, revealing a dark, sculpted anchor tattoo that rose from about two inches above his wrist to just under his elbow. "You were supposed to get a dolphin on your back. Only you hit the floor when the needle hit me, and when you woke up, you ran from that needle."

Trey spoke with an easy familiarity. *I know all of your secrets.* They'd come to Dauphin Island hoping someone would shed light on Eve's past. Gabe just hadn't expected the riot of anger and jealousy to hit him.

I want to know her secrets. He wanted to have the easy familiarity with her.

Why the hell am I jealous? Eve needed to get her life back. She needed her memories, and if this guy could help her . . . *then I have to step the fuck off.*

Eve should be happy. Whole.

Gabe took a step back.

"Check your left upper thigh," Trey told her quietly. "You've got three small moles there. Or, hell, maybe they're freckles, but they are there. Flat, smooth. And they form a triangle." His breath heaved out. "I've seen them plenty of times."

Gabe hated the guy. *Get it together, Spencer. This is Eve's life. If the police chief can help her . . .*

"And you've got another one of those little moles right on your pinky toe." Trey laughed, the sound low and intimate. "Cutest little damn thing I ever saw—"

She has those marks. Gabe had seen her feet. And

when he'd had her under him in that bed, he'd seen the little freckles on her thigh. He had kissed them.

"But you want some concrete evidence, is that it? The marks aren't enough?" Trey cocked his head. "Well, Jessica never had braces, and her dentist—hell, that guy retired years ago and I doubt you'd be able to find any dental records, so good luck with that."

He needed more than luck. *It's no coincidence that she and Jessica have those same freckles, in the exact same spots.* Gabe didn't think Eve was trying to con anyone. He thought that she was Jessica Montgomery, a woman who'd escaped from a killer.

But he'd realized that it didn't really matter what he thought. It was what *she* thought that mattered, and he didn't think she'd accept her identity as Jessica, not until her memories were back.

That is why we're on this island. To get those memories back.

Eve was standing there, her eyes huge, her body trembling faintly. She looked far too fragile right then, and he wasn't sure that she was up to any more big revelations right at that moment.

She'd been attacked the night before. She was too raw, and he was far too ready to kick the ass of anyone who even looked at her sideways. *Like that feeling is normal.* His protective instincts were in overdrive where Eve was concerned.

Gabe wrapped his arm around her shoulders. "I think we need to head to the condo."

She nodded.

They turned for the door.

"I'm telling the truth. I knew it when I kissed you. I knew it when I *saw* you," Trey called after them.

"Things might have ended between us, but you know I'll always care about you. You can trust me."

Things might have ended.

Yes, that had been in the report his employees had created. Jessica and Trey had broken up several weeks before her disappearance, but Pierce had acted as if they were still together. Gabe needed to understand exactly what had occurred between the two of them. *And if Jessica still loved the cop.* He looked back at Trey. "You and Jessica Montgomery were involved."

"Obviously," Trey muttered.

Eve was stiff at Gabe's side. "Who broke it off?" she asked.

Trey hesitated, but then he replied, "You did. Said we were always better friends than lovers, and that it was time for a change." He put his hands on his hips. "You know how folks say you don't realize what you've got until it's gone?"

He was closing in on Eve again.

"The last few months have been hell." Emotion roughened Trey's voice. "When you were gone, I learned what my real priorities were fast."

Eve edged closer to Gabe.

Her hand brushed his arm.

And for some reason, his anger eased. The tension he'd felt, the jealousy, receded. He could breathe without wanting to drive his fist at the cop.

"I'll do everything I can to help you," Trey told her softly, but Gabe saw that the man's hands were clenched into fists. "Because I won't lose you from my life again."

SHE NEEDED TO breathe. Only it felt as if her lungs were filled with water and she was drowning, choking on nothing.

"Eve?"

They were in the condo. And, jeez, but she hadn't expected it. She should have, though, considering how much money the Montgomery family seemed to have.

First off, it wasn't just a condo. It was a penthouse . . . one that would have given Gabe's place in Atlanta a run for his money. It was a gorgeous, insane place filled with furniture that she didn't recognize. Floor-to-ceiling glass windows wrapped around the penthouse, giving her nonstop views of the island. On one side she could see the Gulf of Mexico's waves hitting the sandy white beaches. On the other side she could see the gleaming inlets on the bay side of the island.

So much beauty.

And I can't breathe.

She rushed for the balcony. Shoved open the doors. The wind brushing over the ocean waves hit her, and she sucked in a deep breath.

I'm Jessica. I'm Jessica.

She heard the faint tread of Gabe's footsteps behind her. Then his hands curled over her shoulders. "You remembered him," Gabe said, voice quiet, barely carrying over the crash of the surf.

Eve shook her head. "But he remembered me." The man had been no more than a stranger to her, but he'd known her body. She had those freckles on her. On her upper thigh. On her foot. There was no way for Trey Wallace to know that unless . . . "I'm Jessica."

She was supposed to feel better now. She had a past. A family. But instead of feeling better, she was terrified.

Jessica was hunted. Jessica was tortured. Jessica was left for dead.

"I'm Jessica," she said again as she turned in his hold. Her back brushed against the edge of the balcony. They were on the seventh floor of that condo complex, the highest building on the island, and they were totally alone up there. She should have felt safe.

She didn't.

"I'm Jessica Montgomery, and the man who tried to kill me is out there." She was convinced that the Lady Killer was the man who'd attacked her in Atlanta. Was he going to follow her back to Dauphin Island, too? The part that scared her the most . . . "I don't know who he is. He could come right up to me, and *I. Wouldn't. Know.*" Terror clawed at her. How was she supposed to trust anyone that she met? She could be staring straight at a killer and she wouldn't know it.

His hands rose as he cupped her chin. "He's not going to hurt you."

That was so easy to say. "I've been afraid of him since the moment I opened my eyes in that hospital. I was afraid, and I didn't even know why." Trey had just confirmed her identity. A cop—a police chief!—had said she was Jessica Montgomery. So where was the relief? Where was the—dammit, the feeling of *something* other than the fear? The gnawing in her gut that wouldn't stop? She'd expected more. "He knew me, and it changed nothing."

Gabe gave a hard, negative shake of his head. "I'll call Pierce. I'll tell him about Trey—"

"We were lovers."

Gabe's nostrils flared. "Trey was involved with Jessica."

"I'm Jessica!" Even though the woman felt like a total stranger. Too rich, too beautiful, too perfect Jessica—who'd been taken by a killer. Tortured. Murdered.

No, Jessica survived . . .

"He knew me." She was absolutely certain about this.

"I could feel it in the way Trey touched me. The way he looked at me." Too intimate.

Gabe's hand fell away from her.

"He wanted me to remember him, but I couldn't." *I'll always care about you.* Trey's words echoed in her mind. "And when he touched me, the only thing I felt . . . it was fear."

Gabe's brows slanted down. "He scared you?"

He terrified me. "I didn't want him to touch me. *I didn't want Ben Tyler touching me.* I only want *you.*"

But he backed away.

The surf kept pounding below.

"Trey said that he and Jessica—that he and I were done," she fumbled, trying to make sense even as her mind seemed to splinter on her. *I'm not Eve, I'm Jessica!* But Jessica was still a stranger. No, worse, she seemed like a ghost. "If I'm not involved with Trey, then that means there isn't some lover in the background for me. There's no one waiting—"

"Eve . . ."

"You're the man I want, Gabe. Only you." And he was just standing there. She needed him to say something. Too much was happening inside of her. Emotions were gutting her. She wanted to scream. She wanted to rage. She wanted—

Him.

Eve surged forward. She grabbed his shirt, fisting it in her hands, and she rose onto her tiptoes. Then she kissed him. Wild. Hard. Hot.

She kissed him.

She knew it was too late to turn back. Too late to let go.

It was too late for them both.

HE COULD SEE them, up on that balcony. With his binoculars, he had a perfect view of them. But then, he'd always had a perfect view. He could see her clearly—every moment. *Always.*

He'd made certain of that.

She was kissing Gabe Spencer. Wrapping her arms around him. Holding onto the man as if her very life depended on him.

But it didn't.

Your life depends on me. You can't forget that, not like you've forgotten everything else.

Gabe's arms locked around her.

You should have pushed her away, asshole.

But Gabe was taking her back in the penthouse. He was going to fuck her.

When they vanished from that balcony, he jerked down his binoculars, swearing. *You can't have her. You—*

"Uh, excuse me?"

A woman's voice. Soft, one tinted lightly with what sounded like a drawling Texas accent.

"Could you possibly help me?"

His teeth locked as he turned toward her.

But then he saw her. The light shone off her blond hair. She'd perched a pair of sunglasses on the top of her head, and her eyes, hesitant, hopeful, met his.

Her eyes were green.

Not that perfect, deep green of Jessica's, but close enough.

Close enough . . .

They always were.

Oh, you just might work wonderfully . . . The tool he'd needed had just walked right up to him.

"I heard there was a lighthouse around here," she

said, waving her hand. The light caught the expensive diamond tennis bracelet that she wore. "How do I get there? I mean, where—"

He caught her wrist in his hand. *You shouldn't wear jewelry like that. Not in the water. It just attracts predators . . .*

Sometimes, you didn't see the predators until it was too late.

She looked at his hand, then back up at him. She smiled, a bit nervously, a bit flirtatiously.

He was handsome, he knew it. His looks made things easier. The women didn't hesitate when they were approached by a handsome man. Not the women he hunted. Women used to using their own looks to get what they wanted.

"I'm afraid you have to travel by boat in order to reach the lighthouse. It's about a forty-minute boat drive." He gave her a smile. "There's a lighthouse tour that leaves from the main marina each day, but I think you missed that boat. I saw it head out about twenty minutes ago."

"Oh." Her plump lips curled down in a pout.

His gaze slid over her. She wore a white bikini, and a wraparound skirt that twisted into a tie at her hip. She was slim, but curved in all the right places.

And the blonde looked as if she were the right age . . .

"You vacationing down here alone?" he asked her, keeping his voice light.

"Alexa!"

She jerked at the call, glancing over her shoulder. "No, my best friend and I are on a getaway."

And the best friend was closing in. A pretty redhead with blue eyes.

Not my type.

But Alexa . . . she had potential. He'd have to do a little research on her and make sure she was just right.

"Maybe I can give you a ride out to that lighthouse sometime," he offered, letting his fingers trail lightly over her wrist.

He felt her pulse jump beneath his touch.

"I've got a thirty-foot boat that I think you'd love . . ."

"Alexa?" The best friend was coming closer. She hadn't spotted him yet. That was good. It wouldn't do for anyone to see him with the lovely Alexa. Not if he decided to use her.

He dropped Alexa's wrist and pushed his sunglasses onto his nose. "Where are you going to be tonight?"

Her smile spread. She thought he was interested, and she was loving the attention. One of her shoulders rolled in a light shrug. "I heard there was a band playing on the West End of the island. I thought I'd check them out."

Perfect. That would give him plenty of time to learn more about her. With his resources, he'd know everything necessary about her within a few hours. "I'll see you then." He eased away from her. "And maybe later I can give you that ride . . ."

A ride she'd never forget.

The last ride of her life.

CHAPTER EIGHT

H E SHOULD GET HIS HANDS OFF HER.
But he was holding her too tightly.
He shouldn't be kissing her.
But Gabe couldn't get enough of her taste.

And they were in the bedroom. A big four-poster bed waited for them. They were alone. *She's not involved with the cop.*

She wants me.

And he'd be a damn fool if he turned her away again.

He lowered her onto the bed. He should be seducing her. Taking things slow and easy. Making her moan and tremble with her need.

But he was stripping her. Nearly tearing her clothes in his haste because he wanted her naked. Wanted *in* her more than he wanted to draw another breath right then.

She kicked off her shoes. He yanked down her jeans, tore away her panties.

He was still kissing her. Her tongue licked over his, and his cock jerked—the damn thing was so full and heavy with arousal that he was pretty sure the indentation of the zipper marked him.

He'd shoved protection in his wallet earlier. Because he'd known that he was too desperate for her and he'd wanted to be prepared in case his control broke.

Yeah, it had cracked when she kissed him. He was barely holding on to the tattered remains of that control then.

There will be no going back.

He heaved up and finally managed to pull his mouth from hers. Her green eyes stared up at him. No fear, only desire.

He caught her shirt in his hands. Yanked the T-shirt up and over her head. The plain white bra that she wore just might have been the sexiest piece of underwear he'd ever seen.

But he still wanted it gone.

He fumbled—twice—and managed to unhook the bra. *So much for finesse.* He felt big and awkward and clumsy and all he wanted—

In her.

The blood pounded in his veins, his body seemed to burn from the inside out, and when she parted her legs for him, when she reached for his cock and her fingers touched him . . .

Gabe was gone.

His control shattered. No other word.

Desire consumed him. He sheathed his cock in that rubber, and he caught her hands. She *couldn't* touch him, not then. He caged her hands in his grip even as he thrust into her. He should have used restraint. She deserved care.

But he was too far gone for that. He was beyond anything but desire. A need that controlled, a hunger to consume and take everything that she had to give.

Her hips arched toward him and he drove down, plunging deep into her. She gasped when he filled her—

Don't want to hurt her, don't—

Then her legs wrapped tightly around his hips. Her eyes seemed to go wild with pleasure.

And he didn't hold back. His thrusts were hard and strong, and he kissed her as he took her. His tongue plunged past her lips even as his cock plunged into her body. More, again, deeper, and she was so tight. So incredibly tight and hot and wet as her body gripped him. His eyes were nearly rolling back into his head because sex with her was that fucking good.

Have to make it good for her, too . . . she has to feel . . . what I feel . . .

He freed her hands. His fingers slid between their bodies. He found her clit, stroked her even as he kept thrusting. His head lifted as he stared down at her.

So fucking beautiful.

He needed to feel her climax around him. He wanted to see her when she came. Wanted to see the pleasure on her face.

Her breath caught. Her nails raked down his arms and she surged up with her hips.

"Eve . . ." Her name was a growled rasp from him, all he could manage because his climax was bearing down on him.

Eve first, I want to feel Eve come first—

She did. Her sex clenched around him in a wild, greedy grasp that sent him surging straight into the most powerful release of his life. She was whispering his name, arching, and her delicate inner muscles were trembling around the length of his cock. He kept thrusting, driving into her again and again because he didn't want the pleasure to end.

His heart was a drumbeat in his ears, fast and furious. Her nails still bit into his flesh, and he loved that sting.

He loved the way he could smell the faint scent of sex in the air. Her. Him.

And he loved the gut-wrenching pleasure that still shook his body.

Her breath came out in soft pants. He thought those little pants sounded sexy, and when she said his name, her voice that husky roll of temptation, the cock that should have been tired started twitching again, hardening once more.

Pull out. Get some damn control back. Get sanity.

Slowly, staring into her eyes, he withdrew. Inch by inch.

She locked her muscles around him and moaned.

Fuck, is she still coming?

He could feel the ripples of her release around him, and it was the sexiest thing in the world.

Then she smiled at him.

No, that's the sexiest thing.

He leaned down and kissed her. Her tongue slid over the edge of his lower lip, licking him.

"I didn't know what I was missing," she whispered.

The woman was *gutting* him.

He locked his muscles and pulled out. He had to ditch his condom and get back to her.

"No, Eve," he heard himself say, "I didn't know."

A small line appeared between her brows.

He knew he'd just revealed too much then.

"I'm supposed to believe a guy like you hasn't had dozens of lovers?" Her voice was light, teasing. Her cheeks were flushed pink and her green eyes sparkled with pleasure.

He wasn't going to lie or bluff his way through this. He wanted Eve to know that she mattered. "There's sex," he told her simply, "and then there's what we just had."

The faint smile on her lips slipped away. Some of the pleasure seemed to fade from her gaze. "What did we just have?"

"Fucking I'd-kill-to-have-it pleasure." A dark, disturbing truth. The kind of white-hot passion that ignited and burned straight to the soul. The kind he'd known that he'd have with her . . . *and that's why I tried to warn her to stay away. That if I had her once, it would be too late for me.*

"Sex isn't always like . . . this?"

"No." He turned away. Stalked into the bathroom. Ditched the condom. His cock was up and more than ready to go again with her. *Again and again.* He stared into the mirror, saw his hard eyes and the lust that was still stamped clearly on his face.

The floor creaked and he looked over to see Eve standing in the bathroom doorway. She had a sheet wrapped around her body. Her hair was tousled, her lips still red from his mouth.

"Then what's it usually like?"

"Hot. Good. A release that leaves your body sated."

She licked her lips. "I thought this was . . . better than good."

Hell, yes, it had been. His left hand slid under her chin and he tipped her head back. "Just so we're clear, that was ripping-me-apart great."

Her smile came again. "It was for me, too."

She didn't see the danger. Didn't realize how much he still wanted her.

She would, though. She'd realize that he'd tried to warn her.

Now it was too late.

He lowered his head and kissed her again.

GABE'S PHONE RANG, jerking him from a light sleep. His eyes opened, and he saw the light spilling into the bedroom. The balcony doors were open and he could hear the rush of the surf outside.

The phone rang again.

"You should get that," Eve murmured.

His eyes locked on her. She was in the bed with him, the sheet draped over her body as she curled toward him.

With his eyes on her, he reached out and grabbed his phone. He'd tossed it on the nightstand at some point before. Hell if he remembered when. He put it to his ear. "Spencer."

"The team's here," Dean told him, voice sharp. "Most of the team, anyway. Sarah and Victoria are settled in their rooms and I'm on the fourth floor."

And Gabe wasn't so sleepy and relaxed any longer.

"Wade said you gave orders for him to stay in Atlanta until he learned more about that attack on your girl."

Your girl. His eyes were on Eve right then. Her hand was on his leg, very close to a part of his anatomy that loved her touch.

"You ready to start scouting the island?" Dean asked.

Gabe cleared his throat. "Give us five minutes."

"Right. We can start hitting Jessica Montgomery's old hangouts and work back from there. If we can figure out her movements the last few days leading up to her disappearance, then we might catch the guy who took her."

Yes, they might.

Gabe put down the phone.

Eve was staring up at him, her gaze aware and—determined. "Don't worry. I'm not going to break apart again."

"I've never seen you break."

This time her smile was sad. "Liar."

He shook his head. "I've never lied to you."

Her gaze searched his. His words seemed to give her pause. "No, I don't guess you have."

"And I won't." He needed honesty between them. As more of her past was revealed, she had to know that she could count on him. "The things we find out here . . . they're not going to be easy for you to handle."

Because they both knew she was Jessica Montgomery. DNA test or not, the truth was there for them. In the cop's reaction to her. In Eve's own startling response at the bakery.

The freckles! The fucking freckles!

And as they explored the island more and more, the past would come back to her.

He hoped, anyway.

When he'd talked to her at his office, Sarah had been pretty confident that heading back to Dauphin Island was in Eve's best interest. Familiar environment. Familiar people.

Since it looked as if the killer already knew she'd escaped once, there had been no point in trying to keep her hidden in Atlanta.

"I was tortured. Nearly killed," Eve had told him then, her voice strong. "I already know that, so it's not as if I'll be discovering something new there."

No, but having the memories and reliving the terror were two entirely different things. "I'll be with you."

Her delicate jaw hardened. "And I told you, I won't break."

Now, he heard a knock at the door. Hell, so much for five minutes. Dean must have hauled ass up that elevator. Gabe slid from the bed. Grabbed his jeans and T-shirt and dressed as quickly as he could. "I'll handle Dean while you dress."

She was in that bed, watching him with her deep, gorgeous eyes.

He should say something else. Something about the sex. Something about *them*.

Gabe opened his mouth.

"Thank you," Eve said as she rose from the bed. She didn't bring the sheet with her. She stood there, naked, making his cock ache, and inclined her head toward him. "You stopped making me feel afraid . . . and you just . . . you made me *feel*."

The pounding on the door came again.

Why the hell was it that every time he had Eve in a bedroom, some jerk from LOST had to come knocking on his door? He needed to have a serious talk with people about the importance of *timing*.

"Thank you," he told Eve, without moving toward that pounding. "Because you fucking gave me pleasure I won't forget."

She smiled at him. A quick flash of warmth that had him taking a step toward her because the bed was close, she was naked, and—

Eve put her hand on his chest.

"Get the door."

Right. Shit. The door.

He turned away. Made sure that he closed that bedroom door, then made his way to the condo's entrance. But when Gabe peered through the peephole, Dean Bannon wasn't on the other side of that door.

The Dauphin Island police chief was.

And Trey Wallace was lifting his hand to pound again.

Hell. Gabe jerked open the door.

He saw that Trey *hadn't* been lifting his hand to knock that last time—the guy had a key grasped in his fist—a key that he'd been about to use on the condo's door. *What the hell?*

"So breaking and entering is allowed on this island?" Gabe asked him quietly. "Good to know."

Trey's smile looked like a tiger's. "She gave me a key. Like I said, we were lovers once."

"Past tense," Gabe reminded the guy. As of the present, *he* was her lover.

Trey's hand opened. "Take it."

He damn well did, and shoved the key into his pocket.

"She looked shaken back at the station. I just wanted to make sure that Jessica was okay."

Jessica. The name just didn't come easily to him. When he thought of the sexy blonde he'd just left, naked, in that bedroom . . . *Eve. My Eve.*

"I know you're fucking her." Though Trey's words were low, the anger in them was clear.

An elevator dinged down the hallway. Gabe looked over the cop's shoulder, and when the elevator doors opened, he saw Dean stride toward them.

"One of yours?" the cop asked.

"Yeah." *I know you're fucking her.* Trey's words replayed in Gabe's head. "Dean Bannon's ex-FBI."

A hard sigh slipped from Trey. "Right. 'Cause we need more Bureau assholes running rampant over my island."

"Dean's one of the best agents at LOST," Gabe said, making sure to keep his own voice even.

Dean's brows rose.

"You said we'd have the access we needed here," Gabe continued. What, was the cop about to back out now because—

Trey glanced back at him. "Do you always have this much of a vested interest in your cases?"

"All of my cases are important."

"Especially when the cases look like Jessica."

Gabe narrowed his eyes on the cop.

Trey swore then, and reached for some packages set on the floor, to one side of the door—two bags and what looked like canvases. "Look, I was worried about her, and I wanted to make sure she was all right."

She is all right.

"She paints when she gets stressed." Trey shoved the supplies at Gabe. "She paints when she's happy, too. Her brother sold everything she had, but . . . they have an art store near the station. I just . . . I picked those up for her, okay?"

The bedroom door creaked open. Eve's footsteps padded toward them.

Trey's gaze instantly shot to her. Gabe could read the longing in his stare. Longing, pain, and . . . anger?

Yes, there was definitely some rage there. Gabe's shoulders stiffened.

"I know that look," Trey muttered. "The way her cheeks are flushed and—"

"Don't say another word," Gabe warned him. Cop or not, if he did anything to make Eve feel uncomfortable or ashamed for what they'd just done, he'd slug the guy.

"I already knew you were fucking her." Trey took a step back and nearly bumped into Dean. "So it's not a surprise." His gaze raked Gabe. "But what the hell are you going to do when her memory comes back? When her life is back? Because Jessica Montgomery's life *doesn't* include you."

He spun away. His words had been low, so Gabe didn't think Eve had heard them, but—

"Trey?" Eve called, in the doorway now.

Trey stopped just in front of the elevator.

Eve slipped around Gabe. He wanted to grab her and pull her back but he locked his muscles and held still. *If the guy says anything to hurt her . . .*

"You brought me . . . paint? Canvases?"

Trey didn't look at her. His gaze was on the closed elevator doors. "When you were eight, you picked up your first paintbrush. After that, I don't remember a time you didn't have some paint on your hands or under your nails." He looked over at her. "Except for now." That anger was still back, and Gabe shot forward, dropping the items Trey had shoved at him because the cop was reaching for Eve—

Trey's hands closed around her shoulders. "Don't let Jessica be dead. Bring her back. *Remember.* I need Jessica back."

The elevator dinged. The doors opened.

Trey let Eve go and hurried into the elevator. The cop stared back at her. Then, just before the doors closed, he looked at Gabe, his hand flew out and he stopped the doors from shutting. "I'll do everything in *my* power," he said, jaw locked tight, "to uncover the truth about what happened to Jessica. So send the Bureau guy . . ." Trey jerked his head toward a watchful Dean. "Send your anthropologist. Send everyone you've got to investigate. *Because I want Jessica back.*"

His hand fell away.

The doors closed.

You're not getting her.

Silence.

"Well . . ." Dean said easily. "By my estimate, you two have been on the island about two hours . . . and it looks like you're already busy making friends."

Gabe glared at him.

Dean lifted his hands, palms out, toward Gabe in a classic "my bad" pose.

"I think he is my friend," Eve said, her gaze on the closed elevator doors. Her voice was thoughtful.

"With friends like that . . ." Dean muttered, "this case is going to be even harder than we thought."

Eve squared her shoulders and turned to face Gabe and Dean. "Where do we start?"

Wade could see that the emotion was gone from her eyes. If Trey's words had cut her, there was no sign of the wound. No sign of anything but her stark determination.

And Eve was worried she'd break?

Hell, no, she wouldn't even fracture.

Dean coughed a bit into his hand. "I think we, uh, we need to go and see where the bodies were found. Victoria is already heading over there. Maybe something at the dump site—"

Gabe cut his gaze toward Dean.

"Maybe something at the *recovery* site," Dean corrected carefully, "will help to jar your memory."

Eve nodded. "Maybe it will."

Or maybe the place would just give her fresh nightmares. Either way, he would be by her side. Every step of the way.

WAS SHE SUPPOSED to still be able to feel Gabe's touch on her skin? Because she did. She could almost feel him all around her, *in* her, and her body just seemed . . . different.

Eve kept glancing at him. He'd been so silent during the ride to the old golf course. His gaze had been dead ahead, focused, while she was too aware of him.

Trey knows that I was with Gabe. Was she supposed to feel shame about that? She didn't. Gabe was the man she wanted now, her present—the only man she'd wanted since waking in that hospital. So, no, she didn't feel shame.

But she felt . . . guilt. Because she knew Trey wanted her to remember him. When he'd been in that elevator, she'd seen the need in his eyes. Not a passionate need. The need for—

"This is the place," Dean said from the backseat. His deep voice made her jump. He'd been silent during the ride, too. No small talk for those two.

Just unnerving silence.

She looked back at the road and saw an old gate and a sign that proclaimed: MEMBERS ONLY. NO TRESPASSING.

"I'm guessing there haven't been members here in a very long time," Gabe murmured.

"The country club shut down about twenty years ago," Dean said. He'd leaned forward and his voice was louder now. "With no activity here, the killer knew this was the perfect place to hide his victims."

Gabe drove past the old gate. It had been left open for them. By Victoria? Gabe had told her that Victoria Palmer, the forensic anthropologist, was already in that place. Somewhere.

I wouldn't want to be alone here.

And it was strange . . . because the place was so beautiful. Tall, almost mountainlike sand dunes surrounded the narrow road. The sand was that bright, perfect white, seeming to reflect light all around them.

The road twisted and snaked around the dunes, and they drove up, up, until Eve saw a two-story round building. It was dark, its main windows hazy.

"That's the old clubhouse," Dean said. "Victoria's SUV is parked right there."

The SUV sat next to a Jeep. Gabe slid their rental

into a spot beside it. Eve hurried out and the wind hit her, tossing her hair around her face. There was a giant stretch of beach right below them, empty, and she could see a dolphin breaking the surface of the water down there.

"The bodies were found to the east," Dean said as he came to stand beside her. "That's where the beach took the big hit from that last storm. The SOB probably thought he was safe, that no one would find his girls—"

"But he didn't count on Mother Nature," Gabe said. His voice was so careful, so controlled. He'd been that way since Trey had come to the condo.

Was he regretting what they'd done?

She didn't have time for regret in her life. When you only lived in the present, how could you regret anything?

"Gabe!"

Eve turned at the call, and she saw a woman waving toward them. She was down below, near the edge of the water. Her dark hair was pulled back in a ponytail and a pair of sunglasses were perched on her nose.

"Viki," Dean said, "always keeping it low key." But he hurried down the slope toward her. Two other men were behind Victoria—they also wore dark sunglasses, but unlike Victoria, they weren't dressed in shorts and a T-shirt. They wore khakis and white dress shirts.

"Your men?" Eve asked without taking a step down the slope. It was so hard to meet people, because she worried every instant that she was actually seeing someone from her past.

The killer?

"Those are FBI agents. Dean pulled strings to get us a tour of this area."

Her breath came a little easier. She started down the slope. When the sand shifted beneath her feet, Gabe caught her arm, steadying her. Only once she was steady, he didn't let go.

"I should have backed away," he said, his voice low, carrying only to her ears and not the group below. "It's too late now."

"The pleasure we shared isn't anything to regret," she told him, clinging to her pride because it was one of the few things she had. "It's something to be repeated."

He wore sunglasses, too, dark glasses that hid his expression from her, but she easily saw the hardening of his jaw.

"Eve . . ."

She pulled away from him and headed below.

Victoria hurried to meet her, offering her hand. "Isn't this place amazing?" she said, giving Eve's hand a quick, hard shake. "I mean, talk about your body preservation. With the sand here, the Lady Killer could just put his victims down and then—"

"Victoria." Gabe's voice snapped like a whip.

Victoria slapped a hand over her mouth. "I'm sorry!" Her hand dropped and chagrin flashed over her face. "I'm so used to working with the dead! I forgot that you were one of his victims. I mean, I knew you were a victim but—"

Dean cleared his throat. "Viki gets caught up in the scientific aspect of her work. Sometimes she forgets the bodies that she sees are actually real people."

Red stained Viki's cheeks. "No." Her voice had gone soft, stilted, "I never forget that."

Eve reached out, her hands brushing lightly over Victoria's shoulder. "It's okay. I forget things all the time." She offered the woman a smile, trying to lighten the hard tension that had settled over everyone. "It's kind of my thing."

Victoria's mouth dropped open in shock, then she laughed, a light, quick peal of sound. She covered her mouth almost instantly, as if horrified that she'd just laughed at Eve's memory loss.

Eve kept smiling at her. "It's okay," she said. "Really."

Victoria gave a quick nod, then turned on her heel and motioned toward the FBI agents. "Avery and Douglas have the perimeter secured up ahead, and the search is still going on for—for more victims."

Eve fell into step beside her. The scent of the ocean washed over her, and that scent brought with it the whisper of fear.

She glanced out at the water. It was a bit hazy out there, as if fog were planning to roll in that night and . . . *something is out there.*

She stopped walking and stared out at the waves. Her eyes narrowed as she strained to take in that shadowy shape. Was it an oil rig? A gas rig? She'd seen a few of those as they drove around the island. Maybe it was just a fishing boat or—

"It's a lighthouse," one of the FBI agents said. Eve glanced at him. A tall blond guy with a faint cleft in his chin. "The Sand Island lighthouse."

Eve couldn't take her gaze off the place. "Does . . . does it still work?"

"No, that place hasn't been used in decades." He offered his hand to her. "My name is Avery Granger, and this is my partner . . ." He nodded toward the African-American man a few feet away, "Douglas Stonebridge." Douglas had warm brown eyes and a strong handshake.

Was she supposed to say it was nice to meet them? Because those words were literally on her lips, like some sort of long forgotten manners protocol, but she bit them back. It wasn't really nice to meet people at a body dump site. Saying it was would be anything but proper etiquette. "Thanks for giving us access," she said instead.

"Consider it an information exchange program," Avery said as he cocked his head to study her. "You get to see what we've found, and if your memories come back . . ." His gaze slid toward Dean. ". . . then you get to lead us to the Lady Killer."

"*If* you really are a survivor," Douglas added, voice more than hinting that he didn't fully believe she was.

Fair enough.

Victoria hadn't stopped walking. Eve hurried to keep up with her. She crested another small slope and then—

Graves.

The holes had been dug into the cleared sand. Only they weren't really holes. They were long, very clear rectangular shapes. Four of them.

"The first two bodies were uncovered by the storm," Victoria said as she headed toward the graves. Stakes had been put into the ground, and rope circled the stakes, marking off the area. "A guy and his dog found them . . . and once the FBI started digging . . ."

"We uncovered the remains of four more victims," Douglas finished.

Eve inched forward, staring down into the holes. The insides of those graves . . . totally empty. "How did you push the sand back?" she asked softly. "Because it just keeps falling in, the more you push, the more you fight . . . it just pours in on top of you . . ."

"We had an excavation team—" Avery began.

Eve squeezed her eyes shut. *The sand keeps falling in.* "Were they buried alive?"

"Eve." Warm, strong hands wrapped around her arms. His hands. "Eve, look at me."

Her eyes flew open. Gabe was right in front of her.

"Do you remember this place?"

She remembered something. "The sand . . . I can feel it all over me. I—I think . . ." Her eyes went back to the graves. "I think he buried me." Her hand rose, touching the scar on her neck. "He . . . I . . ." Her head was splintering. "Were the victims tied beneath the sand? Their . . . their hands . . ."

Avery advanced on her. "Why do you ask that?"

Because she could feel a rope cutting into her wrists. And her hands . . . "When I woke up in the hospital, I had rope burns."

"We found rope with them," Douglas said as he, too, advanced toward her.

But she wasn't ready to face them. She crept closer to the stakes, to those graves. *Was I in one of his graves, too?*

The answer was there, pushing forward in her mind. *Yes.*

She blinked away tears that wanted to fill her eyes. "How long were they tortured?"

"Days."

Her heart jerked. "You didn't . . . you didn't answer me before . . . Were they alive when he buried them?" That part hadn't been in the paper. Neither had the information about the victims being bound beneath the sand.

I remembered that.

She could feel the crushing weight of sand all around her . . .

"Based on what our examiner found . . ." It was Douglas who answered. "Yes, we think he buried them alive beneath the sand."

Horror choked off her breath.

CHAPTER NINE

THE SUN WAS SETTING. AT THE WEST END OF THE island the band had already started to play, and bikini-clad women and men in swim trunks were dancing in front of a makeshift stage.

A string of lights had been draped over the stage and crisscrossed the small dance floor—a floor made of sand. The setting sun turned the sky a deep red behind that stage, and, soon enough, that sky would turn black and the stars would appear. A million stars, glittering overhead.

"Hey there!"

Her voice.

His prey.

Keeping his cap on and his sunglasses in place, he turned toward her.

"I was hoping to see you," Alexa said, giving him a bright smile.

And he'd been planning to see her. Especially since she'd checked out so perfectly. Information these days was so readily available. People freely put their whole lives up on the Internet, always wanting attention.

Alexa Chambers was twenty-six, the only daughter of

a wealthy Texas attorney. Two months ago poor Alexa had broken up with her fiancé.

As she'd posted online, it was, "Time for me to get back in the game!"

He did love to play games . . .

Alexa's smile flickered with uncertainty. "Did you . . . I mean . . . are you here with someone?"

"I am now." He caught her hand. Brought it to his lips. Kissed her knuckles.

She laughed softly, nervously, and the setting sun glinted off her bracelet. Had that been a gift from Daddy? Or the ex?

"I knew someone with a bracelet like that once," he said.

Her laughter faded. "Let me guess. A—A former girl-friend?"

Alexa was so delightfully uncertain. Probably the work of her ex. With her good looks and family back-ground, she should have been confident, in control.

But I'm the one with the control.

Soon, all Alexa would have . . . would be fear.

"Not anymore," he said, smiling at her. "You still up for that boat ride?"

Alexa started to nod, but then she bit her lip. "Should I trust you?"

No, you should run screaming from me.

Staring into her eyes, he pulled out his wallet. Offered her the ID there. "Does that make you feel better?" The badge glinted.

Her smile flashed again.

"I'm off duty," he told her, keeping his voice low and easy. "So how about we take that ride? The water is gor-geous when the sun is setting."

And Alexa . . . eager Alexa . . . nodded.

THEY'D STAYED OUT on that beach, next to those graves, for hours. The FBI agents had grilled Eve, again and again. But she hadn't been able to tell them any more.

Just about the rope . . .

The sand . . . crushing down on her . . .

She hadn't been able to remember anything about her attacker.

"It will come to you."

Her head turned. They were back in the golf course parking lot. Gabe was a few feet away, talking with Dean and the FBI agents. Victoria waited next to Eve, sympathy on her face. "It will," Victoria said, her voice stronger with certainty. "You just need more time."

Eve wished she had her certainty. Plenty of time had already passed since she'd woken in that hospital.

"Unless you . . . you don't really want to remember." Now Victoria looked back down at the beach. The sun had fallen low into the sky, and shadows were starting to stretch out onto the water. "I read the coroner's reports on those women. Maybe you're better off—"

"I'm not," Eve said.

Victoria nodded. "I understand."

Did she? Eve wasn't so sure about that.

Gabe strode toward her. The FBI agents were heading back down the beach, back toward those graves.

Four graves. The remains found there had been linked to four women—Kate Ryan, Cassie Blankenship, Sharon Douzanis, and Lyla Strong.

"I need a drink," Eve muttered.

Gabe stopped.

"Um, say again?" Victoria asked, her hands fluttering lightly by her sides.

"Don't act like you don't need one, too." Eve rolled back her shoulders, trying futilely to push away the tension that had lodged there. "We've been staring at graves all afternoon and for most of the evening. We need to unwind." Talk about an understatement. "Let's get a *drink*." She marched for the SUV. "I want music. I want dancing. And I want to think of something other than death."

She jumped into the vehicle. Slammed the door behind her.

A few seconds later the driver-side door opened. Gabe climbed inside. "Are you okay?"

No. "Buy me a drink, Gabe," she said, her hand rising to brush across the scar on her neck. "I don't want to be the woman who can't remember. I don't even want to be the woman who crawled out of a sandy grave. For a little while I just want to drink and listen so some music, okay? I need it to wash away everything else."

Dean opened the back right door. "The island is only fourteen miles long. If you're looking for a good time, I figure we just need to roll down the windows and follow the music."

Eve grabbed Gabe's hand. "I need this." How was a drink and some dancing too much to ask?

Gabe cranked the engine. The windows rolled down.

"You coming after us in your car?" Dean called to Victoria. She was still standing in the same spot.

She gave a quick nervous nod.

"Then let's follow the music," Gabe said as he backed up the SUV. "Let's do anything that you want . . ."

He should be careful what he said. The guy had no idea what she really wanted right then.

Music and dancing—they weren't the release she craved. They weren't going to banish the cloying fear that was suffocating her.

Being in his arms? In his bed? *That's what I need.*

The wild pleasure that he could give to her. But right at that moment she'd take any oblivion she could get.

Drinks. Music. Dancing.

The SUV pulled away from that old country club. They headed back down the narrow road that snaked between the massive sand dunes. She caught a few glimpses of the old golf course as they headed out. A patch of green here, an abandoned cart there. The area just seemed to stretch before her.

Are more bodies hidden beneath the sand?

She was afraid that there were. Three victims had been marked as missing by the FBI. Three women who matched the profile of the Lady Killer's victim. Jessica Montgomery was one of those women. The other two were Chantal Grant and Helen Humphrey.

Chantal had disappeared from Dauphin Island two years ago. At first the authorities had thought she was a drowning victim. The others had been listed as drowning victims, too—until their bodies were discovered.

When the remains of Kate, Cassie, Sharon, and Lyla were discovered, the FBI got to work creating victim profiles. From their profiles, they'd realized that Jessica, Chantal, and Helen could all be victims of the Lady Killer.

Eve didn't think there was any "could be" about the situation. Her gaze slid over the sand. *You're out there, aren't you?*

She knew the Lady Killer had given Chantal and Helen their own sandy graves.

"YOUR BOAT IS incredible!" Alexa said as she jumped on board. She was smiling as she glanced around. "Now this is truly the way to travel in style."

He grinned as he followed her, knowing exactly what

role he had to play. "I take it you like traveling in style?"

She was already heading below deck. *Talk about making things easy.*

"Who doesn't?" Her voice floated back to him. "This is incredible down here!"

Yes, the boat was rather impressive. "I have a confession," he murmured as he entered the main cabin.

She was already helping herself to the champagne he'd stocked there.

"A confession?" She held up the champagne bottle. "Let me guess. You're planning to seduce me." Her voice had dipped to a seductive purr.

He shook his head. "It's not my boat."

"It—It's not?" Her smile slipped and she started to lower the champagne bottle.

"I borrowed it." The lies were so easy. "My boat was wrecked in the last storm. This belongs to a friend of mine."

"Oh." Her smile was back. Even bigger than before. "Some friend you've got."

"Yes . . ." He reached down. His fingers curled around the neck of the champagne bottle, and his knuckles brushed against her hand. "And as far as seducing you goes . . ."

Her mouth was just inches from his. She stood onto her tiptoes, stretching eagerly before him.

"Yes . . . ?" Alexa breathed against his lips.

"I'm not going to seduce you."

She blinked. "What?"

He pressed a kiss to her lips and said, "I'm going to kill you."

It took her a few lost, desperate moments to understand his words, and by the time Alexa tried to pull back from him, it was too late. He'd snatched the champagne bottle from her grasp and slammed it to the side of her head.

She didn't even have a chance to scream.

The champagne bottle thunked into her head. Blood spattered and down she went, tumbling right back on the bed.

He stood there a moment, watching her. Her chest was still rising. She was obviously alive. Good. Because if she'd been dead, what would have been the point?

He put the champagne bottle on the floor. Got some rope—he'd planned ahead, he always did—and he tied her up. Then he wrapped her up in the bedclothes and tossed Alexa's ass in the closet.

"Don't worry, I'll be back. I just need to check up on my island." He stripped off his clothes. Pulled a fresh set from his bag, the same bag that had contained the rope. It wouldn't do to walk around the island with blood on his clothes. You never knew when a bit of spatter would wreck you.

He'd killed to cover up a bit of spatter before. A spring breaker who'd been a bit too observant had needed a fast trip to hell. The kill had been brutal and quick, the same way he'd taken out Pauley McIntyre. Killing that way never gave him any pleasure.

I like to work with my girls.

When he was done changing, he double-checked the lock on the closet. He tapped lightly on the door. "Sweetheart, don't worry, I won't be gone long."

No sound came from the closet.

"When I get back," he told Alexa, "the real fun will begin."

He'd take her far away, so far that no one else would hear her when she screamed and screamed and screamed.

This time you won't get away.

He was whistling when he headed back to the main deck.

EVE DOWNED HER rum and Coke in a flash. Her hand tapped on the counter and her body swayed lightly with the pounding music.

Gabe made sure that he stayed close to her even as his gaze swept the gathering crowd at the beach. It was summer, peak season on the island, and even the discovery of a serial killer's dumping grounds hadn't slowed down the activity there.

"Yeah, baby, sure thing," he heard the guy on the other side of Eve saying to a pretty brunette. "I can get you on the golf course. I can show you where all those graves are . . ."

The brunette put her hand on his chest. "Really, Johnny, you can do that?"

"Hell, yeah, and it's *freaky*. They were all lined up, side by side. Fucking dead girl parade in the sand—"

The brunette's eyes widened with avid fascination. "I want to see."

Hell, so maybe the serial killer *had* attracted some people to the island. He'd seen crap like that before. Almost like serial killer groupies. He would never understand that shit.

"Another one," Eve snapped to the bartender.

He immediately set her up with another rum and Coke. She drained it in an instant.

"I want to go now, Johnny," the brunette said. " 'Cause I heard you can hear the ghost of those women screaming right after sunset, and I want to hear—"

"Oh, yeah, baby," Johnny said eagerly. "Let's *go. I'll get you in that sand, I'll show you—*"

A tremble ran through Eve's body.

"Johnny, stop being a fucking dick," Gabe snapped.

Johnny whirled around and his gaze shot toward him. The guy was in his early twenties, with a weak-looking chin and bleary eyes that said he'd already had plenty of booze.

"That's a crime scene, and you aren't getting your ass near it." The guy wanted to take his girl out there and screw her where women had died? Hell, *no,* that wasn't going down.

Where Eve could have died? The guy wanted to have a fuckfest out there?

"It's none of your business, asshole," Johnny fired back, his cheeks flushing. "You need to step away!" Then he made a mistake. Well, another one. He shoved at Gabe's chest.

Gabe shoved back, only he hit much harder, and Johnny wound up sailing over the bar.

"And there goes the night," Dean muttered as he came to stand at Gabe's side. Some of the folks around them were cheering. "Kid, word of advice?"

Johnny had heaved himself up and appeared to be prepping for another attack. He didn't seem overly interested in Dean's advice. Pity. The dumbass should listen to his elders.

"You don't want to tangle with an ex-SEAL," Dean told him, apparently deciding to give his advice whether Johnny wanted to hear it or not. "You'll just wind up kissing the floor."

Johnny snarled and leapt at Gabe.

And the kid wound up kissing the floor. Or, rather, the sand.

Johnny groaned as he tried to push himself off the sand and back to his feet.

Gabe crouched next to him. "Those women had families. Friends. They aren't some sideshow for you to use just so you can get laid." He grabbed Johnny's head and tipped it back so the guy had to look into his eyes. "Try having some respect for the dead."

"Gabe?" Eve's voice was soft, worried. Shit, he hadn't meant to scare her. But seeing violence up close like that would scare most people. He rose, keeping his hands loose at his sides. If Johnny boy came at him again, he would take him out.

"Hell . . ." That sharp voice *wasn't* Eve's. And it didn't belong to the advice-giving Dean. "Am I gonna have to arrest you the first night you're on my island?"

Gabe glanced over and saw Trey Wallace making his way through the crowd. Trey glared at him. Then the police chief focused his glare on Johnny—who was almost back on his feet.

Before Gabe could respond, Eve stepped in front of him. "That man—" She pointed to Johnny. "He attacked first. Gabe was just defending himself."

Now she was defending *him*. Well, damn.

Dean coughed a bit. "Uh, yes, that's exactly what happened." He moved to Eve's side. "The little prick was spouting off about sneaking up to the crime scene and showing his girl a good time there." He jerked his thumb toward the girl. The brunette was even younger than Johnny, she looked barely eighteen, and her blue eyes had gone huge.

She gasped even as her face flamed. "I was *not* going there with him!"

Gabe rolled his eyes. What the hell-ever. And it was nice that Eve and Dean had his back, but he had this covered.

"That true, Johnny?" Trey asked as he craned his

neck and glanced around Dean. "You throw the first punch again?"

Again? So the kid made a habit of bar fights. Big surprise.

Johnny just glared.

"I told you before," Trey said, voice hard, "you're gonna tangle with the wrong person one night."

Johnny growled at him.

"Seriously? Stop that shit," Trey fired, "or you'll be sleeping in a cell tonight." He looked at Johnny's girl. "Drive him home, Gia. Now. Take him back to his uncle Clay's place."

Gia grabbed Johnny's arm and dragged the guy away.

Trey glanced around. The crowd was still watching. He shook his head. "Show's over, people! Get that music going. It's supposed to be a party, right?"

The band started playing again. Couples danced. The drinks flowed.

The tension drained away from Eve's shoulders. She stared back at Gabe, and she looked tired. Drained.

Trey eased onto one of the bar stools. His fingers reached for Eve's glass. "Rum and Coke, huh? Always your drink of choice, especially when you're stressed."

The jealousy was there again, sliding its way into Gabe's gut. The man seemed to know everything about Eve.

And that should have been a good thing. They needed to know her past.

But the intimacy between them pisses me off.

"Do you feel the stares, Jessica?" Trey asked as he picked up her empty glass and stared into it. "I mean, folks are acting like they aren't looking this way, but they're glancing at you from the corner of their eyes. You still feel the look, right?"

"Yes."

Gabe could feel those stares, too.

"Some folks here recognize you. Sure, we've got a lot of out-of-towners, but . . . Sam over there—the guy playing the guitar? He knows you. That's why he keeps missing the beat every few moments. 'Cause he thinks he's seeing a ghost. And Clara? The redheaded wait-ress? She dropped a whole tray of drinks when she got a look at your face. 'Course, that was when your lover boy was beating up on the kid, so you probably missed that part, too."

Gabe's eyes narrowed on the cop.

"Even Johnny knows you, though he was probably too shit-faced to make the connection tonight. You and his uncle Clay Thompson were friends . . . we all were, back in the day." His smile was sad. "There are lots of folks here who know you, Jessica."

The cop was deliberately calling her Jessica, Gabe knew that. *He wants her to be the woman she was before.* Because that woman had been his?

"When you want to talk to them, they'll be there. But until then, until you're ready, I told them to stay back. Well, everybody but Johnny, I didn't get a chance to tell his fool self anything about you. I'll go see him and Clay later." He looked over at her. "I know you only go for the rum and Coke when you're at your limit. When you're scared or when you're about to break."

"She's not about to break," Gabe said. *Maybe you don't know her that well.*

Trey's gaze was on hers. "Have you painted?"

Eve shook her hand. She flexed her fingers. "I don't remember how to paint."

"Try picking up the brush," Trey said softly, the words

sounding almost like a dare. "You might be surprised at what comes back to you."

Eve looked down at the sand beneath her feet. "My fingers were broken. That was . . . that was one of the injuries I had."

"I read the medical report on you."

Her head snapped up.

Trey flashed a wry smile. Gabe hated that smile. "What? A ghost from my past walks right in front of me, and you think I won't do everything in my power to find out what happened to her?" He stood, moving away from the bar stool and toward Eve. His hand reached out.

Gabe stiffened.

Trey's fingers brushed over her neck. Over the scar there. "I know he cut you here." His hand fell to her side. "And here."

"Move the fucking hand," Gabe warned, voice low and lethal.

"Here we go," Dean muttered a second later.

The handsy-cop wisely took a step away from her. "You had a concussion, but the docs don't think that is what caused the memory loss. You're blocking it all because you're scared. You don't have to be scared with me."

Eve stared into his eyes.

"I've always protected you," Trey told her. Emotions were heavy in those words. "And I always will."

"A word." Gabe managed to push it out as he locked his hand around the cop's shoulder. "Alone."

Trey gave a nod, but he didn't take his eyes off Eve. "I'll be waiting. When you remember, I'm here."

Gabe pulled the cop away from the crowd. As they left, he turned back and saw Victoria striding to join Eve and Dean. And . . . just as Trey had said, there were stares on Eve. Watchful gazes. People who looked as if they were seeing a ghost.

"You're going to lose her," Trey said as soon as he and Gabe were away from the crowd. "Go ahead and get used to that fact, Spencer."

The hell he would. "My job is to keep her safe. To help Eve find out what happened to her."

Trey laughed, but the sound held no humor. "We both know what happened. The killer took her, but she got away from him. Now she's fighting her way back to the life she had before."

Back to me.

Trey didn't say those words, but they hung in the air between them.

"A killer is hunting on your island." The cop needed to be tracking him. "Why the hell don't you seem more concerned about catching the guy?"

Trey's eyelids flickered. "You think I'm not trying?" He stood toe-to-toe with Gabe on the beach now as the waves crashed near them. "You think I'm not up nearly every night, trying to put the puzzle pieces together? Trying to figure out who it could be? The FBI gave me a profile—a white male, late twenties, early thirties, attractive, confident, able to move in wealthy circles . . . do you *know* how many men fit that profile? Every day, people come in and out of this place. And I'm watching them all. I'm trying to watch them every moment." His breath heaved out. "So don't tell me that I'm not doing my job. I'm doing the best I can. I have *four* full-time officers who work for me. Just four. We are doing everything we can to keep this island safe."

"And I'm trying to keep *her* safe." The whole island wasn't his priority. Eve was.

"Are you? Or are you just interested in keeping *her*?" Trey tossed back. "I get it, hell, if anyone can understand, it's me. Once you have Jessica, you—"

"Stop."

Trey lifted a brow. "I'm not some drunk twenty-one-year-old kid that you can toss over a bar."

"Don't talk about Eve."

"Jessica. Her name is Jessica. Eve doesn't exist!"

She was standing not far away, watching them with a nervous stare. "She does to me," Gabe said.

Trey didn't reply to that.

The cop turned, and a redhead nearly slammed into him. "Officer?" She grabbed for his arms. "I can't find my friend . . . she—she was supposed to be here."

Trey focused on the woman. "Have you tried calling your friend, ma'am?" His voice was calm, courteous, but the cop's body was still tense.

Gabe took a few steps back toward Eve.

"Alexa isn't answering. She's not at the condo . . . she's not here. I—I'm worried about her."

Gabe stopped short, next to the redhead. "What does your friend look like?" The question came because of the sudden knot in his gut.

The woman gave a nervous laugh and she pointed toward Eve. "A lot like her. I—I thought that was Alexa when I first got here, but it's not." She grabbed onto Trey's arm. Her blue eyes were filled with worry. "This isn't like her. We've been friends for years. She wouldn't just leave me. Alexa doesn't ditch her friends without a reason."

"Maybe she met someone," Trey said, but there was a new, harder intensity in his voice.

Maybe she met the wrong someone.

The redhead bit her lip. "There . . . there was a guy she was talking with earlier . . . when we were outside of the condo . . ."

"Just which condo are you staying at?" Gabe asked, the suspicion he felt getting stronger.

The redhead glanced at him, her hands fluttering nervously in the air. "Are you a cop, too?"

"Something like that," Trey muttered.

"We're at the Dauphin View." She gave a weak smile. "We're on the fifth floor, with a real killer view of the water."

That was Eve's condo tower, the Dauphin View. "Tell me about the man your friend met."

"I—I didn't see much of him." She glanced between Gabe and Trey. "He was big, muscled, like you two. He had on a ball cap and sunglasses. He turned away before I could say hello."

"You saw him talking to your friend Alexa, at that condo tower?" Trey pressed.

"Yes . . . earlier today." She shook her head. "But Alexa wouldn't just leave with the guy. I mean—she broke up with her boyfriend about two months ago, but she is so still stuck on Mark. There is no way she would hook up with a stranger and not at least *text* me so I wouldn't worry about her."

Trey looked at Gabe. The cop's gaze was deadly serious. Gabe nodded, understanding exactly what the guy feared. "We'll help you find her," he promised the woman.

After all, that was exactly what he did.

SOMETHING WAS WRONG. Eve kept her eyes on Gabe as he and Trey closed in around a pretty redhead. The woman was talking quickly, and nervously waving her hands in the air.

"What's going on over there?" Victoria asked as she peered toward Gabe.

Eve shook her head. "I don't know." But she was worried. Especially when Trey reached for his radio.

Wait, was the redhead crying?

Gabe glanced over at her. His face was hard, tight, and then he stalked quickly toward her and Victoria.

"Is she all right?" Eve asked, craning to see the redhead.

Instead of answering her, Gabe said to Victoria, "I want you to take Eve back to the condo. Stay with her until I get there."

He was sending her away? "What's happening?"

His jaw locked. "It could be nothing, could be just a woman who decided to hook up with a new lover and ditch her friend—"

She grabbed his arm and her fingers curled around his wrist. *"What's happening?"*

"A blond woman named Alexa Chambers is missing. She was supposed to meet her friend here, but Sydney is worried because she can't find her anywhere. Alexa isn't answering her texts or her calls and—"

"Do you think he has her?" Eve asked, breaking through his words.

Gabe's head inclined toward her. "It's far too soon to say anything like that. Trey and I . . . we're just going to see if we can find this woman's missing friend."

But he wanted her away from the scene, that much was obvious to Eve. Because he was afraid the Lady Killer was hunting? "If it's him, why would he go after someone else?" *And not me?*

The faint lines near his eyes deepened. "We're just looking for Alexa. That's all right now. With the island's history, Trey doesn't want to take any chances, and neither do I."

Victoria hopped off her bar stool. "I'm not much for the party scene anyway. Come on, Eve, let's get out of here."

Dean was already heading toward Trey and the redhead. "I want to help," Eve said. She wasn't as eager to leave as Victoria seemed to be.

Gabe shook his head. "Not until we know more—"

"But—"

His hands closed around her shoulders and he lowered his head. His lips brushed across the shell of her ear when he said, "Maybe Alexa is just making out with some new lover someplace, or maybe . . . maybe something else has happened. I need you to stay safe until we find out more. I can't risk you."

Yet it was her life to risk, and she couldn't stand the thought of another woman out there, suffering.

Being buried alive in the sand.

"He could even be trying to lure you out." Gabe's lips feathered over her ear once more, and Eve shivered. "I need you to be safe. Go back with Victoria. Stay at the condo until I get there."

Fine. She nodded. Mostly because . . .

I could walk right up to the killer and not even know him. So just how much help could she really be in the hunt?

Gabe slid away from her.

Then he turned and headed back toward the redhead—Sydney. Eve glanced at Victoria. The other woman was watching her with wide eyes.

"Are you okay?" Victoria asked her with a nervous hitch in her voice.

No, she wasn't, but that was nothing new. She hadn't been okay in a very long time.

"I hope they find her," Eve said. Because that was all there was to say.

I hope the Lady Killer doesn't have a new victim.

ALEXA'S LITTLE FRIEND was screwing things up for him. Spencer and his agent were walking around the West End of the island, asking after Alexa, if anyone had seen her. And of course that little redheaded bitch had a picture of Alexa on her phone, so everyone could get a fast and up-close view of her.

Gabe was asking if anyone remembered seeing her, if she'd been talking to anyone . . .

Yes, she was talking to me.

He backed into the shadows. He wanted to get back to Alexa. Wanted to rush and take that boat out and vanish with her. But he had to be careful.

If he drew the wrong attention, things could go badly for him. He had to play the game just right.

It was a good thing that he'd been playing this game for so long.

For over ten years . . .

And they haven't caught me yet.

They never would.

AS SOON AS Victoria and Eve pulled into the parking lot at the Dauphin View, Eve saw the man waiting there for her. He was standing in front of a big beast of a motorcycle, his arms crossed over his chest. Their headlights hit him, revealing Wade Monroe's tense face. He had his helmet perched on the back of the bike, and, with those stark lights hitting him, the guy looked more than just dangerous.

He looked deadly.

"I guess Gabe sent in reinforcements," Victoria said as she parked the Jeep. "Figured Wade would show up sooner or later."

Eve opened her door. As Wade headed toward her, she saw the weapon at his side. A gun. For an instant, fear had her heart racing.

Wade must have seen the fear on her face. He shook his head. "Easy. Gabe just wanted me to keep guard until he got here."

Now she had two guards.

"You should be out there, helping to find that woman," Eve said. The missing woman—she was the one who mattered right then.

But Wade shook his head. "Sarah's joining the team out there. They've got things covered."

He sounded confident. Good for him—she wasn't confident. She kept picturing a woman being swallowed alive by sand.

Only the woman I picture is me.

"Let's go inside." Wade cast a quick glance around the area. "I don't like staying out in the open like this."

The night air wasn't cold, but Eve still shivered as they made their way inside and up to the seventh floor. As soon as she entered the condo, she saw the paint supplies that Trey had brought to her. Gabe had set them up near the balcony. Her hand flexed, almost as if by instinct when she saw the brushes.

Eve walked toward the supplies then stopped, staring at the blank canvas.

"You okay?" Victoria asked her. The woman had crept up behind her.

Wade was securing the door. Checking in the closets. Eve was pretty sure she even saw the guy peak under the bed. *Overkill.*

Or was it?

"I don't like being helpless." She hated the thought that another woman could be out there, hurting, while she was safe in here.

Pauley had already been hurt by this sadistic bastard, Eve was sure of it. She didn't want anyone else to suffer.

I'm sorry, Pauley. His death would haunt her for the rest of her life.

Wade opened the balcony doors—the doors that led out from her bedroom, not the den, and he stepped outside.

"Whether we like it or not, we're all helpless sometime." Victoria's voice was low, sad.

Eve glanced over at her.

Victoria smiled, but the smile appeared forced. "Everything will be fine."

"Stop," Eve told her. Wade was outside. He couldn't hear them. "You don't have to . . . to pretend with me." And it was very clear to Eve that Victoria was pretending. Giving a fake smile, trying to act as if they were totally safe.

They weren't.

Victoria's smile slipped as Eve turned back to her.

"Why did you join LOST?"

Victoria's stare darted toward the balcony. Toward Wade? "Gabe made me an offer that I couldn't resist."

"Money?"

Victoria shook her head. "That's not why I do it. That's

not why any of us do it. I mean, Gabe's got money to burn, but that came from his family. We charge our clients as little as possible for our services."

Gabe hadn't even charged her. He'd just . . . helped her.

The balcony doors squeaked open as Wade returned.

"We've all lost someone," Victoria told her softly. "It's not like I woke up when I was six and thought, 'Hey, studying the bones of the dead would be fun.'"

"No, I didn't think you did."

Wade was in the room with them now, but he was a silent, watchful shadow.

"It took them a year to identify my mother's body," Victoria said. There was no smile on her face. And behind the lenses of her glasses, her eyes just reflected her sadness. "No family should ever have to wait that long." She swallowed. "The not knowing . . . it can be the worst part, right?"

"Right." It sure as hell was for her.

Victoria blanched. "Oh, jeez, I'm an idiot, that's not what I meant to say—"

Eve hugged her. Just pulled the other woman close and gave her a quick hug. "I'm sorry about your mother."

Then she stepped back, a little shocked by her own display. It was just that—Victoria had seemed to need someone.

And I wanted to help someone.

Victoria blinked. Her lips pressed together, as if she were trying to hide their tremble. "Thank you. And I'm sorry . . . I'm sorry for everything that happened to you."

Eve studied her a moment longer. "Did you find the person who killed your mother?"

Victoria's shoulders stiffened. "He was pretty easy to find. I . . . always knew where my father was."

Wade swore, and there was surprise in that vicious curse. "Viki, you never said—"

She held up her hand, warding him off. "He's dead now, so he can't hurt anyone."

But Eve could see that she *was* still hurting.

"I think I'll check in with Gabe," Victoria mumbled as she turned away. "See if he's found the missing woman or got any new leads for me to follow."

Eve watched her flee. "I didn't mean to hurt her."

"You didn't." Wade's voice was flat. "But you did get her to open up more than I ever have."

Eve glanced at him. Victoria had said, *We've all lost someone.* As she stared at Wade—

He shook his head. "Not happening, blondie. One soul-baring is all you'll get tonight."

"I didn't mean . . ." Wait, she had. Eve exhaled on a long sigh. "I think I'll get some air."

She headed outside. Put her hands up on the railing that surrounded the balcony and stared out at the darkness.

We've all lost someone.

Yes, Victoria was right about that.

I want to find the woman I was. The woman who is lost.

The moon's light hit the water, and Eve saw a boat racing away into the darkness.

CHAPTER TEN

"A LEXA . . ."

Her name came to her. Soft. Low.

She whimpered as she tried to lift a hand to her throbbing head, but . . . she couldn't lift it. Something rough and thick was wrapped around her wrists.

She pushed out with her feet and hit something hard. A door? Where the hell was she? What was happening?

"We're here, Alexa."

Darkness was all around her. She couldn't see anything. "Help me!" She shoved against covers that were on top of her. Where had they come from? The last thing she remembered was—

Something creaked—the door?

Light hit her.

He was there. The handsome cop.

Relief flooded through her. Ridiculous relief that turned to confusion in an instant as she realized—

I'm tied up.

And he's holding a knife.

Alexa shook her head. This whole scene was wrong. The handsome guy in front of her—wait, what had his name been?—he wasn't going to hurt her.

"Wh-What's happening?

He crouched down so that they were on eye level, and Alexa realized she was crumpled in some sort of closet.

"We're here."

Here?

"Let me help you." And he put the knife back in a sheath on his side. Then he reached for her, pulling her up by the rope that bound her wrists and he—he slung her over his shoulder.

Alexa grunted because that move *hurt*. Her head was throbbing and nausea rolled through her stomach.

What was his name? She normally didn't hook up with strangers. But Mark—that jerk Mark—had left her two months ago for his ex. She'd just wanted some payback. No . . .

I just needed someone to want me. She'd wanted to feel desired again.

"L-Let me go . . ."

They were climbing upstairs, and a few seconds later fresh air hit her, air carried on the wind and the waves.

We're on a boat.

"It's just us out here, Alexa." He jumped off the boat, still carrying her, and then he dumped her onto the sand. Alexa scrambled back.

This is wrong.

"Just you and me . . . for miles and miles." He pulled that knife out. Only the glow of the moon shone down on them, seeming to reflect off the sand. "So no one will hear you when you scream, and, believe me, Alexa, you *will* scream." A brief pause, "They always do."

This was a nightmare. It had to be. She was *not* on some little strip of sand with a man holding a knife. She was Vince Chambers's daughter. She'd gone to Stanford. She had a trust fund. She had a cheating ex-fiancé back in Texas.

She had . . . a life.

A home.

And he was coming at her with the knife. "Please . . ." she whispered.

He stilled. "Sometimes they beg first, but that doesn't do any good . . ."

Her hands fisted in the sand.

"They beg and they scream, but, Jessica, you know that doesn't change anything."

"M-My name's not Jessica."

His body stiffened.

"Y-You have the wrong woman." Right. That was what had happened. This whole thing was a mistake. Every single bit of it—*a mistake.* "Let me go. Just let me go and I—"

"You wanted to see the lighthouse."

He was closing in on her again.

"Look behind you. The lighthouse is right there. I brought you out, just like you wanted."

She risked a fast glance over her shoulder. Saw the shadowy outline of the lighthouse.

And then she felt the slice of a knife across her side.

Alexa screamed.

EVE PROPPED THE canvas against the wall. She'd already spread out a sheet to cover the floor. Sleeping wasn't an option for her—yes, big surprise—so maybe . . . maybe she'd just see if Trey had been right.

Jessica could paint anything. I'm Jessica. I can do this.

Victoria was asleep on the couch. Wade, ever watchful, sat just a few feet away. She'd learned fast that the guy wasn't much for conversation. He'd meant it when he said that he wasn't baring his soul. He'd told her pretty much *nothing*.

Eve reached for a paintbrush. Her fingers trembled. Was she seriously trembling just from holding the thing? She pulled in a deep breath and tried to steady herself.

The brush kept trembling. She had the paint ready, but—

I can't even hold the brush steady.

"Your fingers were broken." Wade's voice made her jump. Mostly because he wasn't sitting in the over-stuffed chair any longer. He was right beside her. "Maybe you just need some time for the strength to come back to them."

Eve dropped the brush on the table. "The strength is fine. I just don't know what the hell I'm doing." She looked up and got caught by his stare. "Suspicion," she whispered.

One brow lifted.

"That's what I see when I look at your face, in your eyes. You don't trust me."

He shrugged. "Don't take it personally. I can count the people I trust on one hand."

She waited.

"Gabe. Sarah. Viki. And Dean."

"Your team."

"My team."

"And you think I'm—what? Scamming Gabe? Scamming you all?"

"There's a lot of money at stake with your case. Just look around you." He waved to indicate the lush condo. "The Montgomerys know how to live in style."

"And I was living in a homeless shelter when I first

went to Gabe." The guy thought she was some gold-digging schemer?

"Gabe believes you're legit." He exhaled. "But then, Gabe wants to fuck you, too."

She backed up a step. "You don't pull your punches, do you?"

"Don't see the point in pulling them. Polite lies are still lies."

Well, yes. "But at least they're polite," she mumbled, rubbing the side of her neck. "A little politeness won't kill you."

His lips twitched. "Don't be too sure about that."

Eve didn't understand him. And she wasn't sure she wanted to. *Schemer, my ass. You try waking up to nothing.* "What time is it?"

He glanced at his watch. "Two A.M."

"And they still haven't found her." That hollow feeling in the pit of her stomach told Eve they *wouldn't* be finding Alexa. *Alexa Chambers.* Viki had learned the missing woman's full name and shared it with her.

"There were no signs of a struggle at her condo . . ."

A condo in that building. She swallowed.

"And no one can remember seeing her at the West End. She was just another blonde in a crowd. It's so easy to vanish in a crowd."

And it's easy to die alone.

"You should try and get some sleep."

She almost laughed at that. "I don't sleep much." But she would retreat to the bedroom so that she didn't constantly feel his watchful stare.

She'd taken five steps when she heard him say, "I don't sleep much, either. The damn nightmares just won't stop."

We all lost someone. Viki had been right, after all.

Eve pushed open the door to the bedroom. She changed quickly, putting on her sweatpants and a T-shirt before she slipped into the bed.

Then she froze.

Why do I do that? She glanced down at herself.

She . . . always dressed before getting into the bed. She always had to be covered *underneath* the bedding.

Biting her lip, Eve eased off the mattress. She took off her shirt. Her sweats. Just in her panties, she slid back into the bed.

Her body was as tense as a board.

Wrong. Wrong. Wrong!

She yanked the covers up to her chin. This was ridiculous. Why would she be—

Shuddering, trembling . . . crying?

He'll see, he'll see . . .

Eve jumped up and put her clothes back on.

When she crawled back into the bed again, she wasn't shuddering. But her skin felt iced and her stomach was twisting.

What is wrong with me?

Gabe kept saying that she was strong, that he wasn't worried about her breaking apart. He didn't seem to realize the truth.

She already was broken.

GABE OPENED THE condo door, his steps slow, fury the main force keeping him moving.

The light fell on Victoria's sleeping form. Viki—she'd always been able to sleep anywhere, anytime. Despite her past, the nightmares didn't plague her.

Or maybe . . . *because* of her past they didn't.

"Your lady's in the bedroom, but I don't think she's sleeping." Wade's voice was low. He was in the chair near Viki, and, being Wade, of course the guy was wide-awake.

Gabe rolled back his shoulders. "We didn't find her."

Wade rose. "You think she vanished on her own or do you think—"

"She fits his profile. Sarah said that Alexa Chambers fit the killer's profile to a perfect T." Dammit. "And he took her—right under our noses." His hands fisted. "The guy wanted to prove that he could do it, and that there wasn't a thing we could do to stop him."

Wade rose and marched toward him. "Victoria said that he doesn't kill his prey right away."

No, he didn't. "Torture is part of his M.O."

"So Alexa—if he has her—she could still be alive."

Gabe nodded. "And that's why the FBI agents are swarming. They've taken over the investigation and . . . *officially* . . . asked us to back the hell off." So much for cooperation.

Wade grunted at that. "And you're backing off?"

"Hell, no. Dean is going to learn everything he can about them, and Sarah's interviewing Alexa's friend Sydney. We can't keep searching in the dark, but as soon as the sun rises, I'll be out there again." The FBI agents could screw off. This wasn't a pissing match about turf dominance. This was a woman's life.

"If it is the Lady Killer," Wade spoke slowly, "we have an ace to use against him."

The fuck they did. "Don't go there."

"She's remembering—*that's* what you told me when you called and told me to haul ass down here. She remembered the bakery. She remembered the drinks she used to like. The more she's here, the more she sees of the island, hell, she could lead us right to him." Wade glowered at him. "Are you seriously not going to use her? A woman is missing. This isn't just about Eve—"

The bedroom door opened. "No, it's not just about me."

He should have known she'd overheard. It wasn't like Wade had been whispering. *Could* the guy whisper? Victoria was still asleep, but that woman had slept through a near-explosion on one of their previous cases.

"I have to help, Gabe. I need to do this."

She wore a white T-shirt and a pair of jogging pants that hugged her hips. He'd seen her in those clothes before. She looked tousled and sexy and he wanted her in his arms. He also wanted her far, far away from the killer's reach.

Alexa Chambers is out there.

And Eve was the key.

"Tell me what to do," Eve said.

He exhaled . . . and knew that he was giving in.

"THE FBI IS searching the marina and the beaches," Gabe said, "so we're going off the beaten path."

And their path was taking them to . . . "A fort?" Eve asked as she stared at the looming wooden structure. A large sign welcomed them to Historic Fort Gaines.

The sun had risen, and with the new day, Gabe had taken her out to search. Only she hadn't expected this place to be their first stop. It was a little after eight A.M., and the place appeared deserted.

Damn the torpedoes! Full speed ahead! Eve read the text beneath the fort's name. *General James Farragut. The Battle of Mobile Bay.*

Gabe led the way into the fort. They crossed over what looked like an old moat, then made their way into the shop to pay the fort's admission fee. Eve thought the door to the shop might be locked because the place looked so deserted, but Gabe easily swung it open and led the way inside.

"You be careful out there," the man behind the counter said after Gabe had paid their admission fee and he was handing back some change. "This here fort is one of the most haunted in the U.S. Our ghosts walk in the day and the night."

Eve's eyes widened. Was that guy serious?

Gabe caught her hand, his fingers threading through with hers. "We'll be careful, don't worry."

The guy behind the counter gave them another grin. "They'll be firing the cannon out there later this morning. You don't want to miss the show."

A cannon? Was he for real? Eve kept glancing back over her shoulder at him as Gabe led her out of the shop and into the heart of the fort.

The place seemed massive from inside. The ramparts stretched out, surrounding them on all sides as the heavy stone walls rose toward the sky. Stairs—old and heavy—led up to those ramparts, as did sloping trails of land.

Gabe was striding toward the wall on the east side, and Eve hurried to keep up with him. "Why are we here again?"

"Because we're going to every main stop on this island. If something happened to you at one of these spots, if one of these places can trigger your memory, then dammit, we're going to make that happen."

Her heart was racing by the time they reached the top of the eastern ramparts. Eve tried to suck in a deep breath to steady herself, but then she lost that breath as she took in the view. The crashing waves pounded below, rolling in again and again, and, in the distance, she could just see . . . "The lighthouse."

"There are plenty of places to hide in this fort. Plenty of places to . . . get rid of a body."

I don't want Alexa to be dead!

He still had her hand in his grip. "Are you ready for this?"

Eve had to drag her gaze off that lighthouse. "Yes." *No.*

"Then let's go." And he turned to the right. They weren't heading back down below, into the open field that spread in the middle of the fort. Instead, he was taking her down into what felt like the bones of the fort. A twisting, brick staircase led them lower and lower. The stairs seemed to be crumbling beneath her feet, and she put her left hand on the cold wall for support. Light barely cracked inside as they entered the bowels of the fort.

When they reached the bottom of the staircase, cold air seemed to blow against her face.

"There's a tunnel here," Gabe said.

She could see it. A rounded ceiling curved down, and old lights flickered about every ten feet. The tunnel was so long and—

Eve tensed. "Someone's down there." Or at least she'd thought that she'd caught sight of someone down there. Now she couldn't see anyone.

No wonder the old guy thought this place was haunted. The fort was sure giving her goose bumps.

But Gabe had her hand and was leading her forward. The tunnel was so narrow that they had to walk in single file.

"Does it seem familiar to you?" Gabe asked.

"No." Her answer was immediate and maybe too fast. Because as they headed down that narrow tunnel, Eve did feel something, but it wasn't familiarity. It was fear.

I don't want to be here. "We should stop."

Gabe kept going. "The tunnel ends up ahead."

She didn't want to go up ahead. She pulled on his hand. "I don't remember this place."

He turned toward her, stopping just a few feet from the tunnel's exit. His body caged her against the old bricks. "It's all right."

It was getting harder for her to breathe. "I don't want to be here. Let's go look outside for Alexa. The killer wouldn't . . . he wouldn't bring her here. How would he even get inside? I mean, it's a fort! The place is secure!"

Gabe shook his head. "There are always means of getting inside and methods of sneaking out."

For a SEAL, maybe. Those guys specialized in their covert operations.

"Don't be afraid."

"Easy for you to say," she whispered back.

"Yes." He was so close. Or maybe the tunnel was just ridiculously narrow. Either way, she couldn't seem to take a breath without feeling him against her. His body was so close and his warmth was surrounding her as he . . . just stared into her eyes.

"Gabe?"

"Don't be afraid," he whispered again, and then he kissed her. Just leaned forward in that dark, too tight tunnel, and, with her trapped against the bricks, his mouth captured hers. The kiss wasn't light. It wasn't some brief caress.

His lips took hers. His tongue plunged into her mouth. He licked her. He seemed to savor her, and when he pulled her against his body, squeezing them in that tight space, Eve didn't give a damn where they were.

"Still scared?" The words were a growl against her lips.

Her breath heaved out. "Not exactly." She was focusing on another emotion.

"Good." He kissed her again. "Because anytime you get afraid . . . just remember that I'm right . . ." Another long kiss, one that made her breasts ache and her toes curl. " . . . here."

Her hands tightened around his shoulders. "You can't always be with me."

He kissed her again. In the darkness of that tunnel, in a place that caused an instinctive terror within her . . .

But I'm safe with him. And maybe that was the key for her. Gabe wasn't tied with her past. He hadn't known her until she walked into his office.

He can't be the man who hurt me.

But the others that she met on that island . . . all the people who rushed in and out of her life, people who claimed to be friends, former lovers, even family . . . she couldn't trust them.

Because it was too easy for people to lie.

Her eyes squeezed shut as she kissed Gabe back, kissed him with a wild desperation. She wanted to hold tightly to him and never let go. To give in to the feelings he stirred so effortlessly within her.

Be stronger.

But Eve made herself push against his shoulders and pulled her mouth from his. She *could* do this.

He stared into her eyes. The light in the tunnel was so dim, she wondered how he could see her expression, but he gave a slow nod and backed away.

Then they were heading down the tunnel again. She could still taste him, and her lips seemed to tingle a bit from his kiss. Her steps were faster now. The shadows didn't seem as thick as they walked, and a few moments later, they were out of that tunnel and walking into a big open room. One that had thick, faded bricks lining the walls. And . . .

"Are those names?" Eve asked as she crept closer to the far wall. She lifted her hand and touched the bricks as her eyes narrowed. Yes, there were names there. Dozens of them. It looked as if some had been carved into the bricks while others were written in chalk. Some even appeared to have been written with a marker.

"Guess the kids like to tag the place," Gabe said as he approached the wall with the names.

Yeah, she guessed they did.

Her eyes slid over the names. John. Ally. Beau.

"This room is so deep in the fort that the park officials probably can't ever catch the people tagging the bricks." He was walking ahead, slipping even deeper into the fort. Eve followed him and found another room. Smaller. Even darker. He turned on his phone and used a flashlight app to light up the interior.

More names.

Kate.

Cassie.

Sharon.

Lyla.

Chantal.

Helen.

Jessica.

All of those names had been scratched into the bricks. Not written in chalk or marker, but carved into the bricks—maybe with a knife?

Jessica. Her hand lifted and touched the letters of that name, but when she looked below and saw the last name on that wall . . .

Alexa.

Her heart stopped.

"Gabe!"

"The others are victim names, too." His voice was grim. "Every one of them in this room."

She whirled toward him. "What is this?" Fear was back, beating hard and heavy within her as her heart thundered in her chest. All of the names were females, all appeared to have been scratched in a similar hand-writing, and . . . *my name is there. Alexa's is there.*

We're all there.

The light from his phone drifted to the left, to the right, as Gabe seemed to inspect the wall. "That section of bricks doesn't look as old as the rest."

He was missing the huge damn point! "Those are his kills!"

"The bricks are different." Gabe stalked forward. Pressed against the bricks with those scratched names on their surfaces. "Newer."

"We need to get out of here."

Sweetheart, let's play a game . . .

The voice seemed to whisper through her mind. "We should get out of here, now." She was already backing away from that wall.

But Gabe was trying to use his phone to call some-one. "No signal," he muttered.

Right. They were in the bowels of hell. No big sur-prise that there wasn't a signal there. She turned from him and began hurrying back through the tunnel. They needed to get out of that place ASAP. They had to go find Trey and tell him what they'd discovered.

All of the victims' names are on that wall!

The killer had been keeping track of his prey. Right there. The guy in the fort's shop had been right. There were ghosts in that fort, and Eve could swear she felt them all around her then.

Her feet thudded faster and faster in the tunnel. The lights overhead seemed to dim, and—

Darkness surrounded her.

Suddenly, Eve couldn't hear Gabe's voice or his footsteps. She could only hear the sound of her own heaving breaths and her desperate heartbeat. She knew she had to run. She had to get away. Because if she didn't escape, he was going to kill her.

Her hands flew up and slapped against the bricks on either side of her. They were cool to the touch. She could follow those bricks, keep touching them and make her way to safety.

A hand had grabbed Eve, jerking her back.

Time for the game to begin, sweetheart. I've waited for you, so long . . . it's all for you.

Eve screamed and punched out, hitting as hard as she could.

"Eve!" Gabe shook her lightly. "Baby, it's me!"

And she realized that she'd just punched him in the face. "Gabe! I'm sorry!" In a blink, the darkness vanished. She was back in the dim tunnel, back with Gabe, but that voice—it was still whispering in her head . . .

Time for the game to begin, sweetheart.

"He brought me here," Eve said, body shaking. "This is where it started. *Here.*" And she'd been running from him, trying to get away.

But he'd caught her. In that tunnel. It had been pitch-black, and he'd caught her.

"I've got you," Gabe said.

She pulled away from him because those words—they were too familiar.

He had me, too.

Eve ran for the stairs, desperate to get out of that fort

because the place felt like a tomb to her, and she was very afraid that was exactly what the place was.

"IT'S A HISTORIC site," Trey muttered as he and one of his officers stood with Gabe and Dean in the bowels of the fort. "You expect me to just tear into the wall of a historical place like this? Do you even know what kind of paperwork and government red tape you're talking about?"

The FBI agent, Avery Granger, was peering at the bricks with a close eye and a very bright flashlight. "Let me worry about the paperwork."

"Those bricks are newer," Gabe said. The guy had to see that and stop spouting about his paperwork bullshit. "You can look at them and tell that they're different." And they were different for a reason. The fire in his gut told him that reason wasn't going to be good. *We need to get behind those bricks.*

"The killer was here." Dean's voice was flat. "We all damn well know it."

Trey tapped the bricks. "And what do you think I'm going to find if I rip out these bricks?"

Gabe wasn't one hundred percent sure, but he had his suspicions. "If I wanted to hide a body, that might be one real good place."

"Shit." Trey jerked his hand away from the bricks. "He *buries* them. In the sand. He doesn't pull some twisted Edgar Allan Poe crap and seal his prey up in the walls!"

Footsteps rustled behind them, and Gabe turned to see Sarah making her way toward them. Her head was cocked, her eyes on the illuminated names. "He *would* seal up the prey, if this victim was special to him."

Gabe had called and asked Sarah and Victoria to haul ass over there. Sarah would need to examine the scene so that she could create a stronger profile for the killer, and Victoria, well, if a dead body was there, then she was the woman they needed on point for this one.

"I don't get it. Wouldn't someone have noticed freaking new bricks going up at this place?" Dean paced around them. "Hard to miss, don't you think?"

"They could have been put in years ago," Gabe said, because he'd already considered that point. "The other bricks have been here for a hundred years, but these . . . hell, they look like they've been put up in the last decade." A rough estimate. Techs would be able to tell them for sure.

Avery was poking around the top of the wall. "These bricks . . . two of them are loose."

Trey swore.

Avery poked harder. He shoved. He yanked, and one of the bricks came flying back at him. "Definitely loose."

"So much for doing paperwork," Trey muttered. "So how about now you worry about not destroying more evidence, *Agent* Granger."

"If I see something inside," Avery said as he leaned up on his toes and shone his light into the darkness, "then I'll worry about paperwork and I'll—"

He broke off.

Gabe kept his eyes on the agent.

"We're going to need that paperwork," Avery told them all, "and an excavation team, *now*." He looked back at Gabe. "Because I can see a fucking skull in there."

CHAPTER ELEVEN

DARK CLOUDS WERE ROLLING IN WHEN GABE returned to the condo. The cops and the FBI agents had worked for hours, painstakingly removing the bricks until they'd cleared the remains.

Bones wrapped in old clothing—a dress. A woman.

He shut the condo's door behind him. Wade had just left the place—the guy had been keeping an eye on Eve, and Gabe knew Eve was pretty pissed about that fact. But after the way she'd reacted in that tunnel, he'd needed someone to keep watch on her.

He rubbed his jaw. *Mental note. The woman has a killer right hook.*

"Who is she?" Eve asked. She was standing in front of the balcony doors. Her hands were wrapped around her stomach. She was wearing a pair of shorts and a T-shirt. He'd made arrangements for more clothes to be brought to her.

"Gabe." Her voice snapped, and he realized he'd just been staring at her. *"Who is she?"*

"We don't know." That was true, so far. Because the woman's remains were indicating that she'd been down in that fort for about ten years, but the other missing women—women they'd thought were the Lady Killer's victims—hadn't been missing that long. "Victoria is working on IDing her, and when it comes to this kind of thing, Victoria is the best."

"How long was she down there?" Eve hadn't moved from her position near the balcony's doors.

This he could tell her. Victoria had already been able to make an estimation, based on the victim's decomposition rate. "About ten years."

She sucked in a breath. "That's a long time." She turned away. Glanced out the glass balcony doors. "A very long time to be locked up in the dark."

He stepped toward her. The thick carpeting swallowed the sound of his footsteps. "Sarah thinks we may be looking at the guy's first victim."

Eve glanced back over her shoulder.

"He kept her away from the others. She was special. The first always is." There was usually a trigger involved with the first kill, then, after the serial got a taste for the power that came with killing . . . *there was no stopping him.* "But with first kills, the perp can be sloppy. Disorganized. He hadn't perfected his technique yet—"

Eve flinched.

Shit. She wasn't a LOST agent. She was a victim. And he was screwing this up by being too clinical. "He may have made mistakes with her," Gabe said carefully. "Left DNA on her. Left behind some clues that we can use to track him."

Eve nodded.

"Finding that woman was key."

Her gaze dropped. "I was in that tunnel before . . . I remember being there."

Careful now, he advanced on her. "That's why you took that swing at me."

"I heard a man's voice, he was telling me that it was

time to play." She turned back toward him. Eve licked her lips and again she wrapped her hands around her stomach. "He called me sweetheart and said that he'd been waiting for me."

Another step brought him close enough to touch her, but he didn't, not yet.

"He said . . . he said that it was all for me." A faint furrow appeared between her golden brows. "And I hear his voice—over and over—a rasp in my head that won't stop."

"Do you recognize that voice? Does it sound like anyone you've met on the island?" He nearly held his breath as he waited for her response.

She shook her head. "No. I just . . . I can't stop hearing him now. 'It's all for you.' That's what he said. 'It's all for you.' " Eve sucked in a deep breath of air. "Those women who died—the other victims were all blondes with green eyes. Just. Like. Me."

He knew where she was going with this. "Eve . . ."

"I thought I was just another victim. Unlucky enough to look like the others." When her gaze lifted to meet his, there was no missing the guilt in her eyes. "But what if all of those women were unlucky enough to look like *me*? What if they all died because they reminded him of me?"

"Eve, that's not likely." He had to touch her. He kept his touch light as he grasped her shoulders. "If Victoria is right and the guy killed the first victim on the island ten years ago, then you would have just been a teenager—"

"Jessica Montgomery's birthday is April second. If I'm her . . . I—I . . . I would have been sixteen then."

"You fit his pattern," he told her, because that was obvious. "But you didn't cause him to kill anyone."

"I'm not so sure of that." Her voice was a stark whisper. "He was playing a game, and he said . . . he said he'd been waiting on me."

ALEXA WAS STARING at him.

Not screaming. Not begging. Just staring. He smiled at her, loving the stillness that surrounded her.

His hand went to her wrist and he carefully removed her bracelet. It was so like Jessica's. They both must love diamonds. Diamonds had always looked so lovely against Jessica's skin.

"You don't mind if I take this, do you?"

Her eyes kept staring at him.

"Don't worry. I'll give you another one to replace it." Because he needed Jessica to understand what was happening. She had to realize who she was and why she mattered so very much.

He pulled the second bracelet from his pocket. Carefully secured it around Alexa's wrist.

"There," he said, satisfied, "that's much better." Now, he just had to make sure that Alexa was found. "You'll be different," he told her. His fingers brushed over her cheek.

So cold, so very cold.

He smiled at her. "I love you, Jessica."

"IF ALEXA IS alive out there, she's running out of time," Sarah Jacobs said as she paced along the eastern rampart at Fort Gaines. She'd been over that fort, again and again, all day as she tried to learn more about the killer.

The chief of police stood a few feet away, watching her carefully. "Does being out here really help you, ma'am?" Trey Wallace asked her.

She stopped her pacing and glanced at him. "I'm

trying to figure out why this place was so important to the killer."

He shrugged. His sunglasses tossed her reflection back at her as he said, "It was a dumping ground, same as the golf course. Easy. Accessible."

"It's not always about easy." She tilted her head as she studied the cop. He'd been withdrawn, so very careful in his conversations with her during the investigation that day. Why? Was he afraid of what he might reveal?

Usually, when folks found out that Sarah was a psychiatrist, they tended to back away, fast. Most of them were afraid she'd take one look at them and somehow magically know all their deepest, darkest secrets.

If only it worked that way.

"If that woman was his first kill, then he chose to hide her body here for a very specific reason. Sealing her up inside, using those bricks . . . that's a time-consuming process." She motioned to the water around her. "If he just wanted to dump a body, he could have done that. Instead, he wanted to . . . keep her."

"Uh, keep her? Like she was some kind of damn souvenir?" Trey sounded both repulsed and curious.

"Yes," Sarah answered him slowly, as the wind caught her hair and tossed it over her shoulders. "Something like that." She wanted to head over to Victoria's makeshift lab and find out what her friend had discovered. Victoria could always learn so much from the dead.

While she herself learned from the killers. And this man, the Lady Killer . . .

You know the island well. You knew when to come in and seal up your prey, knew exactly when the fort would be empty for you and you could work undisturbed.

You're meticulous. Detailed. Those bricks were laid perfectly. And then . . . you came back. You came back

*to her again and again. You wrote the other victims'
names right on top of her. Why? Because you wanted
her to know about the kills? You wanted her to know
what you'd done?*

"Uh, Dr. Jacobs?" Trey stalked toward her. "You
okay?"

She blinked. Sometimes she got a little lost when she
tried to connect with the killers. "I'm fine." She tilted
her head back to stare up at him. He was tall, just like
Gabe, muscled.

The right age, the right access to the island . . .

Trey cleared his throat. "If you're sure that you're all
right, then I need to get back to the station and see how
the search is going for Alexa Chambers."

Sarah nodded. "I'll be heading back that way soon. I
just want to do one more walk-around."

He hesitated. "The excavation team is still working
down there, and if you need them . . . the FBI agents
are close by."

Surprise rolled through her. "You think I'm in some
sort of danger?"

He motioned toward her. "You fit, right? I mean, with
the guy's victims? He likes blondes and—"

"He likes green-eyed blondes. Tall, curved. Socialites." Polished, seemingly perfect women . . . that he
tortured and destroyed.

"So what?" Now Trey looked curious. "Since you've
got brown eyes, you think that makes you safe?"

The wind whipped her hair again. "With killers, no
one is ever safe. Even serial killers will break their pat-
terns. They'll attack when threatened. They'll kill if it
means protecting themselves." *Is that why the guy had
killed Pauley McIntyre?*

His hand dropped to rest on the handle of his gun,

a gun that was holstered at his side. "I thought it was compulsion. They *had* to make the kills. Same vics, same M.O.'s."

"Not always." She glanced across at the water once more. "But it is the victims who matter. You find out why the killer picks them, and then you know more about the perp you're after."

"You must like hunting killers."

"No." Her voice was soft. "I actually hate it." Sarah made herself look back at the police chief. "But I'm good at my job, and I will find this man."

He rubbed his jaw. "But will you find him before or after Alexa is dead?"

She didn't have an answer for that question.

"That's what I was afraid of," Trey said as he turned away. "I don't want to find another body on my beach."

"A STORM IS coming in," Eve said. She'd gone out onto the balcony because she'd needed to breathe, and she couldn't breathe in that condo. Or, at least, she didn't feel like she could. *It's suffocating me.* "Not a big one, not yet, but you can feel the storm in the air."

A streak of lightning lit up the sky. "And you can see it," she added.

Gabe was at her side. His arm brushed against her shoulder. "The storm will halt the search."

Her hands tightened around the railing. "I don't want her to be dead."

He turned toward her. "You escaped. Maybe she will, too."

She didn't tell him that it was hard to have hope. She hadn't exactly had a lot of that in the last few months.

"Your . . . brother called. He's on his way down here. He wants to see you, to talk with you again."

Eve nodded. She didn't think of Pierce as her brother, though. He was just a stranger, but then she also didn't think of herself as Jessica, and she wasn't sure she ever would.

"We should crash for a few hours," Gabe said. "When the storm passes, I want to head out again on the search. Alexa is running out of time."

Yes, Eve was afraid that she was. "I don't want to crash." She faced him fully. More lightning flashed.

"What do you want?"

To not be so afraid. "I want to be with you." Was she using him? Part of her was worried that she might be. Whenever her feelings got too strong, when the darkness around her became too great, she reached out for him.

Mostly because she didn't want to face the emptiness inside of herself. And Gabe—the last thing he did was make her feel empty.

"Eve . . ."

"Don't you want to be with me?"

"Fuck, yes."

She caught his hand. Brought it to her mouth. Pressed a kiss to his knuckles. "Then be with me. Please, Gabe, I—I need you." Something was going on inside of her, and that stupid voice—that low rasping whisper— wouldn't stop. *It's all for you.*

"Gabe?"

Rain began to fall on them. Lightly at first, then in harder, heavier pelts as it drove down. She didn't move to run inside the condo. Eve stayed right there, letting the rain wash over her.

"I can't figure you out," Gabe said as he lowered his head toward her. "Why do you keep pulling me close?"

"Because I trust you."

"You don't know my secrets." Something was there,

in the roughness of his voice, something that should have warned her to back away.

She edged closer. Her clothes were getting wet, the fabric sticking to her skin. "I know you're a good man. You fight to stop killers. To help victims."

"Maybe I'm not so good."

Eve shook her head. "You're the SEAL, the hero who helps all of us who are lost." She tried to smile for him. "That's who you are."

If possible, his expression became even darker. "I'm not a hero. Far from it."

She could see he didn't understand. "You are to me." She'd already lost her only friend—Pauley. Every time she thought of him, an ache filled her heart. He'd been so good, kind to his core, but now he was gone. *Because of me.*

The killer had tracked her. He'd taken Pauley's life, and now Gabe was the only bright spot that she had left. Not a connection to her past, but a link to her present.

"If you knew who I really was, you wouldn't want me near you."

His words seemed to be such a strange warning. Especially when . . . "You're the only man I want this close."

Lightning streaked overhead. Thunder rumbled, and he kissed her. Kissed her with the same mad passion of the storm. Kissed her with fury and need, and she loved it.

He lifted her into his arms, carried her back inside the condo, but this time, this time, he didn't take her back to the bedroom.

Gabe pressed her to the wall just inside that condo, right past the balcony's doors. Held her there with his body. His mouth was hard on hers, his tongue thrusting past her lips, and as he kept her there, Eve felt the long, hot length of his cock pressing against her. Gabe wanted her, just as much as she wanted him.

He pulled his mouth from hers, his breath coming out in ragged rasps that she loved. Then his gaze slid over her. The wet clothes stuck to her like a second skin, and her nipples were tight with arousal, jutting out toward him.

He wrapped one arm around her waist and lifted her up again, holding her effortlessly, and his mouth closed over her nipple, right through that wet shirt. She gasped at the contact because a bolt of pure electricity seemed to spike her blood. His tongue laved over the aching tip, then she felt the rough edge of his teeth in a sensual bite. A bite that had her sex clenching in anticipation.

Then his mouth was moving to her other breast, caressing her through that wet cloth, and he was making her crazy. Need shouldn't be so strong, so consuming. She wanted to rake her nails down his back. Wanted to tear his clothes off and feel him, flesh-to-flesh against her.

She wanted to forget everything else—every single thing—but the passion he made her feel. The pleasure that they gave to each other.

She felt like an animal in lust as she fought to shove his clothes away. He lowered her back down until her feet hit the carpet, and her fingers immediately grabbed for the button of his jeans. She managed to unsnap that button and yank down his zipper, and then his cock was in her hands. Eve wrapped her fingers around him, his thick size spilling over in her grip. He groaned at her touch, his teeth scraping together, and she could see the hot desire on his face.

I want everything from him.

Eve eased down in front of him, moving slowly, and then her knees hit the floor.

"Eve?"

She leaned toward him. Put her mouth on his cock. Licked the head, tasted the salty moisture there.

"Eve, baby, you don't have to—"

She took him inside her mouth.

I control the pleasure. I make the choice. My lovers. My pleasure. Me. Me!

She licked him, took him in deeper, and wondered why control mattered to her so much. She loved the way he shuddered. Loved it when his hands fisted in her hair and Gabe groaned her name.

He can't watch me anymore. He can't stop me.

Eve licked the head of Gabe's arousal once more, then she was pulled back. Stared up at him. "Fuck me." She barely recognized her voice. Something was happening inside of her. Something that felt . . . wild.

Wrong.

No, nothing with Gabe can be wrong. Not with him.

"Fuck me now. Right here."

He pulled her back to her feet. Grabbed for a condom from his wallet—the man was so prepared like that—and then he locked his hands around her waist. His strength should have scared her.

It didn't.

Her legs curled around his hips, and he drove into her. Deep and hard.

I can fuck who I want.

Even as that thought pushed through her mind, Eve shook her head. No, no, that was wrong. She didn't want to fuck just anyone—she wanted Gabe.

"Eve?" Her name was a guttural demand from Gabe. "What's wrong?"

She shook her head. Her legs locked even tighter around him. "Nothing." Eve kissed him. Dark shadows were whispering in and out of her mind. She hated those shadows. "Make it stop."

"What?" *He* stopped.

No, no, she needed him to move. "Gabe, please!"

His body was rock hard, his cock embedded in her, but he wasn't moving.

He caught her hands. Pushed them back against the wall. "Eve, look at me."

Her eyes were closed. *I don't want him seeing . . . so tired of him seeing—*

"Eve! Fuck, wherever the hell you are in your mind, come back to me, *now.*"

Her eyes flew open. "I'm with you." With him—that was the only place she wanted to be. She hated the shadows in her mind. The weird whispers that had started in the fort and just wouldn't seem to stop. "Make me forget everything else." She squeezed her sex around him. Held him as tightly as she could. "Make me feel the way I did before."

Lightning flashed outside of their balcony. She heard a loud crack, and the room plunged into darkness.

He started to pull away from her.

"Fuck me, Gabe, *please . . .*" She needed him more than anything else.

And . . . he withdrew.

"Gabe?"

He thrust into her. Hard enough to steal her breath. Deep enough to make her moan.

Just what she wanted.

He kept her hands against the wall, kept her in place with the power of his body. In and out. Over and over. The pleasure was so close. So maddeningly, achingly close, and she needed it. She needed him. Her sex was quivering with every stroke, wet and swollen, and he glided deep into her, claiming every inch of her in the darkness.

"You're with me. *Stay with me.* Only me." His voice was all she heard. His body all she felt. The strange whisper in her mind was gone. There was only Gabe. Just the way she wanted it to be.

Pleasure hit her. Crashing over her in a fast, shuddering wave that swept over her entire body. She gasped, trying to pull in a breath, because the climax hit harder than she remembered. Her sex was pulsing, quivering, trying to hold tight to his cock—

But he'd withdrawn. "Gabe!"

In a flash, he spun her around. Her hands slapped against the wall.

"We're not done," he growled.

And he was lifting her hips, arching her back toward him. She turned her head, trying to see over her shoulder, trying to see him, but he was a shadow in the darkness.

The shadow follows me . . .

Fear quivered inside of her even as her sex still shuddered. "Gabe?"

His hands grabbed her hips, and holding her from behind, he slammed into her. "Couldn't . . . touch you . . . like I wanted . . ." And his right hand left her hip as he thrust and withdrew, thrust and withdrew.

That hand snaked around her body. Slid between her legs. Found her clit.

When he touched her there, her hips slammed back against him in a frantic roll.

"Much better." His mouth found her throat. He kissed her. Licked her. Sucked the skin.

And kept stroking her clit.

Her nails were about to scratch their way down that wall. "Gabe!" Another orgasm hit her, this one even stronger than the first, so strong she totally lost her breath because all she could do was moan and arch back against him.

"That's it . . . that's what I needed . . ." And Eve felt Gabe erupt into her. Her sex squeezed him as he came, and he kept stroking her clit, moving his hand so skillfully even as he groaned her name.

When it was over, she felt limp. Hollowed out. He withdrew from her, and Eve's knees did a little jiggle. She was pretty sure that she was about to wind up on the floor, but he caught her before she fell. She thought he might have carried her to the bedroom. Or maybe she just stumbled in there. Things were kind of hazy.

Then the bed creaked beneath her. The soft mattress touched her head. She shouldn't be in bed. Not naked. She had to get her clothes. Eve tried to push her way through the sated lethargy that had swept over her. "Have to . . . dress . . ."

"Not for me you don't."

He moved away. She heard the faint rustle of his feet.

Eve tried to shove back the covers. *Have to dress . . . he sees . . .*

"Eve? Baby, lie with me."

He pulled her back into the bed. It was so dark there. The power must still be out. Shadows were all around them.

"Need my clothes," she murmured.

"Why?"

"Because he sees me."

She felt his sudden stiffness against her. "Who sees you, Eve?"

"He watches me . . ."

"Who?"

Her eyes were sagging closed. Maybe they were already closed. It was so dark—because the power was out? Or because she was sinking into dreams? She hated to sleep near him, but her body had other plans. "Sorry . . ." She tried to get the words out. "If I scream . . ."

"EVE?"

She didn't stir.

Gabe brushed her wet hair back from her cheek. Eve was asleep in his arms.

His phone rang, and keeping one arm around her, he reached for the device. He'd tossed it on the bedside table moments before. "Spencer," he said, keeping his voice low.

"What?" Wade's sharp voice demanded. "Man, are you whispering?"

He was, because he didn't want to wake Eve. By her own admission, she hardly ever slept. But she was sleeping with him, her body soft, sated, her breath passing lightly from her lips. "What do you want?"

"The outage hit half the island. The police chief says that the condo should be on a generator, though, and he's got a man working to bring it online in—"

Lights flashed on—lights in the den, not the bedroom.

"The generator's working," Gabe said, still keeping his voice low. "What's happening with the search?"

"Still suspended," voices rose in the background, "until the storm passes."

Eve curled closer to Gabe.

"You should try to get some rest, too," Gabe told Wade. "We'll hit hard as soon as—"

"The island is fourteen miles long. We've all covered those miles, again and again. The woman isn't here. Either she left on her own—"

Damn doubtful because she hadn't checked in with her family, and the authorities couldn't get a link on her phone.

"—or the killer took her away. Since the cops found his dump site, it only stands to reason he had to find a fresh site for his bodies."

Yes, it did. "I'm not giving up on her yet."

Silence.

"You know I don't give up. Not until we find the victim alive or—"

"Or we find the bodies." Now Wade's voice was soft.

Wade knew all of his secrets. Unlike Eve, Wade realized that Gabe was far from a hero.

"Are you getting in too deep on this one?" Wade asked him carefully.

He was already in too deep. "No."

"You sure, man?"

"I'm trying to help Eve and Alexa."

"Just . . . don't go over the edge." Now there was worry in his old friend's voice. "At least not unless I'm at your side. After what happened with Amy, well, you don't want a repeat of that shit."

Ice coated Gabe's skin at the mention of his sister's name. The only place he felt warm—that was where Eve's body touched his. "You backed me up then."

"That bastard deserved the death he had coming to him." Wade's immediate reply.

But Wade had lied for him. Years ago. *The secrets we keep—they can fuck up our lives.*

"It was my fault." Wade's breath rasped over the line. "I told you I'd keep an eye on Amy. You were in that VA hospital, fighting for your life. *I was supposed to keep her safe.*" The guilt was there. The same guilt that had eaten at Wade for years.

Guilt because he thought he'd failed in his friendship with Gabe.

Guilt because he thought he'd let Amy die.

It wasn't your fault. It was mine.

"I thought getting her away from Derek—I thought that was the right thing. He was trouble. He was hurting her. As soon as I found out . . . shit, I made certain they were apart."

Derek. He'd been Amy's boyfriend. A jerk with a penchant for pushing around women. Too much money, too little fucking sense.

When Amy vanished, the detective working her case had just thought that she'd run back to Derek. Amy had been young, only twenty-one, a nursing student who'd stopped attending her classes. The detective—a fellow named Roger Hobbs—had thought that she'd turn up in a few days.

But when the days slipped by—and when Derek had proved that Amy wasn't with him—Hobbs had stopped looking for a *live* missing woman. He'd been sure that, with so much time lost, Amy was dead.

Wade had fought with the dick detective. Again and again. Conducted his own investigation. Been censured by the department because he'd been stepping on toes. Going outside of his bounds. Interfering with another detective's case.

Then Gabe had finally gotten released from that VA hospital. He'd teamed up with Wade. Said fucking screw the police department's rules. He'd been determined to find his baby sister, determined to make the man who took her *pay*.

But things hadn't ended the way he'd expected.

Wade had left the force. He'd given up everything for him, and he . . .

Gabe glanced over at Eve's sleeping form.

Baby, I'm so fucking far from the hero. When you learn the things I've done, you'll see me for the monster I am.

He'd started LOST because he wanted to atone for his sins. For the crimes that haunted him, and because . . . because he knew that he had to channel his rage.

The darkness inside of him kept growing, with each passing day and night. Sometimes, he felt like that darkness was going to swallow him whole. Sometimes, he wanted it to.

"No matter what happens," Wade said, "you know I have your back."

He did. Wade had traded in his badge for Gabe's friendship. Gabe knew he could count on the other man to walk through fire for him. And he would do the same for Wade, in a heartbeat.

Good and bad, white, black, and every shade of gray in between, Wade understood him. And Gabe understood Wade.

They'd both crossed the line before. Been pushed too far before.

And, maybe, they'd cross that line again.

Gabe put down his phone. He bent, and his lips brushed over Eve's cheek. She whispered something when he touched her, and Gabe frowned. "Eve? What is it?"

Her lips moved again.

"Eve?"

He could just barely make out . . .

"I did it," she whispered. "It was . . . me."

He blinked. "Eve?"

Her breath rushed out, and there were no more words from her.

WADE SLOWLY LOWERED his phone. He was worried about Gabe. He knew his friend was getting tangled up with Eve. A looker like that, sure, hell, yes, it would be easy to want her.

But he knew Gabe didn't just want to screw the woman. *He's falling deep.*

Wade turned around and saw the police chief watching him. Hell. Just how much of the conversation had the guy overheard?

"Everything okay?" Trey asked as he lifted one brow. "Is Jessica—"

"Gabe's taking care of her. She's safe."

Trey's eyes narrowed. The cop carried a lot of anger. It was easy for Wade to see that rage because he carried the same fury within him.

Trey Wallace wasn't exactly what he'd expected. The fellow might be a small-town cop, but he had an edge, a hard intensity that Wade had seen in seasoned veterans of the force.

"Does your boss always screw his clients?" Trey asked.

Wade shoved his phone into his pocket. "No," he said, and that was the flat truth. "He doesn't."

If anything, that answer seemed to make Trey angrier.

"I don't get it . . ." And Wade was curious about this. "You two were done, right? So why do you care if Gabe hooks up with her now?"

Trey just stared back at him.

"Not my business, huh?"

"No, it's not." Trey gave him a grim nod. "Search resumes at dawn. The storm will have passed by then, and we'll be out in force." He ran a hand over his face, and, for the first time, Wade saw a flash of weariness from the cop. "Damn National Weather Service is starting to say that we could have a tropical storm forming out in the Gulf. That shit is the last thing we need."

Wade had already heard those reports.

"If that storm turns this way, we could lose Alexa."

Because there would be no searching then.

"I don't want to lose another woman," Trey said grimly.

Voices called out then. Trey turned around. Two men had just entered the station.

One guy was young, maybe about twenty-one, and his nervous gaze drifted over the place. The other guy was older, maybe early thirties, with sandy brown hair.

"Johnny? Clay? What the hell are you two doing out here?" Trey strode toward them.

Wade followed, much slower.

"Johnny told me about the asshole move he made down at the West End." It was the older one who spoke. He glared at the younger guy—Johnny. "I wanted to drag his ass down here so you'd know he didn't mean that shit."

Wade's brows rose. The guy had dragged the kid down in a storm?

"Thanks, Clay," Trey told him. "I knew he was just drunk, though. Gia took him home after he tangled with—" Trey glanced over his shoulder. His gaze met Wade's. "—with an out-of-town consultant that we have working the Lady Killer's crimes."

Wait, an out-of-town consultant? Had that kid tangled with Gabe? With Dean? He would have to get the story soon.

"I was out on the boat with a big fishing tour," the one called Clay said. "I didn't realize . . . *is it true?*" His voice had roughened. *"Is Jessica alive? Is she back?"*

Trey's hand curled around Clay's shoulders. "Let's go into my office and talk."

Trey steered him away. The kid, Johnny, stood there, looking damn out of place.

Wade took his time walking toward the guy. "You in some kind of accident?" he asked the kid. It looked like the man's lip had been busted, and a dark bruise was under his eye.

Johnny's jaw locked. "Nothing I couldn't handle."

Right. The kid had some serious attitude rolling off him.

Trey had closed the door to his office. "Your brother?"

"My uncle."

Wade nodded. He'd spent years questioning suspects at the Atlanta PD, so he knew how to play the game, all nice and easy like, to find the intel that he needed. "And your uncle . . . he was close with Jessica Montgomery?"

Johnny's eyes narrowed. "Who are you?"

"I work with the . . . out-of-town consultant."

Johnny grunted. "The guy who was with Jessica at the bar?"

Sounded right.

"Tell that dude . . . he won't catch me off-guard again."

Johnny wasn't exactly sounding repentant. "I'll pass along the message." But the guy hadn't answered his question. "Did you know Jessica?" Because it sure sounded like he'd recognized her.

"Not as well as my uncle." His lips twisted. "And damn sure not as well as Trey."

Trey's office door opened. Clay appeared, looking

shaken. "We'll be here at first light," Wade heard him tell Trey. "You can count on us for the search."

Clay strode toward Wade. He took the man's measure. Tall, strong, determined.

Scared?

It almost looked like there was fear in his eyes as he said, "Johnny, we have to go. We need to secure the boats at the marina before this storm gets worse."

Then they were gone. Hurrying out.

Trey took his time heading back to Wade's side.

Wade waited until the door closed behind their new rescue volunteers, then he asked, "Who the hell were they?"

"Johnny . . . he made the mistake of mouthing off about the victims near your boss."

Right. So that busted lip had been given by Gabe. *I knew he was walking the edge.*

"And his uncle Clay runs the marina. He can give us access to any boats that we need for the search." A pause. "And . . . he knew Jessica."

Knew her? There had been some definite inflection there.

"I told him not to say anything to her, not until she's ready."

"Just how well did the guy know Jessica?"

Trey's jaw had locked. "They hadn't been involved in years."

Another lover on the island. Didn't this puzzle just keep twisting?

"Sometimes, you can't let the past go," Wade pointed out.

"Yeah, you can," Trey snapped. "Especially when the past didn't matter." The cop stormed away.

But what if that past did matter? To Jessica? Or to the guy named Clay?

SHE COULD HEAR seagulls. Eve couldn't see them, but she could hear them, crying out so close by. And waves . . . crashing.

"Sweetheart, do you like the game?"

That voice—that rasping voice—made goose bumps rise on her arms.

"What are you going to do with that knife?"

She glanced down, and a knife was in her hand. The blade was bloody.

"Oh, Jessica . . . did you really think I didn't know?"

Why did she have a knife?

"I've been watching you, all this time. I know your secrets."

She dropped the knife. It fell, tumbling end over end down a staircase. An old, rickety staircase.

"You aren't the good girl that they think. I know . . ."

She hated that rasping voice. Eve shook her head. "Stay away from me."

"Or what? You'll use that knife on me . . . ? You'll use it again?"

There was blood on her hands.

"Do you like the idea of killing?"

Eve shook her head.

"Don't lie." Anger was thick in his voice. "I've seen what you do. I've seen it all . . . you like the game. You like the blood. Do you even like the screams?"

"I—"

Rough hands grabbed her. Shook her. She screamed.

"EVE! DAMMIT, BABY, wake up!"

Eve's eyelids flew open. The lights were on, glowing so brightly, and Gabe was over her, staring down at her with worried blue eyes.

"You were crying."

She lifted her hand and touched the wetness on her cheek.

"Do you remember your nightmare?"

She did. The nightmare. The man. More. Eve rose from the bed. A rush of cool air hit her body, and she glanced down, startled. "I always wear my clothes to bed." She stumbled around a bit, found her sweatpants. Her shirt. Dressed as quickly as she could.

Gabe didn't move from his position in the bed. "Why do you always wear them, Eve?"

Eve. The name felt wrong. Alien.

"Because I have to be ready. Because . . ." It was there, nagging at her. But something else was pushing even stronger, something that had to get out.

She turned from Gabe. Made her way out of the room. Lightning still flashed beyond the balcony and she could hear the roll of thunder in the distance.

The canvas was just where she'd left it. The paint brushes. The supplies.

She reached for the tools almost as if by rote. Her fingers were trembling again, but she ignored the tremble. An image was in her mind, and she wasn't letting that image go.

Her breath heaved out as she painted. Gabe came to stand behind her, clad in a pair of jeans that clung low on his hips. He crossed his arms over his chest, and he just . . . watched her.

Paint soon covered her fingertips. It spattered her T-shirt. And that canvas didn't stay blank. Color filled it. The turbulent blue-green of waves. A patch of white sand. Seagulls.

The stark, dark form of a lighthouse, one that stood— almost impossibly—in the middle of an ocean. No light shone from that place, just shadows that stretched from the inside, out. A darkness without end.

"What is that place, Eve?" Gabe asked as he came closer.

Her fingers clenched around the brush.

"There's a lighthouse just beyond the island," he continued when she was silent. "Is that what you're painting? Do you remember being there?"

"Maybe. I—I don't know." The lighthouse was just in her mind, a hulking place that was burning in her head. She'd painted the damn thing, so that meant she *must* have been there.

Eve dropped her paintbrush and turned toward Gabe. "I need to go there, now."

He shook his head. "The storm hasn't passed. It's the middle of the night—Trey isn't going to send a search party out there right now—"

"Not a search party." She was sweating. Her gut twisting. "Me. You. I want us to go out there."

His gaze was still worried. He watched her as if he thought she was having some sort of breakdown. Maybe she was.

"You wanted me to remember. I'm remembering." She threw her hand up toward the balcony's glass doors, pointing to the dark water outside. "I need to get to that lighthouse. Come on, Gabe, you're a former SEAL! That means you're supposed to be able to do anything in the water, right?" There was no way he didn't know how to drive a boat. She'd bet her life on it.

His jaw locked. "Let's wait until it's light out."

"Please." A terrible intensity ate at her. The image of the lighthouse wouldn't stop burning in her mind. "I—I think something bad happened there."

He reached out to her. His slightly callused fingertips slid over her arm, pulling it back down to her side.
"What did you do?"

"What?"

"When you were asleep, you said . . . 'I did it. It was
me.' " His fingers curled around her wrist, chaining her
to him. "What did you do?"

"I don't know." Said softly.

"Eve?"

She pulled from his grip. "I'm going out to that lighthouse. Either you're coming with me or I'll find a way
to go on my own."

Because something had happened there. Something
terrible and dark. Something that made her cry in her
sleep.

And Eve was going to find out just what the hell that
something had been.

CHAPTER TWELVE

"THERE'S NOTHING OUT THERE," TREY SAID AS HE watched Gabe ready the rented boat. The cop was on the dock of the marina, not being a damn bit of use. "That place hasn't been used in decades. More than half of that island washed away, and the lighthouse itself is barely standing."

"I need to go inside," Eve said. She was on the boat with Gabe, despite Trey's protests. When they first arrived at the dock and the cop had seen them, Gabe thought the man might physically stop Eve from getting on the boat.

Trey still looked as if he wanted to grab her and make a run for it.

That would be a mistake.

From the edge of the dock, that punk Johnny was watching them. Turned out that Johnny's uncle, Clay, actually owned the marina, but when they arrived, Johnny had quickly told them that Clay was out, already searching for Alexa.

Johnny sure as hell had acted as if he didn't want to rent them a boat. But with Trey there, the guy hadn't been able to refuse. Now the kid kept skulking around with his busted lip and glaring at him. *Way to be a fucking help, kid.*

Wade called him earlier, when Gabe had just arrived at the Marina, and warned him about Johnny's uncle.

Looks like your lady had another lover on the island.

Gabe was planning to find Clay later that day. Men connected so intimately to Eve were automatically on his suspect list. He'd be questioning the guy soon enough.

"You can't go inside that lighthouse," Trey said now, stalking closer to the water's edge. "I told you, the place is sealed off. There's *nothing* in there."

The cop hadn't realized a body was stashed in his fort, either.

"Sand and bird shit," Trey snapped as he jerked off his cap and waved it at them. "That's all you're gonna find out there."

"Then that's what we'll find." Gabe kept his voice mild. Eve was determined to go out to that lighthouse. He'd stopped her from going out in the storm—because that would have been suicide in the dark—but he wasn't holding her back any longer. Especially since he wanted to search the place, too.

Trey swore. "Do you even know how to handle that boat?"

Gabe smiled. Since he'd owned a boat just like this one when he was fifteen, he figured he could handle it just fine. "I'll get by."

"Look . . . don't stay out there long, okay? The forecaster is saying the storm in the Gulf is stalling, and the longer it stays over that warm water, the better chance it has of turning into a depression, or, hell, even a tropical storm." Trey ran a hand through his hair. "That's the last damn thing I need. If a storm that strong comes this way, the power company always cuts off the feed to the island."

"We lost power last night," Gabe reminded him. The boat was almost ready.

"For less than an hour—and don't even get me started on the number of calls I got then." Trey was still glowering. "And half of those calls were from Pierce."

From the corner of his eye, Gabe saw Eve stiffen.

"He's worried about you," Trey said quietly. "Just like I am."

Eve crept toward the cop. "Is he . . . here?"

Johnny edged nearer to them, not even trying to hide the fact that he was eavesdropping.

Trey turned to glare at him. "Don't you have something else to do? Shit, I thought you were supposed to be helping Clay with the search, too."

Johnny seemed to pale. "I . . . always will help Clay. *Always.*"

Right, like that wasn't a little too intense. But Johnny turned and backed toward another boat.

When Johnny was out of range, Trey said, "Pierce was in Mobile an hour ago, so he'll be on the island by the time you get back. I think . . ." Trey looked down at the cap he cradled in his hands. "I think Pierce was trying to give you space, but he couldn't stay away. He *knows* you're Jessica, just like I do. The guy had to know when he took one look at you."

But Eve shook her head. "In Atlanta, Pierce acted as if he weren't even sure I was Jessica. Why show such concern now? Why would he—"

"Fear," Trey answered flatly. "It can make a man act insane. He's afraid of finding you, then having to lose you all over again."

The boat's motor growled to life.

"I know just how he feels," Trey said, his words barely rising over that growl. "I found you, then had to watch you go off with this asshole."

Gabe didn't exactly like being called an asshole.

"Alexa's parents are coming in." Trey pushed away from the boat. "They'll arrive after lunchtime. And I get to tell them—hell—what? That we don't know if their daughter ran away or if a serial killer has her?"

"Let the FBI do the talking," Gabe advised the cop as his hands tightened around the wheel. "That's the shit they're good at."

Trey's eyes met his. "Keep a close eye on her. That lighthouse is crumbling apart, and one misstep could send someone to the hospital."

He didn't plan to make any missteps.

Carefully, he took the boat out of the marina. Eve was silent as they slipped away. He glanced at the boats, taking in his surroundings carefully and—

Gabe's eyes narrowed when he caught sight of Johnny. Still watching them. Glaring. While Gabe stared at him, Johnny lifted his hand and flipped him off.

Then Johnny hurried inside the marina.

That little jerk was getting on his last nerve. When he came back, he'd deal with Johnny . . . and he'd find out just what Clay Thompson knew about the days leading up to Jessica Montgomery's disappearance.

But first . . . first he had to let Eve confront a nightmare that had kept her up all night.

The lighthouse waited.

WHEN TREY SAW Johnny stalking toward him, he barely contained an eye roll. *I don't need this shit.*

But he wasn't particularly surprised to see Johnny there. The kid's uncle owned the marina, and Johnny was always hanging around the place. *Clay should have taken the guy out on the search.*

"Who is that jerk?" Johnny demanded. His nose was still swollen and his lip was busted.

"Someone you don't want to mess with again." He had enough on his plate without having to worry about Gabe beating the shit out of Johnny.

"He a cop?"

"No." The boat was chugging ahead. *The lighthouse.* Of all the places, why the hell would Jessica want to go there? No one went out there, not anymore.

Sure, a few years back some folks had gotten together and tried to raise money to protect the place. They'd spent a fucking fortune shoring up sand out there to try and make the island bigger, but then that sand had just broken away—the "new" island had split in two, and folks turned away from the place.

There wasn't any damn thing out there.

"I know the woman with him. I knew her as soon as I turned around and saw her on the West End."

Now that wasn't real surprising. Johnny had been living on the island with his uncle for the last five years.

"You don't forget a woman who looks like that."

Where was the guy going with that?

"I remember . . ." Johnny mused as he tilted his head to the side. "You two used to hook up, right?"

"Don't you have work to do?" He and the FBI agents had commandeered some of the boats and pulled in the locals to help search for Alexa's body.

Because the options don't just have to be that the woman ran away or a serial killer took her. We live on a fucking island. She could have just drowned. Every year, some drunk tourist did.

"She left your ass."

He could totally understand the temptation to punch Johnny in the face. No wonder Gabe had sent the guy flying over the bar. *But I'm supposed to be the cop, and people are watching.*

Early morning fishermen were all over the place. Too many eyes and ears.

"Heard she caught you cheating on her with some other blonde . . . and she threw you to the side."

He tried to keep his body loose. "That's not what happened. You shouldn't listen to gossip, kid."

"Then you tried to get her back, right here at the party at the marina, right? But she ran out on you, left in the middle of that big dance."

She had. He'd called after her, but Jessica hadn't stopped. What the fuck had he been supposed to do? Beg? So he'd stayed put, watched her leave.

Then she'd vanished.

"Bet it pisses you off that she's with that other guy now, bet it makes you so mad you want to pound his ass into the ground."

You're supposed to be the cop.

"If it were me, I'd go after him. I wouldn't take no sh—"

"It's not you." His voice was low, lethal. When he'd been a kid, his father's voice had roared every time he got angry. Trey wasn't like his old man. When he got mad, he went soft. His voice a whisper of hate. Of fury.

Johnny backed up a step.

"Get to work, Johnny. And forget everything you *think* you know about me and my business."

He looked back out at the water. Gabe and Jessica were gone.

"When Clay comes back, tell him to come see me. We need to talk some more." About Jessica. About the past. About the hell that could come calling to paradise.

"When he comes back," Johnny repeated, but the fellow's voice was low, hoarse.

Trey gave a grim nod, then he headed toward the boats.

THE PLACE LOOKED just like her painting.

Too much like it.

Eve stared up at the lighthouse. Gabe had anchored the boat near the narrow sandy stretch of beach—beach that wasn't near the lighthouse, or at least not touching it. The narrow strip of sand—Sand Island—was actually to the west of the lighthouse, and she had to cross the water, sinking and struggling as the waves pushed her, in order to reach the rocky spot that was the home of the lighthouse.

Her shoes were in her hands. She wore a pair of shorts, and her legs were wet from the crashing waves. As Eve was crossing that divide of water—the narrow beach on one side of her, the lighthouse on the other— the saltwater stung her skin. It splashed toward her face when she sank deeper, and she remembered—

The taste of saltwater in my mouth. Swimming, struggling to stay afloat even as my limbs burned.

The rocks seemed to bite into her bare feet and she was desperate to get out of that water. And as she trudged forward, she tilted her head back and tried to see the top of the lighthouse.

Seagulls cried out.

"Doesn't look as if anyone has been here in a while." Gabe made his way to the lighthouse entrance, or what Eve guessed was the entrance. He shoved against an old door, but nothing happened. Grunting, he tried again.

The door didn't open.

Eve slowly made her way around the other side. She didn't see any other entrances. The lighthouse was made of heavy bricks, surging high into the sky.

Above the entrance she saw the number 1871. *Must have been when it was built.* It was odd to think of this place out there, on the little pile of rocks, lasting for so long.

Gabe turned away from the door. His gaze swept the narrow section of rocks that was their perch. "I need something to pry it open."

There were two rectangular windows higher up on the lighthouse. For an instant Eve could have sworn she saw someone in that top window, staring down at her. "Gabe!"

He'd grabbed what looked like a long metal pole that had washed onto the rocks. He was pushing it against the door, straining with all his might, his muscles bulging—

And the door opened. It swung in with a hard screech, the cry just like a woman's scream. Eve froze at that sound.

Gabe dropped the pole. Stepped inside.

Sweetheart, come with me . . . let's play a game.

Eve hurried forward. She put her hands on the old bricks of the lighthouse. She expected terror to hit her.

It didn't.

Just as before, when she'd first set foot on Dauphin Island, she had the feeling that she was home. *Where I belong.*

Wary, she moved inside. The place smelled of the sea, and sunlight trickled through the windows from above. The spiral staircase was old, rickety, and it looked as if one wrong or too hard step would send it crumbling to the ground.

Gabe was at the base of the staircase, about to go up—

"Stop."

He turned toward her.

Eve shook her head. "I don't want you to get hurt." She motioned toward the railing he'd been about to grab. "That always comes loose. Be careful."

"Always?"

Her breath was heavy in her lungs. "Always." Because she'd been here. She had the memories. Running up those stairs. Nearly falling when the railing had wrenched loose beneath her hand.

But . . . someone had caught her. Wrapped an arm about her.

Be careful, don't want to ruin the fun . . .

And she'd laughed. She could hear the echo of her laughter in that place. When she'd painted the lighthouse, she was terrified, but now that she was there, inside . . .

I'm not scared here. I like this place. I belong here.

And that felt wrong.

"I want to go up first," Eve said.

His dark brows climbed, but Gabe didn't argue. Good. She slipped by him, didn't use that railing, and started climbing up all of those steep, twisting steps that led to the top of the lighthouse. The waves pounded outside, loud, rough.

"Watch out for step number nine," Eve said without looking down. "It's cracked." Because she could see herself, jumping over that step, laughing.

You won't get me . . .

"Just how much do you remember?" Gabe asked as he followed her up.

"Not enough." She kept climbing. They reached the first window. She looked out. "I . . . that's the fort."

His shoulder brushed against hers. "Yes."

They had a perfect view of the fort from that vantage point. A perfect view of the place where the poor woman's body had been entombed.

Gabe leaned closer to her. "I'm betting if you use a pair of binoculars, you'll be able to see the golf course perfectly, too."

She could already see the beach that led to the old country club.

Eve turned away from that window. Went up higher. Smelled the ocean.

Her hand slid over the scar on her neck.

"*Eve.*" Gabe's voice was sharp because—

She didn't just smell the ocean any longer. With every step she took, she was inhaling a deeper, cloying scent.

"Eve, stop."

But she was almost running up those rickety steps now, her footsteps pounding so hard they reverberated and—

Someone was looking out from the second window. Eve had thought that she'd seen someone, just for a moment, when she was down below.

Eve staggered to a stop. Her right hand fisted around the shaky railing.

And she stared at the woman who was half tucked in the nook that led to the second window. A woman with blond hair and a bloodstained body. The woman's head was tipped forward, that length of blond hair hiding her face.

The scent of death—now she understood that cloying scent.

"Alexa?" Eve whispered. Then she reached out. Her fingers slid under the woman's chin.

"No, Eve, *don't!*" Gabe jerked her away from the blonde.

The woman's head tilted back an instant and—*sand* poured from her mouth.

"Oh, my God." Nausea rolled inside Eve and she thought she'd be violently ill, right there. Her cheeks went ice cold, then flaming hot as she stared at the woman.

"Alexa," Gabe whispered.

Her throat had been cut and . . . sand was there, too. Falling from her wound, mixing with the blood on her clothes.

Eve spun away from that woman. She grabbed for the windowsill because her knees were knocking together. This place—it was too much.

Let's play, sweetheart . . . His voice, that rasp, but . . .

You'll never catch me. I'm better at this game. Her nails scraped across the windowsill. That echo of a response—it was her echo. She could actually see herself, shouting back those words and laughing as she ran down the twisting stairs of the lighthouse.

The lighthouse that the killer used.

Her head lifted. She stared out that window. She could see straight across that water, all the way to the fort. There was a faint rustling sound behind her, but she refused to look back. Gabe was checking the body. She *couldn't* see that. She wouldn't.

Eve tried to suck in a deep breath, and then—then a light, a flash, hit her eyes. She raised her hand, blocking the glare instinctively, and that was when she saw the second boat.

A boat that was idling in the water, just a few feet away from the small, sandy island. They hadn't heard it approach. Because of the waves? Because they were so far up the lighthouse?

"G-Gabe?"

Someone was down there. A man in a baseball cap, running back toward the other boat. A sleek motorboat with a blue covering on the top and blue stripes on the side.

"What the fuck?" Gabe demanded, then he was running back down the stairs, heading below, rushing toward the guy in the baseball cap. Eve wasn't about to be left behind with Alexa's body. She ran after him, her feet flying recklessly over those stairs.

Gabe beat her outside, and as soon as she shot out of the door after him, Eve could hear the other boat's engine as it roared away. The guy was fast—and he was driving straight for Dauphin Island.

"Stop!" she shouted. Right. Like that was going to do any good at all. Then she sprinted toward her and Gabe's boat. He was already in the little stretch of water between the lighthouse and Sand Island. She snatched off her shoes again and followed him, scrambling up the sand.

Their boat was just a few feet away and—

It exploded. The whole boat flew up, sending a ball of fire flashing up into the air, and Eve fell back into the churning water.

WADE WALKED ALONG the ramparts at the old fort, his gaze on the waves in the distance. The skeleton had finally been removed from its tomb in the fort. *All of that time . . . trapped in the walls.*

He fucking hoped the woman had been dead before the sadistic prick walled her in.

Victoria would do her thing with the remains. How that woman could stand being around the dead . . . he'd never know. And Victoria talked to the bodies. He'd heard her on too many occasions. Talking as if the dead could respond to her.

They can't, Viki. They're long gone.

His gaze slid over the water once more—

What. The. Hell.

He could see a black plume of smoke out there, rising high, billowing into the sky. Smoke meant fire . . . and that location, that was where the lighthouse was.

Gabe had gone to the lighthouse. When he'd called Gabe with the news about Clay, his buddy had told him he was renting a boat to go out there. Gabe and Eve.

And the place was burning.

He shouted for the cops even as fear tightened around his heart.

"EVE!" GABE ROARED her name. Their boat had been blasted into a hundred pieces, chunks had flown everywhere, and the blast had sent him hurtling into the waves.

He pushed through the water, standing in depths to his waist, and shouted for her again. *"Eve!"*

But she didn't answer. He couldn't see her. And he was going out of his mind.

That bastard on the other boat was long gone. He'd come, rigged their boat to explode, then gotten the hell out of Dodge.

"Eve!" He swam to the left, heading closer to the rocky shore of the lighthouse. Eve had been on that side—hadn't she? He'd been so determined to get to the guy who'd blown up the boat that he hadn't paid attention to Eve.

Now she's gone.

No, no, no! "Eve!" He swam blindly because the water was so murky there. His hands were reaching out, desperate to find and grasp her.

What if she'd been hurt by the blast before she went

under? What if she were unconscious? She could be drowning while he dicked around out there shouting her name.

He swam deeper. Harder. His lungs started to burn, but Gabe didn't care. When he'd been a SEAL, he was trained to stay under during every imaginable condition. He could keep holding his breath. He knew from grim experience that he wouldn't pass out for a while yet.

That would give him time to find her. He would find her. Eve. *Eve!*

Then he bumped against something soft. Something that reached for him and held on tightly—something precious.

He locked his arms around her and kicked to the surface. When his head broke from the water, he sucked in a desperate gulp of air, and so did the woman in his arms. Eve choked a bit, but then she was heaving in her breath, gasping desperately and clinging tightly to him. As tightly as he clung to her.

He managed to fight his way back to the beach, never letting her go, not for an instant.

When they reached the sand, he heaved them both up on the shore. The scent of fire and gasoline filled the air, and smoke still rose from the boat's remnants—those that littered the little shore.

Eve rolled over, laying on her back and still breathing deeply. He leaned over her, pushing her wet hair away from her face. "Are you hurt?" When she didn't answer fast enough, his hands slid over her, looking for a wound, "Baby, tell me what's wrong."

"I swam." Her voice was quiet, strangely devoid of emotion. "Until I couldn't swim any longer. Then I . . . I drowned."

What. The. Fuck? "Baby, look at me."

She didn't look. "Then I was a ghost. I walked. I walked and I walked . . . and strangers picked me up. We drove. Just drove . . . because I couldn't turn back."

He caught her chin in his fingers, sending sand sliding over her smooth skin. "Be here, right now, with me." Because he was afraid that her past had reached out to her. They'd wanted to stir up her memories, but—

Right now, I need her with me.

"You didn't drown. You're with me." He leaned over her. Pressed a frantic kiss to her cheek. Her forehead. Her mouth. "You're with me." The terror was still with him, too. The gut-wrenching fear that he wouldn't be able to find her in the water.

He pressed his forehead to hers. Just held her there for a moment. His fingers were shaking. He'd been through countless battles, faced hell again and again, he'd killed . . .

And his fingers were shaking because he'd come too close to losing her.

"Why?" Eve whispered. "Why did he . . . do this?"

Gabe forced his head to rise. Then he stood, his feet sinking into the sand. He'd lost his shoes somewhere in the water, and his clothes clung tightly to him. "I don't know." It sure didn't fit with the killer's M.O. "Maybe he knew we'd found Alexa, and he was trying to buy some time in order to escape."

She sat up, pulled her knees close to her chest and wrapped her arms around her updrawn legs. "Time to escape?"

Yes.

"Did you see his face?" Gabe asked her, because she'd been the first one to spot the guy. He'd only seen the baseball cap and the boat.

For an instant Eve hesitated, then she shook her head. "I don't know who he was."

But her words . . . they were still too stilted. *Is she lying to me?* Why would she lie?

"Do you have your phone?" Eve asked him suddenly. "Can you call for help?"

He shoved his hand into his pocket. Big surprise . . . the phone was gone, and he doubted the fates would shine on them and his phone would magically wash up on shore. "Help will come," he said as his gaze slid over the water. The fire had shot plenty of smoke up into the air. Someone would see those black clouds. Someone would come this way.

It was just a matter of time, time that they didn't have. Because every moment they spent trapped on that island was time the killer could use to vanish.

"He's running because he's scared," Gabe said grimly. The lighthouse waited, with Alexa Chambers's body inside. "He's been bringing them here. Maybe torturing them here before he dumped their bodies—"

"But they were alive when they went into the sand."

His laugh was cold. "Look around, Eve. There's sand here. What's to say he didn't kill them out here, where no one would see them? Where no one would hear them? Fuck, maybe he dug them up when he was sure they were dead and moved the bodies then." He didn't know what the sick freak could be doing.

But he was going to find out.

He bent. Caught her hand in his. "Come on." He hoisted her up in a fast move. There was no way he'd just sit there and wait for help to arrive. Sitting on his ass wasn't his style.

"I don't want to go back." Eve was still. She'd dug her

heels into the sand. Vaguely, he noticed that her shoes were gone, too.

"We won't touch the body." Hell, no, they wouldn't. He wanted Victoria to work her magic on the victim. "But he could have left something behind in that place."

In the distance, thunder rumbled. His head jerked. Way back out over the waves, far past the lighthouse, Gabe thought he saw the flash of lightning. The storm that he'd been warned about? How long did they have before it rolled in?

"We need to search the lighthouse." The waves were already getting rougher around them. What if Trey had been right about the storm? If the weather roughened and a depression or a tropical storm came their way, there was no telling what kind of damage might be done to the lighthouse.

It had withstood storms before, sure, but the ragged appearance of that rocky shore was proof that the lighthouse wouldn't stand forever.

"I don't want to go back." Eve's voice was soft and sad. "It's not what I—I thought."

She wasn't making sense. He turned toward her. There were no marks on her body that he could see, but maybe he'd missed an injury. Carefully, his fingers slid through her wet hair. "Baby, does it hurt?"

"Yes," she said, her eyes on him. "It feels as if I'm breaking apart."

"Eve?"

She pulled away from him. "I'm sorry."

"You don't have anything to be sorry for! You're just as much of a victim as that woman up there!"

Eve flinched. "What if I'm not?"

"I don't even know what you're saying." He grabbed

her hand again. He wasn't about to let her out of his sight or out of his grasp. "Let's see what we can find in that place."

"But help—"

"Help is coming," he promised her grimly. "The Coast Guard, the local cops, Wade—*someone* will be hauling ass out here for us." But he didn't tell her about the worry that nagged at his mind.

Without a boat, they were trapped on that island. Sitting ducks. What if the killer came back? Armed with a gun?

They had to go back into the lighthouse. It was the only bit of shelter, protection, available to them.

The door was still open, and as soon as he had Eve inside, Gabe pushed his shoulder against it and strained to close it—not fully, but enough to slow down anyone who might come after them. He would have shut the thing all the way, but the door was already so old that he worried he might just wind up sealing himself and Eve inside—and wouldn't that be a fucking kick?

He saw that her stare was on the stairs.

"Not up there," he told her, making sure that he brushed his body against hers. He had the weird feeling that Eve was pulling away. Crazy, when she was right in front of him. "I think I saw a room, down below the stairs." Maybe it had been part of the old lighthouse keeper's quarters. Maybe it was just a storage room. Either way, he was going in there.

"I . . . remember being here," Eve said.

"He brought you here?" Gabe demanded.

She was still looking up at those stairs. "I should be afraid."

He was afraid. Worried that freak out there would make another attack. *I have to protect her.*

"But I'm not." Her lips pressed together. "And that's wrong."

He shook his head. "Shock and adrenaline. Just trust me, okay? We'll ride them out together." Then he pulled her away from the stairs and toward what he thought was a room. Only . . . the door there was stuck, too. Stuck and rusted, and he drove his body into it again and again—

"Push it at the bottom," Eve said softly. "The weak spot, near the hinges . . ."

He looked down, found that spot and heaved. The door opened with a groan.

The room inside was small, barely five feet long. The only light came from behind them as they crept inside. He saw that there was a map on one wall. "Dauphin Island," he said, recognizing the shape. He narrowed his eyes, struggling to see in that dim interior. There were scratch marks on the map. Four marks near the area he knew would match with the old golf course. One mark at the fort and . . .

At least a dozen other little scratch marks, careful X's all scattered around the island.

No, the fuck, no.

Something crashed behind him. He spun around and saw that Eve had bumped into a little table, an old wobbly table that had been crammed into the corner. When he'd come into the room, he'd been so intent on the map that he hadn't noticed the table.

A small black box—a jewelry box?—had been on the table, but now it lay smashed on the floor.

"I—I'm sorry," Eve stammered as she fell to her knees and grabbed the box. "I didn't mean to break it!"

She lifted it up and jewelry came tumbling out. Brace-lets. Necklaces. She started to grab for the jewelry, but he lunged forward and caught her wrist in a too-tight grip. "Leave it."

Because there could be prints on the jewelry.

"Is that blood?" Eve asked him, her gaze on a glittering, diamond tennis bracelet.

"Yes." Dried blood.

"Why . . . why are these things here?" Her tortured gaze rose to his. "Why?"

"Because sometimes killers like to keep trophies from their kills."

"There's too many pieces of jewelry." Her voice was hushed.

"Yes." Too much jewelry, too many tally marks. They'd thought that the Lady Killer had only taken seven victims.

Are there more?

"This is why he ran." Gabe's words were a growl. "He knew we'd find his little treasure chest, and the bastard is trying to get away."

By the time they got back to the Island, he could be long gone.

"That's . . . that's a lot of jewelry." Eve rose to her feet. Stared down at the gems. There was sorrow on her face. And what looked like guilt. "It's wrong," she whispered.

"Eve?"

"Maybe it's better not to remember." A tear leaked from her eye. "Maybe the doctors were right. Maybe I don't *want* to remember."

She backed away, trying to rush out of the room, but he grabbed her and held tight.

"I don't want to be here!" she nearly yelled. "There's a dead woman upstairs—a woman who looks too much like me!" Her voice rose more with each word. "Sand came out of her mouth, and I can taste sand on my tongue!"

"Eve!"

"That's not my name!" She shrieked, then froze, her eyes widened in horror.

He knew then that she was at the edge of her control. The place had obviously brought parts of her past back. Parts that she wanted to face. Parts that she didn't. "Jessica," he said softly, but the name rolled awkwardly from him. He didn't know Jessica. He knew Eve. He'd fucked Eve. Eve had cried out for him. She'd—

She pulled from him and ran to the front of the lighthouse. "Dammit, stop!" He hadn't heard a boat approaching, but he hadn't heard it before, either. He lunged forward and grabbed her from behind, locking his arms around her and pulling Eve back against him. *Jessica. Her name is Jessica.*

"I have blood on my hands." Her voice was so low he could barely hear her. "I can see myself. Running in this lighthouse. There's blood on my hands . . ."

"Because he probably brought you here." Her wet hair was against his mouth. "Baby, he brought you here, but you escaped."

"*I* have the knife. I used it. We were playing a game."

"So you got the weapon away from the prick and you stabbed him. Fucking good. Maybe we can get an evidence team out here and they can find his DNA—"

She shuddered against him. "I was laughing. He was laughing. It's *wrong*."

His muscles tensed. "What?"

She heaved against him, trying to break free, but he didn't let her go.

"I'm wrong," she said, her voice lower. "Everything I'm remembering, it's wrong." She whispered, "*Please,*

please, let me go. I can't breathe in here. All I smell is her blood."

WADE RAN FOR the police boat that was tied to the edge of the marina.

"Hurry the hell up!" he shouted to the cop who was trailing him. He hadn't been able to find Trey—the guy was out somewhere on the island doing a search, and since the cell connection on that place was a crapshoot, he hadn't wanted to waste time trying to find the man.

Not when fire had been in the sky.

"W-We can radio for the Coast Guard. They'll be able to help us!" Officer Dennis Sebastian said, his words huffing out as he hurried to keep up with Wade.

Wade jumped onto the police boat. He really didn't know shit about boats so he needed that guy to get him to the lighthouse.

Dennis leapt on after him and got the boat moving into the water—*hurry, hurry, hurry!* Dennis looked like he was in his early twenties, with sun-streaked blond hair, and his hands were shaking as he steered them away from the marina.

Wade grabbed the radio.

"You have to get the channel . . ." Dennis quickly pressed some buttons for him and took the radio with one hand. Then he was talking to someone on the emergency channel, telling him about the fire on Sand Island. Asking for all available hands to report to the lighthouse.

As far as cops went, Wade knew the kid was a good one. He'd been working hard during the case, doing his damnedest and not getting too shaken when he saw the skeleton in the fort's wall.

"Make this thing go faster," Wade ordered him.

Dennis didn't question him. His jaw just locked and they went even faster as the boat's emergency sirens sounded. Good. They would make everyone else get the hell out of their way.

Hold on, Gabe. I'm coming. He'd let his friend down before, and Wade had sworn that he'd never make that mistake again. He'd seen Gabe hit rock bottom, seen him get lost to rage and despair as he'd held his sister's broken body. *I'm coming, Gabe.*

He grabbed for the binoculars near the steering wheel. They had to go around the side of the island before they'd spit out into the open water that led to the lighthouse. *Hurry, hurry . . .*

Water flew around them. Dennis's hands stayed tight around the wheel.

The minutes crawled by.

They passed another boat, one with blue stripes and a blue top that was moving just as hell fast as they were.

"Johnny!" Dennis yelled. "Get out of the damn way!" But the roar of the motors and the waves snatched away his order.

The blue-striped boat shot to the left, heading around them and back to the marina.

"That kid always races too fast," Dennis said, eyes narrowing as he turned the boat a bit. "He's gonna kill someone one of these days."

Right then, Wade wasn't concerned with some speeding punk. When they got back, Dennis could put the fear of God into the guy. The only thing that mattered to Wade right then was getting out to that lighthouse and finding out if his best friend was alive or dead.

CHAPTER THIRTEEN

Gabe was watching from the lighthouse window. Not the top window, because Eve wouldn't go near Alexa's body, but from the perch about twenty feet up in the lighthouse.

He saw the police boat racing toward them with its lights flashing. "The rescue party," he said. He turned to look at Eve, wanting to reassure her. "We're getting out of here."

She didn't move.

"Eve?"

She'd begged to leave the lighthouse, but . . . but he'd been afraid to put her at risk. He'd had to protect her, and kept her at his side.

He touched her cheek and found it ice cold. "Baby?"

He realized that she wasn't even blinking. Just staring straight ahead. Swearing, he yanked her against him, holding her tightly, rubbing her arms. "It's all right. Sweetheart, we're safe, we're—"

Eve screamed. A terrible, high-pitched sound, and then she was fighting him. Kicking him. Punching him. Slicing her nails over his face. He let her go because he didn't want to hurt her, not ever, and Eve spun around. She raced back down the stairs, moving so fast and frantically that he feared she'd fall and break her neck.

"The rescue boat is here!" He didn't run after her, not while she was on the stairs. "It's okay."

Eve didn't stop. She finally reached the bottom of the stairs and then tried to yank the heavy door open.

"Eve?"

He made his way down to her. She'd broken her nails—either on the door or on him—and was about to break her fingers as she struggled so hard with the door. "I got it, I've got it . . ."

He pried the door open. Eve raced outside and she ran straight to the water's edge. For a minute he was afraid that she was going to just jump in and sink—he was ready to leap right after her—but then she stopped. On those rocks, she fell to her knees and her head sagged forward.

Slowly, because he sure as hell didn't want to frighten her more, Gabe crept toward her. "You'll be safe and dry soon." The rescue boat was only a few hundred yards out.

"I did it."

What memories had come back to her in that place? "What did you do?"

Her shoulders hunched forward. "I . . . killed someone."

He wanted to touch her, but she was already on the edge. "How do you know that?"

"I—I could see it. I told you . . . the knife. The blood on my hands. I can remember how it feels. To shove that knife into someone's skin. To see the spray of blood." Her hands slammed into the water, sending spray all around her. "I was so wrong. I thought I needed help, that I was . . . a victim."

"You are, Eve."

"There is no Eve!" She lunged to her feet. Whirled to face him. "I smelled that blood, I stayed in that lighthouse with you . . . and I remembered . . ." Her eyes burned with emotion. "I'm . . . I'm not a good girl, Gabe." Said so simply, as if she were a child. *I'm not a good girl.*

"Who did you kill?" he asked her.

She blinked. "I . . . I don't know."

"Are you even sure you *did* kill someone?" The boat was almost on them.

"I saw the knife! The blood!"

"But did you see a body? Maybe you were defending yourself. Maybe that memory was of you fighting off your attacker."

She shook her head. "I was laughing. I . . . liked it." Her eyes closed and she said once more, "I'm not good."

The boat was close enough that he could see the cop on board—not Trey, but the younger guy, Dennis. And Wade was there, too. Wade who, as a rule, fucking hated boats. But he'd known that Wade would come to help him.

Debris from the explosion littered Sand Island and the water around them. Gabe wanted to pull Eve into his arms and hold her as tight as he could, but he was afraid of making the wrong move with her.

"I'm sorry, I'm so sorry," she whispered.

And—screw it—he did pull her into his arms. "We'll figure this out. You don't know what happened or even if that memory is real. *We'll figure this out.*" Because he knew, better than anyone else, that a person could be pushed too far. Even someone who valued life, who thought he knew the difference between right and wrong . . . even a person like that could be pushed too far.

A person like me.

Deep inside, everyone had the potential to kill. But people usually held back. They stayed in control.

Until someone ripped that control away.

"Gabe!" It was Wade, shouting to him. The young Dauphin Island cop was securing the boat, but Wade had jumped out and was running toward him. "What the hell happened?"

Where to start? "We found Alexa Chambers."

"What?"

Eve pushed against Gabe's chest. "She's dead."

Wade glanced over at the lighthouse. "Sonofabitch."

"His souvenirs are inside," Gabe told him. The cop was trying to rush toward them now. "And . . . there are more victims than we thought. A lot more."

More bodies . . . buried on Dauphin Island. They'd have to take the map that guy had left behind, and they'd see just what they could discover.

"What the hell happened to your boat?" Wade was right beside him now. "And Jesus, man, you look like you took a beating!"

He felt the blood on his cheek. Eve stiffened in his arms. She'd scratched him. Punched him. Fought like a wildcat as she battled to escape her hell.

He stroked her back. "He was here," Gabe said grimly. "The sonofabitch rigged our boat to explode. We saw him as he was racing away." Dennis, the Coast Guard cop, was close enough to hear now. "Get an APB out on that radio. He was on a twenty-foot boat, white, with blue racing stripes on each side and a blue top. I didn't get a clear look at him, but we're looking for a white Caucasian"—he'd seen the guy's hands—"over six feet. He had on a blue baseball cap and black shorts."

"Johnny," Dennis said as he ran a hand over his face. *"Johnny."* Then he was spinning around and rushing back to his boat.

"What does that fucking kid Johnny have to do with this mess?" Gabe demanded.

Wade swallowed. "We saw that fucking kid driving a boat that looked just like that one—when we were racing hell fast to get to you."

Gabe could only stare at him. Johnny had looked barely twenty-one. He was a *kid*. "He can't be the killer. He's too young." Too young for the profile. Too young to have taken the victims that had been recovered at that golf course.

Wade gave a sad shake of his head. "You and I both know . . . sometimes, evil can start early. It can take root in some people, get in them, twist them, until there's nothing good left inside of them."

Eve pulled away from Gabe's arms.

"He can't be the killer," Gabe said once more. Sarah had been the one to come up with the profile. Sarah wasn't wrong. She'd never been wrong. "But maybe that little prick knows who we're looking for." Because maybe . . . maybe the killer had taken on some help as the cops closed in . . .

Eve hurried away from Gabe, heading toward the rescue boat.

Gabe took a step after her.

Wade's hand landed on his shoulder. "Those are scratch marks on your face."

Gabe glanced at his friend.

Wade lifted his brows. "You think I wouldn't know? I'm calling bullshit on those marks coming from the blast." His jaw hardened. "What went down out here?"

I'm not good. "It was just like I told you. We found Alexa. Found the killer's trophies, and then our boat was blown to hell." By some punk kid? "We need to dig deeper," Gabe told Wade. "Because this whole mess is bigger than we thought. There are more victims. They're out there."

Wade nodded. "And our job is to find them."

Yes, it was. No matter what the cost.

VICTORIA PALMER STARED down at the skeleton before her. She'd been working meticulously with the bones, arranging them so carefully on her table in the anatomical position—the exact pose the body would be in if she had a body lying there, and not just bones.

She already knew that she was looking at a female victim. That was obvious from the pelvic bones. Now she needed to figure out the victim's age, her ancestry . . . and how she'd died.

But Victoria had already seen some of the marks on the bones. The indentions that had cut deep—*when the killer sliced her to the bone.* She'd seen marks like that before, and she knew a knife had been used on this woman.

Had the knife attack killed her? Well, that would be determined soon enough. But first . . . "Who were you?" Victoria asked the woman. "And how did you wind up with that bastard?"

She measured the bones, moving carefully. Taking her time. "I want to get everything right for you." Victoria had been given a small work space in the back of the police station. The FBI had wanted her to get to work right away. Sure, they'd be bringing in their own experts, but her credentials and clearance had gotten her fast access to the victim's remains. It wasn't the first time that she'd worked in conjunction with an FBI investigation, and it wouldn't be her last.

Who were you?

She made notes on her laptop. The bone measurements would help her to determine the victim's stature. She already suspected that she was looking at a victim who'd stood at approximately five feet, four inches.

Gloves covered Victoria's hands as she leaned forward to expect the victim's teeth.

No wisdom teeth. Dental growth was key when determining a victim's age. The bones and the teeth—they could tell you so much.

Bones changed over time. When people were babies, their "bones" were made up of a lot of soft cartilage. That cartilage had to harden as the person aged—growth and fusion took place throughout the body. It was those fusion sites that could tell her so much.

After she'd checked her fusion sites, Victoria moved on to the skull. Most people thought the skull was just one piece—they were wrong. The skull consisted of sutures—fusions that closed over time.

It's all about time.

She checked her notes. Measured again.

And felt more sadness sweep over her.

Based on the length of the bones and the projected height, she'd thought the killer had taken another adult female.

But she'd been wrong.

Her gloved fingers slid over the skull. Not for any sort of measurement this time, but in sorrow. "You were so young," she whispered.

So young to be attacked. To be murdered and walled away.

The door opened behind her. Victoria blinked quickly, but she didn't turn to face whoever her visitor was. She was afraid that her face would give away her emotions.

"Viki?" That was Sarah's voice, and Sarah was her friend, but she'd seen far too much.

I don't want her knowing all my secrets. So Victoria was always so extra careful around Sarah. Most people at LOST were.

"I'm working on my report," Victoria said, hoping her voice sounded normal. "I'll have my notes to you soon." Because what she was discovering would completely change Sarah's profile of the killer.

"Something has happened at the lighthouse."

Victoria glanced at her. Wade had mentioned that Gabe and Eve had been heading to the lighthouse that morning. "Gabe—"

"He's okay. We just got a radio from one of the cops on the scene . . . Gabe and Eve are both okay." Sarah stepped closer. "But they found Alexa Chambers."

She could tell by Sarah's voice that the woman hadn't been found alive.

"They also found the killer's trophy stash."

Victoria flinched. Yes, she could work with the dead all day long, but the way Sarah got into the minds of the killers, the way she talked about them as if their horrific actions were totally normal—*I could never do that.*

But then, Victoria knew Sarah's secrets. Most of them anyway. *Maybe it's not fair that I know so much about her.* But with Sarah, well, it was hard to hide her past.

When your father was a notorious serial killer and his exploits were splashed all across the media, you didn't exactly get the luxury of privacy. Or secrets.

"Gabe thinks that there are more victims than we realized."

Victoria glanced back at the skeleton. If she was right about that victim's age . . . "Yes." Her voice was soft. Sad. There were going to be more out there.

Sarah walked toward the table. Stared down at the bones. Sarah was never squeamish, never scared. She didn't show much emotion at all.

How much did you see, Sarah? When you were growing up with that monster of a father?

Though it sure wasn't like Victoria could judge. Her father hadn't murdered ten women—*Sarah's held that distinction*—but her own bastard of a father had killed her mother in a jealous rage.

"Do you think she suffered?" Sarah asked as she stared down at the bones.

"Yes," Victoria said again. Normally she had plenty to say, but here, with the girl's remains, too much sorrow filled her.

Sarah glanced at her. "They all suffer, don't they? Or else, what's the point?"

Victoria shivered at Sarah's words. Sometimes, her friend terrified her.

A CROWD WAS waiting at the dock when the rescue boat pulled in. Eve glanced at the sea of faces—most of their features were a blur to her. It was the emotions that she saw. Curiosity. Fear.

They don't want the killer on their island. They don't want to be victims.

Neither did she.

But I'm not a victim . . .

Eve was afraid she was something else entirely.

"Jessica!" Her head jerked to the right at that call. The tall blond man there—she knew him. Pierce Montgomery. The brother who'd been so hesitant to claim her in Atlanta. But he was on the edge of the dock now, and the emotion on his face—*it's fear, just like the others.*

Trey was at his side. "Dammit, everybody, get back!" he barked to the crowd.

As soon as the boat was secure, Eve jumped onto the dock. It seemed to tremble beneath her feet. A strong hand steadied her—Pierce's hand. She looked up into his eyes. Saw the fear there and thought—

He's looked at me that way before. With fear in his eyes.

"You shouldn't have gone out there," he murmured. "Not without me."

"Am I your sister?"

A muscle jerked in his jaw.

"Do you know me . . . know all my secrets?"

His eyes widened and there was a realization there. "Yes . . ." But the word was low, like a warning.

Trey had gotten the crowd back, mostly. "This place is a damn circus!" He marched toward Eve and Pierce. His gaze swept over her. She had a blanket around her shoulders and her wet clothes still clung tightly to her. "Are you okay?"

Eve pulled that blanket closer, trying to shield herself. Gabe was still on the boat. Wade had stayed back at the island, he wanted to work with the FBI and the recovery team that was being sent in.

"I'm not hurt." That was the truth. As far as being okay? *No.*

"We've got a full search on for Johnny," Trey said, voice curt. "We'll find that guy. You can count on it. Dammit . . . *Johnny. Johnny Thompson.* The kid was always trouble, from the minute Clay brought him into town."

If he'd already left the island, Trey wouldn't be finding him. And why would the guy have stayed?

"I should have been here," Pierce said. His hand closed around her shoulders. "I thought it was better to stay away—*I'm sorry.*"

What was he sorry for? He hadn't done anything to her.

Gabe made his way off the boat. She didn't turn to look at him, but she could see him approaching from the corner of her eye. Her body was too attuned to his. Whenever he was near, she reacted.

He's the only man I react to. Trey is handsome, strong, a cop. I look at him, and, despite our past, I feel nothing. She didn't even feel safe around him. Why not?

She cleared her throat. The images in her head were about to drive her crazy. "Can we go to your office?" Eve asked Trey, ducking her head toward him. "I—I need to talk with you."

"Of course," Trey said quickly. "You know you can always tell me anything."

"*Eve.*" Gabe's voice held a sharp, warning note.

Pierce stiffened beside her. "You remember, don't you?" His hold tightened on her.

"I remember . . . a knife." *Blood on my hands. Laughing.* And she couldn't carry this guilt around in her mind. "I—I think . . ." The crowd had dispersed but her voice still dropped to a whisper. "I think I killed someone."

Shock flashed over Trey's face. "What?"

"Eve, no," Gabe snapped.

But in the next instant it was Pierce who took charge. Pierce who pulled her up against him, wrapping his arm around her side and holding her in a too-tight grip. "My sister doesn't know what she's saying."

She knew exactly what she was saying.

"And she has *no* more comments, not for the police. Not for the FBI." He gave Gabe a hard nod. "And your services are no longer needed."

What?

"Come on, Jessica, I'll take care of you." Then he started half pulling, half carrying her away from that dock. "Not another word," he whispered. "Please, Jess, *don't.*"

And she realized that Pierce knew exactly what she'd done.

"Hold the hell up." Trey ran around and blocked their path. "She just said she killed someone." Disbelief was on his face. "Sweetheart, what are you talking about? I've known you all my life. You aren't a killer."

Sweetheart. "Yes, I am." Gabe had moved to Trey's side. Another obstacle in her path. "And I think I liked it."

"No more!" Pierce's near-yell. "She doesn't know what she's saying. My sister is having a psychotic break. She's had one before, Trey, shit, you *know* I had to put her in the hospital before—"

"What?" Eve's shocked question cut through his words. She'd had a breakdown before?

"We're done here," Pierce said, pulling her close. *"Done.* Any questions for Jessica will need to go through my attorney."

Her body was shaking, splintering. *Wrong. Wrong. Wrong.* The word blasted through her mind again and again.

Trey's radio crackled to life. He yanked it up. "Wallace."

"Johnny was just spotted running into one of the fishing houses near the bridge. He's *there!*"

Trey whirled around. Over his shoulder Eve could

see the line of fishing houses, about ten of them. Big boats were behind those houses—shrimping boats with heavy nets that skimmed the top of the water.

"Keep him there!" Trey yelled into his phone as he began to run. "Do not approach, do you hear me? Do not approach! I want that kid brought in alive."

And he was racing away. As if she hadn't just confessed to murder. The guy didn't even have one of the other cops take her into custody.

But Gabe wasn't moving. Gabe was still there, staring down at her. His expression was unreadable. His body tense.

"You need to get out of our way." Pierce spoke in a low voice. "Your job is done. I have my sister and I'll take care of her from here on out."

He'd take care of her? He hadn't even been there . . .

Why didn't you help me?

Eve's breath choked out because that desperate question was like an echo in her mind, from so long ago.

And the dock disappeared. She saw herself in a white room. Her hands had been bound to the sides of the bed that she lay in. She'd been crying, thrashing. *Why aren't you helping me, Pierce?*

"Why didn't you help me?" she said now as she turned toward the man who was her brother.

He flinched.

"My job *isn't* done," Gabe said into the thick silence there. "And I don't fucking work for you." He reached for Eve's hand. "Come on. If Trey is arresting that Johnny bastard, we have to find out what the kid knows."

"Don't touch my sister!" Pierce yelled, his handsome face suddenly turning very dark. "You don't know—" But he was turning away from Gabe and pulling Eve closer to him. "I didn't want you to remember that part."

His voice was hushed. "That's why I stayed back. I was afraid that I'd make you remember, that by being with me . . . the past would come back." His words roughened. "I thought it might even be better, at first, if you *were* someone else. Because those memories have been ripping you apart for years."

She heard shouts then. Coming from that line of fishing houses. Trey was closing in on his prey.

A gunshot blasted.

"I said to stand back!" The roar of Trey's voice reached them.

More gunfire erupted. Pierce pulled Eve down beside him, taking shelter behind a boat that was tied close to the dock.

Gabe didn't crouch down with them. He ran toward the sound of that gunfire.

"Gabe!" Eve called out after him, frantic.

But he didn't turn back to her, and Pierce was holding her tightly.

"He can handle this, Eve." Pierce's gaze was on her. "We have to protect you. We have to figure out what to tell the cops, we have to—"

She broke away from him and ran after Gabe.

CHAPTER FOURTEEN

THE KID WAS SHOOTING AT TREY. GABE SAW THE police chief duck down behind a garbage can even as the guy called out a warning for Johnny to "Drop your weapon!"

Gunfire was Johnny's response.

There was another Dauphin Island officer there, a guy who was skulking low near the side of the fishing house on the right. The fishing houses were a narrow group of buildings, barely ten feet wide each, all brightly painted in island colors. Boats surrounded them.

Were you trying to get on another boat? Trying to get away?

But Johnny had been spotted before he could make that escape.

"You won't take me in!" Johnny screamed.

Yes, they would. Gabe kept close to the side of those fishing houses. He made sure not to present his body as a target. Trey and his officer had Johnny distracted up front. Now he just needed to work his way around the back and catch the guy off-guard.

But another shot rang out, and Gabe heard a sharp cry.

"Bastard hit me!" That wasn't Trey. The other officer had been hit.

And as Gabe watched, Trey broke from his cover and ran toward the fishing house that Johnny was inside. Trey had his gun out. Johnny was coming outside, not firing any longer. But walking straight out like a prisoner to his execution.

And Trey was lifting his gun, getting ready to shoot.

What the hell? What had happened to Trey's own words not to shoot the guy?

Trey's weapon was up. Gabe ran ahead and he leapt across the small porch of the house, grabbing for Johnny. He expected to hear the crack of gunfire.

But he didn't.

His body slammed into Johnny's, and when they hit the concrete, Johnny landed under Gabe. The idiot tried to fight him, so Gabe just grabbed the man's head and shoved it down. Johnny groaned.

Gabe looked over at Trey, thinking the man must have come to his senses before he'd fired, but—

Eve was there. Her hands were still wrapped around Trey's right arm—and the gun was still gripped in Trey's right hand.

She stopped him from firing.

Pierce rushed up behind her.

"I'll . . . never talk . . ." Johnny vowed.

"Yeah, you fucking will," Gabe promised him as he yanked the guy to his feet. The other officer rushed from the shadows, and blood gushed from the wound on his shoulder.

Johnny's gun had fallen when Gabe hit him. Gabe bent and grabbed that weapon, but he made sure to keep his hold on Johnny.

"This isn't . . . over, bastard!" Johnny told him.

"It is for you." That response came from Trey. He'd closed in on his prey. He yanked out his cuffs. Slapped the metal around Johnny's wrist. "After trying to kill two cops in front of witnesses, you can damn well bet that things are definitely *over* for you." He shook his head. "Your uncle is going to fucking not believe this shit!"

The cop started reading the guy his rights. Johnny was just laughing.

And then—

Johnny's laughter stopped. "Dead girl."

Gabe stiffened. Johnny was staring straight at Eve. Smiling at her.

"I remember you, dead girl. Do you remember me?"

Trey pulled the guy away from Eve.

Her expression had flickered, just a bit, when Johnny taunted her.

Dead girl.

And Gabe realized that Eve did remember the younger man.

"We need to go, Jessica." Pierce wrapped his hand around Eve's arm. "We need to get out of here *now*."

Trey froze, Johnny right at his side. "That's not happening." He glared at Pierce. "I want her at the police station. I want you both there. No one confesses to murder and walks away." His voice lowered as he stared at Eve. "Not even you, sweetheart."

And in the distance, thunder rumbled once more.

"DON'T SAY ANYTHING, Jessica. Do you understand? Not a word."

Gabe watched as Pierce paced in front of Eve—*Jessica.* Dammit, he had to get used to calling her that name soon.

They were in a small conference room at the PD. Pierce had tried to throw Gabe's ass out, but *Jessica* had refused. She'd said that she wanted him there with her. And with her was exactly the place he wanted to be.

"So . . ." Gabe leaned his shoulders against the wall. "Your memory is back."

She was seated at the small table in a slightly wobbly chair. He noticed that every few moments she would rock to the side in that chair. A movement prompted by fear?

"Not all of it." She looked up from the table and her green gaze focused on him. "Not even close. Just bits and pieces. Flashes that are . . . terrifying."

"Jessica." Pierce's face was so red that Gabe thought the man might literally explode. "Please, I'm begging you . . . *stop.*"

But she shook her head. "I don't have secrets from Gabe. He's been the one to help me, from the very beginning."

Pierce reached for her hand. "You have secrets, you just didn't know about them—"

She snatched her hand away from him. "Because *you* didn't clue me in to them. You walked in Gabe's office wearing your fancy suit, and you said you didn't even know if I was your sister." Anger hardened her delicate jaw. "You lied, Pierce. You knew then. *You knew.*"

Pierce's shoulders hunched. "Yes." Shame was in that confession.

Gabe shot away from the wall. "Then why the hell didn't you say something?" The guy had just walked out that day, and left his sister behind. *With no money, no help . . . nothing.*

Pierce spun to face him. "Because if she didn't have

her memories, then she didn't have her nightmares! I thought it might be better for her!"

What a freaking idiot. Gabe's hands had fisted at his sides and he sure loved the idea of plunging his fist into Pierce's pretty-boy face.

"Better?" Eve repeated. She was still in the chair, but now her hands had flattened on the tabletop. "To think that I was unwanted? That no one out there cared at all that I was alive? Or dead?"

Anguish seemed to twist Pierce's face. "You don't know what your past was like. Dammit, Jessica, I had to put you under suicide watch when you were just sixteen!"

Sixteen . . . the age she'd been when her parents died in that boating accident.

Sixteen . . .

Ten years ago.

"You took a bottle of pills. I—I barely found you in time. Your stomach was pumped, you were delirious, and you were just saying that you wanted to die. *That's when I had to have you hospitalized.* You were under the suicide watch."

Gabe's heart stopped. His eyes were on Eve—*fuck, to me, she will always be Eve.* And he couldn't look away.

She held herself so still. No more rocking in that unsteady chair. Her skin was too pale. Her hair had dried, so had her clothes, and she looked . . . lost.

"Did I kill someone?" Eve asked quietly.

Pierce's gaze flew to Gabe. "You need to leave. I have to talk with my sister—"

Eve leapt to her feet. Her chair screeched as it flew back behind her. *"Did I kill someone?"* Her voice was a shout.

"No!" Pierce shouted back at her. Then his eyes widened in horror. "I'm sorry. I didn't mean to yell at you." He raked a hand through his hair. "You tried, okay? You tried to kill the bastard, and he totally had it coming."

Eve looked so fragile. Like she'd shatter at any moment. *She won't. She's strong.* "What bastard?" Gabe demanded.

Pierce glanced toward the door. "Is this place wired? Is Trey listening to us?"

He had no clue, and right then he didn't care. "What bastard?"

But Pierce shook his head. "When we get out of here, Jessica, I'll tell you everything. Just not a word now, okay? Trey won't let his feelings for you hold him back. He's a black and white guy, always has been. That's why you left him at the end. You knew if he ever found out, he'd turn away from you. You said you couldn't count on him. That's what you told me."

"I was laughing." Eve stared down at her hands. "And there was blood on my hands. Why would I do that?"

"Because he deserved the pain you gave him."

The guy just needed to stop with the bull and come right out and *say* what he meant.

Eve's hands clenched into fists. "I don't think I was the Lady Killer's victim."

Now *that* sure as hell surprised Gabe. He crossed to Eve, unable to stay away.

"I have these flashes . . ." She waved her fist in the air. "I can hear his voice, low, rasping, and he's telling me that we're playing a game together."

The door opened then. Trey stood on the threshold, looking weary but determined. FBI Agent Avery Granger was behind him.

"We've got some information you all are going to want to hear," Trey said as he marched into the room.

He motioned toward the table. "Jessica, you're gonna want to sit down."

Considering she'd just jumped up from that table, Gabe wasn't particularly surprised by the negative shake of her head.

"Right. Fine." Trey was holding a manila envelope. He opened the envelope and a plastic bag spilled onto the table. A bag that contained a gleaming diamond tennis bracelet.

Gabe frowned at the evidence. "Is that one of the pieces recovered from the guy's trophy box?"

"No." Trey's voice was clipped. "This piece was around the wrist of Alexa Chambers, only it didn't belong to her." His gaze was on Eve. "It belonged to you."

She shook her head. But this time the shake was slow, uncertain.

"There's an inscription inside, one that I'm pretty damn familiar with, since it says, 'To J, with all my love . . . P.' "

Surprise flashed in her eyes.

"The bracelet was yours." Pierce's voice was wooden. "I bought it for you after . . . after our parents' death."

Eve didn't speak.

Trey exhaled on a long sigh. "There's blood in the diamonds. Maybe that blood is Alexa's. Maybe it's yours. Maybe it's both—"

"Why would my bracelet be around her wrist?"

"Why indeed?" It was Agent Avery who asked the question. "Why do all the victims look like you? I thought the guy was just fixated on blondes, that *you* were unfortunate enough to fit his victim profile, but now I'm not so sure."

There was another knock at the door.

Avery called out, "Come in."

And the door opened to reveal Sarah.

"I figured it would be best if your psychiatrist joined us for this part," Avery said. "Especially since she's been working so hard to understand the killer for us all."

Sarah looked . . . nervous. And she wasn't meeting Gabe's stare.

What the hell?

"Why would the killer put that bracelet on Alexa's wrist?" Avery asked.

Pierce moved closer to Eve. "I don't understand what's happening here—"

"Oh, sorry," Avery said, sounding anything but. "Let me clarify . . . we're trying to catch a killer, and I'm using the best psychiatrist in the area to try and explain the psychopath's motivations. Does that clear things up for you?"

Silence.

Sarah cleared her throat. "Victoria . . . she's determined an age for the victim that we found in the fort." Now she did look at Gabe. "She was only sixteen."

Shit.

"And Victoria thinks that she was killed ten years ago."

When Eve would have been sixteen, too.

"Tell me more . . ." Avery murmured, and Gabe realized that the FBI agent already knew this information. The guy was too certain, his gaze too assessing as it stayed on Eve.

What did they discover while I was out on that island?

"I've been doing an age chronology for the other victims that we've identified," Sarah said. "Their ages vary slightly, and I think . . . I think he was increasing the age of his victim, as he aged."

Gabe wasn't sure he followed. "So he started killing sixteen-year-old girls . . ."

"When I think he was younger. And as he aged . . . and as the target of his—his affection aged . . ." Sarah seemed to stumble a bit as she used that word. "So did the ages of his victims."

Gabe cut his eyes back to Eve.

The target of his affection.

"It's unusual." Sarah's voice was mild, clinical. "Typically in cases like this, the serial has a type—a set age, a set hair color, a vision of the perfect victim that doesn't change over time."

Eve crept closer to Sarah. "But his vision changed."

Sarah nodded. "Yes," she said softly.

"Why?"

Sympathy flashed across Sarah's face. "Because I think you changed."

Eve froze.

"Avery told me about the bracelet on Alexa's wrist . . . your bracelet. I suspect the killer placed that bracelet there to send a message."

"What message?" It was Pierce who made this demand. "The man out there is crazy, he—"

"He wanted us to know—wanted you to know, Eve—that he's always been killing you. Each woman, *she's you*." Sarah's expression was grim. "He put that bracelet on Alexa because he wasn't killing her, he was killing—"

"I get the picture." Her voice was low and husky—far huskier than it normally was. Her gaze flashed to Gabe, and he was stunned to see the guilt in her stare. "But I don't think *you* fully understand," Eve said. "What if I'm not his victim, what if I'm—"

"Dammit, Jessica!" Pierce erupted, and he grabbed her arms. "Enough. *Enough.*"

"Yeah, that is fucking enough, buddy." Gabe's voice

was low and lethal. Because the guy was holding her far too roughly, his fingers digging deep into Eve's skin. "Get your hands off her. *Now.*"

Pierce's hold eased, but he didn't let her go.

"I don't want you to throw away your life. You weren't helping that freak out there," Pierce said. "You *weren't.*"

"Move your hands." Gabe advanced with intent. Eve's fear was killing him. "Or I will move them for you."

And Trey was also leaning in close to Pierce. "If Jessica has a confession to make, I want to hear it."

Pierce shook his head. His gaze never left Eve's. "Please," he whispered. "I'm trying to protect you."

His hands slid from her shoulders. Straightening his spine, he glanced over at Trey. "Don't you have a suspect in custody? Shouldn't you be interrogating *him*?"

"I will be . . . right after I hear Jessica's confession. After all, she did tell me that she killed someone."

"She doesn't remember what she did or didn't do! My sister is troubled, always has been."

Sarah frowned at that. Gabe and Sarah had done their best to pull up Jessica Montgomery's medical records. They hadn't found, any notation of her suicide attempt or her hospitalization.

"Why is she so troubled?" Sarah asked.

Pierce's lips clamped together. "There are no more questions. No more answers. Leslie Van Knight is my attorney. *Our* attorney. All questions will go through her."

Trey shouldered Pierce out of his way. "Is that really how you want to play things?" he asked Eve. "Hiding behind a lawyer? 'Cause I never would have thought that was your style."

Gabe didn't move. He was waiting to see how this scene played out.

"Maybe you don't know my style," she told Trey softly.

Anger slit his eyes. "Like you do? You can't even remember your own damn name, your lover, your art—nothing. It's all gone for you, and you're screwing this asshole over here"—he jerked his thumb toward Gabe—"because you'd rather be with a stranger than someone who actually gives a shit about you."

Enough. "The asshole can hear," Gabe said, "and you need to watch your step, police chief." It was the only warning he'd give the guy. "You aren't going to talk to her like that." Gabe stepped in front of Eve. He rubbed her shoulders, deliberately keeping his touch light and reassuring. "Your brother's right. You're done here. Anything else you need to say to the cop, it can go through your lawyer." Then he caught her hand. Her fingers were shaking as he twined his fingers with hers. "It's time to get the hell out of here."

"She's not leaving!" Trey shouted. Avery was in the background, silent, watchful. "I'm not letting her leave again, I'm not just going to let her—"

"She's not under arrest." Gabe's voice was flat. *Cop, back the fuck off.* "You have nothing to hold her on. And as you just said yourself . . ." He turned to glare at Trey. ". . . she doesn't have her memory, so Eve doesn't know what she was saying before. No confession can be trusted from her."

Gabe's fingers squeezed hers. He wanted to reassure Eve. But he also didn't want to say too much, not with Trey and Avery watching them too closely.

Then he led her to the door. The sooner he got her out of that place, the better he would feel. Pierce hurried to keep up with them, but he was still spouting off and telling Trey to stay away from the Montgomery family.

Ordering Trey to do his job and to question Johnny Thompson.

Sarah watched Gabe and Eve, and he sure as hell wanted to know what she was thinking. Sarah inclined her head, and he knew they'd be having a private talk right away. *Good. Because I don't like it when I feel like my own team is working against me.*

Or . . . against Eve.

Then they were out in the hallway. More cops were there. Dean and Victoria were milling around, too. He'd have to get the team together, away from the cops, and find out what they'd all discovered.

Gabe paused next to Dean. "Use your pull with the FBI," he muttered, his voice low and only carrying to Eve and Dean. "Get into the interrogation with Johnny." Because that would be going down soon. "I want to know exactly what that little prick has to say."

Dean's head moved in the slightest of nods.

Gabe glanced down at Eve. "It's going to be all right." He needed her to believe him.

Eve glanced down at her hand.

"You can trust me," he told her.

"But can you trust me?" she asked him. The pain in her voice tore at his heart. "Because I'm not even sure I trust myself."

"You can't keep me locked up in here!" Johnny Thompson yelled as he yanked on his cuffs. Those bastards had *chained* him to the table. It was freaking bull. They couldn't do this to him! "I know my rights!" he shouted toward the closed door. "I want a lawyer! I want a phone call! I want—"

The door opened. "I want you to calm the hell down."

That wasn't Trey standing in the doorway. It was

some blond jerk in a dress shirt—some fool who looked like he'd never worked a day in his life, and he was shadowed by another guy—tall, dark hair, eyes that were freaking ice.

"Who the hell are you? Where's Trey?"

The blond man pulled out a chair and sat across from him. "I'm FBI Agent Avery Granger. I'll be the one questioning you."

The FBI?

His gaze cut to the other guy. The silent one. "You FBI, too?"

"Dean Bannon is a . . . consultant on this case," Avery said smoothly.

Well, big fucking deal. Johnny leaned forward. "I want the cuffs off."

Avery shrugged. "I want answers. You help me, and maybe I'll help you."

He wasn't helping the bastard at all.

"Were you at Sand Island today?" Avery asked him.

Johnny smiled even as his heart thundered in his chest. "Never heard of the place."

Avery's stare didn't leave his face. "Did you take your uncle's boat out there, and did you rig Gabe Spencer's boat to explode?"

"Gabe Spencer," he repeated, rubbing his nose. His *broken* nose. "That jerk needs to get his ass beat."

Finally, the dark-haired guy spoke. "And you think you're the one to do it?"

Johnny laughed. "Trey should . . . if he had balls. I mean, that Gabe guy comes rolling into town, and he's obviously fucking Trey's girl. Shit, if it were me—"

He broke off because he knew that he'd just made a mistake.

"If it were you, what?" Avery asked.

Screw it. He was already in too deep, but there hadn't been a choice. "I'd teach the bastard a lesson."

Dean cocked his head. "The kind of lesson where you make his boat explode?"

He didn't answer.

Avery pushed a manila file across to him, then opened the file and started spreading pictures out before him.

"Shit!" Johnny's gaze jerked away from the photos. "What the hell is this?"

"A dead girl parade," Dean said. "I mean, that is what you called it the other night, isn't it? When you were trying to convince your girlfriend that it would be a good idea to go and have a screw where all these poor women were buried."

They didn't really look like women, not anymore. "Get that shit away from me!"

"We found evidence of more murders out at the light-house. We found the body of Alexa Chambers—"

"I didn't have *nothin'* to do with that!" Were they trying to pin this shit on him?

"We also found other trophies that the killer had taken and a map that we believe may lead us to additional victims."

Johnny jumped out of his chair, but the cuffs didn't let him move far. "I didn't kill those women!"

"But you *did* go to Sand Island today, didn't you? You caused the explosion."

Johnny's gaze flew to the door. "I want to see the police chief."

"You're seeing me." Avery's voice was flat.

Johnny kicked out at the table. "I want Trey in here! I want him in here, *now*! He's not going to pin this shit on me! I did my part. I did exactly what I was supposed to do, and I'm not going down for this—"

"Your part?" Dean asked him. "Just what part was that?"

His breath heaved in and out, seeming to burn his lungs. "I ain't saying another word. Not until I see Trey, do you understand?" Those FBI bastards were trying to railroad him. Trey would help him.

"You shot a cop."

He swallowed. "He was shooting at me." *Kill or be killed . . .*

"Bullshit," Avery snapped. "You were trying to run away, and when you got caught, you decided to go down fighting."

Because he wasn't about to get tossed in a cage.

"You're going away," Dean said, as he took his time walking toward Johnny. "For a long time. So if you want any leniency from the government, now's the time to talk. Now is the time for you to tell us everything that you know about the Lady Killer."

His frantic heartbeat was shaking his whole chest. "What makes you think I know anything?"

Dean stared at him. "You shot a cop. You attacked Gabe and Jessica Montgomery. You wouldn't have done that for no reason."

The cuffs bit into his wrists.

"Tell us the reason, Johnny. Tell us why you went over the edge."

His chin jerked up. "I didn't go over no edge."

"Then tell us . . . *why?*"

The door to that little room opened again. Only this time Trey was there. Looking furious, his cheeks red, his eyes blazing. But he directed that fury at the FBI agent. "You started the interrogation without me?"

Johnny saw Avery's shoulders stiffen. "The FBI is in charge of this investigation—"

Trey stalked closer to the guy. And closer to Johnny.

Johnny's gaze dropped. Trey had his weapon holstered on his right hip.

"*My* man was shot," Trey nearly yelled at him. "This is my island, my people—"

"And your people have been dying for a while."

Trey jumped closer. He was just two feet away from Johnny. "You don't interrogate my people without me!"

Johnny leapt forward then, trying desperately to get that gun—

But Dean grabbed him. Shit, he'd forgotten about him. He'd been so silent—

Dean shoved him back into the chair, held him there with a grip of steel. "Not going to work like that," Dean told him in a voice that made Johnny's whole body tense. "You're not going to attack us, and you're sure as hell not going to go out the easy way."

Easy way.

Johnny tried to heave against his hold. "Nothin' easy . . . about it!"

Suicide wasn't easy. His mother had gone out like that, because she'd been so sick of being an abusive bastard's punching bag. But it hadn't been easy. She'd bled out so slowly. That blood had soaked her rug before she died.

"Why did you go after them?" Dean asked him.

"L-Lawyer . . ."

"Did you kill those girls?" Dean pressed. "Your 'parade of dead girls' out there?"

Johnny glared back at them.

"I don't think you did. I think you were too young for some of those murders. But I think . . . I think you know who did kill them." Dean shoved him away.

Johnny sat back down. The cuffs were still cutting

into him. He tried to look like he wasn't scared. That he didn't give a shit. That was the way *he* would look. *I can do this. I can—*

Trey had paced away from him but suddenly whirled back around. "Where's your uncle, Johnny?"

Johnny blanched.

And Trey's narrowed eyes said he saw the telling movement. "We tried to contact him at the marina and I sent a man to his house . . . but he wasn't there."

"He was . . . helping with the search," Johnny lied. "You know that. He's probably still out on one of the boats."

Now Avery was leaning over the table. "We're going to search your house. Your marina. We're going to tear your life apart."

"And your uncle's life," Dean added.

Johnny stared down at the table. He didn't have anything else to say to these SOBs.

"Where is Clay?" Trey asked him.

Trey and his uncle used to be such good friends. Back in the day. Before a woman had torn them apart. Johnny started laughing then, because he just couldn't help it. "She screwed you over in the end, the same way she did him."

Trey slapped the table. *"Where is he?"*

"It's over," Johnny said. "All fucking over." He forced his head to lift. "Now get me a lawyer."

EVE WAS BACK on the balcony at the condo. Pierce was a few feet away, watching her too carefully, and Gabe—he was close. Not touching her, but watching, just like Pierce.

She was tired of everyone watching her.

Pierce cleared his throat. "You need to . . . let me know how much I owe you, Spencer. I can give you a check and you and your team can be off the island by dusk." He waved toward the ocean's waves. "There's talk of a tropical storm rolling in soon, so it'd be better if you were—"

"I'm not leaving Eve."

"Jessica," Pierce fired back. "Her name is—"

"I like Eve," she said, staring out at the water. She could see the dark clouds in the distance. They reminded her of the smoke she'd seen before, back on Sand Island. "I know Eve. Jessica . . . I'm not sure I want to know her."

"What?" Pierce caught her arm and pulled her around to face him. "You're not making sense."

"Secrets," she said, the word sad as it fell from her lips. "How many have you been keeping?"

His gaze darted to Gabe. "I told you before, we could talk privately—"

"I trust him."

Gabe edged closer to her. The wind tossed locks of her hair around her face.

"He's helped me from the beginning, when no one else would. And he asked for nothing in return."

Pierce's cheeks reddened. "You've known him for days—"

She laughed. "Yes, well, currently, that's my record, you see. Because I don't think the hazy memories count. And since I've known him longer than I've known anyone else . . ." She gave her brother a weak smile. "I'm trusting him."

Anger glinted in Pierce's eyes. "Because you're fucking him."

Why was everyone so concerned about her sex life?

She took a step back and her shoulders bumped into Gabe.

"Yes," he said flatly. "She is."

Ah, okay.

Pierce shook his head. "I thought you were past that."

Past having sex?

"But I guess . . . with all the trauma . . . you reverted."

He'd totally lost her. Probably because the guy was running around and keeping his secrets. "What are you talking about?"

Pierce's lips thinned. "It's because of what he did . . . what he tried to do. That's why you . . . acted out with men when you were younger."

Her own mouth parted in surprise.

"The shrinks said you were trying to take control back, by taking those lovers." He turned from her. Stared out at the water. "You were so young. And you were running wild. Sleeping with Trey. With Clay Thompson . . . with others that I don't even know about."

She backed even closer to Gabe.

"With anyone who caught your eye. You didn't have to *know* the guys for long. And, hell, it's not like you really wanted them. Though they sure wanted you. The men took one look, and they wanted you." Pierce glanced back at her, at Gabe. "That's what's happened with you, right, Spencer? You took one look, and you wanted. And I guess Jessica fell back into her old habits."

He sounded furious with her.

But . . . whatever, so Jessica had enjoyed lovers. Men did that crap all the time. They had plenty of lovers and no one cared. Why did that make her—

"Each lover you took just made things worse for you,"

Pierce said, and some of the anger had slid from him. "The darkness he'd made inside of you just got worse."

He'd made?

A half smile—one that looked both sad and angry—twisted Pierce's lips. "Do you still sleep with your clothes on, Jessica? Those long sweatpants and the T-shirts that swallow you?"

An ache was in her stomach. She pressed back, edging ever closer to Gabe. His arm curled around her shoulder, holding her tight. "Y-Yes . . ."

"Want to know why you do that?"

No. "Yes."

"Because he would watch you when you were younger. He'd come into your room . . ."

She shook her head even as she felt tears begin to sting her eyes. *This isn't right. This isn't—*

"I didn't know, not for so long. You didn't tell me, and I thought you realized you could tell me anything."

Come with me, sweetheart, let's play a game . . .

That voice was in her head, but she couldn't see the man it belonged to. She never could.

"The lighthouse . . ." Eve murmured.

Pain flashed over Pierce's face. "He used to take us there. And there . . . he tried to hurt you."

A tear slid down her cheek.

"You must have known what he had planned." Pierce's voice was so low, like a growl. "Because you had a knife. I—I heard you laughing, screaming and laughing, and I rushed inside. You'd stabbed him."

Blood on my hands.

"Who was the fucker who did this?" Gabe's voice was savage.

"Our father," Pierce said. "The man who had the ear

of presidents. The man who sat on the board of a dozen charities. The man who was a damn monster."

I won't let him touch me. She could almost hear herself saying those words. *I'll kill him first.*

"I stopped you." Pierce's shoulders hunched. "Maybe I shouldn't . . . you . . . you broke after that."

Gabe's arm tightened around her.

"Started sleeping with Trey, with Clay, with them all . . . one after the other. You were choosing, you said. *You* were in control."

Her skin was itching, burning. No, she was burning, from the inside out.

"Then he and our mother died in that accident, and you—you tried to take your own life." He stepped closer to her. Torment was clear to see on his face. "You were all I had left. Was I supposed to just let you go? I did everything I could . . . *everything* . . . to save you. I sent you to that hospital, I got you therapy, I got you help, and you were strong again. You were better, until . . ."

Until she'd vanished?

"I just want you better," Pierce whispered to her. "And there is nothing to be gained by telling Trey about your past. That will only raise suspicion. He'll wonder . . . did you kill them? He'll wonder because, Christ, *I wondered,* too."

That hole inside of her was getting bigger with every moment that passed. "Is it any surprise . . ." Her voice was so cold. ". . . that I wanted to forget my life?"

Pierce shook his head. "No."

"I . . . I need you to leave." She was about to bowl over with the pain. She couldn't do that. She needed *control.*

Pierce drew in a long breath. "I kept telling you that Spencer needed to leave. Now he should—"

She grabbed for Gabe's hand. Held tight. "Not him.

You. I need you to leave. I—I can't talk to you right now." Too much was happening. She didn't want to shatter in front of him. He was a stranger.

Pierce actually backed up a step, as if she'd just struck him. "But I love you. I want to help you."

She believed him. He did love his sister.

"I should have helped before. I should have seen it. But he was my *father*! The damn great Montgomery legend. When I came home from college, I kept noticing that you were more withdrawn, I knew something was happening, but I couldn't figure out what. Not until it was too late." His voice was hoarse. *"I don't want to be too late again."*

She shivered. She couldn't keep talking to him. Couldn't keep hearing more about her past. She didn't want to be Jessica. She wanted to be Eve.

Eve . . . who'd woken in that hospital, scared but not shattered. Alive.

Eve . . . who'd met Gabe. Who looked into his eyes and found a man she could trust.

Eve . . . who'd wanted Gabe, not for any other reason than that he made her *feel*. Passion. Need. Desire.

"Leave now," Gabe said as he pulled Eve so that she was standing behind him. "Can't you tell she needs time? You just—"

He broke off and she was afraid of what he might say. *You just destroyed her.*

Because that was how she felt.

So her father had molested her? She'd tried to kill him? Maybe she *had* killed him? Her own brother thought so.

She'd slept with men she couldn't remember.

And she kept seeing blood on her hands.

"When you broke up with Trey," Pierce's voice was

haggard, "I was afraid you were . . . falling back into your old routine. He told me that you—you'd been spotted with different men in town, that you were flirting wildly at the marina party that night."

Did I sleep with the man who tried to kill me?

"Go," Gabe gritted again. "She's had enough for today."

Her knees felt like they were about to give way.

This isn't me. This isn't me. He's wrong. He doesn't know.

But . . . her brother should know.

Gabe stopped waiting for Pierce to move on his own. As Eve watched, eyes widening, he grabbed Pierce and hauled him off the balcony and back into the condo. She watched them through the glass doors. Before Gabe pushed Pierce out of the penthouse, he bent and whispered something to her brother. Something that made Pierce jerk back and shake his head.

Gabe spoke again, the words too low for her to hear.

And Pierce left, hurrying away. He looked over at her right before the front door shut.

Then he was just . . . gone.

Let's play a game . . .

Eve shook her head, hard.

No games. No more. Not ever.

Her hand curled in, as if . . . as if the fingers were curling around a knife.

No games.

"Eve?"

Her head whipped up. Gabe was there. Staring at her with a gaze she couldn't read.

She needed to know what he was feeling. Disgust. Pity. Fear. What did he feel when he looked at her? *What?*

He was about five feet from her. She couldn't force her body to move an inch in order to get closer to him.

"We need to talk," Gabe said, voice quiet. Too quiet.

He's going to leave . . . he doesn't want me anymore. Not now that he knows about me.

"Yes." She had to move, but she couldn't. She had to—

"I'm not the man you think."

He was moving slowly toward her. His blue eyes were on hers, staring hard and deep.

He was so wrong, though. He was exactly the man she thought he was. True and strong and—

His hand lifted. His knuckles brushed over her cheek. "You're afraid."

Afraid that he was going to leave. That she was a monster. A killer. Yes, she was afraid of plenty right then.

"Why?" His hand was warm against her cheek.

"Because of . . . what I've done."

He kissed her.

Eve was so stunned that her heart actually seemed to stop in that instant. It wasn't a rough kiss. Wasn't wild with passion or fury. Just . . .

Tasting.

Claiming?

"I'm not the man you think," he said against her lips. "And if anyone can understand darkness, baby, it's me."

He was wrong. He—

"It's time you knew the truth about me." His head lifted, just a few more inches. His eyes . . . so blue . . . so deep. "I tried to tell you before that I wasn't some hero."

To her, he was.

"If you're pushed far enough, anyone can go over the edge."

Her breath seemed too ragged. "Have you been pushed . . . ?"

"You know someone took my sister."

She managed a nod.

"By the time the cops realized she wasn't with her ex, she'd been missing for days . . . fucking *days*. They thought there was no chance that she was still alive. They gave up on her."

Eve had goose bumps on her arms.

"I'd been in that VA hospital, fighting for my life, fighting to get free so I could go to her." The lines near his mouth deepened. "When I finally got loose, Wade and I didn't give up on her. Wade wasn't like the rest of those jerks in the homicide department—he wasn't backing down. But the days kept slipping by, and soon I thought . . . maybe I'll just be finding her body. Maybe that's what I'll be bringing back home."

"Gabe—"

"I had to bring her home."

Her lips wanted to tremble so she pressed them together. Her hands wanted to reach for him, so she wrapped them around her stomach.

"We realized the guy who had taken her had been a patient she'd seen at the hospital. We found him at an old cabin in the mountains." He swallowed and the soft click was almost painful to hear. "My sister was dead . . . but she hadn't been dead for long. It was still *her* when I looked at the body. He'd kept her alive all that time. Tortured her. She'd fought to hold on, fought to live long enough to come back to me, and I got to her *too late*."

Too late. Those were the same words that Pierce had said, only now they knifed right into Eve.

"He was there, that bastard who'd taken her. Talking about voices in his head, voices that made him hurt women. He *told* me that he'd killed her two days ago. He just told me. Wade had his badge, so I guess the guy thought we were just going to take him and get him locked up in a psych ward once he started spouting his stories."

"He . . . he didn't realize she was your sister."

"Not until I started punching him."

She backed up a step, instinctively. His gaze noted the movement, but no change of expression crossed his hard face.

"Wade had to pull me off him. I wanted to beat the bastard to death with my bare hands."

He looked down at his hands now. So did she. Strong, powerful hands. Hands that had caressed every part of her body.

"I've got blood there, too, baby. Blood that won't ever wash away."

He understood.

"The guy went for a scalpel . . . a scalpel he'd used on her. Seemed the man liked to play doctor with the nurses, only he wanted to cut them open, not heal them. He came at me with that scalpel . . ." His gaze lifted. Held hers. As if he had to be sure that she was paying attention to this part. "And I shot him in the heart."

Her breath exploded from her lungs. "Y-You were defending yourself."

"I was a SEAL. I could have disarmed him in a dozen ways. I didn't want to. I wanted him dead. Wade knew that, he knew exactly what I'd done, but he still backed up my story."

She wasn't retreating any longer.

"There was plenty of suspicion, but I was the grieving brother, and the guy's guilt in Amy's murder was obvious. So the cops closed the case, and I learned to live with the darkness in me."

He'd told her about that darkness before. She hadn't believed him. Or . . . had she?

Why was I so drawn to him? Because I sensed he was like me?

"I started LOST so other families would have a choice, so they could find their loved ones and not have to face the monsters out there." A muscle flexed in his jaw. "I didn't want them pushed to the edge the same way I was, because when you're pushed too far—"

"There's no going back," she finished softly.

"No. There isn't."

The crash of the waves seemed so loud, and a chill had swept over her. The sky seemed to be darkening around them.

"Say something, Eve."

"I—I understand."

"You're afraid."

Not of him. "Are you afraid of me?" Because she'd attacked her father. Killed him? *I don't know.*

"Never." His hands wrapped around her shoulders. He pulled her closer to him. Closer was exactly where she wanted to be. "I want you just as much as I always have, and that is fucking *more than anything else.*"

That was the way she wanted him. It wasn't about having control. About taking control . . .

It was about Gabe. About how he made her feel.

"I'm a killer, Eve. You need to understand that."

She shook her head.

But he nodded. "If anyone tried to hurt you, I *would* kill that bastard."

If anyone tried to hurt me, I'd kill him myself. That whisper was inside of her. Dark. Cold. And . . . true. She knew it. Whoever she'd been in the past—she hadn't just cried and taken her pain. She'd fought back.

And she would keep fighting. Jessica . . . Eve . . . she would keep fighting.

She rose onto her toes, and her mouth pressed to his.

TREY POUNDED ON the door. "Clay!" he yelled. "We have a warrant to search the premises! Open the door!"

Agent Granger was behind him. Dean Bannon was there, too. He'd argued against bringing the guy, but Granger had insisted, saying that Bannon had previous FBI experience they could use.

Freaking FBI—they stuck together too much.

"Doesn't look like he's opening the door," Granger said.

No, he wasn't. But that was because Trey didn't think Clay was there. Half a dozen boats were still missing from the marina. People out searching . . . *Clay out running?*

But, screw it. He was done waiting. He had a tropical storm bearing down on him, an injured officer, and another dead body in the town's too little morgue.

The mayor was having a shit fit, and this was ending. *Now.*

Trey kicked open the door. Rushed inside. "Clay!"

No answer. Had the guy already gotten off the island? Used any of the dozens of boats housed at his marina? That was a definite possibility. Talk about your perfect access. With the marina his to control, Clay could have taken out his victims on different boats anytime he wanted. No one would have known what he was doing. Not until it was too late.

Footsteps pounded in behind him. Granger and Dean. They were all searching through the house.

"Found something!" Granger yelled.

Trey whirled away and ran toward the shout. The FBI agent was in a bedroom, one that looked out over the water and one with—

A shrine?

"That's Eve," Dean said. "I mean, Jessica."

That *was* Jessica Montgomery. Dozens of pictures of her. Pictures of her as the beautiful teen that Trey remembered. Pictures of her as the woman she was now. Pictures of her running along the beach. Pictures of her naked in bed.

"Were Eve and Clay lovers?"

Trey's back teeth locked together. "Once." A fucking *long* time ago.

"We need all available resources looking for this man," Granger said. "The bastard got his nephew to try and cover his tracks . . . *we have to find him!*"

Because they thought Clay was their killer.

Trey stared at those pictures of Jessica. Beautiful, perfect Jessica. In her bed. The silken sheets around her . . . and . . .

Someone had been in the photos with her.

His eyes narrowed as he tried to make out more in them. But the man with her was blurry, a bit indistinct. He was— "*Sonofabitch.*" He whirled for the door. He needed to get to Jessica. Right then.

"What the hell?" Dean jumped in his path. "Where are you going?"

"Jessica—"

"Is with Gabe. She's safe. We have to work at finding this bastard here."

The guy didn't get it. No one understood. He threw back his hand toward that creepy shrine. *"It's him!"*

"What?"

Jessica wasn't safe with Gabe. She wasn't safe at all. He had to get to her while there was still time. "It's him!" He snarled again. "Gabe!" And he shoved Dean out of his way.

He was getting to Jessica. No one was going to stop him.

No. One.

CHAPTER FIFTEEN

GABE HELD EVE AS TIGHTLY AS HE COULD. HE had the feeling that if he didn't keep her close, she'd slip away, right out of his hands, and that wasn't going to happen for him. He'd been looking for her—he hadn't even realized it—for too long. He had the woman he wanted, the woman who fit him, and he wasn't going to let her get away.

He took her back into the condo. Kissing her, stroking her, fighting to strip those clothes off her. Death had come too close that day. Secrets. Sins. They were tangling around them both, but that didn't matter.

Only Eve mattered.

He pushed her back onto the bed. Tossed away the last of her clothes. Spread her out beneath him.

He wanted to give her so much pleasure that she couldn't stand it. Wanted to banish every fear that she'd ever had.

He wanted to give her everything.

His mouth went to her breast. Her nipple was pink and tight and perfect. And when he took that peak into his mouth, her nails dug into his back. Her hips eagerly slammed up against his.

She moaned his name, and he loved the sound of her need.

He kissed his way to her other breast. Lust was a fury within him, demanding that he take and take and—

Use care.

That fast warning came from deep within him. His hand flew out and fisted around the sheets. He wanted to drive into her as hard as he could. To know that she was safe and alive and with him.

Care.

She deserves care.

His hand slid down her stomach. Her shorts and underwear were gone. He touched her silken, bare sex.

I want to take everything she has. I want her to take all of me.

Fuck!

His hands jerked away from her and he fisted the covers.

"G-Gabe? What is it?"

His head lifted. Gabe searched her gaze, but he didn't see fear. Just passion. "I want you . . . to be okay . . ." Okay with his possession. With his passion. Her fear was the last thing he wanted.

"I'm always okay," was her soft response, "when I'm with you."

Because he would do *anything* for her. Did she realize it? Just how far he'd fallen? He'd been falling, ever since he'd looked up and seen a woman who told him that she was lost.

"I don't want you . . ." Speaking was hard. When his cock was that big and all he wanted to do was drive balls deep into her. ". . . afraid."

Her hand slid between their bodies. She shoved his clothes out of her way and then her fingers were curling around his cock. Warm and tight. Good. So good. But not as good as it would be when Gabe was in her. Nothing was that good.

Her past . . . her past . . . don't hurt her. Don't—

"You and me," Eve said, and she pressed a kiss to his lips. "That's all that matters right here, right now. You." She stroked him. "Me."

He wouldn't let his control go. Couldn't. "I never . . . want to hurt you." He should pull away. After what she'd learned—

Then the fear came. Flickering in her eyes. Her hand rose. Pushed against his shoulder. "St-Stop."

I'm a fucking bastard.

"It's because of what he said . . . what I did with the— the others . . . you don't want—" Her breath heaved out. "I don't even remember those men!"

She tried to twist out of the bed. Carefully, he held her there. Carefully, he kissed her there. "Other lovers don't matter to me." Well, they'd better never come at her again with desire in their eyes or they'd deal with him. With an effort, he kept his voice soft. "I wasn't a virgin, and I didn't expect you to be."

She was still beneath him.

He mentally told his cock to calm the hell down, for the moment. This was important. She was important.

"That's your past," he told her. "Good, bad, everything in between. *Past.*" He had to kiss her again. A little harder. A little deeper. "I'm your present." He wanted to be her future. "Be with me."

"I am!" The pain in her voice cut through him. "You're the one trying to pull away."

He rolled them, twisting them on the bed so that she was on top of him. He needed to give her as much power as he could. He wanted—

"Control," Eve whispered.

Yes.

"I don't want it."

What?

"Not with you. It's not a power play . . . a—a game . . ." She shook her head. Her hair slid over her cheeks. "I just want you, exactly the way you are."

But he could be a dominating bastard, and he wanted to be different with her.

Her lips brushed over his. "I just want you. There's nothing else. No one else. Just you. Just me."

His hands were curved around her hips. Her legs were open, her sex bare and sliding over him. He pushed his fingers between their bodies. Stroked her sex. She was warm, her heat glistening on his fingers. But she wasn't ready enough. Not even close.

If she wanted him, just the way he was, then she'd have him.

Good, bad, everything in between . . .

He rose up. Pushed her back. Spread her legs even farther apart. Her breath hitched, then came faster.

He put his mouth on her. On that perfect, pink flesh. He put his mouth on her and he feasted.

There was no past. There was only them.

She came against his mouth. Eve shoved up against him and gave a wild cry. He kept licking her, kept stroking her with his tongue and mouth, and she was wet now. Creamy. He loved her that way.

Eager for him.

But he didn't climb on top of her. He settled back on the mattress, leaning against the pillows. He lifted her over him once more.

I can be a dominating bastard . . .

But I'm hers.

His tight grip on her hips guided her to him. When she slid over his cock, a ragged groan tore from him because she was a hot paradise. Squeezing and hugging his cock like the best dream he'd ever had.

He pushed her forward, wanting her clit to slide against his cock as he arched against her. His hips left the bed and he shoved into her as deep as he could go.

This time she was the one to grab for the covers. To hold them tight in a fisted grip. Eve's head tipped back and she began to ride him. Not some smooth, controlled passion. Hot and hard and driving.

Deep and consuming.

Sweat slickened his body, and he didn't care. He was surging toward fulfillment, taking every drop of passion that she had to give. In and out, his cock slid home, and it was *perfect*.

She was perfect.

Eve started coming again, trembling around him, her body shuddering, and she was touching herself as she came, pushing her hand over her clit and calling out his name.

He'd never seen anything more beautiful. In that moment he realized how very far he'd fallen, for Eve.

He surged into her once more and the pleasure overwhelmed him. He held her as tightly as he could, in a grip that he feared would bruise, but he couldn't let go. *I never want to let go.* Eve had come to mean far too much to him, in just a few short days.

He emptied into her, his whole body shuddering because the pleasure was enough to make a man crazy.

Especially a man who was already on the edge.

TREY WALLACE SLAMMED his car door shut and glared up at the condominium complex. The sky was too damn dark behind that building, and he could already feel a roughness in the wind blowing against him.

His phone rang, and swearing, he jerked it up to his ear. "Look, I don't—"

"We have more victims," Agent Granger told him.

What? He'd just left the guy!

"My partner followed the map that was recovered at the lighthouse. Douglas is only at the first location, near the Nature Preserve, but he's found . . . remains."

Shit.

"We need you back at the station," Granger said. "We have to work at recovering as many of these bodies as we can. The National Weather Service has just said that the tropical storm is definitely turning. It's not heading east toward Pensacola. It's coming here. We'll be the ones getting the direct hit."

I don't have time for this.

"If we don't recover those bodies before the storm hits—"

"Have you ever been through a tropical storm, Agent Granger?" Trey shouldered his way inside the condo's lobby. When the guard tensed, Trey flashed his ID. Seriously, Rick *knew* him. The guard should be waving him right through, not looking all dumbass suspicious.

"Uh, no. I haven't," Granger replied.

"Right. Didn't think so. I've been through dozens, and you know what happens? Evacuation orders come through. They are probably already on the way. Parts of the island will flood. The power company will cut our connection long before the storm reaches land, so we'll all be in the dark. There won't be time to find those bodies—there's only going to be time to board up and get the hell out." Because even a weak tropical storm could wreck the place.

He marched toward the elevator. Jabbed the button.

"Those bodies could be lost!" Granger said.

"If they weren't lost in the last storm, then maybe they'll just keep staying right where they are." He knew he sounded like a cold bastard, but his priority was the living, not the dead. With a storm coming, all of his already meager resources would be strained to the limit. "Now I'll be back at the station as fast as I can. You want advice?" Probably not since the jerk had taken over the investigation. *My* investigation. "Secure the evidence that you have and get off my island while you can."

He shoved the phone back into his pocket just as the elevator doors opened. Trey came face-to-face with Pierce Montgomery. Hell.

Once upon a time, he and Pierce had been friends.

Once.

Those days were long gone.

As soon as he saw him, Pierce stiffened. The guy didn't march out of the elevator, instead he seemed to take root in there. "What are you doing here?" Pierce asked him.

"Going to see Jessica." He jumped into the elevator. Pierce didn't get off. So Trey held the doors for him. *I don't have time for this.*

"I told you to stay away from my sister! She has nothing to say to you!"

He really wanted to take a swing at him, but a cop wasn't supposed to do that. A cop wasn't supposed to do a lot of things. *But I do them anyway.* "I'm not here to question her. I'm here to help her."

He gave up on ditching Pierce and let the doors close.

But Pierce lunged forward and stopped the elevator, freezing them between floors. "Bullshit," Pierce growled at him. "I know what you've been doing to her. For *years*."

Trey shook his head.

"You used Jessica. Took advantage of her."

The hell he did.

"I know you cheated on her. The stories about you and that blonde reached me . . . all the way up in Birmingham."

Trey's jaw locked. "We'd broken up then." And he'd been drunk. The woman had meant nothing. None of the other women had ever meant anything, just Jessica.

"You don't get a second chance with her."

"Look, Montgomery, I get that you think I'm not good enough for your sister, that I never was. But my job is to protect the people on this island, and that includes *her*." With a jab of his fingers, he had the elevator rising again. "She's in danger, and I'm not going to stand back and let her get hurt."

"How did you ever help her before?'

The question pissed him off. "Maybe you didn't know your sister as well as you thought." Jessica hadn't been a perfect angel. Hell, no one was. They all had plenty of sins on their souls.

"I knew everything about her."

The elevator opened. Good. He marched out, not waiting to see if Pierce followed him. He headed for Jessica's condo and pounded on the door. "Jessica! Jessica, open up!"

And he had a flash of himself at Clay Thompson's home, pounding.

The images of Jessica on that wall . . . naked . . . smiling.

His fist pounded into the door once more. "Open the fuck—"

The door swung open. Only Jessica wasn't standing there. Gabe Spencer was. He was just wearing a pair of faded jeans, and the hard lines on his face clearly said the man was pissed.

He was about to become even more furious.

Trey started to shoulder past him.

Gabe grabbed him, surprising Trey with his strength as he was shoved back.

"I need to see *Jessica*."

"Why?" Gabe Spencer was a freaking immoveable object in front of him.

And Pierce was behind Trey. Crowding in close. "I told him to stay away from my sister!" Pierce was nearly snarling.

Too bad. "I'm here because someone's been watching her." He held Gabe's stare. "Someone has been watching you both."

A line of confusion appeared between Gabe's brows.

"Let me show you," Trey said. "Give me two minutes. Just two." That would be all he needed.

Gabe backed up. Trey stormed inside, and then he saw Jessica. She was standing in front of the bedroom. Her hair tousled. Her cheeks flushed. She was wearing a pair of sweats and a loose T-shirt.

Jessica always wore—

He cut off the thought. "You're not safe here."

She'd been having sex with Spencer. He knew it. He could see it in her gleaming cheeks. Smell the faint scent in the air. His hands fisted.

She tensed, but he walked right by her. Headed into the bedroom. The bed was wrecked.

He jerked his gaze away from it. Whirled around the room. Checked the angle. Figured out—

There.

The smoke detector. He grabbed a chair and yanked it toward the detector, the one placed in the far left corner of the room.

"What are you doing?" she asked, sounding worried.

She should be worried, Trey thought. That guy had been watching her nearly twenty-four seven. *For how long?*

He yanked down the smoke detector, and when he did, the fake cover fell off, revealing the small camera that was there.

"What the hell?" That was Pierce's shocked voice.

Trey stared down at the camera because he didn't want to look at Jessica or at Gabe. "We searched Clay Thompson's house a bit ago. The guy has a freaking shrine to you in there. Dozens of pictures. Old and . . . new." Now he did look at Gabe, who had moved close to Jessica. Protectively close. He had his arm around her side.

I fucking hate him.

"One of those pictures . . . you were in bed, Jessica. And you—you were naked."

Spencer swore.

"I saw the scar on your neck, and I knew the photo was recent. Had to be . . . it was a picture of you and Spencer. The guy was watching you, even when you had a guard right next to you." A guard who'd been screwing her.

Rage pumped through him, but he held it back. *I lost her long before Gabe Spencer appeared.* He knew that truth, even if she didn't.

"The guy's in the wind," Trey said, because they all needed to know that. "His place is empty. He must have sent his nephew after you both. It figures Johnny would do anything that the uncle he idolized said to do."

Pierce was trying to grab for the camera. Trey held it out of his reach.

"He's still out there, and he's obsessed with you." You didn't have to be a shrink with fancy diplomas to know that. "So you," he said, talking to Gabe now, "need to get her the hell out of here." Because he was starting to think there might not be any safe place for Jessica.

HE'D BEEN WATCHING her.

Eve stared at all of the pictures in Clay Thompson's house. Pictures of her. A woman she barely recognized. A woman who looked so happy in some of them and so sad in others.

"I don't know him." She turned toward Sarah. The other woman had also been studying the pictures in silence. "If we met before, I don't remember him."

"Your brother says that you and Clay were lovers, years ago."

How was she supposed to respond to that? Eve threw her hands up in the air. "And a spurned lover does what—starts killing women who look like me because he can't let go? Attacks me?"

"It would appear that way, yes." But Sarah's voice was carefully controlled. "This is almost textbook what you'd expect to find at a scene of this nature. Pictures, mementos of you."

But it wasn't just pictures. There were videos, too. They had been discovered by FBI Agent Granger and were stored on Clay's computer.

How long was that camera in my bedroom? She was afraid to ask just how many videos had been recovered. Eve didn't think that she wanted to know.

Violated. Yes, that was exactly how she felt.

"Textbook," Sarah murmured again.

Eve shivered. FBI Agent Granger had wanted her at the scene, to see if anything jogged her memory there. Nothing was jogging her memory, but the place was creeping her out. All of those pictures . . .

She turned away. Hurried outside. Thunder was rumbling in the distance. It always seemed to be thundering now. An alert had been issued on the island. Tropical Storm Henry was heading for them, with an expected arrival just before daybreak. Everyone was being asked to leave the island, for their safety.

When she rushed down the narrow steps that led back to the ground, she saw Pierce waiting for her. His expression was tormented. He hadn't wanted her in Clay Thompson's house. He wanted to protect her.

And the man she seemed to need protecting from?

Where is Clay Thompson? He appeared to have vanished.

"FIVE MINUTES," AGENT Avery Granger told Gabe with a hard nod. "That's all you get with him. And I'm breaking the rules just by giving you that."

Yes, the guy was, and Gabe was real grateful for that rule breaking because he had to get in there with Johnny Thompson. He had to find out just what the hell that kid knew.

Where is your uncle, Johnny? Where is he?

Gabe reached for the door. He was choking back his fury, using all of the self-control that he possessed. To know that he and Eve had been watched, during their most intimate time . . . *I am going to destroy that bastard.*

"Is that such a good idea?" Wade asked softly.

His head turned. Agent Granger had walked away a few steps, and Wade had closed in.

Wade crept closer. "Why don't you let me go in and ask him the questions?"

He knew Wade had been out with the other FBI agent, Douglas Stonebridge, and that they'd recovered the remains of another woman near the Nature Preserve.

How many more will we find?

"You're too close on this one," Wade murmured, his expression intent. "I don't want you going over the edge—"

Like you did before.

Gabe lifted his chin. "I'm not going to walk into this room and discover my sister's brutalized body, so I think I'll be fine with my control."

"Gabe—"

"I need to find out what he knows. The agents can't get jack from him, but I can." He knew it with certainty. Why?

Because Johnny feared him.

Fear could be a very powerful motivator.

"I won't cross the line," he promised his best friend. *But I will get close.* This was too important—he had to learn the truth for Eve's sake. Everything he did now . . . it was all for Eve. Because she mattered more than anything else to him.

Wade stepped back, and Gabe went in to face his prey.

Agent Granger had left Johnny in a small interrogation room. The guy was cuffed to the table, though Gabe didn't really think those cuffs were necessary. The kid looked a bit pale, and, when Johnny's gaze centered on him, Gabe could see the man's fear.

"Johnny . . ." He sighed out the guy's name as he settled across from him. "You're in a mess here."

"I told them—*I ain't talking without my lawyer!*"

"Yes, well, since a tropical storm has forced an evacuation of the island, that's not happening." Johnny would be evacuated soon, too. Transferred to the jail over in Mobile for holding.

So we don't have a lot of time here.

"Where's your uncle?"

Johnny's lips thinned. "Guessing you didn't find him at home."

"No, but we found the pictures."

The guy's angry gaze slid away.

"We know your uncle was quite . . . obsessed with Jessica Montgomery."

"Was he?" Now Johnny was looking at him again.

Gabe leaned forward. "I'm not a cop."

"I know—"

"I'm not an FBI agent. I'm not some D.A. who has to play by the rules." He smiled at Johnny. "I'm her lover—the lover of the woman that your uncle tried to kill." He knew his eyes would show his rage.

Johnny's Adam's apple bobbed.

"So how do you think I'm feeling about *you,* right now, Johnny? You set that explosion on the island. She could have been *killed* out there." He hated thinking of those moments. He never wanted Eve to be threatened or to be afraid. *Never again.*

Johnny was starting to sweat.

"I know how to kill," Gabe said. "I know how to make a man scream for mercy."

Johnny's chin jutted up. "I won't be screaming for you."

"I'm just trying to figure out how you fit into all this. Why would you protect the guy? Is it because he took you in? When your mother died?"

Johnny's eyes narrowed. "You don't know nothin' about me."

"And you know too little about me." He leapt up then

and grabbed Johnny. He hauled the guy across the table toward him. "I won't have her hurt. I'm not going to let her be the victim—"

Johnny laughed. "That woman isn't a victim. You've got her all wrong."

The hell he did. He knew Eve, inside and out.

"She was sleeping with him, pushing him to kill," and, just like that, Johnny was talking plenty. With no force, just with glee. "She was the one who wanted him to do it. She was the one always in his head, telling him to do it. She screwed him, over and over—"

Gabe drove his fist into Johnny's face. Johnny jerked back, then the cuffs jerked him down. And Gabe slammed the guy's face into the table. Blood spilled across its worn surface at the same instant the door behind Gabe flew open.

"What in the hell are you doing?" Trey demanded.

Gabe thought the answer to that was rather obvious.

"He doesn't like hearing the truth," Johnny yelled. "He doesn't like hearing that bitch is the one who pushed Clay! Who made him hurt those other girls!"

Trey pulled Gabe away from Johnny. For the moment, Gabe let the cop pull him.

"She's messed up," Johnny said, as the blood dripped from his busted lip. "Fucked in the head."

Gabe tensed, but Trey still had a too tight hold on him. *The little prick will pay for talking about Eve that way.*

"He knows," Johnny said, nodding toward the cop. "He has to know, as close as they were, and he's just protecting her. Trying to make sure his piece of ass doesn't get thrown in jail."

Gabe yanked back on his rage and studied the man with new eyes. Despite the blood and the fear, Johnny was meeting his stare directly.

Why isn't he afraid? A young guy like him, tossed into jail, he shot a cop . . .

Johnny *should* have been terrified and trying to work a deal.

"Clay didn't deserve what happened." Johnny's chin jutted up again as he said that. "He never did any-thing—*he didn't deserve this.*"

And those words held the ring of truth.

"Are you going to attack again?" Trey asked Gabe in a low whisper.

"Not yet." But he would be making another move, sooner or later.

Trey let him go.

And Gabe studied Johnny with new eyes. "Where's Clay?"

Johnny stiffened. "In the wind. Long gone and—"

"You don't know, do you?"

Johnny's eyelids flickered, just a bit.

"You love your uncle." That was obvious. The guy was going to jail for him.

"He always protected me. Wouldn't let anyone talk about my mom." Johnny licked his lips. "She tried her best, dammit. She didn't take the easy way out."

He was so pale.

And Gabe knew he was missing . . . *something.*

But what?

SARAH JACOBS WALKED slowly through the inte-rior of Clay Thompson's home. FBI Agent Douglas Stonebridge was there, talking to a tech, muttering about how they had to move fast with their evidence collection.

Because a storm was coming. A powerful storm.

Sarah stood in Clay's bedroom, right in the doorway,

watching the scene before her. It just didn't . . . feel the way it should.

All of the photos of Jessica Montgomery were there, hanging on that wall, photos that had obviously been collected over time, but . . .

He just had them out in the open? Not even hidden? What if someone had walked into his bedroom? There wasn't even a lock on the bedroom door.

And the files on his computer hadn't been password protected. They'd just been right there, for anyone to access. It was the same computer that the guy used for his work, and she knew dozens of people were in and out of that marina every day.

"Your profile was dead on," Douglas said as he came to stand near her. "A Caucasian, early thirties, one who could fit in wealthy circles. Hell, he was always chartering out fancy boats for rich parties. The guy had plenty of knowledge of the area and of boats."

Yes, Clay fit, but . . . the scene didn't.

"It feels staged." That was the problem. There was no emotion there. Just pictures. Spread out for her. She'd read the background info that the PD had on Clay Thompson. The guy didn't have any past history of trouble with the law. He'd been on the island, running his marina, ever since his father had retired and he'd taken over the business.

That marina gave him access. He could pick up the women, use any boat that he wanted and take them out.

Or . . . or maybe he'd seen the killer take the victims out.

"It's too perfect," Sarah said.

"What?" Douglas stared at her in disbelief. "How is it perfect? The man is on the run, he sent his nephew out to do his dirty work—"

"And *that* is what's wrong." Because Clay had taken care of Johnny ever since the guy's mother had committed suicide. "He wouldn't use Johnny that way." She might not be sure of the scene, but she was sure of that part.

"This guy is our killer." Douglas didn't seem to have any doubts. "We've got a nationwide manhunt in effect for him now. He will be brought down."

A manhunt . . . right. She'd heard the news report. Clay Thompson was considered armed and dangerous, and that meant when the cops approached him, they'd go after him with their weapons out.

The scene doesn't fit.

She needed to talk with Johnny.

Sarah hurried out of the house. It was up high, built on stilts because it was so near the bay side of the island. She looked out, saw the glistening water.

Then she looked down. Pierce Montgomery was down there, with Jessica. He had his hand on her shoulder. His posture was protective, concerned.

He'd sure changed a lot since she first saw him at LOST.

Dean Bannon was close by, too, watching the scene, and keeping his gaze on Jessica. Sarah knew that Gabe had ordered Dean to stay close. The guy was very good at following orders.

I'm not so good at that.

She pulled out her phone. Called Gabe. The phone rang, once, twice . . .

"This isn't a good time." Gabe's voice was curt.

"Are you with Johnny?"

"I'll call back—"

"Ask him what he'd do for his uncle." She needed to be there. To *see* Johnny.

It was a good thing the island was so small. She could be in the police station in five minutes.

"Keep asking him about his uncle," Sarah said as she ran down the stairs and rushed past Jessica and Pierce. "Ask Johnny where his uncle is. Ask Johnny if—if someone was threatening Clay . . ."

She jumped into the car near Jessica. Sarah saw the other woman frowning at her, but she didn't have time for explanations. Dean would keep Jessica safe.

Sarah spun out of the narrow lot, speeding as fast as she dared for the police station. The wind had already picked up, and she could hear the howl around her car. The rental shuddered a bit under the force of that wind.

"YOU SHOULD LEAVE the island," Pierce said as his hand tightened around Eve's shoulder. "You don't want to be here when the water starts rising."

Eve stared after Sarah. The woman had been running so fast.

Ask Johnny where his uncle is. Ask Johnny if—if someone was threatening Clay . . .

She had overheard part of Sarah's phone conversation. But who would threaten a killer?

"I thought . . ." Eve cleared her throat. "I thought the condo complex was supposed to be safe in a storm."

"The building was built to be as strong as it could be, but no place is one hundred percent safe," Pierce said as his green gaze swept slowly over her face, concern in the depths of his eyes. "You don't need to take chances. You should be safe. I can take you off the island. We can head up to our house in Birmingham until the storm is over. Hell, you don't *ever* have to come back here. It's not as if the place has good memories for you."

But it must have . . . once. If she'd chosen to make her life there.

"Who would threaten him?" Eve murmured.

Dean edged closer to her. Gabe had put the guy on guard duty, and he'd been her shadow every step she'd taken that day.

"*I'd* threaten him!" Pierce said, obviously not having caught Sarah's words on the phone. "He's after you— he's *obsessed* with you."

Was he? "Why didn't he try and talk to me?" Since she'd been on that island, why hadn't he approached her?

"You don't want him talking to you."

Rain began to fall. Thunder rumbled.

"You don't want him anywhere near you," Pierce added, voice sharp. "Now, we need to get off this island. If we don't hurry, it will be too late. The roads on the other side of the main bridge flood as the bay rises, and we won't be able to pass."

Yes, they did need to hurry. The island seemed to hold nothing but death and secrets everywhere she turned.

So . . . why did she want to stay?

Eve shook her head. "I'm not leaving without Gabe."

"WHERE IS CLAY?" Gabe asked Johnny quietly as he shoved his phone back into his pocket.

"It's time for transport," Trey said. "The prisoner has to be removed before the waters rise more."

Gabe leaned toward Johnny. "Who's threatening your uncle?" Sarah's question, one that he didn't fully under-stand and—

Fear flashed in Johnny's eyes. Bright, hot, terrified.

Sarah. She'd been dead to rights on that one. Some-one had threatened the guy.

"You can't ask him questions!" Trey snapped. "Not until his lawyer is here . . ." He unhooked one of Johnny's cuffs. "I don't care what the FBI agent told you, that's not how things work down here. We follow the law."

Johnny didn't move. His fearful gaze was on Gabe's.

"You love your uncle, don't you?"

"H-He looks out for me. Always has."

Now they were getting somewhere, because the cocky mask was fading from Johnny's face. "And you look out for him."

A faint nod was his answer. Trey unhooked the guy's other cuff. Johnny stayed in his chair.

"Is someone hurting Clay?" That was a stab in the dark, but when Johnny blanched, Gabe knew he was right.

Shit. He needed Sarah there. She could figure this kid out, she could—

"I have to protect him." Johnny's voice was low. "I *have* to!"

And then Johnny grabbed for Trey's gun. The cop had dropped his guard, maybe because Johnny had seemed so broken in that instant. But Trey reacted quickly, his own hand flying over the weapon.

Trey and Johnny fell to the floor. The table crashed down beside them. Gabe lunged forward because they were struggling with the gun and someone was going to get—

Shot.

The blast echoed in the room, deafening in its intensity.

The door burst open and Agent Granger ran inside.

Gabe grabbed for Trey's shoulder, but the cop was already rolling back. Blood covered the front of his shirt, but it wasn't his blood because Gabe could see the gaping hole in Johnny's stomach.

Shit. *"Medic!"* Gabe yelled even as he shoved a stunned-looking Trey back and put his hands on Johnny's wounds. "The kid needs help!" More help than he could give. He'd seen wounds like that in the field, and the wounded men hadn't survived the gut shots.

Johnny's blood soaked his fingers. "Look at me!" Gabe demanded, because the guy's body was shaking and his eyes were rolling back in his head.

Trey swore behind him. "He didn't give me a choice . . . dammit, he didn't give me—"

Agent Granger tried to help Gabe. They were both desperate to stop that blood flow. But that shot had been at point-blank range, and the damage was massive.

Too massive.

"Un . . . uncle Clay?" Johnny's voice broke.

"Stay with me," Gabe told him. They needed a hospital!

But there wasn't one on the island . . . shit, shit, *shit!*

A gasp sounded behind him. More frantic footsteps. Then—Sarah was there. Sarah had her MD. She could help.

And she was trying to help. Studying the wound, looking at Johnny's eyes, attempting to hold him still.

"H-Help . . ." Johnny gasped.

"I'm trying, Johnny," Sarah said, her voice soothing. "I want to help you."

Johnny's rolling eyes managed to fix on her. "H-Help . . . un-uncle . . ."

The man was spitting up blood.

"Please . . ."

"I want to help you first," Sarah said as she leaned

toward him. "You need to stay calm." She glanced back at Gabe. "He needs a hospital! Is there a helicopter that can airlift—"

"Help!" Johnny's voice was ragged, so desperate. And his hand lifted. He grabbed for Sarah's hair and he yanked her closer.

"Un . . . cle Clay . . . good . . . help . . ."

Trey pried Johnny's hand away from Sarah. Johnny looked up at the cop, and the terror flashed across his already pain-filled face. "Wh-Why? I—I did . . . what I was . . . s-supposed to . . ."

The man's blood was gushing from his body. Gabe and the others tried to lift him so they could get Johnny out of there.

They ran to the parking lot. Trey was shouting that the airfield was close. That they could try and get Johnny to Mobile and the hospitals there—

But Johnny died before they even made it to the helicopter.

CHAPTER SIXTEEN

SOMETHING WAS WRONG. EVE HURRIED INSIDE THE small police station. Dean was at her side, and Pierce followed right behind her. She could see Gabe up ahead, near the counter, and—

He turned toward her. His hands were covered in red. Blood. And blood stained his shirt, his jeans.

The blood is on my hands.

"What the hell happened?" Dean surged toward him.

And Eve saw Sarah then, standing near Gabe, her shoulders hunched. There was blood on her clothes, too. A smear of blood on her cheek.

"Johnny Thompson got Trey's weapon." Gabe's voice was hollow. She'd never heard quite that tone from him before. "They fought, and the gun went off." His bloody hands fisted. "Right fucking in front of me. The kid died—"

"No loss," Pierce muttered.

Gabe's gaze snapped toward him. "He was a twenty-one-year-old kid! Scared and *just* starting to tell us what was really happening on this island!"

An alarm sounded then, a long, shrill siren's call that came from outside.

"Evacuation," Eve whispered, just—*knowing*—that sound. "It's time to leave the island."

"We tried to get Johnny to the airfield," Sarah said. "He just . . . didn't make it." While Gabe's voice had been hollow, hers was thick with sadness.

Dean headed toward them. "Sarah?"

She jerked back. "He was protecting his uncle."

Wasn't that what they'd already realized? Goose bumps were on Eve's arms. *How many more people are going to die?*

Would it ever stop?

She crept toward Gabe. His gaze was shuttered. "I'm sorry." She could feel his pain. It seemed to hang around him like a shroud.

"He was talking to me. There was more there, Eve, I *know* it." His bloody fingers fisted. "He was scared and he was desperate."

Pierce was right beside them now. "The guilty often are."

She reached up and wrapped her arms around Gabe. She pulled him toward her, not caring about the blood, only wanting to be close to him. "I'm sorry," she said again.

"There was more to his story," Gabe growled into her ear. "I was so close, so fucking close, and he died."

Over his shoulder she saw Trey. His gaze met hers and he stiffened. Then his jaw locked as he strode toward them. "Evacuation is in effect. Everyone needs to get off the island right now."

She pulled away from Gabe. Trey had just killed a man. She expected to see emotion on his face, but there was none. Eve hesitated, then moved toward him, her steps slow. "Are you . . . okay?"

"I shot a prisoner who tried to escape." Said flatly, as

if he were just stating the facts. "I wish things had ended differently but they didn't. He gave me no choice."

He was hurting. He had to be hurting. Her hand lifted. Touched his shoulder. "Trey—"

He pulled away from her. "Get off the island." His stare moved toward Gabe. Sarah. Pierce. "All of you. Get the hell off my island before the storm comes." Then he strode away, heading for the front of the station.

Eve stared after him.

"I don't think he's killed before."

She flinched at the voice because she hadn't heard Agent Granger approach.

You're wrong. That whisper was there, in her mind.

Eve frowned as she glanced at Granger.

"The first is always the hardest," he said, giving a sad shake of his head.

"They are always hard," Sarah snapped back. Eve was surprised by the snap in her words. Sarah had looked almost defeated, but she sure sounded pissed. "He didn't have to die. If I could have just talked to him—"

"You can't save everyone," Dean told her quietly.

Sarah sucked in a sharp breath. Then she was spinning away and heading for the back of the station.

Dean followed after her.

"We need to leave, Jessica," Pierce told her as he caught her hand. He tugged her toward the door. "Traffic will get backed up—hell, it probably already is. We need to go."

"You go ahead." She wasn't leaving. "I'm staying with Gabe."

Gabe's eyes met hers. "I'll get her off the island safely." The words were for Pierce, but Gabe didn't look at him.

Pierce kept pulling on her hand. "I have more resources—"

Eve slid her hand out of his grasp. "I'm sure you do, but I'm not leaving my friends yet." Her friends . . . Sarah. Victoria . . . Dean. Yes, she'd started to think of them as friends. Not just guards. Not agents she'd hired. And they needed her, just as she needed them. "Get off the island," Eve told Pierce, managing a slight nod. "And I'll see you soon."

"But—"

"I've got her," Gabe said, and he did look at Pierce then. "I promise, I'll keep her safe from the storm."

Eve hurried away from them. She needed to find Sarah. She opened the door to the right, nearly ran down the narrow hallway, and then she saw Dean, standing a few feet away from Sarah. Looking both helpless and furious.

Sarah was crying.

"Sarah." Eve said her name softly.

Her head snapped up. "He—He died when my hands were on him."

Eve advanced carefully. Dean eased back. Watched them.

"I know there was more to the story." Sarah sucked in a heaving breath. "The pieces didn't fit. The scene was *wrong* . . . and at the end, he kept asking me to help."

"He wanted you to help him?"

"No." Sarah shook her head. Stared at Eve with stark eyes. "He wanted me to help his uncle. He was dying, and with his last breath he was begging me to help Clay."

"Your relationship with my sister is completely inappropriate," Pierce fired, his voice low. "She can't even remember her past, and you—"

"You don't want to push me right now," Gabe warned

him as he flexed his hands. "I just saw a man die, the woman I love is in fucking danger, and my control really isn't what it should be."

Pierce's eyes widened. "You . . . think you love my sister?"

He didn't think it. He knew it. His feelings had been crystallizing ever since that damn explosion out at the lighthouse. He'd come too close to losing her, and he'd realized just how much she truly meant to him. Only he shouldn't have been saying that shit to Pierce. He needed to be talking with Eve. But since he'd already started down this path . . . he advanced on Pierce. "Yeah, I love her." He'd fallen fast and hard, and there was no going back for him. "So you know what that means? It means I won't let anyone or anything," even fucking Mother Nature and her storms, "hurt her."

"Jessica—"

"*Eve. That's who she is now. Deal with it.*" *Deal with me.* "Follow her advice. Get off the island. Cover your ass. And I'll be taking care of her." Then, because he didn't trust his control to last much longer and Eve's brother just rubbed him the wrong way, Gabe spun away from him.

"She won't stay with you." Pierce's voice was low. "She'll leave you just like she did them. She uses men. I love her, but I know her weaknesses."

Gabe glanced back at him. "You don't know her at all." Then he stalked after Eve. He needed her close. The scent of death was all around him and Eve was his one light in this madness.

He needed her.

He headed into the hallway. Sarah was near the interrogation room door, her body so stiff. Tears drying on her face. And Eve was there, talking softy to Sarah.

It wasn't the first time that someone had died in Sarah's arms. Unfortunately, with Sarah's past, too many had lost their lives that way.

And she hadn't been able to save them.

He knew the grief that ate at Sarah and he wished he could help her. But the demons she carried were her own, and she couldn't seem to shake them.

You will, Sarah, you will.

"Let's get the hell off this island," Gabe told them.

Dean immediately nodded, but Sarah hesitated. "I—I need to check Clay's home once more. I want to make sure—"

"You need to be safe," Eve told her firmly. "It can wait. He can wait."

Sarah looked at Gabe. "He wanted me to help . . ."

And Sarah always would. She couldn't turn away from those who needed her. Sarah was too busy trying to atone for her past.

He nodded because he understood her so well. "Wade is outside of the station." He'd been there when they tried to get Johnny to the airlift. "Sarah, get him to go with you to the Thompson house. Do your sweep, then get off the island." He pointed to Dean. "Victoria is still in her makeshift lab. Tell her it's time to go. I want you and Victoria to head out together." Each one of them needed to be with a partner. With the killer on the loose, he wanted them covered.

And he'd get Eve out of that place.

The alarm was still sounding. He could hear its distant cry.

He lifted his hand toward Eve. Shit. He still had blood on him. He dropped his hand, but Eve—Eve still came to his side.

I love her.

He'd meant what he said to Pierce. He wasn't going to give up Eve, not now.

Not ever.

EVE HURRIED INTO the condo. The lights were blazing but she still felt . . . nervous. Scared. Because she'd thought the condo was a sanctuary. When all along . . .

He was watching me.

"We'll get our stuff," Gabe said behind her, "and then get on the road out of here."

Her gaze slid to the right. To the painting of the lighthouse that she'd done before. Painting furiously, wildly, at an image that wouldn't leave her alone.

Eve hesitated as she stared at that painting. Then she found herself inching closer to it. The paintbrushes were in a cup of water, sitting there as if forgotten.

Let's play a game, sweetheart . . .

Her fingers reached for the brush.

"WHAT ARE YOU hoping to find here, Sarah?" Wade asked her as Sarah hurried toward Clay's house. A yellow line of police tape roped off the stairs.

Sarah hesitated at the tape. "Something that isn't perfect."

"You know that makes no damn sense, right?"

Lightning sliced across the sky. Rain was pelting down on her. The first bands of the storm were already coming onshore.

"Go back and stay in the car," she told him, because she needed to be up there alone. Needed to be able to think and search without someone else breathing down her neck. *What did you leave behind?* And Wade would just distract her if he went up there. "I'll be as fast as I can."

"Yeah, how about you make that *fast* . . . as in ten minutes, and if you're not done then, I'm coming up there and dragging you out."

When she glanced at him, he was standing beside the rental car, glowering at her.

"We're not getting caught in that storm," Wade told her. "I'm not going to risk you."

Because Wade always followed orders.

I don't.

Sarah slid under the tape and hurried up the stairs. The door was locked, but she had skills that most people weren't aware of. When you grew up with her particular background, you learned all about breaking and entering.

And killing.

Sarah had the door open in seconds and slipped inside. The lights were off, darkness everywhere, and she hated the darkness. She flipped on the lights.

But the lights didn't make the place any better.

What did I miss?

She went back to Clay's bedroom. All of the pictures of Jessica Montgomery had been removed. Tagged and bagged as evidence. Agent Stonebridge had been very thorough. The wall was now a stark white, staring back at her. White except for . . .

Sarah leaned in closer. There was a streak of red across that wall. Faint. That red could have been anything. Paint. A marker.

Blood.

The red had dried, and she'd have to get a sample to figure out just what she was looking at. She didn't have any evidence collection bags with her, so she hurried into the bathroom. She reached for the mirror behind the sink, knowing by its shape that the medicine cabinet was hidden behind it. Sarah opened the mirror, saw cotton swabs in there and grabbed a few. She began to shut the cabinet then, and as the glass swung closed—

She saw the reflection of the man standing behind her.

Sarah opened her mouth to scream, but he grabbed her head and slammed it into the mirror.

The glass shattered around her.

"I knew you were going to be trouble, sweetheart . . ."

"EVE, WE NEED to go."

Her fingers slid away from the paintbrush handle. She headed for the balcony, her steps feeling slow. Sluggish. The sky had darkened so much out there. The setting sun was giving way to the night, and angry clouds stretched as far as she could see.

"It was storming then, too."

"Eve?"

She pushed open the balcony door. Headed out until she reached the railing. The waves were rough, the surf heaving against the shore as the water rose to swallow huge chunks of the beach.

"I was drowning." She could still taste that salty water, water that was choking her. "And even that was better than being with him." The memories were there, struggling so hard to push through.

Lightning flashed.

Lightning flashed then, too. The thunder rumbled. The waves were so rough. "So rough," she said quietly.

"Are you remembering what happened?"

I don't want to remember. "I don't want to die."

Gabe's fingers curled around her shoulders. He pulled her toward him. Stared down at her with a gaze that gleamed in the growing darkness. "I won't let that happen."

She stared into his gaze, smiled, and told him, "I want to fly."

"What?"

She tilted her head back. Stared into the darkness. "He can't hurt me when I fly. I want to fly away."

She saw the lightning flash across the sky. Thunder cracked right after it, and Gabe was pulling her into the condo. Forcing her back inside.

It was too bright in there. Far too bright. It had been dark when she died, dark in that murky water that pulled at her and pulled at her. Greedy hands to hold her tight.

"It's too bright," Eve heard herself whisper.

Then thunder rolled once more and they were plunged into darkness.

SARAH'S TEN MINUTES were up. "That's it, Sarah," Wade said as he shoved open his door. Rain immediately started plummeting down on him. Figured. He hoped Sarah had found whatever she was looking for in that place.

His phone rang. He grabbed it and saw Dean's name and face flash on the screen. "You guys safe?" Wade asked him.

"Victoria and I are at the bridge," Dean told him, "and we're about to clear the island. You?"

"Getting Sarah now," he said as he leaned forward and peered through his windshield. Only . . . the light in the house up there had gone out. He looked around and realized everything was dark around him. "The power company must have cut the feed." He'd been warned that would happen.

"The FBI agents are in the van in front of us," Dean told him. "The police chief and his men stayed behind to keep folks there safe."

Because there would be some who didn't heed the warnings. There always were.

He glanced back toward the darkened house. He knew Sarah didn't like the dark.

Except it wasn't dark up there. Not anymore. Light was flickering, he could see it, moving unnaturally. "Fuck, *fire!*" Wade shouted, and he dropped the phone. He leapt out of the vehicle and ran right through the thin police tape. He ran up the stairs, shoved open the door, and the scent of smoke and flames hit him. "Sarah!"

She didn't respond. He ran through the living room, turned to the side—the flames were coming from that room, from Clay's bedroom. The fire was eating at the walls, rushing around the bed, chasing over the carpet.

And in the middle of those flames, Sarah lay on the bed. It looked like something wet was on her face. She was sprawled out, eyes closed, not moving. "Sarah!"

The flames were growing higher around her.

Locking his jaw, Wade shot forward. He tried to jump over the fire, but it scorched his legs. He didn't stop to see if Sarah was alive—*be alive, be alive!*—he just yanked the covers around her, trying to protect her as best he could even as he started coughing because the smoke was so thick. He scooped her into his arms and ran back through the flames. The fire was even hotter and it burned across his right arm. He didn't cry out, just ran as fucking fast as he could out of that place and back down—

His car was gone.

The rain fell on him as he held Sarah in his arms. He hurried down the stairs, being as careful as he could with her, and then put Sarah on the ground.

Where the hell is the car?

He pulled the covers away from her face and he realized that blood was on her, dripping down from heavy gashes in her head. "Sarah?" He put his fingers to her pulse. Felt the thready beat. "Who did this to you?"

Lightning flashed.

He glanced around. The houses nearby were all pitch-black. They were boarded up, protected against the storm, and the cars were gone. His phone had been in the car that some jerkoff had taken. The same jerkoff who'd torched that house and left it to burn.

I guess Clay Thompson didn't go far after all.

Maybe it was pretty smart of the bastard to ride out the storm in his own house. The cops sure wouldn't have gone back there. But Sarah had returned there. Sarah . . . who could think like a killer so well.

It's in my blood. She'd told him that once, sadly. Shamefully.

He lifted her into his arms once again. He didn't know where her phone was, probably back in that burning house, but he'd get her help. He started running with her, holding her tight. He'd get her help.

THEY ARE MY prey.

Most people had already left the island. Those who hadn't were hunkering down, hiding behind their boarded-up windows. Taking shelter until the storm passed.

He liked the storm. Liked the roar of the waves and the whip of the wind. The storm was the perfect cover for him. No one was watching. He didn't have to pretend anymore.

The condominium tower came into view. It was as dark as the rest of the island. He'd made sure the generators wouldn't work there. He had full access to that place—hell, he had full access to every place on the island. No one ever stopped him. They wouldn't dare.

He parked the car. Took his time entering the tower of condominiums. The guard, Rick, had left long ago. So had the others there . . . Tourists always fled first.

Not Jessica.

She was there, waiting for him.

That fool Gabe thought that Jessica would leave. That she would be his. Gabe was wrong.

Gabe will die.

So would Jessica. Back in this place, where it had all started for them. Jessica . . . she'd found his video camera, months ago. She'd found it, and she'd started to put the pieces together.

He'd gone to her. Slipped into her bedroom because he'd wanted to be close to her. She'd woken up and seen him, but she hadn't screamed.

I thought that meant she understood.

Instead, wearing her sweatpants and her T-shirt, she'd risen from the bed. Stared at him. He'd thought her calmness meant that she understood. He'd even begun to smile—

Then she tried to run away from him. *She tried to trick me.* So he'd punished her. And then she *had* screamed.

He made his way into the stairwell.

You'll scream tonight, too, Jessica.

He pulled out his gun. He usually preferred his knife, and that was certainly what he'd use on Jessica, but for Gabe . . . the gun would work perfectly. After all, he just wanted that bastard out of his way.

Jessica was the one who would give him pleasure. Her kill was the one he longed for.

WHEN THE LIGHTS went out, Gabe thought the emergency generator would kick on. The damn thing was supposed to be fixed and ready to generate power automatically, but the darkness kept surrounding them.

When lightning flashed, he saw Eve . . . standing near the balcony doors, staring out at the storm.

"I hate it," she whispered. "I'm responsible. It's all my fault. Those women, Pauley . . . it's all on me."

The rain was coming down harder. He reached out to her, but Eve flinched away.

"I saw him. We both realize I did. I *know* the killer, but I can't identify him. I blocked him from my mind because I was too scared to face him."

"Or because you nearly died." He pulled her toward him. Screw getting her things. They'd be there when the storm cleared, or hell—he'd just get her new stuff. He'd wanted to shower her with things from the moment he'd seen her walking into that homeless shelter. *I will give her anything she wants.*

Eve didn't fight him when he started leading her back to the condo's main door. "The elevator won't be working," Gabe said, "so we'll have to take the stairs."

He had his phone. He could use the flashlight app to get them out of there, no problem.

When he shoved the condo door open, he could hear the angry howl of the wind and the crush of the waves against the shore.

The stairwell was to the left. But he stared out at the island for a moment, aware of the darkness—everywhere.

Eve's nails dug into his arm.

He looked back toward her. Kissed her, because he needed to do it right then. Needed her to know that he was there, they were both safe, and that everything was going to be all right. "I love you," he told her.

"Wh-What?"

He knew he had shit for timing. A tropical storm bearing down on them, a killer on the loose, but he had to tell her. Adrenaline and instinct were pushing him. He wanted Eve to know how he felt, no matter what happened. "I think I started falling for you the minute you walked into my office."

"That's not—you're just— *Why?*"

Why did he love her? "Because you're strong and brave, and when I look into your eyes I want to do anything and everything within my power to make you happy." To protect her. The wind kept howling. "Because I look at you and I see a woman who is a fighter. A woman with spirit and passion. A woman I want more than any other."

He wished that he could see her expression. Her silence was making him realize—

She doesn't love me.

But then, he'd expected that. "When all of this is over, give me a chance, Eve." Simple.

"A chance to do what?"

"To make you love me." No, not to *make* her. Shit, but he was screwing this up. "To show you what we could have."

Lightning flashed again.

He kept his hold on her and drew her toward the stairwell. When he opened the door, the yawning darkness stared back at him. He lifted his phone, pushed the screen so the flashlight app would come on, and—

A gunshot rang out. The blast hit him in the chest, and as he fell, Gabe heard Eve scream his name.

CHAPTER SEVENTEEN

THROUGH THE FALLING RAIN, HEADLIGHTS HIT Wade. Bright lights that pierced the darkness and blinded him. He pulled Sarah closer to him, wishing that he had a weapon because who else but their attacker would be coming out in this—

"Wade!"

That was Victoria's voice. And she was jumping out of the passenger side of the car and rushing toward him even as Dean leapt out from the driver's side.

Hell, yes.

"What the hell happened?" Dean demanded as he ran to Wade's side. His breath hissed out when he saw— "Sarah?"

"She's hurt, but she's gonna make it." But if he hadn't gotten her out of that house, Sarah would be dead. Another victim of the Lady Killer? "Get on your phone," he told Dean. "Gabe needs to know that Clay Thompson is still on the island. The bastard might be coming for him and Eve."

Dean yanked out his phone as they all hurried back to the SUV. Carefully, so carefully, Wade put Sarah in the backseat of the vehicle.

"She needs a hospital," Victoria whispered. Then . . .

"Wade, your arm!" The car's interior light glared down on them.

He glanced at it. The thing had been hurting like a bitch, but he didn't have time to deal with the burns.

"He's not answering," Dean said, a worried edge in his voice.

"The cell signal on the island is always hit and miss," Victoria said. "With the storm, maybe the call just didn't go through."

Wade yanked his door closed behind him. "Get me to those condominiums."

In about two seconds Dean had the SUV spinning into reverse.

Sarah moaned and her eyelashes flickered.

"It's okay," he hurried to soothe her, stroking her shoulder lightly. "You're out . . . you're safe . . ."

The SUV splashed through the rising water.

"Drop me off," Wade said as he kept stroking Sarah's shoulder, "and get Sarah to a hospital. Get her off the island! I don't want Clay taking another shot at her—"

"N-Not . . ."

What was Sarah trying to tell him?

"N-Not . . ." she said once more, the word a bare breath that he had to strain to hear. "C-Clay . . ."

"GABE!" EVE GRABBED for him as he fell. His phone crashed into the stairs, splintering, and its flashlight went out, plunging them back into darkness. She touched his chest. Felt the wet warmth of his blood. "Gabe, no! Please!"

His hand flew up. Locked around her wrist. "R-Run . . ."

"I'm not leaving you. I'm not—"

"Jessica . . ."

She screamed. That low, rasping voice was coming

from the darkness of the stairwell, and it was the same voice that haunted her dreams. No, her nightmares.

"R-Run," Gabe ordered again.

If she ran, he was dead. The bastard hadn't shot again, but he would . . . he *would*. Eve knew it with utter certainty.

"Stay away!" Eve yelled into the darkness, but the stairwell just sent her own voice echoing back to her.

"Let's play, sweetheart . . . do you remember the game?"

And images flashed through her mind. Dozens of them, one right after the other.

The long blade of a knife . . .

Sand surrounding her, burying her.

Seagulls flying over her head.

Waves turning red with her blood.

Dying . . . dying . . .

"Run, Eve," Gabe begged. "Please . . ."

He was going to die. If she left him . . .

Eve rose to her feet. She didn't back away and try to get out of the stairwell, though. That bastard in the dark was talking, rasping about his *game* . . . and how they would—

"Let's play again, Jessica."

"Play with your own fucking self!" she shouted and then launched herself straight into the darkness. Straight at him. A gunshot blasted again, but it missed her, and she collided with him. Then they were falling. Spinning, twisting, and tumbling over the stairs. Pain snapped in her knee, in her shoulder, and her hip when she crashed into—the landing?

She was on top of him. She couldn't see a thing about him and leapt back into the darkness. "You want to play a game?" she threw at him. *Keep him away from Gabe. Keep him away.* "How about hide and seek? Come find me, bastard."

Her hands slapped against the walls—heavy, concrete walls. If she didn't *find* a way out, she'd be dying soon. But then her fingers closed over the door handle. Hell, yes. She'd been right. She was on a landing. Maybe at the sixth floor? She hadn't fallen that far.

Eve jerked the door open and she ran.

"Jessica!" he yelled.

"Come after me!" she shouted back. "Come and get me!" Because if he was coming for her, then he couldn't hurt Gabe. Gabe would be safe. Gabe would survive.

I love you.

Gabe had to survive. Because she loved him, too.

Eve ran down the hallway, her hands slapping out, trying to find doors to the condos there.

Locked. Locked. Locked!

Okay, hell, her plan had a serious flaw.

And she could hear his footsteps, rushing out behind her. He was coming . . .

"I'll play, sweetheart." That terrifying rasp that she knew to the core of her being.

She yanked on another door handle. This one turned. *Yes!* She burst inside. Shut the door. Locked it.

"Help!" Eve gasped out. "We have to call—"

No one was there. The condo was dead silent. She ran forward and didn't hit any furniture. Lightning flashed, illuminating the room in one instant of time, and she realized that she was standing in the middle of one of the open units. Gabe had told her that a few units hadn't sold at the condo complex.

This is one of them.

So there was no one there to help her.

The lightning gone, Eve turned back toward the door in the dark. She'd locked it. He *couldn't* get in.

He . . .

A soft knock sounded at the door.

HIS BLOOD WAS pumping out with every breath he took. That bastard had been aiming to kill—*only his aim missed.*

Gabe hissed out a breath at the pain as he staggered to his feet. He almost went back down again, slipping in his own blood, and he grabbed frantically for the railing. "Eve!"

She'd gone after the killer. He'd fucking not been able to believe it when she leapt at the man.

Don't risk yourself for me, baby! Don't!

Eve had gone down the stairs. He'd heard the sound of her screams, then . . . nothing.

He started walking down into the darkness. Each step sent pain surging through him. The blood wouldn't stop, but neither would he. Not until he'd found Eve.

"I'm coming," he whispered.

And he'd kill the man who was trying to hurt Eve.

THE CONDOS WERE pitch-black.

Dean brought the SUV to a screeching stop near the parking garage, and Wade immediately shoved open his door. "Take care of Sarah," he ordered Dean. "Get her to a hospital."

"You need backup, man," Dean snapped at him.

"He has it." Victoria's words. She was already out of the car. Already at his side.

And that was all there was to say. Dean tossed Wade

a flashlight. Good thing it had been in the SUV. Wade's fingers tightened around it.

"And take the gun," Dean ordered him.

Hell, yes, he'd be taking that. Especially since the bastard out there had taken *his* weapon when he stole his vehicle. Dean turned the SUV in that flood, and as he drove away, Wade and Victoria hurried into the parking garage. They'd only taken a few steps when the light from the flashlight hit on the vehicle there.

His vehicle. The bastard was already inside.

They'd tried calling Gabe again. Over and over during the ride. But he hadn't answered. Because he couldn't answer?

Wade didn't want to rush up to the penthouse and find his best friend dead, because if he did, he was afraid that this time he would be the one to lose control.

His fingers tightened around the gun.

HE WAS UNLOCKING the door. Eve could hear the soft sound, and it had her body trembling.

She backed away, fast, looking for any kind of weapon that she could get her hands on. There had to be something. Somewhere.

Her body slammed into a door. Her hands pounded across the surface. *Doorknob. Door—*

She wrenched open the door, raced forward and— fell. She'd tripped on something soft.

Her hands flew down and she touched . . . skin?

"Help me!" Eve cried.

She heard footsteps. Coming toward her.

"Oh, sweetheart . . . he can't help you . . ."

He was there. Right freaking *there*. And that voice . . .

Eve backed away, moving crablike on her hands as she

tried to escape. More memories pushed into her mind. The lightning flashed, spilling right into that room.

In that moment, she saw the man on the floor, the man she'd tripped over. The man who wasn't moving at all.

"You found Clay Thompson."

Bile rose in her throat as darkness enveloped her again.

"Can you keep a secret?" He still spoke in a rasping voice, and she wanted him to stop. She wanted to hear his normal voice. Wanted to hear him, and see him, too.

She wanted the darkness *gone*.

"He's been dead for a while, but Johnny didn't know that. Johnny thought if he did *exactly* as ordered, I'd let his uncle live."

She was still on the floor. Staring up into the darkness as she heard him creep forward. "You never let anyone go."

"No," he said softly, with certainty, "I don't." Then he reached down for her. "I missed you, sweetheart."

And when he touched her, she knew. Pain seemed to explode in her head because she'd been in this exact scene before. On the floor, cowering, terrified . . . and he'd been there, reaching down for her. Coming to kill her.

"No!" Eve screamed as she kicked out at him.

Lightning flashed—and she saw her brother's face above her.

Him, always . . . him!

"Pierce, no!"

He laughed. "Ah, there she is," he said, the rasp leaving his voice as he spoke louder, in a harder, angrier tone. "The girl I know and love . . . welcome back, sweetheart." She felt the gun barrel push into her chest. "Welcome back."

GABE NEARLY FELL when he reached the landing on the sixth floor. Every single step was agony, but he wasn't about to stop. Eve was out there. His Eve, and she needed him.

I need her.

He swallowed, digging deep for more strength. Would Eve have kept going down the stairs or would she have run out, seeking help on the sixth floor?

He pushed open the door. He had to check that floor. Had to see if she was there.

Only darkness greeted him.

Gabe crept forward. He knew he was leaving a trail of blood in his wake. "E-Eve?" Her name was a whisper from him. If he shouted and the killer was close, he'd give away his location. He couldn't take another hit. He had to be ready to fight.

"No!" That scream froze him. It had come from up ahead. *"Pierce, no!"*

It was Eve. He followed her scream, running forward desperately. His hands pounded against the doors. He'd heard the cry from that area. She had to be close.

"Eve!" Gabe bellowed. He didn't care if he gave away his location now. He wanted the bastard in there to know that he was coming after him. "Leave her alone, you bastard! *Leave her alone!"*

GABE WAS STILL alive. Eve's breath stilled in her lungs when she heard him.

"Guess I left the door open," Pierce murmured. "But since we're the only ones here, I didn't think anyone would come when you started screaming."

He'd thought wrong.

Pierce shoved the gun barrel against her harder. "I bet

he's half dead, and when he rushes in here, desperate to save you . . . *boom*."

She shuddered.

"I'll shoot him and I'll keep shooting until your lover can't move anymore."

"Don't—"

"And then it'll just be us, Jessica. The way it was always supposed to be. Before they tried to send me away from you."

The memories were still pouring through her mind, one right after the other, and now Eve realized . . . "M-My father never touched me." He'd made her believe that her father had tried to molest her, when all along . . .

It was always Pierce!

He laughed then. Soft, taunting laughter.

"It was you. *You* were the one who watched me too much. You made me feel . . ." *Scared. Dirty.* "I told them—"

"And they sent me to dozens of shrinks. Like it was wrong for me to want you."

That gun was still close, and . . . was Gabe coming? She didn't hear him crying out any longer. Maybe he was trying to sneak in there. She had to keep Pierce distracted so that Gabe could attack.

"You weren't my blood sister. I could desire you. Wanting you was natural, especially when you were so perfect for me." His fingers slid against her cheek.

That lying *bastard*. "I didn't attack my father." The image of the lighthouse . . . her running . . . the knife in her hand . . .

I'd gotten away from him! Pierce held me in that lighthouse, and I'd taken his knife. I thought I would get free . . .

But he'd caught her at the foot of the stairs.

"I'm the one who killed him," Pierce confessed, "and dear mother. When you found out, though, you *did* swallow all those pills." Anger roughened his voice. "Such a bad girl. *Why* would you do that? Why would you try to leave me?"

Because she'd known . . . deep inside . . . that Pierce had hurt them. There'd been no proof, and when she'd tried to tell people—tried to tell Trey—no one believed her. Because Pierce had been so good at presenting his perfect mask to the world.

All of those trips to the shrinks . . . the doctors had never found out his secrets, they'd only skimmed the surface of just how dark Pierce truly was. He'd been far too adept at hiding his true self.

Only I saw him. I saw the real man. The monster.

But when she got out of the hospital, Pierce hadn't touched her.

Because . . . dear God . . . he'd started killing other girls then . . .

"I never wanted to hurt you." His voice was low.

Had she just heard a creak in the other room? Was Gabe in there?

"But you found my camera that night . . . I—I needed to see you, so I snuck in. You saw me at the foot of your bed . . ."

And she could see that terrible night, right then, in her mind.

She'd woken to the faintest of creaks, and she'd known that she wasn't in that room alone. He'd moved, the shadows cloaking him, and fear had twisted inside of her. She'd known then . . .

He's come for me.

She'd tried to tell Trey about her fears, but he never

believed her. *Why not? Why not?* Why had everyone been so quick to believe that Pierce was perfect?

He'd used his money to hide his past, she knew that. Her parents had even helped to make those early visits to the shrinks disappear. *They wanted perfect, too. A perfect family*—but instead they got a nightmare.

She'd risen from the bed, trying to stay calm. He'd crept toward her.

"Let's play, sweetheart." Those words from her memory were the same words he said now, as past and present merged.

Her hands flew up and she grabbed for the gun.

"Eve!"

That was Gabe's bellow. So close—right outside.

"He's dying," Pierce promised her as he shoved her back. Her head hit the hardwood floor and then he was whirling around.

Gabe would burst through that door at any moment. "No!" Eve screamed. "Stay back, Gabe! Stay back!"

Lightning flashed—

Gabe wasn't staying back. They were in a bedroom and he was running toward them as Pierce lifted his weapon.

Eve leapt up and slammed her body into her brother's. They hit the floor together, tangling in a mass of limbs. The gun flew out of Pierce's hand, but then that hand slammed into her jaw. He hit her—

"No," Gabe roared. *"Not her!"*

He yanked her brother off her and started punching Pierce, hitting him with his fists again and again. The thud of flesh hitting flesh filled the room, a terrifying, savage sound. "You don't—" *Thud, thud, thud.* "Hurt her!"

She wanted to cover her ears. Wanted to slide into the darkness and escape the nightmare. To forget—

I want to fly, Daddy . . .

But she wasn't going to run this time. "Gabe . . ."

He was still hitting Pierce. She inched toward them, stumbling in the dark. Lightning illuminated the room in a flash, and she saw Gabe's hand drawn back, about to pound again. Pierce was limp on the floor. "Gabe . . ."

He hit Pierce once more.

"I'm okay," she promised him. "Please, Gabe, you weren't too late." Because she knew he was in his own nightmare, too. Trapped and remembering when he'd arrived too late to save his sister.

She grabbed for him in the dark, wrapping her arms around him. "I'm all right," she told him, desperate. "I'm all right."

He shuddered. Then he was whirling and jerking her against him. He held her in a too tight grip that hurt, and she didn't care. He'd saved her. They were alive. Pierce wasn't going to win this time. *He wasn't.*

"Gabe!" A shout from the doorway, and then a flashlight beam hit her and Gabe. "Sonofabitch, what the hell went down?"

That was Wade's stunned voice. His shadowy form behind the flashlight.

The beam moved to Pierce's face. It was a mess, smashed, bloody, his eyes swollen and nearly shut. A weak groan broke from him.

"He didn't win," Eve said, her voice cracking a bit. "Not this time." She held tighter to Gabe—

And he slumped against her. "Gabe!"

The flashlight bobbed as Wade ran toward her. He grabbed for Gabe and laid him down on the floor, right next to Pierce's prone form.

"No, man, *no.*" Wade's hands were shaking. "You do not get to do this to me."

Victoria was there now, too, her breath heaving out. She grabbed the flashlight from Wade and shone it on Gabe's body.

His eyes were still open, open and on Eve.

Wade ripped Gabe's shirt open.

"I . . . meant it," Gabe whispered.

"The bullet is still in you!" Wade's voice rose with fear. "Shit, there is a lot of blood."

Gabe didn't look away from her.

Thunder rumbled.

"Love you . . ." Gabe told her. "Always."

Wade growled at him, "Don't give that last rites crap, okay? You love that woman? Then you fight for her. You fight, and you stay with her."

"Stay with me," Eve told Gabe. She could feel tears filling her eyes. She tried to blink them away. "Please."

Pierce groaned again. She saw his fingers sliding across his body . . . he rolled over, hunching, coughing.

"I love you," Eve said, needing Gabe to have those words. Needing him to understand that she would do anything and everything necessary to protect him.

Just as he'd protected her.

She grabbed for the gun at the moment when Pierce lunged up. The flashlight glinted off the knife in his hand, a knife he was trying to swing toward Gabe's vulnerable chest.

Without hesitation, Eve fired. And she kept firing, again and again, until the bullets were gone.

Pierce sagged back against the floor.

"You don't win," she said once more as a tear slid down her cheek.

Then she went back to Gabe. Caught his hand in hers. Held tight.

"St-Stay?"

That one word from him drove straight to her core.

"Always," Eve promised him. "I will always be with you."

THE STORM HAD passed.

Eve watched as the body bags were loaded into the coroner's van. Two bags. One for an innocent man who'd gotten caught in a killer's game.

You wanted to use him as your scapegoat.

And one for a twisted bastard who'd hid his madness too well.

"I'm sorry." Her head turned. Trey was there. Standing by her side. Watching the aftermath. "I remember . . ." A sad smile pulled at his lips. "When we were just kids, you used to say you were . . . afraid of him."

"Yes." Those memories were there for her, too.

Car doors slammed. She looked over. Saw Gabe. Gabe, who *should* have been laying down someplace, but he was trying to stagger toward her.

Even as Wade tried to force her lover back into the ambulance.

"He believed you."

She nodded. Gabe was determined to make his way to her. The bullet had been taken out, he'd been stitched up—courtesy of some fast-acting EMTs.

Victoria and Wade had gone out for help in the storm. They'd come back with the cavalry.

And Eve had stayed with Gabe. Holding him tightly. Telling him that she loved him. *More than life.*

"When the rest of the flood waters recede," Trey said now, "the FBI agents are going to finish the search of the island. They think they'll find at least ten more bodies."

Ten more lives lost . . . because of her brother.

"You remember everything now, don't you?"

She glanced toward Trey.

"I can see it in your eyes," he said softly.

Eve nodded. And . . . *Eve* . . . that was exactly who she was. She had all of her memories, yes, but it almost seemed as if the woman she'd been *had* died, and someone stronger had taken Jessica's place.

Someone who hadn't let fear win.

Someone who had everything to live for.

"I'm sorry. I should have listened to you before. I should have helped you—"

"My parents tried to help. When I kept telling them that something was wrong, they sent Pierce to doctors . . . but he was very, very good at manipulating people." Even the people who were supposed to see evil. Sickness. "And when he got older, I think Pierce learned to buy his way out of trouble." He'd learned to make any . . . incidents . . . from his childhood vanish with the right amount of cash. He'd become the epitome of a successful businessman . . . only a killer had hidden beneath his carefully erected veneer.

"I'm sorry," Trey said again, and she could hear the pain in his voice. "I wish . . . I wish so much had been different . . ."

She leaned up and kissed his cheek. "I'm not afraid anymore." His masculine scent teased her nose. Memories, so many of them, were right there between them. Yes, she had cared for Trey once. And he'd always have a place in her heart—as a friend.

But he was her past, and it was time to put that past to rest. It was time to focus on her future.

She looked back at Gabe. Her tough ex-SEAL. Staggering toward her when he should have been on his way to a hospital.

Gabe lifted his hand to her. Eve hurried to him. Their fingers locked together.

And Eve realized that she wasn't lost, not anymore. She was exactly where she was supposed to be, with the man who stared at her as if she was the most precious thing in the world.

"I love you," he told her, and Eve knew she'd never get tired of hearing those words.

She rose onto her toes, and her lips pressed lightly to his.

"A hospital!" Wade snapped, sounding distinctly annoyed. "That man needs a hospital—you two save that lovey-dovey crap for later."

Because there would be a later. A thousand nights of later. A lifetime.

Eve eased away from Gabe. Stared into his eyes. She wanted to be sure he heard this part. "I love you, Gabe Spencer."

That blue gaze warmed.

"Now get your ass back in that ambulance, because I'm not losing you. Not now . . ." Eve kissed him once more. "Not ever."

Because she would fight anyone or anything in order to keep Gabe by her side. The man who loved her, darkness and all.

The man who was . . . hers.

Always.

EPILOGUE

HER FEET DUG INTO THE SAND AS THE WAVES OF the ocean pounded the shore. Seagulls were above her, crying out.

And she wasn't afraid.

Eve stared out at the water. She could see the lighthouse in the distance. Tall and strong, having survived another storm.

And she wasn't afraid.

Her hand lifted. Touched the scar on her neck. The memories pulsed through her.

And she wasn't afraid.

He caught her hand in his. Brought her fingers to his lips. Kissed them. One by one.

And she smiled as she turned toward him.

There was no answering smile on Gabe's hard face. He stared down at her, almost appearing afraid. But that was wrong. Gabe wasn't afraid of anything.

Except of losing me.

Because she did know his darkest fear. He'd whispered it to her, when he held her tight in that hospital room.

I'd be lost without you.

"The victims have been recovered."

She nodded. Victoria had told her about them. Almost twenty in all. *Twenty.* Not the ten they'd first anticipated.

When she first heard, Eve had broken down and cried for them. For so many lives that had been lost.

No, not lost, but taken, by her brother.

"It looks like his first victim was the girl we found in the fort. And after her, he started burying his victims."

He'd let the sand hide his crimes.

"He wrote their names on the walls of the fort, in different rooms. Hiding them, but always marking his prey."

"Taking credit for the kill," Eve said.

Gabe nodded. "Yes."

She glanced back out at the water. "He was . . . sick. My parents sent him to doctors, so many doctors, but nothing ever seemed to help."

"He fixated on you," Gabe said. "Maybe because you were so close to him, because he saw you, day in and day out . . . you became the thing he wanted most."

She closed her eyes and let the wind slide over her face. "I came here to get away from him, but he followed me." He'd turned her safe haven into a hell.

No, I won't let you take anything else from me! I won't!

Her eyes opened.

She stared at the beauty of the beach. The beauty of the waves. The sand. When she looked down, she didn't see blood in the water. That was just a memory.

"The Montgomery fortune is mine." It would be, once she'd jumped through all the legal hoops. "I don't . . . want it. I'm giving it to the families. To help them—" Eve broke off, shaking her head. "As if money will ever make up for what they lost." Nothing could make up for what was taken. But she was still sending the money to those families. To Pauley's sister. To Clay's father.

She knew that Pierce had been the one to kill Pauley. The one to attack her. He'd been using colored contact lenses the night he came for her . . . they'd found other contacts, some disguises and hair dye, in his house on the island. He'd been such a careful killer.

A tricky bastard who'd been too good at hiding his true self from the people around him.

"What happens now?" Eve asked as she stared at the waves now rising to brush against her toes.

"You live your life." Gabe's voice was gruff. "You start being happy again. You love—"

Her gaze returned to him. "I already do." Her feelings for him were getting her through the darkness.

He smiled at her, and the sight nearly broke her heart.

"I will love you, Eve, Jessica—whatever name you want to use—I will love you for the rest of my life." His voice was low, heavy with intensity. "And I will do everything within my power to give you only good memories from here on out."

But Eve shook her head, and she saw fear flash on his face. She told him, "Life isn't always good. Sometimes, it's ugly and it's dark and it tries to wreck you." That was the way fate worked. "You don't have to promise me perfect times. Just promise me . . . that I'll always have you. That you'll be with me. Because if I have you . . ." And she smiled for him. The first real smile that she could remember in months. "Then I have everything."

He pulled her into his arms. Held her tight, so tight. "You'll have me forever."

When he kissed her, Eve knew that the past was truly dead.

The future—it was what waited.

Gabe waited.

Don't miss the next sexy and suspenseful novel
featuring the LOST team
from *New York Times* best-selling author
CYNTHIA EDEN!
Read on for a sneak peek at

TWISTED

Available in print and e-book April 28, 2015!

PROLOGUE

"WHAT DO YOU SEE FOR MY FUTURE?"

Emma Castille slowly glanced up from the cards that were spread on the table before her. The young girl who sat across from Emma appeared to be barely sixteen. Her blond hair was secured in a haphazard knot at the nape of her neck, her clothes were faded, and her blue eyes were wide with a fear that couldn't be controlled.

Emma didn't reach for the cards that were on her table. She just stared at the girl and said, "I see a family that's waiting for you. You need to go home to them."

The girl's chin jerked. "Wh-What if they won't have me?"

"You'd be surprised at what they'd have." Darkness was coming. The night slowly creeping to take over the day. Emma knew that she would have to leave Jackson Square soon. Her time was almost up.

The others around her were already packing up their booths for the day. Psychics. Artists. Musicians. They were a mixed group that assembled every day as they came out to capture the attention of the tourists in New Orleans.

Emma wasn't psychic. She wasn't gifted when it came

to music or art. But she did have one talent that she used to keep her alive and well fed—she had a talent for reading people.

For noticing what others would too easily miss. Too easily *ignore*.

"You're running from someone." Emma said this flatly. The girl had already glanced over her left shoulder at least four times while they'd been talking. Fear was a living, breathing thing, clinging to the girl like a shroud.

Emma knew what it was like to run. Sometimes it seemed as if she'd always been running from someone or something.

"Will he find me?" the girl asked as she leaned forward.

Emma almost reached for her hand because she wanted to comfort her. Almost. "Go back to your family." The girl was a runaway. She'd bet her life on it.

The blond girl blanched. "What if it's the family you fear?"

At those words, Emma stiffened.

"Aren't you supposed to tell me that everything will be all right?" the girl asked. She stood then, and her voice rose, breaking with fear. "Aren't you supposed to tell me that I'll go to college, marry my dream man, and live happily ever after?"

Others turned their way because the girl was nearly shouting.

"Aren't you?" the girl demanded.

Emma shook her head. She didn't believe in happily ever after. "Go to the police." This she said softly, her words a direct contrast to the girl's angry tone. "You're in danger." There were bruises on the girl's wrists, bruises peeking out from beneath the long sleeves of her shirt. A long-sleeved shirt in August, in New Orleans? Oh, no, that wasn't right. *What other bruises are you trying to hide?*

The girl stumbled back. "Help me." Now her voice was a desperate whisper.

Emma stood as well. "I'll go with you—" she began.

But the girl had glanced over her shoulder once more. The blonde's too-thin body stiffened, and she gasped. Then she was turning and running away. Shoving through the tourists that crowded that busy square. Running as if her very life depended on it.

Because maybe, just maybe, that life did.

Emma called out after her, but the girl didn't stop.

Let her go, let her go.

But Emma found herself rushing after the girl, going as fast as she could. But New Orleans, oh, New Orleans, it could be such a tricky bitch with its narrow streets and secret paths. She couldn't find the blonde. She turned to the left and to the right and she just saw men and women laughing, celebrating. Voices were all around her. So many people.

And there was no sign of the terrified blond girl.

Emma paused and her right hand pressed to the brick wall on her right as she fought to catch her breath.

But that wall was . . . wet. Her hand lifted, and in the faint light she could see the red that covered her palm. A red that was—

Blood.

"OH, JULIA, SWEET Julia, why did you try to run?"

He ran the tip of his knife down Julia's cheek. She was already bleeding, and, before he was done, there would be even more blood.

So much blood.

Behind his left hand, Julia whimpered.

He let the knife slice even deeper into her cheek. "Now I'm just going to have to punish you more. You know that?" His voice was whisper soft because that other woman—the one with the dark hair and too bright eyes—had followed his Julia. The woman was just steps away, less than five feet. She hadn't realized that they'd ducked into the abandoned bar.

She didn't know that he had Julia in his arms right then.

The woman was looking at her hand.

Ah, did you see Julia's blood?

Because he'd slammed Julia's head into that wall. Stopped her from running.

"You're not going to get away from me," he told Julia as the other woman crept closer to the bar. The place's windows and doors were boarded up, but he'd found a way inside. A way that gave him perfect access to Julia. "I always keep what's mine."

The dark-haired woman was almost upon them. Through the thin cracks in those boarded-up windows, he could see the slender shape of her body. The long, flowing dress.

He smiled as the thrill of the hunt filled him once more. *"Always . . ."*

New Orleans was fucking hot. No other way to describe it. *Fucking. Hot.* On a late September day the heat was like a damn blanket wrapping around Dean Bannon. He'd rolled up his sleeves, ditched his tie, but those feeble efforts sure hadn't done any good.

New Orleans was hell, he was convinced of that, and the place was also the site of his latest assignment.

Sixteen-year-old Julia Finney had last been seen in the Big Easy. Her mother was desperate to find the girl, but the local cops weren't giving any of their time to finding the runaway, and he—well, he was one of the agents from LOST who'd been sent down from Atlanta to find her.

He made his way slowly down Bourbon Street. The sun hadn't even set yet, and the place was already hopping. Drunk frat boys and drunk sixty-year-old men staggered down the street in near perfect rhythm. And girls—girls that looked far too young—stood in darkened doorways and waved the men inside.

Ann Finney was worried that her daughter Julia was going to become one of those girls. On the streets, with no money, no connections . . . what else could happen to her?

A fucking lot.

Dean lifted the picture he carried of Julia. Showed it to the girls. But their glassy-eyed stares just passed right over the image. No one recognized Julia. No one knew her.

It seemed that no one had ever bothered to *look* at the girl.

Now he was looking for her, but the clench in Dean's gut told him that he might already be too late. Still, he kept trudging along, kept turning down the streets until he found himself in Jackson Square.

Street performers were out, some kids playing jazz, others dancing fast and frantic rhythm on cardboard boxes that they'd brought out as they worked for tips.

The crowd there was huge. So many people. Too many.

No wonder a sixteen-year-old girl had vanished without a trace.

"Who are you looking for?"

The voice was feminine, low, husky—and very close.

He turned his head and saw her. A woman with a long cascade of black hair and the bluest eyes he'd ever seen. She was sitting beneath the shelter of a big blue umbrella. A small table sat in front of her, and a sign by her said that a "reading" would be twenty dollars.

His eyes narrowed as he studied her.

She smiled at him, flashing dimples in both of her cheeks. "Come now, don't be afraid of me, handsome, I won't bite." Her hand, delicate, tanned, motioned to the chair across from her. "Come closer."

Why? Did it look like he was some tourist in the mood to be conned? Because that sure as shit wasn't his style.

But if the woman usually worked the square, if she saw all the people coming and going . . . then maybe, just maybe, she'd seen Julia.

Dean ducked his head and slid under that umbrella. But he didn't sit. He leaned over her, and the woman tilted her head back as she stared up at him.

Her smile dimmed. Those dimples vanished, and Dean had one thought—

Fucking gorgeous.

The woman's face was eerily close to perfect. High cheekbones. Straight nose. Wide, amazing eyes. A delicate chin.

Her lips were full, sexy and red. Her face might have made her look like an angel, but those lips and that dark mass of hair . . . oh, it made him think of sin.

Not here, not now.

Dean had a rule about mixing business and pleasure. He damn well never did it.

He was there on a case. For him, the mission always came first. *Always.*

"Not a cop," she said as she lifted one eyebrow. "But a government agent . . ." Her lips pursed. "FBI?"

Was he supposed to be impressed? He'd been an FBI agent for ten years, working day and night in the Violent Crimes Division. He'd seen enough shit to give most people never-ending nightmares.

Good thing he didn't have nightmares. He didn't have dreams, either. When he slept, there was only darkness.

He pulled out the photo of Julia. He noticed the would-be fortune-teller's eyes fell to the photo, and she tensed, just for an instant.

"I'm betting you see plenty of people come by this way each day."

Her gaze lifted back to his. "I don't work here every day."

He took a step closer to her. She definitely tensed. Dean put the photo of Julia down on the woman's table. As he leaned in even closer, he could have sworn that he caught the scent of jasmine. He'd grown up on his grandfather's farm, a lifetime ago, and jasmine had been there.

She wasn't looking at the photograph.

"Most people disappear for a reason," she said, staring into his eyes. "They don't like to be found."

Too bad. "My job is to find the lost."

Her head tilted a bit more, and a dark lock of hair slid over her shoulder. She was wearing gold earrings, hoops that moved faintly as she watched him. Those hoops, her hair, her amazing eyes—yeah, they all came together to give her a seductive, mysterious air. He bet the tourists loved her.

But Dean knew there was no mystery about the woman before him. Just another pretty face hiding lies. The woman was a scammer, out there to bilk the people dumb enough to approach her table.

"Look at the girl," he said softly.

Her blue gaze fell to the table.

For just a moment her eyes widened. "What has she done?"

Interesting question. "Her family wants her home."

Her hand rose. Her fingers slid over the photograph. "She should go home. I . . . told her that."

He caught her hand. Grabbed her wrist in a lightning fast move. "You've seen her." He felt the light ridge of raised skin beneath his fingers. A scar?

She was still looking down at the photograph. "It was at least a week ago. She came here right before sunset." Her full lips curved down as sadness chased over her face. "I'm sorry, but I don't think you'll be finding her."

The hell he wouldn't.

She tugged on her wrist. Dean didn't let her go.

"That girl is sixteen years old," he said. "She ran away from her home in Atlanta, and her mother is desperate to find her. Her mother *needs* her back home."

"I don't think she wanted to go back."

She stood then, moving from beneath the shelter of the umbrella, even as he held onto her wrist. She was smaller than he'd thought. He stood at six-foot-three, and the woman was barely five-foot-four. Maybe five-foot-five. When she tried to slip away from him, he tightened his hold.

"Let me go."

He didn't. But his hand slid up her forearm a bit, and he felt more of that raised skin. Just small ridges. Curious now, he looked down as he turned her arm over. Those *were* scars. Faint lines of white that crossed her skin. The marks were at various points on her inner arm, and . . .

His hand pushed open her clenched fist. There were a few more faint scars there, too. Little slices.

A surge of anger caught him by surprise. "Who did it?"

"It's rude to ask questions like that." She actually sounded as if she were chiding him. "Didn't they teach you a better interview technique at the FBI?"

"I'm not with the FBI."

"Well, not any longer, of course," she said. Her smile flashed, only this time he recognized it for the distraction that it was. Hell, he bet plenty of men got lost in that wide smile.

He wasn't plenty of men.

And he knew better than to fall for a pretty face.

"The girl," Dean gritted out. "Tell me everything you know about her."

Her gaze slid to the left. To the right. And Dean realized that the others close by were watching them.

"You are seriously bad for business," she said, sounding annoyed. "It looks like you're an angry lover who's having some public spat with me. You need to let me go, *now*."

An angry lover? Okay, so he was holding her pretty close, but he wasn't backing off. And that sweet jasmine scent was definitely coming from her. "Tell me what I need to know and—"

"Is there a problem here?" A male voice. Close. Sharp.

Dean turned his head just a bit and saw the uniformed police officer, frowning at them.

"Ms. Castille? This guy bothering you?"

Dean mentally filed away the lady's last name even as he made himself step back and release her. "I'm not bothering her." Okay, he had been.

The cop came even closer. His face was tight with suspicion, and it was a young face. The guy was in his early twenties and had ROOKIE written all over him.

"It *looked* like you were bothering her, so I'm gonna suggest that you keep walking now, buddy."

"It's all right." *Ms. Castille* put her hand on the cop's shoulder. "Thanks, Beau, it sure is nice to know you're looking out for me."

Beau smiled at her. Dean figured the cop's smile flashed because she'd just fired him that megawatt smile of hers, dimples included.

"Always here for you, ma'am," he told her, flushing a bit. Then the cop glanced back at Dean, and his frown was back. "I'd like to see your ID, mister."

Hell. But, whatever. Dean tossed the cop his wallet.

Beau pulled out his driver's license. Ms. Castille was right next to him as the cop read, "Dean Bannon, age thirty-six, from Atlanta, Georgia." Beau whistled. "Love me some Braves."

Dean waited.

"What brings you down to Atlanta?" the cop asked him.

"Keep looking in the wallet," Dean said.

The cop's brows scrunched when he pulled out one of Dean's cards. "LOST," he said, and his frown deepened. "I've . . . heard of that group." His gaze shot to Dean. "The LOST team caught that serial killer over on Dauphin Island a while back!"

Yes, they had. And since Dauphin Island, Alabama, was just a few hours away, Dean wasn't real surprised that the cop had heard about that incident. "We didn't bring him in alive," Dean said. Because the Lady Killer hadn't given them that option.

"You stopped him," Beau said, sounding more than impressed. "That's good enough in my book."

LOST. The organization that Dean worked for was gaining more and more attention these days. Last

Option Search Team. Dean's buddy Gabe Spencer had been the one to put the team together. The ex-SEAL had wanted to bring in a group with varied backgrounds, a team that knew how to get the job done.

When local law enforcement gave up the hunt for the missing, when the families still needed hope, they turned to LOST.

Just like Ann Finney had done. No one else had helped her find Julia. Runaways disappeared every day. With Julia being an older teen, the cops hadn't spent a lot of time looking for her . . .

But Dean wasn't going to give up.

"There's a picture of a missing girl on Ms. Castille's table," Dean said. "We were just talking because I thought she might know where I could find Julia."

Beau tossed Dean's wallet back to him. Then the cop went to stare at the photo.

The woman didn't move, though. She kept her eyes on Dean. "I haven't seen Julia in over a week," she said, voice soft. "But I can tell you this . . . the last time that I did see her, she was scared."

His muscles locked. "How do you know that?"

The cop's radio had crackled to life. Beau took a few steps away, turned his back and pulled out that radio.

"Because I know what fear looks like." Her lips pressed together, then she said, "And I also know what bruises look like. She had bruises on her wrists. Some-one had been hurting Julia."

He lunged toward her. "Why the hell didn't you tell me that before?"

She glanced over at Beau. He was on his radio, still staring down at that picture as he paced and talked. "Because you said you wanted to send her back home. Julia didn't want to go home. She was afraid of her family." Her eyes darkened with sadness. "There's a reason people run away, you know. If life were perfect, why would a girl like that leave?"

The cop was coming back toward them. He'd put up his radio. "You need to go down to the station," he told Dean. "You can check in with the detectives—"

"My partner is already at the station." While he hit the streets, Sarah Jacobs had wanted to check with the local authorities to see if they might have any leads. Dean wasn't exactly holding out much hope on that end. But since he had a cop right in front of him, one who worked this beat, he asked, "Have *you* seen the girl, officer?"

Beau shook his head. "She looks just like a hundred others I see every day. Sorry." His radio crackled to life once again. "Got to go. See you soon, Ms. Castille."

Thunder rumbled as the cop headed away. Dean looked up. There were a few dark clouds sprinkling over the sky.

"Storms come up fast down South. They rage hard, then they die away as quickly as they come." She turned away. Started shutting down her booth. "Good luck finding the girl."

Did she really think he was just going to walk away? "You're my best lead." So far she was the *only* person who'd actually seen Julia.

Provided, of course, that she hadn't just been blowing smoke up his ass.

She pulled down her umbrella. "Bourbon Street."

His brows climbed.

"The last time I saw her, she was headed over there. But then, most folks wind up there eventually, right?"

Dean pulled his card from his wallet. "If you remember anything else, call me."

She didn't take the card. "I won't remember anything."

He reached for her hand. Put the card in her palm. Stared at the faint scars. "They're defensive wounds," he told her as another rumble of thunder sounded in the distance.

Her too bright eyes held his.

"Someone attacked you with a knife. You raised your hands, and that someone"—a fucking bastard in his book—"sliced you. The blade cut across your palm. It sliced into your forearm."

Her fingers closed around the card. "You left the FBI because you got tired of all the death."

He stiffened.

"You have scars hidden beneath your clothes. Scars on your skin. Scars *beneath* the skin." Her head gave a little shake. "You don't really think you'll find Julia alive, you don't think you'll find any of them alive."

What the hell?

"But at least you try." She backed away from him. Collected her bag. Her table. Started walking away. "Good-bye, Dean Bannon."

"Wait!" He hadn't meant to call out like that.

She glanced back at him.

"Do you . . . need help?" And why was he stuttering like some kid right then?

"I've never needed help." She turned away. Kept going. "I hope you find her."

Dean's legs had locked as he stared after her. He watched as she disappeared, not heading very far away at all, but going toward a little shop on the corner. A small place that he almost hadn't even seen before.

A crystal shop.

I hope I find her, too.

And the sexy fortune-teller had been wrong. He did

want to find Julia alive. He *needed* to find the missing
. . . still alive.

Because he'd found too many dead already.

He tucked the picture of Julia back into his pocket. A
drop of rain fell down on him, but Dean didn't move.
The dark-haired woman had vanished now. There had
been something familiar about her. Something that kept
nagging at him.

Another raindrop fell.

Where have I seen you before, Ms. Castille?

And . . . *who the fuck hurt you?*

DEAN STRIPPED OFF his soaked shirt. Lightning flashed
just outside of his hotel room. For an instant his gaze
slid to the window. Being on the thirty-eighth floor gave
him a killer view of the city. The river was below, dark
and turbulent, and the clouds were swirling so close that
it looked as if he could reach out and touch them.

Instead, he turned away from that window and
reached for his laptop. In seconds he had the thing
booted up and he was searching—for her.

Castille.

The name had struck a chord with him, stirring up
memories of an old FBI case. Ms. Castille had appeared
to be about twenty-five, and he'd first joined the FBI ten
years ago.

He started tapping on the keyboard. Going through
searches. Accessing records most people didn't know
about but that LOST operatives had managed to reach
long ago.

Castille . . .

The memory of that name teased at him.

So he typed in . . . *Castille . . . psychic.*

The search results were instant.

House of Death . . . Psychic John Castille Arrives Too Late to Save Missing Teens . . .

"I'll be damned," he muttered. He leaned forward as he read the first search article.

HE WAS BACK.

Emma kept staring at her client, nodding her head as the woman talked, but her focus was on the tall, dark, and far too dangerous man who stood a few feet away.

Dean Bannon.

He was wearing another dress shirt today. A crisp white shirt in the ridiculous New Orleans heat. He'd rolled up his sleeves, like that was going to do much good. He was also wearing another pair of too expensive pants.

Seriously, the guy was so out of place . . . and he just *looked* like a federal agent. How had he not expected her to tag him right away?

"Thank you so much, hon," Mrs. Jones was saying. Mrs. Jones was a weekly client. A sweet grandmother in her early seventies. "I love our talks."

Emma almost smiled at that. A real smile, but she caught herself just in time.

Mrs. Jones handed her a twenty. Emma reached for the money, but instead of taking it, she leaned close to Mrs. Jones and caught her trembling hand. "I want you to see a doctor tomorrow."

Mrs. Jones's dark eyes widened. "Wh-Why?"

Because she could feel the tremble in Mrs. Jones's hand. Because the woman's skin was paler than it had been the week before. Because her voice kept getting breathless when it shouldn't have. "Because you need to be checked out. It's been far too long since you've paid a visit to your doctor."

"I . . . *how did you know?*"

Emma stared into her eyes. "I'm worried about you, and I want you to go and see a doctor right away."

Dean inched closer. Eavesdropping? Sad. So sad.

"I—I think I'm fine . . ."

Emma pushed the money back at Mrs. Jones. "Have I ever steered you wrong?"

The woman shook her head. "That's why I come to you."

No, Mrs. Jones came to her because she was lonely and she just wanted to talk with someone who would listen to her.

"Then listen to me now. See a doctor."

Mrs. Jones nodded. Then she was off, hurrying away, and Dean Bannon was closing in. Great. Emma narrowed her eyes on the man. "You're terrible for business." Hadn't she told the guy that yesterday?

He smiled, but it wasn't a real smile. Emma knew because she gave plenty of her own, fake smiles. Dean's smile just lifted his sensual lips, but the smile never lit his dark eyes. The man was handsome, in a too polished sort of way. She'd like to see his hair longer, his tanned cheeks flushed more with a fury or passion, and she'd like—

"You're not who you pretend to be."

Uh-oh.

Her gaze slowly swept over his face as she tried to figure out just what the guy could have learned about her. Unfortunately . . . *he could know too much.* In this Internet-filled world, secrets were just a search engine away.

Dean Bannon had closed in on her, his powerful body moving with a grace that the guy shouldn't possess. He was controlled—*definitely controlled.* Everything about him screamed control, and she . . . well, she'd never had much use for control.

Emma let emotions rule her. She lived for passion, she lived for the moment.

Why live for anything else? Especially when nothing else was ever guaranteed. *The past is a nightmare. The future could vanish.* So why not live in that wonderful here and now?

Only the here and now wasn't always so wonderful.

His hair was cut a bit too short. His expression was too hard. That deliciously square jaw of his appeared to be clenched—again, and his eyes had locked on her as if he were a predator and she his prey.

"I didn't think psychics were supposed to tell bad fortunes."

Now he'd caught her by surprise. *I don't remember saying I was psychic.* Emma always tried to choose her words very carefully. Whenever possible, she opted not to lie.

Her father had told too many lies. Emma had discovered that she didn't really have a taste for them. Even if she had inherited his . . . other . . . talents. Talents that weren't always savory. Talents that weren't exactly legal in some places. *Most places.*

"Were you trying to scare that woman?" he asked, voice sharp.

"I was trying to get her to see a doctor." Emma shrugged. "Horrible, I know, to want to make certain that a friend is in good health." Her eyes widened. "I guess that means I'm just a terrible, wretched person on the inside."

His frown got worse.

Emma sighed. "You'd be so much better looking if you just smiled. Like, a real smile."

He blinked at her.

"Right, no smile." So she smiled brightly for them both. "To what do I owe the pleasure of your company today? Come for a reading, did you?"

Because she really didn't want to waste time talking with him. As it was, she'd spent most of the night staying up, thinking about Julia.

Now I have a name to go with her face.

And when sleep still hadn't come at midnight, Emma had slipped away and gone to Bourbon Street, but there had been no sign of Julia.

He pulled out the folding chair that she'd set up. The guy surprised her by tossing a twenty on the table and sitting down in front of her.

Intrigued now, Emma made herself comfortable in her chair, shifting a bit, as she kept her gaze on him.

"A reading . . ." he said. She almost shivered. The guy had one of those amazing voices that, once a woman heard it, she didn't forget. Deep and rumbly. A voice made for darkness.

And sex.

She'd detected no accent in his voice, and Emma was very good at recognizing accents. Accents, habits, behavior—she noticed them all.

Like the way Dean Bannon had a habit of rubbing his jaw with his index finger and thumb. He did that when he was thinking. When he was annoyed, she'd noticed that a muscle flexed along the left-hand side of his jaw. And—

"Your name is Emma Castille."

She leaned forward. "I can use the cards if you want. Some people like that part." She actually did know what all of the cards meant, so she could shuffle them and give a reading, no problem. But she preferred to work in other ways.

"You're not psychic."

Were they back to that?

Emma put her hands in her lap. She didn't believe in making nervous gestures. She didn't believe in giving away anything at all with her body language.

"What you are . . ." Ah, now he *did* smile. Her father would have called it a shit-eating grin. The more PC term was probably a Cheshire cat smile. Whatever the name, that smile annoyed her. "What you are, Ms. Castille . . . is a criminal. A fraud."

Maybe she should grab her chest and dramatically gasp. She didn't. "Wonderful for you," Emma said. "You pulled up a background report on me." She let her eyes widen a bit. "It's amazing what one can find if a person just knows how to use a search engine."

A furrow appeared between his eyes.

"How about I say what . . . *you* are?" Emma asked him. "A washed-up FBI agent who snapped on the job. You held your control tight every single day, but the bad guys—they just didn't stop, did they? You hunted them, you stopped them, and more appeared. While you were fighting the system, they kept coming, and the bodies kept piling up on *your* watch."

He shot right back to his feet. The folding chair slammed down behind him.

"You and your father bilked desperate people," he accused. "You told them you were psychic, that you could help find their missing children. And you—"

"We found them." Two girls who'd vanished. They'd *found* them. "We just didn't get to them in time." And she would *not* go back to that place.

She motioned toward Manuel. He knew the signal meant he could take over her booth. There was no way, *no way,* that she was going to stay there with this prick while he slammed the most painful moments from her past in her face.

Manuel, pale, tattooed, with piercings in his lips and eyebrows, quickly claimed her spot.

Emma jumped to her feet, muttered her thanks, and fled right past the guy she was starting to think of as Agent Jackass.

She pushed through the crowd. Wasn't there always a crowd in Jackson Square? And that was why she loved the place. It was so easy to vanish in a crowd. To be anyone.

The crowd closed around her.

To be no one at all.

Emma hurried around the back of the cathedral. She knew the streets so well. Her home was close by. She would get inside and forget Agent Jackass.

I'm being followed.

Emma stilled at the intersection. A horse-drawn carriage rolled by her. Voices called out.

And he touched her.

Emma didn't flinch. Didn't scream. She looked down at the hand on her shoulder. "When a woman runs away from you, that means you need to stay the hell away from her."

His hold tightened on her. "You and I aren't done."

She looked up at his face. Had she really thought the man was handsome? Annoying, that was all Dean Bannon was.

"I need to find that girl, and you're the only lead I have so far."

"Then you're not a very good investigator."

Ah, that muscle flexed in his jaw. Lovely.

"You were heading to your apartment." He pointed across the street. "One block over, right? Seems like the perfect place for a chat."

My my, but he had been busy. Only instead of spending all his time investigating her, he should have been looking for the missing girl.

Emma took a step forward. He, of course, followed right by her side. They didn't speak as they made their way to her apartment, a precious little gem that she adored. It was right over a clothing store, nestled up high with a balcony view. She climbed the narrow flight of stairs that led to her room, and then . . .

Emma stopped as her heartbeat increased. The pounding seemed to shake her entire body.

"What are you waiting for?" Dean demanded.

Emma shook her head. "Someone has been here." Her welcome mat had been moved. Moved over one tiny inch, as if it had been hit by a shoe. She could see the outline where the mat *should* have been. A bit of dirt, some dust. A marker that showed her something was wrong inside her place.

"How do you know?"

"The mat's in the wrong spot." She reached for the knob, and it turned. "And I never leave my door unlocked." Given the things Emma had seen, she would never have made that kind of mistake.

Never.

But the knob was turning easily in her hand. Far too easily. And as the door swung open, Emma sucked in a sharp breath.

The place was wrecked. Her mirrors were smashed. The furniture had been slashed. Cushion stuffing littered the floor.

Dean swore, and in the next moment he grabbed her and pushed Emma behind him. "Stay back," he ordered. "The bastard could still be inside."

Then he was rushing inside. Going through the wreckage, but being careful, she noted, not to actually touch anything. He searched the small place. The studio-style apartment didn't exactly cover a lot of square footage, so she could see most of her home from her nervous perch in the doorway.

But then Dean disappeared into the little attached room that she'd made into her bedroom. Emma realized that she was holding her breath, waiting for him to reappear. Only he didn't come right back out.

She crept forward and her right foot slid over the threshold of her home. She glanced down, and her eyes narrowed at the speck of red she saw there. Almost a dot.

Blood?

"He left something for you."

Her head whipped up.

"The house is clear." His voice was grim. "We need to call the cops right away. Maybe the guy left some evidence here." He motioned toward her. "Before they get to the scene, *you need to come here*."

She found herself walking toward him. A huge part of Emma was screaming that she needed to run the other way. To get the hell out of there. She didn't know much at all about Dean Bannon. For all she knew, he could have been the one to destroy her house. He'd known where she lived, after all.

And she stopped advancing.

Dean's eyes widened in surprise. "You're afraid of me."

Hell, yes, she was.

Emma took out her phone. Called 911. When the operator answered, she said, "Someone broke into my house. They've . . . *he* destroyed everything, and I—I think there's blood."

The operator's voice stayed calm as she asked for Emma's address.

"I'm not alone," Emma said quietly. Because she'd learned not to trust anyone. Not in this life. "A man named Dean Bannon is with me." She wanted his name on the record. Just in case . . . hell, just in case of what? That he decided to attack her before the cops arrived? Dean was making no move to come toward her. He was just standing there, watching her with those deep dark eyes.

Emma gave the operator her address. "Get the cops to hurry, please." *Hurry*.

She lowered the phone and glanced around her apartment once more. *Gone*. She'd worked so hard to build this place—her sanctuary—and in one night some bastard out there had destroyed everything.

"I won't hurt you." Dean's voice was low. She wanted to believe him. But she'd heard that particular lie from too many men before. "I didn't do this, Emma. I'm one of the good guys."

She laughed at that. "There's no such thing."

His lips thinned, then he glanced back over his shoulder, toward her bedroom. "You're going to need a guy like me in your life."

Goose bumps were on her arms. "I doubt that."

But Dean nodded and said, "Come with me into the bedroom."

She shook her head.

"He left something you need to see."

Her gaze locked on that bedroom doorway and Emma inched toward it. Dean backed up, but his shoulder brushed against her arm as she passed him. For some reason that one brush against his body had her tensing. Heat seeped into her skin, and she hadn't even realized that she'd been cold. Not until that moment.

"The mirror," he told her. "Look there."

But her gaze was on the bed. It appeared as if someone had taken a knife to the mattresses and sliced them open. Feathers from her pillows littered the floor. Her clothes had been taken out of the dresser drawers, and they'd been slashed, too. Her shirts. Her skirts. Her bras. Her panties.

Her breath choked in as her gaze slowly rose to the mirror. It had been shattered. Long cracks covered the surface. As did . . .

Words. Words written in red spray paint.

You're next.